GOOD AS GOLD

Also by Louise Patten

Bad Money

GOOD AS GOLD

Louise Patten

Quercus

First published in Great Britain in 2010 by

Quercus
21 Bloomsbury Square
London
WC1A 2NS

A CIP catalogue reference for this book is available
from the British Library

ISBN 978 1 84916 247 0 (TPB)
ISBN 978 1 84916 246 3 (HB)

10 9 8 7 6 5 4 3 2 1

Typeset by Ellipsis Books Limited, Glasgow

Printed and bound in Great Britain by Clays Ltd, St Ives plc.

For Mary-Claire,
curriculum currens

1912

RMS *Titanic*, first-class smoking-room: 9.40 p.m.

In that somnolent time between dinner and bed, Kit
Quentance shifted against the wing-backed armchair. He'd
only eaten so much because he was bored, and was already
regretting the jumble of oysters, turtle soup, roast salmon,
chicken Lyonnaise, asparagus vinaigrette and Waldorf
pudding that sat leadenly in his stomach. A walk on deck
might have helped, but he'd promised Harry he'd wait for
him here in the smoking-room. If he wandered off now, he
and his brother might not find each other again all evening,
Titanic being more like a small town than a proper boat.
Leaning his head against the walnut-stained leather, Kit
closed his eyes and wished for the hundredth time that he
was aboard his own little *Cassandra*, or on a sleek, British
Cunarder. Anything rather than this bloated White Star
monster.

'What fun you'll have!' That's what everyone at home had
said when Father announced that he was sending Kit to
keep Harry company on his trip to New York. 'The last word

in luxury, and what an opportunity! You'll rub shoulders with the richest men in the world.'

There had also been the odd hint that, at eighteen, he wasn't too young to start looking for a pretty American heiress, but that was of no interest to him. Kit had already lost his heart. Despite the discomfort in his stomach, he couldn't help smiling when he thought of her. Florence March-Wynter, a vibrant, copper-haired beauty, always happy, always laughing. As soon as he got back from this beastly trip, he was going to ask her to marry him.

Running his eye over the room's ponderous stained-glass panelling, Kit jiggled a foot impatiently. *Titanic* steamed along so smoothly that he'd never had a chance to get his sea legs. On any normal ship, he'd feel the motion of the waves through his feet and he'd move with the fluency that the sea always gave him. But on this lump of floating metal, he'd kept his shore legs. Gangly things, always tripping him up in society ballrooms. He pursed his lips and sighed. No risk of that tonight. It being a Sunday, there was no dancing or any other sort of entertainment on offer, just brandy, cigars and talk.

Impatience was getting the better of Kit and he was about to go and chivvy his brother out of the restaurant when two men sauntered into the smoking-room, one of whom he immediately recognised from his curly hair and fine set of moustaches. It was J. Bruce Ismay, chairman of the White Star Line and one of the grandest panjandrums of the shipping world. Kit had a sudden urge to introduce himself to Ismay as a fellow sea lover and to hell with the conventions. But on second thoughts he didn't feel brave enough to break one of the more rigid of the rules that governed his class. You simply couldn't speak to a man to whom you hadn't been formally introduced. Instead, he watched as a cloud of waiters fluttered round Bruce Ismay. They were re-arranging the chairs in such a way that, whilst he couldn't join in the conversation, Kit was at least unable to avoid overhearing it.

'Last-minute change of plan,' Ismay said as he sat down. 'That's why Pierpont isn't sailing with us. As a matter of fact, I've ended up with his suite.'

In the pause before the other man answered, Kit heard matches being struck, and then the heavy smoke of cigars curled around him.

'I've put quite a bit of cash with Pierpont Morgan.'

Listening to the light drawl of Ismay's companion, Kit felt a thrill of excitement. The man they were talking about so casually must be John Pierpont Morgan, the entrepreneur who not only owned his own bank but was also the ulti-mate owner of the White Star Line and of *Titanic* herself. Harry would love to know all this.

Kit closed his eyes and concentrated as the man went on, 'Morgan tells me your outfit's hoping to dominate the North Atlantic crossing with this ship.'

'Hoping be damned!' Kit heard Ismay smacking a hand down on the leather armrest of his chair. 'It's an absolute certainty. The Cunard line is White Star's only competitor, and *Titanic*'s going to thrash that British outfit off the face of the sea. Look around you – this boat's perfect.'

'She's certainly well designed. You'd never know there was anyone from the lower ranks on the whole ship.'

'Excellent, isn't it? First-class only on the upper decks, proletariat down below. The top of the ship's the top of the social order, just as it should be.'

To Kit's ears, Bruce Ismay's chuckle sounded unpleasantly self-satisfied. Ismay's companion seemed to think so too, because when his reply finally came, the voice was cold. 'All the same, I hear your English aristocracy plans to stick with Cunard. You'll never get a monopoly on the North Atlantic without the Brits on board.'

Kit found himself nodding in agreement. It was exactly what his best friend had told him. Hugo Brink was the son of Viscount Tamar and heir to the Earl of Ivybridge; Hugo understood these things. 'Profitable investments,' he'd said. 'That's all *Titanic*'s about. Fine if you want to hob-nob with bankers, but deadly-dull otherwise. It'll be all pomposity and showing off.'

'Stuff and nonsense!' Clearly Ismay would have disagreed with Hugo. 'Who cares about a few crusty old lords and ladies? This is the twentieth century, and what makes one chap better than another isn't the length of his family tree. The only thing that matters nowadays is how tall a man is when he stands on his wallet. You mark my words, give us a few months and all the big money-men will be crossing the pond on *Titanic*.'

After a polite laugh there was a silence between the pair until Kit heard Ismay's companion say with sudden interest, 'Hey, Bruce. Isn't that your designer just coming in?'

'Designer? Oh, you mean Andrews. Brilliant man. This ship's quite unsinkable, you know.' Kit heard the scrape of chair legs on the linoleum flooring as Ismay got up. 'Come and meet him. We'll get him to give us a tour.'

The two men drifted out of earshot, leaving Kit to reflect on what he'd overheard. *All the big money-men will be crossing the pond on* Titanic. His brother would enjoy that.

Wireless room: 9.50 p.m.

FROM *MESABA*: ICE REPORT IN LAT 42 TO 41:25'N. LONG 49 TO 50:30'W. SAW MUCH HEAVY PACK ICE AND GREAT NUMBER LARGE ICEBERGS. ALSO FIELD ICE. WEATHER GOOD, CLEAR.

'Get a move on, Phillips. Here's another couple of messages for Cape Race. You know the rules. We've got to keep the first-class passengers happy.'

Slipping the iceberg warning under a brass paperweight at his elbow just till he'd finished, Wireless Officer Phillips began to transmit: GREETINGS FROM THE OCEAN. WISH YOU WERE HERE. ARRIVING FRIDAY. GET THOSE WHITE LADIES SHAKEN.

Another knock at his door brought a sheaf of new telegrams. Phillips glanced at his watch: 9.50 p.m. Dinner over, the ship's wealthiest passengers would be downing their liqueurs and in no mood to worry about the cost of sending ship-to-shore messages. He sighed. Better get on with it.

Mesaba's warning message lay by his elbow, forgotten, as RMS *Titanic* made directly towards the reported ice field.

Smoking-room: 9.55 p.m.

'Evening, Quentance.' Shortly after Bruce Ismay had left, and before Kit had had time to get impatient again, he saw two men coming towards him through the thickening fog of cigar smoke. One was a big-boned, fair-haired stranger, the other a younger man to whom he'd been introduced in the ship's gym earlier that day, and who now said, 'I've been telling Mr Guggenheim here about that family bank of yours and how you're planning to set up a New York branch. He wants to meet you.'

Kit leapt to his feet. He might not have recognised the man, but he certainly knew the Guggenheim name.

'How do you do, sir!' Flattening back the forelock of blond hair that refused to stay put no matter how much oil he plastered on it, Kit added hurriedly, 'But you don't want to talk to *me* about the bank, I'm only just starting in the business. Harry's the one you want. Last seen wolfing down fillet of beef in the Café Parisien, but he'll be along here any minute.' Kit hoped his brother would hurry. The American mining king, worth a reputed sixty million dollars, was exactly the type Harry was hoping to meet on this trip.

'Sure I'll wait.' Kit liked the sound of Guggenheim's voice. 'I'm always happy to meet a new banker on the street.' Taking a chair, he gestured for Kit to sit next to him. 'Why don't you join me while we wait for your brother? I hear you're planning to steal the America's Cup from right under our noses?'

Kit was thrilled with the chance to talk boats rather than banks. 'Well I'm certainly going to give it a try,' he said enthusiastically. 'Father's putting up the money for a hundred-footer, a real beauty. We're calling her *The Eagle*, after the family bank's old mark.' Seeing a blank look on the older man's face, he hurried to explain. 'You know, sir, one of those signs that hung outside shops in the olden days, before street numbers were invented?' But it was clear that for Guggenheim the history of commercial signage held no charm.

'*The Eagle*, eh?' His reply was serious. 'I guess the New York Yacht Club will be getting rattled when they hear that name. You've a reputation in yachting circles, haven't you, young man?'

'Oh, that's nothing to do with me, sir! My little gig does the winning for me. She's only got mains'l and mizzen, but she'll make a cracking speed on the river.'

'Is that the River Thames?'

Kit was horrified at the thought of racing on London's sluggish waters but he was far too polite to show it. 'Oh no, sir. My boats are moored at our quay on the River Dart, down in Devonshire. That's where we live, you see, Dartleap Park.' A sudden thought struck him. 'I say, Mr Guggenheim, Father gave me a motor cruiser for my eighteenth birthday, so why don't I take you out in her? Get *Cassandra* beyond the estuary with a good sea running and there's nothing to beat it!'

He felt quite misty-eyed as he remembered that swell of the waves as you shot from the shelter of the river-cliffs and out into the tricky winds of Start Bay. 'Or perhaps you'd rather be under sail?' Not waiting for an answer, he hurried on, 'Yes, of course you would! The crack of canvas, a gale in your mouth, the pull of her heel when she lays her lee rail down to the water ...'

'The pull on your stomach can be pretty unpleasant,' a grave voice interrupted. 'You haven't told Mr Guggenheim that, have you?' Kit grinned as his brother sat down beside him. 'Harry Quentance, sir. Is Kit boring you to tears about his wretched boats?'

Kit watched a slow smile spread across the American's face. Harry always had this effect on people. 'Well I'm darned sure I'd rather be here with forty-six thousand tons of steel under my feet than on one of your brother's skinny little gigs.'

Afraid that the conversation would be dragged away from sailing, Kit ignored Harry completely. 'Oh, but Mr Guggenheim,' he said rapidly, 'you've no idea how much safer a small boat is than this titan. I was chatting to the second officer earlier today. He started his career on a three-skysail-yarder and he's been on every kind of ship you can imagine. He says these mammoths have grown out of all proportion to their strength, and in *his* view a smaller ship's far stronger. In fact he told me how he was once out on the Western Approaches in a mail boat, and as they were luffing up to a squall—'

'Kit!' His brother held up a hand, laughing. 'Give me a look-in, won't you? I want Mr Guggenheim to associate our name with finance, not maritime construction.'

Kit resigned himself as he saw Benjamin Guggenheim's slow nod. Just another businessman. Without taking his eyes off Harry, the millionaire made a signal with one finger. Immediately a waiter floated across to leave a bottle of brandy and three glasses on the table on front of them. Leaning his head comfortably against the antimacassar draped over his chair-back, Guggenheim said, 'Quentance Bank has quite some history, I understand. Why don't you tell me about it?'

'Ra-*ther*!' Taking a sip of brandy and frowning at Kit to do the same, Harry launched into a description of the family business.

As he listened to his brother chatting to one of the richest men in America, Kit had to admit that although it would have been far more fun to cross the Atlantic on something smaller, faster and preferably with sails, in terms of making business contacts this ship was the place to be. It might be dull, but Father had been quite right to send them to New York on *Titanic*.

Bridge: 10.00 p.m.

'Is that you, Lights? By George, it's perishing out here. Aren't you cold?' Having come from the brightness below, First Officer Murdoch had to feel his way up the companionway to join his second officer on the bridge.

'Cold?' came the reply. 'Wait till you've finished your watch and you'll know what frozen feels like.' Lightoller's words were brisk, but Murdoch wasn't sure he sounded as cheerful as usual.

'I'll get used to the temperature, but it's the quiet I can't get over,' he said into the dark. 'This lady's almost silent, isn't she?'

'Too darned silent for my liking, I prefer a bit of noise on a ship. D'you know something, Murdoch? I'd go straight back to sail if I could. Ropes cracking, that gurgling hiss as the water scurls in the scupper holes – now that's how being at sea should sound.'

Murdoch cut across Lightoller's reminiscences with a laugh that rang oddly in the icy air. 'That's all very well, you old romantic, but don't forget how we got pitched and tossed from here to kingdom come. And those days and nights with not a stitch of dry clothing to put on. No, Lights, you can keep your sails. Give me steam any time.'

'Well, this old girl's very steady, I'll give you that, and she's really warming up to her work. We've been making an easy twenty-two knots through my watch and she could surely do more.' There was a pause between them, then Lightoller added softly, 'I just hope no one wants us to put on more speed through field ice, that's all.'

'What?' Murdoch said sharply. 'Have there been more ice reports while I've been below?'

'Yes, as a matter of fact.' In the darkness Murdoch couldn't see Lightoller's face properly, but he could tell from his voice that he was frowning. 'This one came up to the bridge at seven-fifteen. Have a look for yourself.'

By the light of his torch, Murdoch peered at the message. GREEK STEAMER *ATHINAI* REPORTS PASSING ICEBERGS AND LARGE QUANTITIES OF FIELD ICE TODAY IN LATITUDE 41:51'N, LONGITUDE 49:52'W. He stared blankly at the piece of paper, then asked in astonishment, 'This came to the bridge at seven-fifteen, you say? But it's timed as received one-forty-two p.m.'

'I'm as stumped as you are. Apparently the captain saw this telegram when it first came in, but then he handed it straight over to Mr Ismay, who pocketed it. E.J. didn't get it back until after seven.' Murdoch's eyes were getting used to the dark and he could see Lightoller shaking his head. 'I can't understand it. We've both sailed under E.J. many a time, and he's never been one to take risks.'

'Field ice!' Murdoch wished it wasn't his turn to be officer of the watch through what looked set to be a nerve-racking night. 'On this course, we're making straight for it. I can't understand why E.J. wasn't more worried by *Athinai*'s report.'

'Perhaps he was. He came up on the bridge just under an hour ago and all he could talk about was ice.' Lightoller's teeth showed white in the starlight as Murdoch caught his sheepish smile. 'Call me a funk if you like, but I suggested we slow down. I got short shrift for that, I can tell you!'

'To be honest, I'm in a funk myself.' Murdoch felt his heart beating faster than usual as he imagined *Titanic* racing towards ice. 'Suppose an order goes through to speed up? After all, the last watch on a freezing cold Sunday night would be the perfect time to put *Titanic* through her paces. There'll be no passengers hanging around on deck to get worried.'

'A speed trial would be madness.' Lightoller's voice was emphatic. 'The captain would never dream of it.'

'I'm not so sure,' Murdoch replied slowly. 'You can understand why the Old Man might follow an order like that, with the chairman of the White Star Line watching. And besides, this is his last ship, isn't it? He's not going to annoy the bosses and jeopardise his pay-off.'

'You old cynic.' Lightoller's arm reached out to clap him on the back. 'I don't believe a word of it. Just keep those sharp eyes of yours peeled.'

Murdoch looked out to sea. His breath hung in the icy air, a tiny cloud in the black stillness of the star-crowded sky. After a few moments' silence he said, 'Well, I reckon my eyes must be adjusted by now, but I wish there were a moon tonight. Stars are all very well, but there's scarcely any definition between ocean and sky, is there?'

'None at all, though visibility's clear.'

'Let's hope it stays that way, Lights. You've told the lookouts to watch for ice?'

'Certainly. They'll see any iceberg as long as it's got a bit of white to it. Mind you, I've never known a lookout to spot ice before the man on the bridge, have you?'

'Never,' Murdoch agreed. He'd always preferred to trust his own eyes, and didn't mean to take them off the sea ahead for a single moment. 'All I hope is that we don't meet a berg with her black side turned our way.'

'But even so, you'd see the water breaking against its base.' The voice was comfortingly steady. 'On a clear night like this, anything large enough to do any damage would be visible a good couple of miles off.'

'At this speed, that only gives me four minutes to act,' Murdoch grumbled, but Lightoller had already turned away to leave the bridge.

Port boat-deck: 11.40 p.m.

Kit Quentance was standing in his cabin when he felt the jar that ran through the ship. It couldn't be a collision, because anything of that sort would have had him off his feet. It was more an interruption in the monotony of her smooth steaming than anything else. That prolonged, grating shudder reminded him of an embarrassing experience the previous month, when he'd grounded *Cassandra* on a notorious group of submerged rocks just west of the Dart estuary. From the feel of her, *Titanic* had just done the same thing. She must have scraped her keel along some submerged object.

He looked at the Louis XIV-style clock on his desk. A ridiculous extravagance, Kit thought, just like everything else on board, but at least it was bound to be accurate. They even sent a steward in to adjust the time as the ship steamed westwards. The hands showed twenty minutes short of midnight. Harry had dragged him off to bed half an hour ago and was doubtless already snoring in the cabin next door, but Kit hadn't even started to undress and felt full of unspent energy. From a change in the ship's vibration, he guessed that the engines were idling. There'd be a thorough check for damage going on, and he guessed it would be hours before the liner got under way again. Despite the cold, the idea of getting a last breath of fresh air was tempting, and Kit decided he'd go up on deck to find out what had happened.

He'd only got as far as pulling a thick jersey on over the

top of his shirt and evening trousers when he felt the re-assuring forward thrust of the engines again. No point in going up on deck now. If the ship was moving, there couldn't be any problem.

For a few minutes he tried to read, but he couldn't concentrate, and as the gilt clock tinkled out its polite midnight chimes, he threw his book away from him and stood up. He had a feeling that something was wrong. Maybe it was just some subtle change in the movement of the ship, but he had to see for himself. Kit had already opened his cabin door when he caught sight of himself in one of the ornate mirrors cluttering the walls, and saw that his hair was standing on end where he'd pulled his jersey over it. Reluctantly, he turned back into his room. If Harry caught him looking a fright with all these potential clients on board, he'd be furious.

The engine tone altered as Kit was dragging a pair of ivory-backed brushes through his hair. He stood at the dressing-table mirror, staring into the blue of his reflected eyes while he tried to work out what was happening. For a while the engines idled, but then he heard them powering up again. This time, however, there was a different feel under his feet. *Titanic* was moving astern. Dropping the brushes, he hurried out of his cabin.

As he closed the door behind him, Kit glanced along the corridor to where his brother was sleeping, but decided against rousing him. Harry was a great fellow, one of the best, but he didn't understand boats. He certainly wouldn't appreciate being woken up over a strange vibration and an odd feeling. And even if Harry wasn't cross at being disturbed, he'd never believe there might be a problem on the 'unsinkable' ship. Kit decided he'd slip outside on his own to see what was going on. If there was any excitement he could always come back later and shake Harry up.

It was as he emerged into one of the alcoves of the first-class promenade deck that he became certain that something was wrong. His feet told him that *Titanic* was down forward, and glancing over the side, he could see far below that there was scarcely any white wash slipping away from her sides. Putting the engines astern must have arrested any residual forward movement, but then why had she been put into motion at all after she'd struck whatever it was? And why were the engines still running, when, judging by the way she was lying in the water, *Titanic* had damaged herself quite seriously? Just as he was wondering about this, the engines stopped.

There was a second or two of silence before the closing down of the engines triggered a tremendous roar as steam escaped from the ship's exhausts. Pressing his hands to his ears, he dived back inside and made his way to the boat decks. Although they were allocated to second-class passengers, Kit had already been up there several times and greatly preferred them to the promenade decks reserved for his own class, where you were protected from the elements by covered walkways and might just as well be strolling along a Mayfair arcade as the deck of a ship. At least the boat decks were open to the skies, and gave you a clear view of the ocean, while the line of lifeboats reminded him of the open luggers used as mackerel drifters by the fishermen of his native Devonshire.

As he emerged on to the port-side boat deck, the din from the exhausts seemed a hundred times louder. This and the freezing air almost sent Kit straight down below again, but then he glanced along the deck and saw seamen at work coiling down ropes, clearing away the lifeboat covers and making them ready for lowering. So there *was* something seriously wrong. Slapping his shoulders with his hands to try to keep warm, he watched in admiration. The deafening noise meant that there was no way of making any command heard, but despite this, the work carried on efficiently.

Not wanting to get in the way, Kit leaned up against the railings that prevented any passenger on the Boat Deck from getting too close to one of *Titanic*'s four giant funnels. He wanted to find how badly the ship was damaged but realised he'd have to wait until all the steam had blown from the exhausts, at which point the deafening noise would stop. While he waited, he tilted his head back and looked at the sky. There was no moon to distract his eyes from the clarity of the stars against their ink-black backdrop, but as he gazed upwards, it occurred to him that there was something odd about *Titanic*'s direction of travel. That was the Pole Star, surely? The ship seemed to be heading northwards, when New York was undoubtedly to the west. Kit couldn't make it out, and eventually decided that he must have got the direction of the bow wrong. He put it down to his lack of experience at navigating by stars alone.

Turning back to the decks, Kit was impressed by how fast the work had carried along while he'd been star-gazing. The lifeboats had all been cleared of their covers, and one after another they were being swung out on their davits in response to orders conveyed by hand signals. The Officer in charge had moved closer to where Kit was standing, and he recognised him as Second Officer Lightoller, who had talked to him so patiently about sailing ships earlier in the day. He also saw that passengers were starting to mill around on the boat deck. They were clearly anxious, but like him they couldn't make their voices heard above the thundering exhausts. Kit stayed watching in silence, fascinated, no longer even noticing the bitter cold.

It wasn't until the first lifeboat had been lowered level with the boat deck that the din finally stopped. A babble of panicky voices erupted as passengers started to shout questions at Lightoller and his men.

'What's up? I found a great mess of ice on the deck!'

'Did we really hit an iceberg?'

'My valet wanted me to put a life preserver on. Ridiculous nonsense. This ship's unsinkable, isn't it?'

Kit started to speak just as Lightoller held a hand up for silence. In the sudden quiet he was afraid that his voice sounded loud and his question ridiculous. 'Is it serious?'

In an equally loud voice, pitched to sooth, the officer replied, 'Oh no. It's just a matter of precaution to get the boats in the water.'

Kit tried again. Diffidently, he moved closer to Lightoller and said softly, 'I can feel her shifting well down to the bow. She grounded along a submerged ice shelf, didn't she?'

Lightoller was paying attention to him now. 'Either that or she's rebounded against the ram of a berg.'

'So how can I help, sir?'

The officer's eyes rested on him and Kit hoped he'd noticed the 'sir'. He was trying to make it clear to Lightoller that he expected to take orders and would obey them. As a first-class passenger, he knew it was almost unthinkable that he should be put to work, but Kit had spotted that Lightoller was short-handed seven men. He'd understood Lightoller's hand movements when the officer had sent the bosun's mate and six hands down to open one of the lower-deck doors, and as yet, none of them had made it back.

'So how can I help, sir?' Kit repeated.

Lightoller seemed to be appraising him, and Kit grinned with relief as he came to a decision. 'You can help by rounding up the passengers. It's going to be a hard job persuading them to climb into one of these on a freezing night.' He indicated the line of lifeboats waiting to be lowered seventy feet down to the sea. 'Women and children first,' Lightoller added quietly. 'And don't worry which class they're travelling in. It's our duty to care for the weak before we help the strong.'

'Of course, sir,' said Kit, moving off to do as he had been told.

It was indeed very difficult to persuade anyone to get into the lifeboats, and Kit could see exactly why the passengers were so reluctant. Lightoller was loading the first boat, and the process was terrifying. The lifeboat had been lowered until its gunwhale was level with *Titanic*'s deck, and there it hung, swinging gently on its ropes, high above the cold sea. Lightoller was standing with one foot on the deck and the other planted in the lifeboat. Any woman brave enough to venture forwards had to hold out her right hand, the wrist of which the officer grabbed while hooking his left arm under her armpit and practically lifting her over the gap between *Titanic*'s side and the lifeboat's gunwhale. The woman then had to make her way to a seat while the lifeboat rocked perilously, high above the icy Atlantic.

The loading process took a long time, and the first lifeboat was by no means full when Kit heard Lightoller giving the order to lower away. Kit caught his eye, and the officer must have understood the unasked question, because he immediately moved closer and explained quietly, 'I know there's room to spare, but the women in there aren't sea-wise. With all their wriggling about, I'm afraid the lifeboat might break its back if we overload it while it's out of the water.'

As the first boat was lowered to the sea, there was the whoosh of a rocket, which exploded in a shower of white stars high above the ship. This firing of the first distress signal brought home to Kit just how serious the situation must be, and he realised suddenly that he'd seen no sign of his brother. Perhaps Harry had gone over to the starboard side of the ship? Moments later, he was distracted by a surge of passengers who had begun to take the lifeboats more seriously. Lone women and those with children were starting to come forward, but as he carried on with the task he'd been given, he found it hard to persuade some of the married women to leave their husbands.

Looking around, he recognised Isidor Straus, a venerable figure and the founder of Macy's. The old man was leaning up against one of the *faux*-Georgian windows of the deck house and talking quietly with his wife. Approaching the couple, Kit said diffidently to Mrs Straus, 'May I take you along to the boats?'

The elderly woman smiled sweetly at him, but he could see that her answer was addressed to her husband. 'That's very kind of you, young man, but I think I'll stay here for the present.'

'Now, Ida,' Mr Straus pressed her, 'why don't you go along with him, dear?'

'No, not yet.' With a shake of the head, Mrs Straus took her husband by the arm. The two of them turned from Kit and walked slowly away from the lifeboats.

He spotted another couple sitting on the fan casing. They didn't look much older than he was and he guessed they were on their honeymoon. The girl was very pretty, and Kit felt himself blushing as he said to her, 'Won't you let me put you in one of the boats?'

'Not on your life!' Kit wondered if Florence would look at him the way this girl was gazing up at her young husband. 'We've started together and if need be we'll finish together.'

As time passed and boat after boat splashed down into the water, Kit was getting quite hot in his thick jersey, despite the bitter cold. But what with obeying Lightoller's orders and hurrying to and fro between the remaining lifeboats, he never found a moment to tug it off, and would in any case have felt embarrassed about undressing in front of female passengers. Lightoller was still sticking firmly to his 'women and children first' rule and didn't seem to be having any trouble from the male passengers. But Kit could feel the ship's list down at the bow growing steeper, and what with this and the regular firing of distress rockets, he realised that it must be clear to even the blindest optimist that the unsinkable ship was in serious trouble.

He was quite close to Lightoller when he saw Chief Officer Wilde coming over from *Titanic*'s starboard side. Kit didn't catch what Wilde said, but he was near enough to hear Lightoller's reply. 'Revolvers? I can't believe we'll need guns, but let's go and get some if you really want them.'

There happened to be a lull between the lowering of one lifeboat and the loading of the next, and Kit watched as Lightoller and Wilde hurried away. He could see their heads huddled together and it occurred to him that they, more than anyone else on board, would know exactly how *Titanic*'s accident had happened. He gazed after them, wishing he could hear their conversation, until a female voice at his elbow said, 'Any room in a boat for the likes of me and the baby?' and he turned away to carry on with his duty.

Not long afterwards, he saw Lightoller coming back, and felt relieved to know that he had a gun with him. In the short time that he'd been away, the press around the lifeboats had grown. There were men panicking now, and as Kit worked on, there would come the occasional shout, 'Quentance! That man with the gaff topsail collar. He's trying for the boats. Pitch him out of the way for me, will you? If he tries that trick again I'll take a belaying-pin to him.'

Kit was happy to use all his young muscle to push every male chancer away until a particularly firm voice came from behind him. 'You're Kit Quentance, aren't you?' Kit spun round, and recognised the pale eyes and startling moustaches of John Jacob Astor IV. Known to Kit primarily as a great yachtsman, he was more generally known as one of the richest men in the world.

Kit's first thought was how much Harry would like to meet him, and his second was, Where the devil *is* Harry? Both ideas were driven out of his head when Astor spoke again. Pointing to the lifeboat which was just being loaded, he said in a voice of quiet authority, 'Get me a place in that boat. My wife's in a delicate condition and she needs me with her.'

'Oh my goodness!' Kit was dumbfounded. Harry would *kill* him if he offended such a powerful potential customer. 'Colonel Astor. Sir. That is, I mean to say, I don't think . . .'

He was saved by a calm voice behind him. 'It's women and children first. No men are going off yet, I'm afraid.'

Kit watched anxiously as Astor's eyes locked with Lightoller's. Slowly, the American stripped off the pair of gloves he was wearing, and for one panic-stricken moment, Kit thought he was going to strike the second officer with them. But after a long, cold stare it was Astor's eyes that dropped first. Shrugging his shoulders, he threw his gloves to his young wife at her place in the lifeboat and vanished back into the ship.

The encounter had unnerved Kit. He longed to go and find his brother, but he'd placed himself under the second officer's command and he couldn't slip away without permission. To steady his nerves, Kit stood quietly for a moment, holding on to the side rails to brace himself against the slope of the deck. Looking along the line of empty davits, he could see that there were only two lifeboats left, and when he peered over the side, he was horrified by how far the sea had crept up *Titanic*'s sides. There was a strange, submarine glow from rows of cabin lights, still shining out through their drowned portholes.

Kit was overwhelmed by fear. That water was freezing, and it must be miles to the seabed. Would he die by drowning or would the cold get him first?

'Quentance!' Lightoller's shout pulled him back. 'Over here!'

As he hurried along the deck, Kit glanced out across the North Atlantic. Pinpricks of light speckled the water where the sea reflected the stars back up into the night sky. Across the face of the ocean, he could see lifeboats crawling away like fat, black beetles, abandoning him to his death. Kit took a deep breath and turned back to the work he had promised he'd do. He'd just have to hope that, when the time came, he'd find enough courage to die like a man.

2008

ONE

In the final quarter-mile of Edie's downhill sprint, the adrenalin kicked in, and with it the feeling of being entirely at ease with her body. Her arms seemed fluent rather than simply long, while her legs floated her gracefully up on to the top of a crumbling stone wall. She paused there to gaze down into the graveyard. It was a sheltered place, far quieter than Dartleap Park. The Quentance family house might be only a mile and a half away, but it stood exposed on top of its hill, whereas the church of St Barnabas lay lower and was protected by a ring of bosomy slopes from the winds that whipped off Dartmoor.

Edie did a few stretches before hopping down off the wall. She wanted to keep running, leaping the humped tombs, hurdling headstones, slipping between the yews at the lower end of the churchyard and then on down to the Dart. She could see the river in the distance, its waters flicked into little wavelets which sparkled in the June sunshine. If she followed its banks southwards, eventually she'd reach Dartmouth and the freedom of the sea beyond.

Common sense took over. A run like that would take all

day, and she had her research to get back to. She was tempted to make a final sprint across the graveyard, but a residual respect for the dead and a rather stronger fear of offending the vicar constrained her. With scarcely a glance at the daisies speckling the grass, or the more opulent flowers spilling across the fresher graves, she walked round the squat little transept tower to the plot where generations of her family were buried.

Picking her way past the graves of her more remote ancestors, she stopped in front of a basalt memorial. Ever since she was a child, she'd loved the fierce-eyed bird carved into the polished black stone. Wings outstretched, the eagle soared heavenwards, bearing in its talons the drooping body of a young man. The sculptor's skill had given the corpse the impression of having drowned, even to the droplets of water that appeared to fall from its trailing fingers to trickle down the memorial. Edie ran a finger along the heavy gold lettering incised into the stone.

HAROLD QUENTANCE

1887–1912

ERECTED BY HIS PARENTS IN MEMORY

OF OUR MOST DEARLY BELOVED SON

TAKEN FROM US AT THE AGE OF 25 YEARS

BY THE SINKING OF RMS TITANIC

'THE WATERS WERE HIS WINDING SHEET,

THE SEA WAS MADE HIS TOMB.'

That final couplet was grim, because, like those of most of *Titanic*'s victims, Harry's corpse had never been recovered.

Gently she traced the flowing line of the young man's arched spine. *Our most dearly beloved son . . .* Had their parents blamed Kit for escaping without his brother? Had they mourned the older child and rejected the younger? Poor Kit. She knew how that felt.

Wondering if this was yet another link with her great-grandfather, she walked the few steps to his grave.

'BENEATH THIS SPOT LIE THE MORTAL REMAINS OF
FLORENCE QUENTANCE
1895–1935
BELOVED WIFE OF KIT, MOTHER OF RICHARD AND TEDDY

She normally skipped this first part, but today her eye lingered on Teddy's name. She'd never been interested in this particular black sheep, but it occurred to her that he'd been the younger child, too. By now though he'd be either ancient or dead, and besides, the father was far more interesting than the son. Dismissing Teddy, her eyes moved down to the lower part of the headstone.

ALSO INTERRED HERE IS THE BODY OF
CHRISTOPHER (KIT) QUENTANCE
1894–1982
RESPECTED CHAIRMAN OF QUENTANCE BANK
FROM 1920 UNTIL HIS DEATH AT THE AGE OF 88

Edie had often pondered that 'respected'; it was such an impersonal epitaph. She'd been told he was an austere old man, but she couldn't believe that respect was all Kit deserved at the end of such a long life. No one with his passion for boats could be entirely unlovable, and surely the whispers about his cowardice on *Titanic* should be balanced by his heroism at Dunkirk? And taking over the reins at the bank when all he'd wanted to do was try for the America's Cup, that had been another sort of bravery. She shook her head at the thought. She could never give up boats. She wasn't going to work in the bank either if she could help it.

Ambling on between the headstones, Edie came to her grandfather's grave.

RICHARD QUENTANCE

1925–1983

CHAIRMAN OF QUENTANCE BANK FROM 1982 TO 1983

SADLY MISSED BY HIS SONS, ALEC AND MAX,

AND BY HIS GRANDDAUGHTER, IANTHE

Ianthe. Her sister's gravestone with its heartbreaking inscription was just behind her. Edie didn't turn to look at it, but at the thought of her little body lying so close, a shadow seemed to pass over the sun. She shivered in her thin T-shirt and running shorts. Time to jog back up the long hill to the house.

She was just propping a foot up on her grandfather's headstone to tighten a shoelace when she heard the growl of the Dartleap Bentley pulling up beside the church. A few minutes later the world turned bright again as her Uncle Max's face appeared round the corner of the buttress. 'I thought I might find you communing with the ancestors,' he called, picking his way over the graves. 'I'm off to Paris in a couple of hours and I didn't want to miss my goodbye kiss.'

'Hang on,' she put out a warning hand as he came up to her. 'I'm all sweaty from running.'

'Why should I care? You're my favourite niece.' Without giving her time to make the usual reply that she was his *only* niece, Max flung his arms around her. As usual, though he was scarcely more than an inch taller than her, Edie felt comfortingly dwarfed by the breadth of his shoulders. He pulled back and grinned at her. 'So tell me, ghoul, whose tomb are you looking at today?'

'Grandfather's.' Edie waved a hand at the headstone. 'Is it true that he was sadly missed?'

'Dad? That's a laugh.' Max took a stride forwards and stamped down hard on the grave of Richard Quentance. 'He was a ferocious old bastard. Your father and I were thrilled to bung him in the earth.'

Taken aback by his uncharacteristic venom, Edie searched for something to say, until her eye was caught by a line on the headstone. '"Chairman of Quentance Bank from 1982 to1983",' she read out. 'He didn't have much time at the top, did he?'

'No, thank God.' Max gave a hollow laugh. 'He'd have frittered away everything Kit worked for.'

'Was Richard a bad banker?' Edie asked.

'More absentee than bad, to be fair.' There was a flash of blue as her uncle looked at her, then his eyes crinkled into a smile. 'He was obsessed with the idea that Kit had a fortune stashed away in the Dartleap cellars. As soon as the old man died, Dad spent all his time grubbing around down there.'

'You don't mean he believed that daft *Titanic* story?' Edie raised an eyebrow. 'It's ridiculous to think Kit could have carried tons of gold bars into the lifeboat with him.'

Instead of agreeing, Max surprised her by saying, 'Maybe, though if Kit took anything, it's more likely to have been bearer bonds. He could have swapped them for gold after he got to New York.' Max laughed suddenly. 'But there's no point in daydreaming. There are no gold bars, and I need to get back to Dartleap and pack.'

'No gold bars,' Edie echoed as they moved off through the churchyard together. 'I never thought there were any in the first place. I'm only interested in true *Titanic* secrets. My D.Phil. would be brilliant if I came up with anything new.'

'Boat hit berg a hundred years ago.' Max paused to plant a kiss on the side of her head. 'Fascinating.'

Edie knew her uncle was teasing her, but she couldn't help rising to the bait. 'But my doctorate *is* fascinating,' she insisted, lengthening her stride to keep up as her uncle hurried towards the church car park. 'My professor loves my idea of applying modern analytical methods to the *Titanic* story. He says we'll put maritime history right on Oxford's map. And honestly, Max,' she tried to stop her voice rising with excitement as she scurried after him, 'you wouldn't believe how many inconsistencies I've already found in the evidence. It's valuable research. I just need to get proper funding.'

Her uncle didn't even pause. 'Well you're not getting any

from me, sweetheart,' he called over his shoulder. 'The sooner you start working in the bank, the better.'

Max didn't stop till he reached the lych gate, and as he held it open for her, he smiled, as if she'd never mentioned her need for money. 'Do you want a lift back?'

'No thanks,' she muttered, 'I was going to run.'

Used to her uncle ignoring anything unpleasant, she wasn't surprised when he said cheerfully, 'All right then. You can trot behind the car and I'll time you.'

'And eat your exhaust? No thanks.' Edie couldn't help a reluctant grin. 'Maybe I'll come with you.' She didn't approve of gas guzzlers, but relaxing in the Bentley's leather seats would be a lot more comfortable than pounding up the hill in sweaty trainers.

They drove away from the church in silence, and when Max turned through the eagle-crested gates that marked the entrance to Dartleap Park, Edie leaned out of the window to enjoy the mile of driveway. After crossing a couple of fields, the road twisted upwards through dark, hanging woods, and as it curled higher round the hillside, occasional loops of the Dart appeared far below, flashing in the sun like coils in a rope of gold. Eventually, with one final curve of the drive, the trees thinned, and there was the house, shrugging itself from its cocoon of woodland like a butterfly popping out of a chrysalis.

Max stopped the car on the sweep of raked gravel, and as Edie got out she paused to look up at Dartleap. The house had been built in a lemon-beige stone by some eighteenth-century admiral who'd made his fortune from looting Spanish galleons. Over the years, she'd tried to admire its symmetrical façade, but it still seemed to her to be irredeemably bland.

'You've never liked Dartleap much, have you?' Max came up beside her, apparently reading her thoughts.

'Not a lot.' Edie tucked a hand into the crook of his arm. 'I hate its regularity. This sort of architecture's far too polite for me.'

'You're a Philistine, you know that? It's perfect late-Georgian.' Squeezing her hand with his elbow, he moved towards the house. 'And besides, it's our family home. I'd live here all the time if I didn't so hate paying tax when I can avoid it.'

Edie believed that everyone ought to pay their taxes and thoroughly disapproved of her uncle's claim to be non-resident, particularly as she was pretty sure he cheated over the number of days he spent in England, using *Cassandra* and *Cilissa* to slip in and out of the country whenever he felt like it. She was tempted to tell Max how unfair his tax evasion was, but he'd only laugh at her naïvety. Instead, she turned to face him on the shallow steps up to the front door, the word 'exile' having triggered a thought she'd dismissed in the churchyard. 'Your uncle Teddy vanished overseas, didn't he? Do you suppose he's still alive?'

'I certainly hope not – though mind you, I only saw him once in my life.' Max's eyes widened into the vague-eyed stare that meant he was scanning his memory. 'It was down at the church, at Dad's funeral.' His voice was quite normal, but Edie knew her uncle was actually seeing what he described, running the scene through his head like a reel of film. 'We were all in St Barnabas, and Ianthe started shrieking when they brought the coffin in. She had an absolute terror of being shut in the dark and I suppose she didn't like to think of her grandfather stuck in that box. Anyway, Alec was busy with the vicar, so Clio asked me to take Ianthe outside.'

'Did she?' Edie couldn't help interrupting. 'I'm surprised Mum let her out of her sight.'

'Well, we all know how much your mother loved her.' Max's eyes came briefly back into focus, then grew distant again. 'But Clio was heavily pregnant with you and Oscar, so I carried Ianthe off down the aisle. When I got to the back, a stranger stood up and introduced himself as Teddy. Oddly enough, Ianthe stopped crying straight away and just stared at him while he told her what a beautiful little girl she was. She probably thought he looked like me.'

'And did he?' Edie asked.

'Identical. Except Teddy was twenty years older and not quite as handsome.'

Edie looked at her uncle standing beside her on the steps. The sun shone on his golden hair, masking the odd streak of grey, and despite a few smile-lines round his mouth and eyes, he still looked like a film star. Afraid that he'd vanish into the house, she said encouragingly, 'So you saw Teddy at the back of the church. What happened next?'

'Ianthe had calmed down, so I took her back to the front pew where your parents were sitting. And then we had a good laugh.'

'About your uncle?'

'Not at all,' Max said. 'The first hymn was "Sheep May Safely Graze", and I whispered to Clio that it was a hymn for a butcher's funeral, not a banker's. She laughed so much, she wet herself.'

'No!' Edie was shocked at the thought. 'I can't imagine Mum letting go like that.'

'Ah, but your mother was a great giggler in those days.' Max was still smiling, but his gaze was abstracted. 'After the service was over, we had to hang around the graveside waiting for the coffin. I remember her saying, "If I have to stand here much longer, my waters are going to break, and judging by the size I am they'll swamp Richard's grave. Then the vicar won't be able to bury your father's coffin, he'll have to launch it."'

'I don't believe you. That doesn't sound like Mum at all!'

'Not nowadays,' Max said, pushing the front door open. 'It was pretty much the last time I ever saw Clio happy like that.'

Edie nodded. Soon after Richard's funeral, Ianthe was dead too. That must have been when her mother stopped laughing.

'Come on.' Max stood back to let her go into the house ahead of him. 'It's too hot to stay out here chatting.' They crossed the black and white marble slabs of the entrance hall, and Max paused at the foot of Dartleap's cantilevered double staircase. 'You may not like the outside,' he said, 'but you must admit this is perfect.'

Edie stared up at the twin flights. They swept in twisting strands all the way to the great glass dome in the roof that let the clean Devon light wash down through the house. 'It's OK, I suppose,' she conceded. 'If you like regularity.'

'Regularity's all right. It's regulation that's the bugger!'

Max swung off upstairs, while Edie passed on along the hallway to the library.

It was quite her favourite room, having escaped the interior decorators who'd modernised the life out of every other part of Dartleap. She loved the way the sunshine was refracted by the whorled glass in the high, Georgian windows so that it splashed in rainbows across the polished oak floor and shot prisms of colour along the stacks of leather-backed books. Seascapes of exceptionally high quality jostled for space between the bookshelves, and Edie liked to imagine that they were relics of Quentance forebears who had loved the sea as much as she did.

Before she settled down to work, she heaved all the old-fashioned sash windows open to let the hot scents of rose and lavender creep in and mingle with the indoor smells of beeswax and book leather. Then she sank down into the rather too comfortable club chair in front of the desk and dragged her D.Phil. thesis towards her. *RMS* Titanic: *The Application of Historical Source Analysis to Maritime Myth.* Edie blinked hard, but the words seemed to shimmer over the cover of her file like a heat haze. A profound midday silence muffled the Devon countryside for miles around, and the only noise was the soporific thud of the pendulum from the long-case clock just outside the library door.

Her gaze drifted to a silver-framed photograph of her great-grandfather, Kit. It stood on the over-mantel, propped against the dark-oak carving of the family's coat of arms, and showed him on the deck of *Cassandra*. He was leaning against the wheelhouse, his face unsmiling, and even though the photo was in black and white, it was clear that

Kit Quentance had had the blond hair shared by the entire family. Everyone, that was, apart from Edie herself.

He'd died the year before she was born. Eighty-eight was a good age, but she'd often wished he'd managed to hang on a few years longer to explain to her all those incomprehensible riddles about *Titanic*. It was odd to think that Kit had been right there, at the very heart of the disaster. Maybe he was out on deck when the collision happened? Perhaps he'd even smelled the sour breath of glacial ice as *Titanic*'s hull was sliced open? The chair creaked as Edie threw herself back against it. As far as she knew, Kit had never told a soul what happened that night. The story was that her great-grandfather would never speak of *Titanic*. It was said that he was too ashamed of the terrible thing he'd done.

She looked again at the over-mantel, but this time her eyes slid past Kit to a larger photograph of herself, surrounded by her family on the steps of the Sheldonian Theatre in Oxford. It had been taken on the day she'd been awarded her degree, a starred First, with the offer of a post-graduate place to study for a doctorate. Edie had been so blindingly happy that her joy seemed to have rubbed off on everyone else in the picture.

On one side of her was Max, with her father looking almost cheerful beside him. Dad wasn't as obviously good-looking as his brother, but that straight white hair and lean face echoed some noble knight from the Arthurian legends. Edie herself was in the middle of the group, with Oscar on her other side, arms flung casually round her and her mother's shoulders. With her children standing guard between her and her husband, and her favourite twin hugging her, that must have been why even Clio was smiling, lips parted to show her perfect teeth, sooty eyes peering out from under her fringe.

As Edie looked at herself at the centre of the group, it did seem unfair that she was the only dark-haired one in a golden-blond family. But at least the sun was shining through the spikes of her hair and making it look almost pretty, like a halo of bright rays round her narrow face. She was giving the camera that mouth-closed, speculative smile she used when she didn't want the gap between her front teeth to show, and although her lips looked rather more bee-stung than she felt comfortable with, at least they were a regular shape. Unusually, her eyes were open in the photo, and actually, they were a perfectly nice blue. As Edie assessed her face, it occurred to her that maybe she didn't need to look *quite* that academic to be taken seriously. Perhaps her mother was right in nagging her to try make-up?

Idly, she wondered how it would feel to be the kind of woman who always wore eye-liner and painted her nails. To be one of those adorable flirts who made people smile with her silliness, who had men fighting for her attention. She'd known girls like that; some of them had been at Oxford with her. They'd been seriously brainy, but they'd never been serious. Instead, they'd been light-hearted, lovely and lovable. Edie smiled at her own foolishness. She had no idea how to be like that, no idea at all.

Her glance moved to her twin. It was no wonder everyone adored her brother, because Oscar was the male version of those pretty, flirty girls. He seemed to be happy whatever he did, including working for the family bank, but the idea filled Edie with horror. She forced her eyes back down to the papers in front of her. An academic life in Oxford was her escape from Quentance Bank, and if she wanted to keep her postgraduate place, she'd better get on with her research.

Before she'd gone for her run, Edie had been making notes from Commander Lightoller's autobiography, *Titanic and Other Ships*, but Max must have used the desk since, and the book seemed to have disappeared under a morass of his papers. As Edie fumbled under her uncle's documents, her fingers closed around something hard. It had square edges, but it didn't feel like a book. Books didn't come wrapped in soft cloth, and when she tugged the thing out on to her lap, she realised that it was also far too heavy. A bee hummed in through the open windows, and as it whined around the room she prodded the material, trying to guess what it might be covering. It was something solid, sharp-cornered and absolutely none of her business.

Edie sat listening to the bee bouncing drunkenly off the library bookshelves until curiosity overcame her. After some furtive probing she touched the coldness of metal, but at that same moment she thought she caught the creak of floorboards. She froze guiltily, the object half unwrapped between her hands, but now all she could hear was the steady thud of the clock from the hallway. Even the bee seemed to have buzzed its way outside again. Bending over her discovery, she drew the cloth away and found herself staring down at a rectangular block of solid gold.

There are no gold bars. The words Max had said in the grave-yard drummed in her ears. So what was this one doing here? As she looked at it more closely, Edie spotted some patches of thin striation, as if it had been scratched. There was also what seemed to be a hallmark, but she couldn't make it out clearly. Lifting the bar close to her face, she turned it slowly around to try to pinpoint the sunlight on to the mysterious little mark.

'What the *hell* are you doing?' The growl from behind her almost made Edie drop the heavy lump. She spun round in her chair and found her uncle looming over her, looking nothing like the perennially pleasant man she was used to. 'Give that to me!' he said, making a grab at the bar, but Edie instinctively pulled it away from him. A moment later, he had got hold of her upper arm with one hand and the gold with the other. There was a brief tug-of-war in which he turned out to be far stronger than she'd imagined. Once he'd wrenched the thing from her hands, he immediately stepped backwards, away from her.

Edie was too dumbfounded to feel angry at Max's roughness. 'That's gold,' she said weakly. 'Whatever's it doing here?'

'Don't be so damned nosy!' Without another word, her uncle stamped off towards the library door, the bar tucked under his arm.

'Where are you going?' Edie called after him, unable to take in what had just happened.

'Paris,' Max threw over his shoulder, and with that he was gone.

As she listened to the angry skid of tyres on gravel, Edie sat in her chair feeling dazed. She wouldn't be seeing Max again until the weekend after her and Oscar's twenty-fifth. He'd left without even wishing her a happy birthday.

TWO

The rumble of a car over the leaded glass above her head made Clio pause. Cupping a hand under the brush which she'd just loaded with burnt umber, she glanced up at the clock. An hour and a half till the twins were due to arrive, plenty of time yet. As the engine noise faded away round the peaceful Bath square, she went back to painting, sweeping an earthy wash right across the lower part of her canvas, then stippling it with celadon and bistre to create an appropriately sombre base for a woodland floor.

At first, she was perfectly conscious of being in the vaults that opened from the paved area in front of her basement flat and extended out under the road, but as the minutes ticked by, Clio became absorbed within the artwork she was creating until brick walls became the peeling trunks of light-starved trees. Pock-marked caps of fly agaric and the arrow-shaped leaves of cuckoo pint poked up from the meagre soil, so real that she could actually smell the toadstools' fungal decay and the acridity of the nightshade berries. A heavy silence blanketed the wood around her, but from somewhere far beyond the trees came the slow tolling of a bell.

As sometimes happened when she was engrossed like this, the emerging picture took control of her brush, as if it was drawing the painting out of her rather than the other way round. First a clearing appeared amidst the leaf-mould, and then a shaft of sunlight cut through the forest canopy to illuminate a white rose, scrambling over a mound of bare earth. Clio couldn't help herself. Holding her palette under a downlighter to get the colour exact, she mixed steel grey with a smear of ecru before painting in the little gravestone.

'Now that was really silly, wasn't it?' She spoke aloud, breaking her creative trance. Turning her back to the fresh picture on her easel, Clio began to clean the oil paint off her brushes. 'Just look at the time: they'll be here in half an hour. Supper's not even started, they've got their friends coming along later, and I must look a complete mess.' As tears stung the back of her nose, she told herself, 'Don't think about it. Just *don't* think about it!' The twins' birthday was always difficult.

Slamming the studio door behind her, Clio paused to pick a couple of struggling stalks of tarragon before going on into her flat. As she stepped into the comfortable, coat-hung muddle of the entrance lobby, Clio hoped that her twins felt as cushioned from life as she did in this patchouli-scented space where she'd brought them up. She'd bought it as an escape valve after they were born, dreaming that she'd occasionally slip away for a few solitary days of painting, but it had turned out to be a permanent haven when Edie and Oscar were still only toddlers and the downward drift of her marriage to Alec had become unstoppable. Memories. She shook her head to cut them off. This wasn't a good day for remembering.

From the lobby, Clio walked briskly down the broad corridor that bisected her flat. She'd made this central passageway a gallery for her paintings of the twins, and every inch of wall space was crammed with oils marking the various stages of their development. As she passed along, Oscar grinned down at her through his childhood and adolescence, invariably cheerful, unfailingly handsome. Edie, on the other hand, was rather less satisfactory.

Clio paused by a full-length painting she'd done of her daughter the previous year. If only she didn't fight so hard against anything feminine, Edie could be quite pretty. Setting aside those front teeth, her mouth was fashionably large and would look even better if she'd just wear a bit of lipstick. Those clothes though, shapeless, colourless, sexless. Such a waste when a nice floral dress would look so sweet on her. Clio frowned as her eyes travelled over the portrait. Edie would have a really good figure if she wasn't so skinny. If she thought her daughter would listen, she'd tell her to stop all that ridiculous running and eat a bit more.

With a sigh, Clio walked on towards the kitchen, sniffing the green-lemon scent of the tarragon in her hands. She'd chop the herb up finely and slip it under the skin of the chicken before putting it in to roast. Red wine and softened garlic in the gravy would be delicious, and she'd do a green salad and a bowl of that nutty Camargue rice to go with it. Strawberries with champagne sorbet for pudding, and even Edie couldn't say her food was unhealthy.

She'd love to have made the twins a huge, creamy birthday cake and studded it with candles. Oscar would eat it out of kindness, though he worried about his waistline rather too much for a young man, but Edie would reject it outright. It had always been like that. Clio paused at the kitchen door, her mind flying back to their babyhood. While Oscar would be happy to suckle for hours, Edie had arched her back and screamed whenever she tried to breast-feed her. She could remember the guilty relief when she'd finally given up trying and had passed her over to be bottle-fed by the maternity nurse. Such a difficult infant she'd been. So unlike— Clio squeezed her eyes shut to block out the involuntary image of her first baby gurgling in her arms.

As she went into the kitchen, she was momentarily dazzled by the evening sun which flooded in through a bank of glass windows, making the whole room glow. The jumble of art and cookery books became a multi-coloured patchwork. A leather chair took on a deep, oxblood lustre. Even the stub-ended refectory table was transformed from scrubbed oak into burnished caramel. While she was taking in this unexpected beauty, a finger of sunlight touched the single painting on the far wall. Against her ominous background, the child stood out like a jewel. Sad-eyed, Ianthe stared down at her mother.

The tarragon still in her hands, Clio sank on to a chair. 'Mummy! Mummy!' The voice was a thin scream. 'I'm frightened, Mummy! I'm all alone in the dark. Why don't you come to me?'

When they first noticed Ianthe was missing, they'd assumed she'd just got herself lost in the woods, and Clio had actually been more cross than worried. Her daughter was a bright little five-year-old, always wanting to run around exploring, and it had been hard to restrain her, even when she'd complained of that fluttery bird in her chest. An innocent murmur, the doctor had called it, but Clio had never quite believed him and was always getting annoyed when Ianthe rushed about and made herself breathless.

Alec and Max spent all that first afternoon calling. They searched right down as far as the river but there'd been no sign of her. They were going to ring the police, but then the phone calls started. On her hard-backed, kitchen chair, Clio rocked to and fro, muttering, 'Forget it. *Forget* it! It's over,' but she couldn't stop the anger welling up like bile in her throat. The kidnapper wanted millions of pounds and they'd refused to pay. What if it was a hoax, Max said. They couldn't raise that kind of money, Alec said. And so they'd dithered. Eventually they rang the police, but by then it was too late.

Clio closed her eyes. Remembering was torture, but she couldn't stop now. On the third day, she'd been out at dawn and was searching down near the gates. She was hugely pregnant with the twins, she'd hardly slept and was feeling oddly disassociated from the real world. Either she'd forgotten to put any on, or she'd kicked her shoes off somewhere on the drive, because she could remember being distracted by the dew on her bare feet. Glancing down, she'd noticed minute cobwebs shimmering in the grass like doll-sized bridal veils, and she'd squatted awkwardly to try and see the money-spiders that had spun them.

'Ianthe,' she'd called. 'Ianthe darling! Come and help me

look for the baby spiders. Ianthe!' She'd paused to listen, but there was no human voice mingling with the whoops of the dawn chorus. All she'd heard was a car coming along the road, and a moment later the vicar's black Vauxhall had pulled up. Clio found she didn't have the strength to heave herself upright, so she'd waited until the vicar came over to her.

'Clio?' She'd squinted up at him but she couldn't see his face against the brightness of the morning sun. 'Will you come down to St Barnabas with me?'

'If you really want me to.' She'd held her hands out for him to pull her up. 'Though I'm not sure I believe in prayer any more.'

'We're all in God's hands,' was all he'd said as he helped her to his car.

Dizzy with lack of sleep, she'd clung to the lych gate for support as they went into the churchyard. When the vicar spoke, she couldn't take the words in and had to ask him to repeat them.

'Ianthe's here. I've found her.'

Clio had swayed and held tighter to the gate. 'You've found her! Why didn't you tell me straight away?' She could remember exactly how she'd felt. Half stunned, flooded with relief and an uncontrollable happiness. 'Oh my darling Ianthe, safe! I can't believe it! Oh my God, oh my God! Quick, where is she?'

The reply had seemed unbearably slow. 'She's round behind the church, in the Quentance plot, but—'

She didn't stop to listen. Ignoring a warning pain from deep in her abdomen, she'd run off through the graveyard, her bare feet slipping on the grass, stumbling painfully on the low edges of tombstones. There'd been a shout from behind her. 'Clio, wait!' Ignoring it, she'd rounded the buttress and there was Ianthe, asleep on the grass. A sudden stabbing ache had slowed her down. Clutching her stomach and grunting with the pain, she'd walked as fast as she could until she was staring down at her darling little one.

'Ianthe.' The word had come out in a whisper. The child was lying across the grave of Kit and Florence Quentance, still in the clothes she'd been wearing when she disappeared, though there was also a rug half wrapped around her, as if to protect her and keep her warm. A breeze had rustled through the churchyard, lifting the little girl's curls as it passed. 'Ianthe, I'm here now. Are you awake, my angel?' The child's sea-purple eyes were open, staring up at her mother. They were unmoving, fixed in a wide stare.

'Clio, my dear.' The vicar had puffed up behind her.

'She won't answer me.' Clio had swung round to grab his arm. 'What's wrong with her? What's *wrong* with her?' Releasing her hold on the vicar, she'd dropped heavily to her knees and reached for her child. The little hand was so cold. She'd leaned forward and lifted Ianthe up into her arms. The body flopped awkwardly, and as Clio had clutched her daughter to her, a sweet, sickly smell came from her half-open mouth.

The graveyard had turned dark and seemed to spin into the swirling blackness around her. Clio had no memory of putting Ianthe down, but when she recovered her senses, she'd found that she was kneeling beside the lifeless body which lay among the daisies in the bright green grass of the graveyard. With one hand, she was stroking her daughter's cold forehead again and again.

'And so I didn't call the police when I found her, though I probably should have done.' Clio had vaguely wondered how long the vicar had been speaking to her. 'I thought the family ought to see her first.' She'd felt his hand touching her shoulder. 'Your little girl's in God's care now.'

Ignoring him, Clio had gone on silently stroking Ianthe's head until something caught her eye and she'd paused to pick a few strands of fair hair off the child's neck. Sitting back on her heels, she'd looked at them, but nothing had made sense so she'd just tucked the hairs into the pocket of her dress. It was funny how she still remembered details like that. Later, she'd given them to the police but they'd been dismissive about finding pale hairs on Ianthe's body when the whole family was blond. They could have come from any of them.

The kitchen in Bath took shape around her, but after a minute spent rocking back on her chair legs and thinking how useless the police had been once they'd seen that coroner's report, her mind took her back to the graveyard.

As she'd knelt in the grass beside her dead daughter, the bell in the church tower began to toll the hour. Above its mournful clanging, Ianthe's voice floated up to her, sweet as a lark, singing one of her favourite nursery rhymes.

> 'Bell horses, bell horses,
> What time of day?
> One o'clock, two o'clock,
> Time to away.'

The pain was unmistakable, a squeezing ache, like a period pain but of an unbearable intensity. Within moments she'd been on the ground, groaning, only vaguely aware of the vicar taking one horrified look at her before scurrying away to call an ambulance. Later that day, the twins had been born.

With an effort, Clio stood up and fumbled for a handkerchief. If she didn't get that chicken in the oven, there'd be no birthday dinner for them at all.

THREE

'Oscar? Oscar!' Edie scowled at her twin's profile, but there was no answer. He swore under his breath as he was forced to slow down behind a pair of lorries that were crawling over Bathwick Hill, but then he just went on working on some lyric of his.

> 'Cocaine Kate is taking a train,
> She's snorting the dragon's line.
> Crying tears of a different kind ...'

'I wish you'd listen to me!' He could sing very loudly when he wanted to, and she had to shout to make herself heard. 'If *you* wanted something, you know I'd be begging Mum to help out.'

The song stopped as her brother said calmly, 'But I'd never ask you to persuade Mum about anything. Why would I?'

If she wasn't trying to get his help, Edie would have been tempted to punch him. She knew perfectly well how difficult her relationship with her mother could be and she didn't need anyone else to spell it out. Swivelling round in her seat, she stared out of the car, leaving her brother to get on with his composing.

'Kate loses the beat as she walks down the street,
It's hardly the road to heaven . . .'

They were driving with the roof down on Oscar's old Morris Minor, and as the dull suburban boxes on the outskirts of Bath gradually morphed into Georgian ashlar, Edie felt her annoyance melting. She might not appreciate her twin's taste in music, but he had a golden voice.

'Like an alley cat in a headlight beam,
Her nine lives are down to seven.
Weeping tears of a different kind.'

As Oscar's song faded, Edie went on staring out at the city. The setting sun had washed the stone with a soft glow, turning the houses that deep, buttery colour she loved so much at Oxford. Oxford. She must fight for it. Twisting back to face her twin, she picked up the conversation as if she'd never let it drop.

'I only want Mum to go on paying my allowance for another couple of years. She's my last hope. Dad turned me down flat, and so did Max when I asked him, though I bet they've got a fortune stashed away somewhere,' she added, remembering that mysterious gold bar.

'I'm sorry, Eds, but you know Mum's not going to help out any more. She thinks it's time you got a proper job instead of sponging off the state.'

'But I'm desperate to stay on at Oxford and get my D.Phil. finished.' Edie paused. 'All right then. Will you tell her I'll manage if she can just give me half what I get at the moment? I'll find a job in a pub or something to make up the rest.'

'To be perfectly honest, you don't stand a chance, not even of half,' her brother said as he swung the little car down towards the river. 'In the first place, Mum thinks all academics are self-righteous lefties, and in the second place, you're a Quentance and she thinks you should be working in the family bank.'

'Just listen, Oscar. You know I'm clever, and if the economy wasn't going down the tubes I'd walk straight into a lectureship. But as things are, it might take me a bit of time to get a university job. *Please* persuade her for me. She'll never agree if I ask.'

'You know something?' Oscar glanced at her. 'You might get on better with Mum if you made more of an effort. A decent haircut, a bit of war paint and you'd be quite respectable.'

'Concentrate on the bloody road, can't you?' Edie stared at the line of traffic ahead until an appropriate answer occurred to her. 'And I might just point out that even if I'd wanted to throw slap all over my face I wouldn't stand a chance, with you hogging the bathroom all afternoon.'

'That's perfectly true,' her twin conceded generously. 'It takes me an age to get my hair right. We'll need to find a bigger pad when you're working at the bank.'

'I'm not *going* to!' Edie pulled herself up. There was no point getting into a squabble. 'Have you enjoyed working in the London branch?' she asked curiously.

'Well I love the money, obviously, but St James's Square pretty much runs itself, and Dad's never involved me in anything he gets up to. Working with Max will be a lot more fun.'

'So why the bigger place in London? Surely you'll be based in Paris?'

'I'll still need somewhere to see my friends, and you as well, Eds. I'm not having you just vanishing out of my life. Anyway, don't you think it'd be nice to have a bit more space?'

Edie tried to keep her voice firm but it was hard not to smile when Oscar said such sweet things. 'We'd have more room if you didn't leave your clothes everywhere.'

'What about your books?' he shot back. 'I don't know why you can't fill the place with knickers and make-up like a normal girl.'

Edie's reply turned into a yelp as her twin jammed on the brakes and skidded into a pub car park. His Morris Minor rocked unnervingly round a high wall, coming to a halt only feet from a grassy bank leading straight down to the River Avon.

'Bloody hell, Oscar!' Edie said as soon as she could speak. 'Are you trying to scare the shit out of me?'

'Not all over my seats, *if* you don't mind.' He'd put on his camp voice. 'I need a drink. Coming?'

'I'll come into the pub, but I'm not touching a drop. Your old schoolfriends are boring enough to put me to sleep as it is.'

'They're better than your comprehensive geeks. I don't think Mum's ever got over you going there.'

LOUISE PATTEN | 57

'At least it got me into Oxford.' She put a hand on her twin's shoulder. 'You will help me stay there, won't you?'

'I wouldn't hold out much hope, but I'll do my best.'

'Thanks.' She leaned across to kiss him.

Having climbed out of his car, Edie watched Oscar as he tugged up the old convertible's roof, thinking how odd it was that she'd never minded feeling like an ugly duckling while he'd grown from a cygnet into a swan. 'Tell you what, I'll drive the rest of the way to Mum's if you want to get shit-faced. Treat it as an extra birthday present.'

'Eds, you're an angel!' Oscar hurried round the car to grab her hand, which he swung happily as they moved off towards the pub.

'I wonder what presents Mum's going to give us this year.'

'The usual, I suppose.' Her twin's voice was gloomy. 'Something frilly for you, and something manly for me.'

'Cheer up.' Edie swung his arm higher. 'We can always swap.'

When they went into the pub, she knew exactly what to expect. Men and women turned to look at Oscar, bringing his automatic grin in return. Despite his height, he moved easily through the crowd and was standing at the bar ordering their drinks while she was still trying to push her way through. By the time she reached him, the young barman was already laughing at some joke of Oscar's, while a pair of very pretty girls standing near by were openly eyeing him up. No one ever stared like that at Edie, and she told herself for the hundredth time that she didn't care. She might not be beautiful, but she was clever. And she was fit, too. She could outrun any of them.

As she stood beside her twin, she caught something slightly feminine about the way he leaned his hip as he chatted to the barman, but when she touched his elbow, he glanced down at her, then immediately switched his gaze to the two girls who'd been staring at him. They were giggling now, shifting about to give Oscar a clear view of thigh-skimming dresses over bare legs. 'I recognise them, Eds.' He nudged her and pointed. 'I'm sure they're in *Neighbours*. Why don't you ask them?'

'I'm not going to pimp for my brother!'

'Spoilsport.'

'I don't mean to be,' Edie said. 'It's just that I feel a complete tit in this ridiculous dress. I only bought it because Mum likes me to look girly, but honestly, she should try being six foot with a flat chest and see how easy that is.'

Oscar got more looks as they moved out to the pub's beer garden and found themselves a couple of seats right down on the bank of the Avon. Edie would have been quite happy to sit there, chatting in a desultory way and watching the midges dancing on the river, but it wasn't more than a few minutes before the usual happened. Oscar couldn't resist including strangers on the benches nearby in their conversation, others shifted closer to join in, and soon Edie and he were surrounded by a cheerful crowd, all talking as if they'd known each other for ever. Any minute now he'd start singing.

'Give me the car keys,' she shouted in her brother's ear.

'What's that, Eds? Not going already, are you?'

'I think I'd better. Mum's expecting us.' Oscar looked so happy that she couldn't bring herself to nag him not to stay drinking for too long.

'You're a star, you know that.' His eyes crinkled into a smile as he looked up at her. 'Mind you don't scrape my paintwork.'

Edie was more used to cycling than driving and her nerves twitched as she eased the Morris Minor cautiously through Bath's crowded streets. She had a few close shaves with parked cars as she manoeuvred her way along lanes built for horse-drawn carriages before pulling up outside an elegant, six-storey house. A black-leaded causeway bridged the gap between the pavement and the pair of pompous columns flanking the front door, but Edie didn't cross it. Instead, she trotted down the flight of concrete steps that led to her mother's basement flat. She knocked on the front door, and while she waited for it to open she gave herself a quick talking-to. I will *not* answer back. I will *not* lose my temper. I *will* stay calm.

Edie never meant to quarrel with her mother, but somehow they always did. She'd blurt out the wrong thing, Clio would flare up, and it would end with tears and the slamming of doors. She assumed that her mother had loved her unconditionally when she was a baby, but somewhere that love had all gone wrong. Maybe it was simply that she'd been a rebel, not dressing how her mother would have liked her to, refusing the exclusive school that had been chosen for her, picking friends she knew Mum wouldn't approve of. And in truth, it hadn't been hard to annoy Clio, because underneath that artistic hippy-dippy exterior, her mother was deeply conventional.

Hearing footsteps approaching, Edie prepared a warm smile. This time it would be different.

FOUR

'*Monsieur Alec à l'appareil!*' Claudine's voice drifted through the open door of Max's office.

'*D'accord, j'arrive,*' he called back, hunting through the mess on his desk until he excavated the telephone from beneath a replica of the *Golden Hind*. 'Good-morning from sunny Paris.'

'Morning.'

His brother's voice was cool, but then Alec was never anything else. Immediately after Dad had died and they'd started running the bank together, Max had tried to appear older than he was by copying that laconic style. Eventually, though, he'd had to find other ways to win his clients' trust, because however hard he worked at it, he could never manage to stay serious for long, whereas perennial gravity was the source of Alec's charisma.

'How're things in London today?' Max asked, picturing his brother as he did so. Alec would be sitting very upright, the surface in front of him bare apart from a 1950s Bakelite telephone, a fountain pen and an inkwell.

'Ghastly. Have you seen the markets this morning?' Max heard the click of a drawer and guessed what Alec was doing. His brother's office displayed nothing to belie his chosen image of reliable, old-fashioned banker, but that was just for show. A high-tech computer system, data feeds, and a glowing bank of phones were kept concealed in the dummy drawers of his mahogany desk and would slide out at the touch of a button. 'I can't *believe* how much Gordon Brown's borrowing,' Alec grumbled. 'The economy's a debt-drunk disaster and it's going to get worse.'

When his brother was this gloomy, there was usually only one reason. 'Been talking to Clio, have you?'

'How did you guess?' Something between a snort and a sigh came from the other end of the line. 'She rang to moan about some bust-up with Edie on the twins' birthday. Apparently Edie was after money so she could stay on at Oxford, but Clio refused to help.'

'I turned her down as well,' said Max, feeling a touch of guilt about ruining his niece's dreams.

'Quite right too! Edie can finish her D.Phil. in her spare time, but she's going to have to knuckle down to making us some money.'

'Do you think she'll be any good at it?' Max was curious. While Oscar was as keen on cash as any true-born Quentance, Edie seemed to have missed out on the avarice gene.

'To be perfectly honest, I'm more worried about that sanctimonious streak of hers,' Alec said. 'I think I'll lock her up in the basement. Records and Archives should keep her from poking her nose into anything she shouldn't.' Max was wondering whether to mention Edie finding the gold bar when Alec changed the subject. 'How was your date last night, by the way?'

'A washout. Remember me telling you about a redhead?'

'Twenty years younger than you and looking for love. Is it time I gave her the once-over?'

'Sadly not. She turned into a bore and I'm feeling like death.' Max sipped at the *tisane* his secretary had forced on him. 'Claudine thinks I'm having a *crise de foie.*'

'That means your liver's shot, doesn't it?'

'More like a bilious attack, and you'd be feeling rough if you'd dined where I did last night. I tried to persuade the girl to come to my house for a nice quiet supper, but she nagged me to take her to that villainously expensive restaurant at the top of the Eiffel Tower, and now I think I've got altitude sickness.' Max shuddered at the memory. 'It gave me the most horrible feeling that I was flying.'

'Since you've never flown in your whole life, I can't see how you can possibly know what it feels like.'

'I can imagine *exactly* what it feels like, and that's precisely why I'm never going to do it.' Max fumbled through his pockets until he found a handkerchief to wipe his forehead. Even the thought of aeroplanes made him sweat. 'Things went right downhill when she started hinting about taking me home to meet her parents. Can you imagine? I hadn't even got to first base and she was hearing wedding bells.' Max could guess what his brother would say next.

'It's more than time you got married, Max.' He'd guessed right. Here came the lecture. 'Just find some nice young thing who'll breed us another Quentance boy or two. We *can't* risk letting the name die out. Obviously Oscar will do his duty, but supposing his wife doesn't give him any sons?'

Max had the occasional suspicion that Oscar might not be keen on this particular duty, but he certainly wasn't going to raise that with Alec, and anyway, he was probably wrong. 'Of course,' he answered after a pause. 'When I find the right woman, nothing'll stop me settling down and having scores of Quentance sons.'

Clutching the phone to his ear, Max wandered over to examine his face in one of the mirrors that hung around his office. With his free hand, he touched his cheekbones, pulling the skin taut. A few more lines on his forehead maybe, a certain slackness around the jawline, quite a few streaks of grey in the blond curls. But the full mouth and the cobalt eyes were as good as ever. He took a step back and grinned at his reflection. Plenty of time to find a wife. Fifty-two wasn't that old, after all.

In that uncanny way he sometimes had, Alec guessed his thoughts. 'You need to get a move on, Max. Those looks of yours can't last for ever.'

At that moment, his secretary's elegantly coiffed head appeared round the door. '*Dix minutes, Max!*'

'What was competent Claudine saying?'

'Nothing important. She disapproves if I keep the nobility waiting, and I'm off to shift a packet for Isaiah Jerichau.'

'Profitably?'

'You bet, and may God bless the European Union, my haven on earth!' He waited, but there wasn't even a murmur from the other end of the line. Perhaps it hadn't been as funny as he thought. 'No borders, free trade and a single currency,' Max went on. 'I think those adorable Brussels bureaucrats had money launderers specially in mind when they designed the euro.'

'That's quite funny.' This time, when he hadn't meant to joke, he heard his brother laugh.

'Honestly, Alec, I'm serious. The five-hundred-euro note has turned Europe into the perfect laundry-land. I can carry a million pounds' worth of cash in a briefcase. Though I still like shifting gold best of all. It's what *Cassandra*'s built for.'

'That old girl's got the speed of a snail. I don't know why you keep it when you've got the monster motor-boat to play with.'

'Because *Cassandra*'s so much prettier than *Cilissa*, that's why.' Max would have liked to say more about his lovely *Cassandra*, but Alec interrupted.

'Call you back,' he said crisply, and the phone went dead.

Alec quite often cut him off like this, but Max was never offended. Because despite his lack of obvious warmth, he knew that his brother loved him, and it had been on *Cassandra* that he'd first known it for sure. He closed his eyes.

Rain was hurling itself against the attic window. The glass panes were grimy, with cobwebs drooping on either side like tattered curtains. Max knew what he'd see if he walked over and peered out of this eyrie, right at the top of Dartleap. Wet fields with tiny cows grazing, sodden woods cloaking the lower slopes like dark sheets of tarpaulin, and beyond the trees the river, far, far below. If he opened the window and leaned out, he'd be able to see the Dart snaking almost to the sea in one direction and up to Totnes in the other, but if he did that, he'd get soaked. It was because it was pouring that they'd been sent up here to amuse themselves while Dad had a talk with Grandfather Kit down in the library.

Max tried to extract from his brain a picture of how old he and Alec would have been, and after a minute, he caught the image he was looking for. On one skinny wrist, his brother was wearing the watch he'd been given for his birthday. So Alec would have been eleven and Max nine.

Remembering their ages brought back the keen sense of misery he'd felt that year. Alec was leaving for boarding school, and Max would soon be sent away too. Even worse, he was being packed off to be educated with strangers, abroad. However was he going to manage, all alone in Switzerland? The thought had been worrying him for weeks, and when they'd got up to the attics, he'd found himself blurting out all his fear and his loneliness. 'I don't *want* to go away. No one will care about me. Oh Alec, I don't *want* to!' As he talked, he felt himself spiralling into that muddled, dizzy, choking sort of crying that he couldn't get under control unless someone either soothed or shocked him out of it.

He could remember feeling quite grateful when Alec said fiercely, 'Well you've got to go, so stop being a drip. You're to take over the European business when you grow up and you need to mix with the right sort of foreigners and learn their languages. And besides,' his brother had added more kindly, 'you'll be able to sail all the time. Your school's right near Geneva and there's a huge lake.' He'd calmed down after that and they'd looked round for something to do. The attics were empty and Alec was soon bored, but they'd been ordered to stay there and didn't dare go downstairs.

Swinging in his comfortable desk chair, Max smiled at the memory of his nine-year-old self. Insecure and unloved, the only thing he'd had to be proud of was his extraordinary memory. Up there in the attic, he'd have known it was a mistake when he begged Alec to play cards, but in those days he'd always carried a pack in his back pocket and he did so like to show off. If a card had been turned over, even if only for a second, its picture and its exact place in the pack fixed themselves in his brain. For hours afterwards Max would be able to riffle through the pack in his head and 'see' precisely the position of every card. Sometimes Alec would find it funny, but not on that particular afternoon. After half an hour of losing every game, he'd had enough.

'You're a pain, Max. I'm not playing with you any more and I don't care if it makes Dad cross. You can jolly well go and find Nanny.' Scrabbling up from the floor, Alec had set off down the stairs, and after a moment's hesitation Max had followed.

As they crept round the curves of the double staircase, a roar of shouting hit them. Their father was bellowing, but Max had thought Grandfather Kit sounded far more frightening. He'd never heard him raise his voice before, and it wasn't at all like Dad's wild thundering. Grandfather Kit was shouting too, but in a cold, controlled sort of way, like a captain giving orders on a ship.

'Calm yourself, Richard! You're revoltingly drunk.'

'And so what if I am, you old miser! I have to have some pleasures in life, even if you're too bloody mean to pay for them.'

'I am not mean, and nor am I a miser. You live perfectly comfortably on the money you earn from the bank and I'm *not* having you frittering away a fortune just because you want to show off to your London friends.'

'Show off? How *dare* you!'

The boys slid cautiously on down the stairs till they were standing outside the closed door to the library. Max was astonished by how much noise his father could make. 'I work my fingers to the bone for the bank and I don't see why I shouldn't throw the odd party. Just because you're a miserable old skinflint with a dodgy past—'

'You forget yourself, Richard.' His grandfather's voice had cut like ice. 'I don't have money to waste on you. Now get out of here, and don't come back until you're sober. You disgust me.'

As they pressed themselves back against the wall on either side of the door, they heard the crash of a glass breaking, followed by their father's voice, roaring in fury, 'You don't have money? No money? You've a bloody fortune in gold stashed away somewhere, haven't you?' There was another crash. 'Where've you hidden it?'

Max was terrified. Dad was beating Grandfather Kit up. He'd be put in prison and then there'd be no one at all to care for him. Scrabbling frantically with the doorknob, he pushed the door open crying, 'Dad! Don't!' In the doorway, he halted. There'd been no fighting after all. His grandfather's tall, thin frame was silhouetted against the sashes of the window, while his father was standing by the fireplace, a whisky bottle in his hand and a broken tumbler at his feet. 'Dad?' he'd said again, then stopped.

'You little sneak!' his father thundered when he saw him. 'I'll teach you to creep around eavesdropping!'

He heard Grandfather Kit saying sharply, 'Richard! Leave the boy alone!' but his father, face scarlet with fury, had come charging towards him with his fist raised. Max had felt that hand before and stood immobilised with fear, but then there'd been a sharp tug on the back of his shirt and before he was clear what was happening, Alec had pulled him away, had slammed the door in their father's angry face, and was dragging him off along the hall.

Minutes later they were out of the house and darting through the spattering remnants of the rainstorm across the garden and to the edge of the terrace. Without daring to look back, they slipped over it and sprinted down through the long meadow until they were on the edge of the dark woods that lurked, silent and sinister, between them and the river. Max hesitated, torn between the fear behind him and the terror ahead, but then he'd felt wet leaves whipping across his face as Alec grabbed his arm and tugged him in under the shelter of the trees. Then, letting go, still without saying a word, Alec sped off, leaving Max to fight his fear alone. The woods were out of bounds because they were dangerous. There were men who might shoot them by mistake.

Alec was nearly out of sight and Max hadn't dared to get left behind. Lowering his head to avoid being smacked by branches, he'd slithered downhill after his brother. It hadn't taken him long to catch up because Alec kept slipping over in the mud. Being more athletic, Max managed to stay upright and to keep reasonably clean and dry, but Alec's shorts were already filthy. Nanny would be furious with them when they got back. She'd probably tell Dad. The thought made him run even faster.

Three-quarters of the way down the hill, the boys tumbled out of the trees into a clearing and skidded to a halt. The damp leaf-mould underfoot and the wet trees crowding around them muffled every sound. The moment he'd got his breath back, Max whispered, 'I don't like it, Alec, we shouldn't be here. You know it's let to the Navy for exercises. Please can't we go back to the house?' Max's own fear redoubled when he saw that even his eternally calm brother looked scared.

As if to challenge both his nerve and the oppressive silence, Alec said loudly, 'Don't be a weed. This land's all ours, isn't it? And anyway, the Navy's silly. When I grow up I'm going to fly aeroplanes.' Alec began to make flying noises and set off again, twisting down between the trees.

Max was far too frightened to stay alone in the clearing, and as he followed his brother, his voice grew tearful. 'Well I'm *never* going in an aeroplane. I'm going to be a sailor and I'm only *ever* going to travel on boats.'

Alec had paused in his descent towards the river. Max thought he might be going to thump him, but he didn't. Instead, catching hold of a low branch, he'd swung himself clumsily to and fro and said quite nicely, 'You can't *only* go in boats, you know. There are lots of places boats don't go to. You like trains, don't you? Remember when Dad took us with him to Scotland? You liked that.'

Max sniffed and wiped his nose on the sleeve of his jersey. 'I suppose I don't mind trains, but I like boats better. I don't know why Grandfather Kit won't take me out on *Cassandra* more often.'

'It's because you keep pestering him with questions whenever we come here.' Alec fell silent. There were footsteps, then low voices from just up the hill. A branch cracked.

Exchanging one terrified look, the two boys dashed off again through the trees. Brambles scratched their bare legs, branches clutched at their arms as they skidded down through the damp and gloomy wood until, panting with fear, they shot into open daylight, right at the water's edge. In front of them, their grandfather's boat swung gently at her moorings on Dartleap's private quay.

'She's lovely, isn't she?' Max breathed, transfixed by the sight of *Cassandra*. 'Imagine her going all the way to Dunkirk and back.'

'Oh *do* come away,' Alec had urged, for once the less brave of the two. 'I think that boat might be haunted. There were dead bodies at Dunkirk, weren't there?'

But Max was not to be deterred. Bounding across the quay, he peered in through one of the portholes. 'It's all clear, I can't see any ghosts.'

After that, he'd been completely absorbed by what he could see of *Cassandra*'s interior, so it was Alec who heard it first. There was the buzz of an outboard motor, and then a boat swung into view round a bend in the river. At the same time, they heard a shout from the hill above them. They were caught.

In his panic, Alec scuttled between the woods and the water, looking for a hiding place, but Max had confidence in his own sturdy legs. Taking a running leap from the quay, he landed safely and scrambled over the guard-rails that ran around *Cassandra*'s deck. Leaning back over the aft rail, he called to his brother to follow, but Alec had been born with none of his own physical self-assurance. For agonising moments Max watched him scurrying up and down, that white-blond hair of his flopping into his eyes as he tried to see a safe place to jump the gulf between quay and boat. There was another shout from the woods, which seemed to decide him. Head down, Alec ran at the edge of the quay and leapt blindly towards the boat to land half on, half off her slippery foredeck. His legs scrabbled wildly as he began to slide down towards the evil-smelling water.

As always when he was on a boat, Max felt completely confident. Thrusting one end of a rope under Alec's elbow and the other around his own shoulder, he said urgently, 'Come on. Pull on that.' Alec pulled and was soon lying flat on the deck, sides heaving. Max had had to half drag his brother to the wheelhouse door and push him inside. They'd crouched there, breathing in the smells of brass polish and engine oil, while the outboard motor buzzed on by. The shouts from the woods had grown louder, then gradually faded away into the distance.

Max was so caught up in the memory that it took him a while to realise that his phone was ringing. When he picked it up, his brother's crisp voice asked, 'Were you asleep?'

'Course not,' he smiled into the handset. 'I was taking a

memory trip. Remember when we were running away from Dad and we hid on *Cassandra*?'

'Vaguely,' said Alec. 'Do you mean the day we found the letters?'

'The letters. Of course.' Max closed his eyes and saw the corner cabinet down in *Cassandra*'s saloon and the irregularity he'd spotted in its mahogany base. There'd been a concealed handle, a secret drawer, and an iron-bound box sitting snugly inside it. He and Alec had been so excited. They'd assumed the box would hold hidden treasure, but when they'd opened it, all that had spilled out were unhappy family secrets.

'How funny, I'd almost forgotten about them.' Alec's voice cut across his thoughts. 'Are they still at Dartleap?'

'As far as I know they're in the bottom of that chest in the library.' Max paused. 'But, Alec. That day. Do you remember what happened when we got back?'

'I got a very sore arse. Father thrashed the life out of me for slamming the library door in his face, and later he thrashed me again for ruining my shorts.'

'But he didn't lay a finger on me,' Max said softly. 'You protected me. I've never forgotten it.'

His brother's reply was lost in the noise of his office door crashing open. '*Vas-y, Max! La voiture t'attende!*'

'*J'arrive.*' He waved apologetically at Claudine's retreating back. 'Sorry, Alec, got to go.'

'*Tu seras en retard,*' floated back through the door.

'Oh God, the woman's such a nag. Talk later?'

'Don't we always?'

*

Prince Jerichau's angular face loomed round the corner of an ebony-inlaid tabernacle. 'So there you are. You do like to meet in the oddest places.'

'Odd? But it's July and the city's heaving.' As a result of Claudine's bullying, Max had arrived ten minutes early and was perched on a bench of cherry velvet studying Carpaccio's *Hippolyta and Theseus*. 'Where in the whole of Paris could you find a more discreet meeting place than the Musée Jacquemart-André? Or a more lovely room than this gallery?'

'Pa-pa-pa!' The Italian flicked his fingers. 'Crude medievalism.'

Wanker, Max thought as Isaiah Jerichau glanced dismissively at the jewels of fifteenth-century Venetian painting.

'My *palazzo* in Genoa, now there is true art. Rubens and Renoir, Boucher and Fragonard.'

'I rather thought you'd sold the Rubens last year? In fact I moved it for you on *Cassandra*, remember?'

'So you did.' Jerichau lowered the lid of one of his deeply hooded eyes. 'You sail close to the wind, Max. One day you and your boat will be stripped by the Customs.'

'They'd certainly never find anything on *Cilissa*, unless they had some extremely advanced technology.'

'But the old one, what about that?'

'You mean *Cassandra*? Dunkirk heroine?' Max opened his eyes wide in mock-astonishment. 'She's like the Queen, no one's going to strip-search *her*.'

'I trust you are right.' Jerichau gave him a slow smile which emphasised the brown rim edging his lips. It made him look suddenly attractive, as if he'd just been sucking on an illicit bar of chocolate. 'My family has used Quentance

Bank for many, many years and I myself have come to rely on your *giuoci di prestigio*.'

Max laughed politely. Sleight of hand, indeed! Was Isaiah being intentionally offensive? Or maybe he'd just forgotten that Max's Italian was fluent, as was his French, his Spanish and his Russian, relics of all those lonely years of multicultural schoolboy exile in Switzerland.

'In truth, Max,' Jerichau went on, 'I saw the financial cataclysm coming and I thought it wise to sell that little Rubens at the top of the market. And now I have traded a Donatello bas-relief on behalf of a gentleman who has sadly lost his fortune in unwise banking investments.' With a careless foot, he nudged a black briefcase towards Max. 'You will take care of this for me, in Guernsey?'

Glancing down, Max noted the cheap plastic with irritation. Jerichau was always immaculately dressed in that narrow-waisted, sharp-seamed style that rich Italians do so well. He'd never dream of carrying anything but the best crocodile or lizard himself, so why was he expecting Max to walk around with this vulgar-looking piece?

To give himself time to recover his temper, Max got up from his bench and glanced through each of the gallery's doorways to check for eavesdroppers. The entire upper floor of the museum appeared to be deserted, but despite this, Max lowered his voice to a near whisper as he came back to sit next to his client. 'You want it in the main family account, do you? YRR7978?'

'*Si*,' Jerichau nodded. 'No need for it to be anywhere more private, the cash is clean.' He stretched widely, then stood up to go. '*Ciao*, Max.'

'*Ciao*, Isaiah.'

Once he'd heard Jerichau's footsteps clicking away down the museum's marble staircase, Max picked up the brief-case and ambled off in the direction of Edouard André's bedroom. The Winterhalter there was just the right style for the portrait he was planning to have painted as his Christmas present for Alec.

It was as Max passed through the enfilade of private rooms running down the far side of the building that he became aware of someone moving ahead of him. Bouts of phlegmy coughing echoed off the gilded panelling and he caught occasional glimpses of a bent back, a long black coat and a broad-brimmed hat. Judging by the uncertain gait, Max assumed it was an old man, and from the way he seemed to speed up whenever Max drew closer, he was an old man who didn't want to be seen. As Max passed from antechamber to bedroom, the figure would shuffle on into the next room, doubtless unaware that he was trapped. But as Max knew well, this particular line of rooms ended in Monsieur André's bathroom. A cul de sac.

Max had been brought up to be a gentleman. If the old man ahead of him had no wish to be seen, then he had no wish to intrude. When their game of grandmother's-footsteps had reached its inevitable end and the stranger was cornered in the bathroom, Max politely turned his back to allow the man to slip past him. Curiosity had, however, got the better of his manners to the extent that while Max positioned himself with his back to the bathroom door, he made sure that he was facing Edouard André's large looking-glass.

As the stranger slid by, their glances met fleetingly in

the mottled mirror. A scarf covered the lower part of the man's face, and with that hat pulled right down over his forehead, Max could see nothing but a pair of blue eyes. And yet in that brief moment, it seemed to Max that those eyes burned, not with the hostility of someone inadvertently cornered, but with an absolute hatred.

Madman, he thought as the sound of coughing faded away through Nèlie Jaquemart's bedroom.

Having noted the Winterhalter, Max wandered out, pausing to admire Boucher's mischievous Venus seducing a peacock in the entrance gallery. His car was waiting for him on Boulevard Haussmann, but it was a beautiful day. Just as he was toying with the idea of sending the Rolls away and walking back to his office, he caught sight of the madman standing not more than twenty yards away on the corner of Rue de Courcelles. It suddenly occurred to Max that anyone could bend over, cough and shuffle, and that the scarf, coat and hat might actually be concealing not an old man but a terrorist. Seeing that his chauffeur was holding the car door open for him, he scrambled inside.

Early that evening, Max was standing at one of the windows of his first-floor drawing-room, looking down on his treasured quarter-acre of garden. It was one of his favourite secrets, being entirely concealed behind high walls, right in the heart of Paris. The setting sun on his pleached limes threw boxy shadows across the grass, though the trees were sad specimens when seen in full daylight. In his impatience to get a quick effect, he'd had them planted too close together, and already they were dying back. He'd have to get them ripped out and was thinking of replacing them with one of those stone-edged rills that were so fashionable at the moment. Seen from up here he could just imagine it, a sapphire ribbon, ravishing against the emerald green of his cherished lawn. Maybe he'd have some agapanthus shipped in for the few months when they were in flower? A splash of amethyst reflected in the water would be perfect.

Of course he'd have to be careful which firm he used to do the work, because of the new vault he'd had put in below a particular flagstone. It was tiny compared to the one in London, but Alec had said it would be very useful for storing cash in transit, and other things too. The gold bar, for instance. Such bad luck Edie finding it on the very day he'd been bringing it here.

Max turned from the window as his mobile trembled in his pocket. No need to look at his watch to know that it would be exactly ten minutes to six in London. Flipping his phone open, he said, 'How's tricks?'

'Good.' There was a satisfied note in Alec's voice. 'Tell me about Jerichau.'

'Oh, I had a great time with him. He's given me a bundle of cash for his Guernsey account. I'm thinking of taking Oscar across on *Cilissa* when I shift it.'

'I know the boy will do well.'

'Hope so. The only thing I'm not sure about is his memory.'

'It was perfectly adequate when he was working for me in London.' His brother sounded offended, but this was business. Max had to make his point clear.

'It needs to be a lot better than adequate, you know that. I'm not having him writing customer details down.' Oscar would have to remember exactly which shells in which tax havens related to any one of multiple aliases for every single client, just as Max had always done.

'Don't push him too hard. He hasn't got your freaky memory.'

Catching a note of parental concern, Max said soothingly, 'Oscar's a Quentance. As long as he loves money, he'll be fine.'

'Talking of which, I've scooped another twenty-eight million into the Adamantine Fund.'

His brother had said the number so calmly, it took a moment for Max to take it in. 'Twenty-eight million pounds? *Twenty-eight!* That's unbelievable! Who is it?'

'A charming old dear called Mrs Coverley-Kissing. Apparently her late husband was into cleaning products in a big way and left her his fortune. I've spent the afternoon being fed sandwiches and sherry at her house in Kensington, but it was well worth it.'

'Twenty-eight million pounds,' Max repeated. He felt quite breathless with admiration. 'Let's hope she lives for a long time.'

'Sadly she's not very well, but I've got that covered too.'

'Already?'

'It's all sewn up. Quentance Bank are to be sole executors and we'll charge four per cent of her estate. I bet her children will be sorry they didn't spend more time with her after she's gone.'

'Brilliant,' Max breathed. 'Let's celebrate at the weekend.'

'The birthday party, of course. See you then.'

FIVE

The July sun was enervating, and Edie was almost glad to have been coerced out of trousers and into a sleeveless linen dress. By staying where the edge of the lawns sloped up to the house, she could look down on her family's extravagance, observing the waiters hurrying around with jeroboams of champagne, while waitresses slipped between the guests carrying trays of beautifully crafted food. It was amusing to see faces growing redder and gestures more exuberant, but she wasn't at all tempted to join in. It was a lot more fun to watch this party than to be a part of it.

As the roar of chatter washed up to her, she caught odd snippets of conversation.

'I say, there's Johnny Tamar. I haven't seen him since prep school.'

'Probably come for the free booze. From what I hear, there's scarcely a bean left in the Ivybridge coffers.'

'Not a lot of poverty here though, is there? The Quentance family always seem to stay quids-in, no matter what shit the rest of the world's in. You have to admire them for it.'

Looking across the Dartleap lawns, Edie thought that

perhaps there *was* something admirable about her family's financial success, especially on set-piece occasions like this. Over the heads of their guests she could see her father, whilst a little further into the mêlée, the glint of sun on a pair of dark-gold heads identified her uncle, with Oscar beside him. They were laughing at some joke, and seemed to be completely surrounded by women. While she was watching, Max glanced up and caught her eye. Something in his look made Edie uncomfortable. In theory at least, this was her birthday party and she really ought to be mingling. Abandoning her viewing point, she dived down into the crush and made her way over to her father.

She found him leaning courteously over an elderly lady who was wearing a triple rope of the largest pearls Edie had ever seen, making her wonder how such a skinny old neck could support their weight. Her father was giving the woman all his attention and Edie got only a nod as she slipped in between him and a podgy, middle-aged man who was listening to the conversation. Taking the hint, she smiled vaguely, then stood in silence at Alec's side.

'My friend Lady Beacon tells me your Adamantine Fund returns are consistently high,' the old woman was saying. 'She says I should invest with you.'

Knowing how keen he always was to keep the money flowing into his wealth-management business, Edie was surprised to hear her father reply, 'I'm afraid that's impossible.'

'Impossible? ' The podgy man looked indignant. 'Perhaps you don't realise that my mother never deposits tranches of less than a million pounds.'

Her father's eyes flicked appraisingly over the man's face. 'No doubt she does, but the problem's quite different. More people want to put their money with me than I can possibly cater for.' Turning back to the woman, he took one of her hands. 'And besides, I'm sure you don't really want to talk investments on a lovely day like this. Wouldn't you rather I show you round the garden?'

Before Alec could lure her away, the son butted in. 'I'm keen for my mother to invest in hedge funds, as a matter of fact.'

'I wouldn't dream of exposing my clients to that level of risk.' Her father's smile lingered, but Edie saw frost in his eyes. 'Hedge funds lose fortunes quite as often as they make them, whereas I've beaten the market every single year since I started investing.'

'My dear Mr Quentance, I do so wish you'd let me into your fund.'

'Not today, we've talked *quite* enough business.' Alec cupped a hand under the old woman's elbow and began to guide her away. 'My secretary will be in touch and we'll have a nice cosy lunch together. But now you must have a nice glass of champagne. Edie?' Apart from that initial nod, it was the first time her father had acknowledged her presence. 'Go and send someone over, will you?' Obediently she went off and found a waiter, but she didn't follow him back to Alec. He clearly needed no help from his daughter.

Instead she wandered on through the milling strangers, half regretting her point-blank refusal to invite any of her friends, though it had become a matter of principle as soon as she realised why the party was being held. The birthday celebration was a sham. It was simply a tax-deductible business entertainment for the rich investors whose conversations she picked up as she passed by.

'2008's turning into a *dreadful* year,' a male voice said. 'Don't know how we're going to get through it.' Hoping she might pick up some insight into the failing British economy, Edie paused, trying not to look as if she was eavesdropping.

'Money problems?'

'Christ, no. Grouse. There's been too much rain.'

Grouse moors! She pushed her way on through the crowd, disgusted by the idea that anyone should have exclusive rights over huge tracts of land just to kill small birds. Society was no more equal now than it had been on *Titanic*, she thought crossly. The poor were still pushed out of sight and mind of the wealthy.

'You're awfully pale, Imelda.' Another conversation caught her attention. 'No Barbados?'

'Bloody Cornwall's all David says we can afford. His bonus was only half a million this year.'

'Poor you! William had a fabulous pay-out from Lehman's. Praise be it's a sound bank, because the whole lot's held in their shares.'

Edie felt a moment's envy for these people, all so secure in their wealth. But supposing their world was more fragile than they thought? What would they do in an earthquake, for example, or some chaotic upheaval among the banks they depended on? Her mind went back to *Titanic*. Men with equally insulated lives had been tested by a catastrophe they had no control over. She shook her head, realising that the outcome had been wrong. Those who passed the moral test drowned, while those who failed it escaped in lifeboats. Depressed by this conundrum, alone in a crush of strangers, Edie suddenly needed to find Oscar.

'Excuse me . . . Sorry . . . Can I come through please?' The crowd seemed to get thicker as she fought her way to where she'd last seen her twin, but when eventually she found him standing under the yellow goblets of a tulip tree, she recognised the couple with him and would have turned tail had Oscar not already spotted her.

'Hi, Eds, just look who's here. Remember Daniel?'

Of course she remembered Daniel Somerskill. He was a lying sneak, and she'd never understood why he'd been one of Oscar's closest schoolfriends. 'Awfully nice to see you again, Edie.' The hand was slippery. 'You haven't changed at all.'

Hoping that she'd actually changed a great deal from her angry, gangly teenage self, Edie was furious to find herself blushing as she turned to face Yves de la Châtaigne. His lips pouted under a silky cavalier's moustache, and the black curls and the sharp eyes were as sexy as ever. No wonder she'd had such a crush on him. She shivered as his mouth brushed the back of her hand.

Yves was still holding the tips of her fingers when Max came over and interrupted them. 'Can I take Oscar away for a minute? There's a rich young lady I want him to charm.'

'*Mais bien sûr.*' Edie was momentarily taken aback. She'd forgotten how high-pitched that French voice was.

'I'm sorry.' Oscar pursed his lips into a little *moue* of apology. 'Duty before pleasure.'

'Don't be silly,' Yves said in his light drawl, 'money *is* pleasure.'

As Max and Oscar moved away, Edie felt awkward. If it had just been Yves, she'd have hung around, but she couldn't go on gazing into his eyes with Daniel Somerskill watching. 'I'd better keep circulating. Lovely to see you both,' she muttered, turning towards the throng of guests.

Long before she was out of earshot she heard Daniel's fat chuckle, 'Remember when I dared you to snog her? You said you'd rather eat dirt.'

Yves' reply was also far too audible. 'Not my teacup, *chéri*. A nice pair of legs, but look at her height, and the size of those feet! The duckling has become *une cigogne*.'

A stork! How dare he? With an idea that she might escape down to the river, Edie forced her way blindly through the party.

When she finally pushed out from the fringes of the crowd and on to the terrace, she was surprised to find her mother there. Edie's first reaction was annoyance, she'd wanted to be by herself to recover from the sting of Yves' words. But there was something not quite right about the way Clio was sitting slumped down on the flagstones, her back against a low wall. She was wearing a cheerful-looking, flower-strewn hat, but beneath it her head was bowed.

'Mum?' The only response she got was a brief flap of a hand. Maybe Clio was still cross after that row at their birthday dinner? Edie sank down on to the hot flagstones, not caring how badly she crumpled the bleached linen of her dress. 'I'm really sorry about the other night. I shouldn't have lost my temper when you'd gone to all that trouble.'

There was no reply, but just as Edie was wondering what else she could say to mollify her mother, she heard a bubbling sniff. She peered at Clio's face and was shocked to see that below the brim of her hat, her kohl-blackened eyes were shiny with tears. 'Mum! Whatever's up?'

'I shouldn't have come.' The voice was hardly more than a whisper. 'This is where your sister vanished.'

Ianthe. It hadn't occurred to her. Edie reached over and took her mother's hand. The palm was roughened by turpentine and paint, and she gave it a little squeeze of sympathy. After several minutes, Clio pulled herself upright and started dabbing at her eyes with a handkerchief. 'Thank you, darling, and I'm sorry to be upset. Are you having a nice time?'

'To be perfectly honest, I'm not. I hate this party and I particularly hate Yves de la Châtaigne.'

'Yves? I never liked him either.' Clio blew her nose, then put the handkerchief back into her bag and closed it with a snap. 'Such a crashing snob, though he's got absolutely nothing to be snobbish about.'

'But he always used to boast that he was descended from the entire *ancien régime*.'

'Completely bogus.' Clio shifted her position to face Edie. 'I remember his parents because Max was rather proud of getting them as clients. They were hugely rich, but there was no "de la" in their name. André and Marianne Châtaigne were just common-or-garden *pieds noirs* who had to hoof it out of north Africa when the French lost their colonies.'

Edie threw back her head and laughed, forgetting that she was wearing a dress. Feeling it riding up well above her knees, she tugged the hem down, but not before she'd caught the eye of a very tall young man who was looking at her legs appreciatively. Viscount Tamar. Trust some bloody aristocrat to be eyeing her up. Meeting his half-smile with a scowl, she watched him amble away.

'I should have worn sandals instead of these wretched things,' Clio sighed as she edged her feet out of a pair of high heels and wriggled her toes. 'You like your necklace do you, darling?'

'It's stunning,' Edie said, fingering the fiddly little turquoise thing round her neck. Thank God she'd remembered to put it on.

'I thought it'd bring out the blue of your eyes. What else did you get?'

Edie swivelled round on the hot stones so that she was directly facing her mother. 'Did you know Oscar and I were going to be given thirty shares each in the bank?'

Clio picked a bit of thyme from between the flagstones and sniffed it before she replied. 'It was always the plan that you'd get them when you turned twenty-five, but I thought Alec might have changed his mind. He'd rather spit on sixpence than give it away.' Edie hated it when her parents moaned to her about each other. There was a silence until Clio said suddenly, 'You do know about the bank shares, don't you? Somebody *has* told you?'

'Told me what? Oscar and I've been given thirty each, Dad and Uncle Max have thirty each, so there are a hundred and twenty shares in all. That's right, isn't it?"

'Not quite. Quentance Bank has a hundred and *forty* shares issued. There's another twenty shares floating around that everyone always forgets.' Looking up, Edie saw that her mother had compressed her lips into a tight line. 'You know your grandfather had a brother, Teddy?'

'Who ran off with Grandmother Eve, yes of course I know.' There was a pause. 'Oh I see. Teddy has the other twenty shares, does he?'

'Exactly.' Clio's hand brushed against her shoulder. 'There are far too many secrets in this family.' A moment later, her mother was standing barefoot on the warm stone of the terrace, her discarded shoes dangling from one hand. 'Come indoors,' she said. 'There's something I'm going to show you.'

SIX

Clio felt a stab of irritation as she followed her daughter into Dartleap. However had Edie managed to get the seat of her dress so filthy in the course of a single afternoon? But as they walked through the entrance hall to the atrium of the staircase, the light pouring down from the glass dome picked out the streaks of Devon's red dirt against the pale linen, while the grass stains shone like bottle-glass. Such a perfect colour combination, she'd have liked to paint it.

When they got to the library, Clio stood in the doorway, again caught by the transforming effect of that strong, July light. The high sun angled down through the windows, illuminating the walls and revealing the true quality of the collection of maritime masterpieces. Ecru clouds billowed across the luminous tranquillity of a seventeenth-century Dutch waterway. A fallen sail dragged a four-master on to an outcrop of black basalt. A modernist painting which she'd always dismissed as formulaic was no longer two oblongs of colour but a representation of the boundary between ocean and sky.

'Heavens above,' she muttered. 'There's a fortune on these walls. I can just guess how the family got hold of them.'

'What was that, Mum?' Edie had wandered over to the desk. 'Is this where whatever you want to show me is kept?'

'No.' Enjoying the feeling of her bare feet on polished wood, Clio walked across to the glass-fronted drinks cabinet which squatted in the far corner of the library. 'It's a bundle of letters, and they're in here.'

'I don't think so. There's just a copy of the family tree in the drawer, and that cupboard's only got room for a couple of decanters and some tumblers. Honestly, Mum, I've been using the library for ages. If there were any letters here, I'd have found them.'

There was something intensely annoying about Edie's certainty that she was wrong, and Clio replied more curtly than she meant to, 'I said there were too many secrets in this bloody family.' Kneeling down in front of the cabinet, she opened the glass doors and lifted out the pair of cut-glass decanters. They'd always been there, with those silver labels hanging off their necks reading GRAIN and MALT, but knowing how rarely her daughter drank spirits, it was hardly surprising that she'd never spotted the false panel behind them. Clio slid it open and pulled out a packet of letters barely held together by a couple of near-perished rubber bands.

There was a gasp behind her. 'I'd no idea! I'm sorry I didn't believe you.'

Clio meant to smile, but as she stood up, the telephone caught her eye. It sat on top of the drinks cabinet where it had always lived, and quite suddenly she felt paralysed by memories. A husky-voiced man ringing, claiming to be holding her child. Herself, collapsing on this very floor. Terror that her little girl was shut up somewhere, alone and afraid. The police waiting here in the hope of intercepting a call from Ianthe's kidnapper.

'I've made you cross, haven't I?' Edie's voice came from close beside her.

'Of course not.' Clio hated the library. No, it was worse than hatred and she had to get out. 'Let's look at these letters in the drawing-room,' she said, going over to the door. 'Will you bring the family tree as well?'

'OK, Mum.' Behind her, she heard Edie sigh, but couldn't wait to explain what had upset her as she hurried off to the drawing-room.

Its perfect cube of high-ceilinged space made Clio feel calm again. The room brought back no memories at all, having always been for show rather than comfort. In fact, apart from entertaining the odd bank client whom they'd wanted to impress, it had scarcely been used when she and Alec were at Dartleap together. Whatever else might be wrong with him, Clio thought as she looked around, her estranged husband had decent taste. The room had been restyled since she'd left, and now it was all stark angles, with a few carefully placed pieces of modern art to emphasise its rigid severity of line. The walls shone with a gunmetal varnish, and she liked the way the saxe-blue curtains had been hung in sharp-edged rectangles to disguise the curves of the bay windows.

Clio perched herself on a low-backed sofa and patted the seat beside her. 'Come and sit next to me,' she said as Edie followed her into the room. 'You can spread the family tree out on the coffee table.' Because of the austerity of the room, it took a few minutes before enough small objects were found to weigh down the curling corners of the parchment, but eventually they were sitting side by side looking down at the family Clio had married into.

AN EXTRACT FROM THE FAMILY TREE OF QUENTANCE
1850 to the Present Day

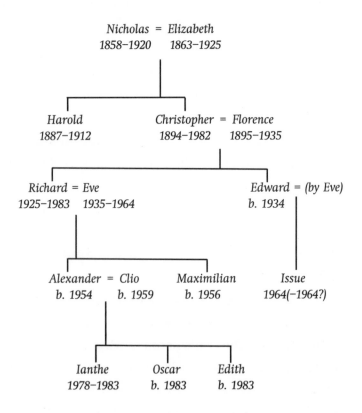

Nicholas = Elizabeth
1858–1920   1863–1925

Harold
1887–1912

Christopher = Florence
1894–1982   1895–1935

Richard = Eve
1925–1983   1935–1964

Edward = (by Eve)
b. 1934

Alexander = Clio
b. 1954   b. 1959

Maximilian
b. 1956

Issue
1964(–1964?)

Ianthe
1978–1983

Oscar
b. 1983

Edith
b. 1983

'It's a funny thing, but I'd never noticed how few men used their full names,' her daughter said after a few moments.

'Harold was Harry, Christopher was Kit, Edward was Teddy.'

Catching the hesitancy in her voice, Clio guessed Edie might be worried that she was still irritated, so she reached out to give her hand a reassuring pat. 'You're right, darling, I'd never thought of it either. Alexander's Alec, isn't he? And Max has never been Maximilian.'

'And everyone calls me Edie.'

'I wish they wouldn't, but I seem to have got used to it.'

Clio was warmed by her daughter's wide smile, for once feeling more charmed than annoyed at the sight of that gap between her front teeth. 'Maybe Eve was short for something like Evelina,' Edie went on. 'What d'you think?'

Clio stared down at the family tree, wondering about the mother-in-law she'd never met. 'To be honest, all I know about her is what's in here.' She stroked the bundle of letters in her lap. 'I don't even know what she looked like because Richard destroyed every single photo of her.'

'Wasn't Dad old enough to remember his mother before she left?'

'I suppose he must have been,' she nodded, 'because he used to tell Ianthe that she was the image of her grandmother. Alec thought that the only difference between them was that Eve's hair was brown.'

'Was it? That must be where I get it from. I don't suppose Max remembers her, does he?'

'I don't think he can, he was only a toddler when she left. Though he always used to say she smelled of sweet vanilla and liquorice.' Clio turned to look at her daughter as a thought struck her. 'Alec and Max were brought up without a mother, and you and Oscar had an absentee father. We're a sad family, aren't we?'

'Not really.' There was that smile again. 'Dad's always been around, and presumably Teddy and Eve lived happily ever after, or at least till she died, didn't they?'

Clio sat in silence, stroking the packet of letters in her lap. Perhaps she was wrong to let her daughter hear the whole story.

'Oh I see,' Edie murmured. 'They didn't, did they?'

With a shake of her head, Clio slipped off the rubber bands and spread out the first letter. The sight of that thick, creamy manila brought back how proud she used to be of Dartleap's writing-paper, with the family's crest of a soaring eagle stamped just above the address. '"My dearest Eve,"' she began, but Edie interrupted.

'Hang on, Mum. Who's this from?'

'This is your great-grandfather Kit's handwriting.' Clio held the sheet of paper out and watched her daughter examine the precise, black italic, touching it with her finger-tips as if she wanted to sense the man behind it. 'Most of these are between Kit and Eve,' Clio explained, taking the letter from Edie's hands and starting again.

My dearest Eve,

    I'm not going to beat about the bush. I know you've had your problems with Richard but he is missing you badly and so are your boys, especially Alec who is quite old enough to understand that something has gone sadly astray in his young life.

    And you have another little one to care about. You shouldn't be gallivanting across Europe in your delicate condition. It's not fair on Richard's unborn child and it's not fair on Richard.

Please, Eve, come back. You must know you are needed at Dartleap, in particular by your fond father-in-law,

Kit Quentance

'I don't believe it!' Edie was staring at her. 'You're not saying that Eve ran off with Teddy when she was already carrying his own brother's child?'

'I'll stop now if you like,' Clio said. 'It's not a pretty story.'

'Keep going. I want to know what happened.'

The paper of the second letter crackled as Clio smoothed it out. She remembered how she'd felt when Alec had shown her these letters and she'd seen her own mother-in-law's handwriting for the first time. There was something endearing about the way it dashed along with no respect for line, as if Eve's thoughts had come pouring out faster than she could write them down.

Dearest Kit,

I can hardly imagine the trouble I've given you but you must know how madly happy I am with Teddy. He's such an angel. I can't bear to be apart from him and everyone loves him here. With my dark hair, I fit in like a native, but he's so glamorously blond and the locals all stare at him.

I do miss my boys badly. I nearly cried this morning when I saw a toddler and his fat little knees made me think of Max. Do please give them kisses and tell them to be good. And say I'll come and see them when I can.

'Christ, that's sad. I'm glad you stuck with us, Mum.'

Edie could say surprisingly nice things sometimes. Touched, Clio turned back to the letter in her hands.

We're staying near Bandol. Did you ever sail round here? Teddy wishes you'd give him Cassandra, by the way, is that out of the question? The harbour would be perfect to moor her in. Old houses, a tiny port and fishermen selling their catch on the shore. I lie on the beach getting fatter by the day, and the baby's fluttering about like mad.

And do tell Richard . . . no, perhaps not. The simple thing is that I married the wrong brother. I'm so sorry, Kit, but so happy too.

With love from your little

Eve

'It must have been awful for Richard, mustn't it?' Edie's voice was thoughtful. 'Dad and Max always talk about him as if he was a brutal bully, but maybe this explains why he was like that.'

Clio was silent. Her father-in-law had certainly had his share of the Quentance charm, always joking and flattering her, and he'd been very fond of Ianthe too. But there'd been an undercurrent of violence beneath his loud-voiced teasing and she'd been careful not to leave her little girl alone with him for too long. 'There were probably faults on both sides,' she said eventually, 'but I don't think Richard was an easy man to live with. Shall I go on?' Not waiting for a reply, she picked up the next letter.

My dear Eve,

I was glad to hear that you are well and that your preg-nancy is progressing safely. I won't trouble you again about coming home until after your baby is born, but do remember that you carry Richard's child. He surely has some rights, and it is hard for him to have to explain that his wife is living abroad.

As I don't want you to have any worries in these last months, I'm enclosing a cheque. It is for you alone, and you can tell Teddy he can't have Cassandra as I have no intention of giving him anything. Besides, Max already enjoys toddling round the deck whenever he gets the chance. Poor little chap. He misses you, though it's Alec I'm more worried about. He's becoming a bit of a loner and he doesn't chatter away like he used to.

Doubtless everything will sort itself out once you are back with us at Dartleap.

With fond love,

Kit Quentance

There was a muffled noise beside her, and Clio caught Edie scrubbing away a tear. Kit's letter slipped to the floor as she reached for her daughter's hand. 'What's upset you, darling? I know it's a sad story but I never dreamed it'd make you weep.'

'I'm being an idiot.' The voice was somewhere between a sob and a laugh. 'It's just the idea of Dad being all lonely and damaged like that. Do you think his childhood's what made him so distant?'

The question took Clio by surprise. She'd never thought

about the cause, but it was precisely Alec's quality of cool composure that had attracted her in the first place. Other men had been all over her, but he'd kept her guessing, so that while she'd been sure of the fire behind those ice-blue eyes she'd never been certain how he felt, even on the day he proposed to her.

'Did you hear me, Mum? Do you think Dad's reticence is all to do with his early insecurity?'

'I suppose it must be.' That aloofness had kept her tantalised at first, but Alec's inability to share her despair over Ianthe's death had driven her away in the end. That, and his ambivalence over the ransom. 'There's nothing insecure about him these days,' she added briskly. 'Money's his crutch. He fought hard to make the bank a success, and now he's rich, he has all the support he needs.'

Turning her attention back to Eve's cheap writing-paper, she noticed how the handwriting had deteriorated. There were lots of crossings-out and the paper was blotched in places.

Dearest Kit,

Thank you for the cheque, it was a lovely surprise. I hadn't realised how expensive living here would be, and of course Teddy does need to get about and have the odd drink. I can't expect him just to sit around with me while I get huge.

I wish you were here to put things straight. We seem to have got into a muddle and I don't know how to get things right again. I know I'm carrying another man's baby, but after all it is Richard's child. I keep telling Teddy that Richard's his

own brother and I am still really Richard's wife. It's just that
– oh dear. It's just that Teddy gets cross sometimes. Resentful.
As if he loves me but he hates my pregnancy.

But still, I am cheerful really. The baby's due in less than
three months and I do love Teddy. Most of the time he's divine
to me. It's just that sometimes he's – well, difficult.

I miss you,

Eve

Clio was about to reach for the next letter when Edie asked, 'Did Teddy and Eve get married?'

'No. Richard and Eve never divorced.'

'Nor did you and Dad.'

Clio frowned. It wasn't something she ever discussed with her children

'D'you know something, Mum? As long as you and Dad were still married, Oscar and I used to think you'd get back together one day, so we could be a proper family.' Edie was looking at her steadily. 'I don't suppose there's any chance, is there?'

'It's far too late for that.' It was also absolutely none of the twins' business, but Clio wasn't going to let herself get annoyed. She shrugged her shoulders, unfolded the next sheet of Dartleap writing-paper and began to read.

Dear Eve

In two months I've heard nothing from you. Surely you can
find the time to let me know about you and your child. It
must be due any day now?

Your last letter filled me with anxiety. I realise that Richard

has a wicked temper at times, but Teddy has his faults too.
He has a will of iron. When Teddy decides he wants some-
thing he will never turn away from it, however long it takes
and however many people he may hurt.

Be strong, Eve. Look after yourself and Richard's baby, and
remember that your duty is here at home. Surely you can't
let Alec and Max grow up without a mother? I don't think
Alec's a happy child, though he's turning out to be clever. Max
is bright too, very agile for his age, and getting into all sorts
of mischief. Really, they are charming little boys but they need
you.

Please write to me straight away. And come home just as
soon as you and the baby can travel.

Your father-in-law,

Kit Quentance

Neither of them spoke while Clio smoothed out the next sheet of paper. It looked as if it had once been badly crumpled, as if someone had squeezed it into a tight ball to be thrown away, but had then decided to keep it after all. She knew what was coming next, but she still felt a lump in her throat as she started to read the letter out loud.

Dear Kit,

There is no baby. Teddy wants me to lie to you, but I can't.
I'm not sure I can bear the guilt, let alone the pains I still
get. I miss you terribly, Kit, and the boys. I think about them
all the time now, how they must be growing, what they're
doing, whether they ever ask about me.

It was a girl. She had real blue Quentance eyes, with a mop of fair hair, but she was too little to live. She mewled a bit and then she died. It was an abortion, Kit, a very late abortion. Teddy bullied me and bullied me. He didn't want to bring up Richard's child. He promised that all would be well if I got rid of it. He went on and on, Kit, on and on. Eventually I just gave in.

We're going away now. I can't bear to stay here. Teddy's trying to find a boat for us to live on, and then we're going to sail off round the Med. We'll go to Italy, or maybe to Greece.

Forgive me, Kit.

Eve

'That's disgusting. Imagine killing her own child! I bet Dad and Max would have loved to have a little sister.'

'Don't upset yourself,' Clio said calmly. She'd forgotten that the pro-life ethic was one of Edie's many moral stances. 'This all happened a long time ago.'

'I don't care, it was still murder.'

Not feeling strong enough to argue the point, Clio picked up the next letter.

Dear Kit,

I haven't heard from you so I suppose you can't forgive me. Believe me, I'm finding it hard to forgive myself. I go to church sometimes but I don't understand the language, and why should God listen to me anyway?

I wouldn't bother you, but we're so short of money and Teddy's still refusing to write to you. Things are very hard for

us at the moment. Could you send something? Even a few
pounds would help.

Eve

PS If you do send a cheque could you write a few words about
the boys?

'If she missed Dad and Max so much, why didn't she just
hop on a plane to see them?'

Clio looked at her daughter and smiled. 'You're the histo-
rian. This happened in the early 1960s, when separation
and adultery were still quite shocking. Eve would have been
really afraid of facing Kit and Richard given what she'd
done. And then Teddy's supposed to have been just as good-
looking as Max and Oscar,' she added. 'Maybe she didn't
want to risk leaving him on his own for too long.'

'I still think she was a wimp not to see her children. You'd
never have abandoned us in a million years, Mum.'

'No. No, I wouldn't.' Touched by her certainty, Clio was
inclined to throw her arms round Edie, but she held back.
Her daughter could be just as reserved as Alec, and hated
any mawkishness. 'Only a couple of letters left now, and
then we really ought to be getting back outside.'

The next sheet was covered with Eve's untidy scrawl.

Dearest Kit

I can't tell you what a life-saver your cheques have been,
but you haven't written a word to me. I know I don't deserve
it, but I long to hear from you.

Teddy's very good to me, but I miss Alec and Max terribly.
Sometimes I don't think I can go on. But of course I must,

especially now. I'm expecting another baby. Teddy's child. It's
due next January, so maybe 1964 will be a better year than
this one's been.

Pray for me, Kit. I don't deserve your prayers, but I need
them and so does your grandchild. The doctors say there is a
risk, a high risk. My own fault for what I did to that darling
little girl. I never even held her.

With my love
Eve

'She must have been pregnant with Issue.'

'Issue,' Clio repeated sadly, looking down at the family
tree. 'I wonder if it was given a proper name.'

'Poor little bastard.'

'Edie!' She tried to look shocked, but laughed instead.

'You should laugh like that more often, Mum, it makes
you look really pretty.' Her daughter gave her an affectionate
nudge.

Clio's smile faded as she picked up the last letter. It covered
just one side of a sheet of lined paper which looked as if it
had been torn out of an exercise book. There was no date
and no address.

Father.

I swore I'd never write to you until you accepted me into the
family again and wrote me back into your will. I wouldn't be
writing now except that I suppose I have a duty to tell you this.

Eve is dead. I'm returning the letters you wrote to her. The
child killed her. It's a pathetic little runt and the doctors don't
think it'll survive. I don't care either way.

You cast me off from your life, so now I'm casting you off from mine. Don't expect to hear from me again. I'm hanging on to my twenty shares in the bank, but as for your bloody gold, you can keep it. I'm going to make a pile of my own.

Teddy

'So you were right about the shares, Mum, but what an awful story. Did Teddy and Kit ever make up?'

'Kit never heard from his younger son again.' Clio paused as a memory came back to her. 'Teddy did turn up at Richard's funeral, though it was more to try and cadge some money than to mourn for his brother.'

'I know, Max told me about it. He says Teddy hasn't been seen since.'

'He's probably dead. Unknown, unloved and unlamented.'

'Unpleasant as well.' Edie tucked a hand under her arm as they got up from the sofa. 'But I'm glad I know what happened now. Thanks for telling me.'

As they strolled back past the staircase, light poured down on Edie's face, illuminating that enviably clear skin of hers. 'You'll never need foundation,' Clio said without thinking. 'Just a bit of lipstick would make all the difference.'

Expecting the usual crisp reply she got whenever she mentioned her daughter's looks, she was surprised when Edie said amiably, 'Do you think so, Mum? Maybe I'll try it.'

Clio felt quite light-hearted as they walked on through the hallway and down the front steps together. Maybe her daughter had finally grown out of what had felt like a life-long rebellion. Giving Edie's arm an affectionate squeeze, she paused by the bottom step to put her shoes on.

'Mrs Quentance?'

Clio squinted up to see a tall figure bending over her. 'Yes, but I can't see who you are with the sun behind you.'

'It's John Tamar, Mrs Quentance. I wanted to thank you for inviting me to this party, and you too of course,' he added to Edie.

Clio stood up and put on her widest smile. Viscount Tamar. He must be around thirty now, because she'd daydreamed about Ianthe marrying him. But now it was Edie standing beside her, and the heir to the Earl of Ivybridge was still a bachelor.

The fantasy was ruined almost before it began. 'You don't need to thank me,' she heard her daughter muttering. 'I didn't ask anyone to this bean-feast.'

'Edie! Take John off and find him some champagne. And you can bring me a glass as well.' Frowning up at her daughter, she was surprised to see that Edie was only at eye level with John Tamar's jawbone.

'Sorry. I honestly didn't mean to be rude. It's just that throwing all this money around feels so, so . . .'

'Feckless?'

'Oh I don't think my family lacks feck.' This was better, there was a half-smile on Edie's face. 'I just feel they should do something more useful than stuffing the overfed.'

'The champagne idea's off then, is it?'

Taking in the raised eyebrow and a suspicion of mockery in his voice, Clio wished she could have warned John Tamar that teasing her daughter was never a good idea. Even more annoyingly, a waiter chose that moment to come up with a tray of drinks and she could think of no other reason to send the pair off together.

Clio looked on helplessly as Edie made some excuse about getting ready for the birthday speeches. As her daughter hurried away, Clio caught John following her with his eyes. The streaks of earth and pollen down the back of that pale linen dress were quite impossible to miss.

SEVEN

'Well I've seen a fire when the flames have died,
Only the atmosphere survived.
And I've seen water. I've seen water washing over a stone.'

Oscar stopped singing and took a deep breath. This sea trip was just what he needed to get the last dregs of champagne out of his system. The party had been great. He'd met several of Max's clients and found he could chat quite easily about money and art. Even better, Yves had come all the way to Devon and despite his sophistication, he'd seemed almost impressed by the show of wealth they'd put on at Dartleap. And now they'd be bumping into each other all the time in Paris. Oscar hugged the thought to himself as a new couplet popped into his head.

Composing had been such a big part of his life. It was a shame he was going to have to give it up, but he'd have no spare hours for music. With Max, he was going to be doing real work, not the paper-pushing Dad had stuck him with in the London branch. Oscar felt a surge of excitement. Max was going to teach him how to be a serious banker, and he'd earn serious money, too.

He leaned over *Cilissa*'s aft rail and tried to assess the value of the other boats moored at the marina. A three-masted sailing sloop looked as if a fortune had been spent restoring it, and there was a blunt-nosed gin palace which must have cost a packet. But nothing in Dartmouth's harbour could hold a candle to *Cilissa*, a million pounds' worth of ebony-hulled, teak-decked, streamlined luxury. She had the technology of a strike fighter and a maximum speed of thirty-seven knots which, as his uncle had explained to him, meant she could outrun pretty much anyone who might want to ask questions.

'Mind you,' Max had said as they walked up the gang-plank. 'Since our lovely government abandoned border controls, we only really need to keep an eye out for the coastguard, and I'm far too well known in these waters for them to bother us. Anyway,' he'd added cheerfully, 'it'd take more than a coastguard's search to find anything interesting on *this* lady.'

Oscar had no idea what he'd meant, but asking would only have highlighted his own ignorance of boats. And besides, he hadn't yet learned when to take Max seriously. His uncle was undeniably successful, but he was an adventurer as well. Or maybe all bankers had a touch of the pirate in them? Either way, Oscar wasn't going to let it worry him. He'd had more fun since he started working with Max than in a whole year grinding away for Dad, and as long as he didn't embarrass himself by being seasick, this trip was going to be great.

Seeing his uncle fiddling about with the ropes, Oscar called along the deck, 'D'you want help with the untying?'

'It's called "casting off", you landlubber, and no thanks. I can manage *Cilissa* single-handed. You stay put and watch the scenery.'

A few minutes later, Oscar heard the grumble of the engines shifting up an octave, and as the boat slid away from her berth he clung to the rail behind him. But before they'd even reached midstream he'd found that the movement of the deck beneath his feet wasn't at all frightening. All that stuff Eds had been feeding him about danger and slipping was nonsense.

Lifting his chin so that he could feel the fitful sun on his face, Oscar gazed out over the river. The towns of Dartmouth and Kingswear clambered up the banks of the Dart while *Cilissa* crept between them around the long bend of the river. Then as the sea came into view and the River Dart widened, the houses petered out into dark stands of woodland which tumbled right down to the water. Oscar felt entirely contented, breathing in the salt-laced air and feeling the heavy vibration of the boat's engines juddering up through his feet. Edie and Max were quite right. This was a wonderful way to travel.

But when they passed between the pair of castles crouching high above the rivermouth, everything changed. Clouds hunched overhead, a gale roared in his ears, and the world started moving sideways and vertically at the same time. Oscar grabbed at the rail as he was almost thrown off his feet. Trying to keep his foothold on the deck, he slithered towards the doorway, feeling as if he was roller-skating on an ice sheet, and as he ducked into the *eau de nil* comforts of *Cilissa*'s interior, his stomach heaved ominously. Clutching his mouth, he collapsed into the deep, bucket-shaped seating that curved round the stern end of the wheelhouse and sat there with his eyes closed, willing himself not to be sick.

'It's always a bit choppy where the river hits the sea.' Max's voice broke into his misery. 'Keep your eyes on the skyline and you'll be fine.'

Oscar was afraid he'd throw up if he looked at anything, and so he sat in silence, eyes tightly shut. He concentrated on taking deep breaths until gradually he began to feel a bit calmer, mesmerised by the regular surge and smack of water on hull as *Cilissa* accelerated out into the rolling swell of the Western Approaches. Eventually he felt sufficiently recovered to open his eyes and, following Max's advice, he looked at the ocean. How could Edie possibly claim to love this? It was like some godforsaken desert, a heaving monotone of waves racing towards the horizon. With a shudder, he turned his head from the void beyond *Cilissa*'s windows.

Fortunately, the interior of the boat seemed as reassuring as the outside was threatening, and there was his uncle, perched with his back to him, occasionally reaching up to turn a dial or to flip a switch. Max insisted on calling this his wheelhouse, but to Oscar, the array of high-tech instruments and brightly lit control panels made *Cilissa*'s helm look more like the cockpit of a military jet than the tiller of a private motor yacht. Comforted by the thought that all this expensive technology would be bound to keep him safe, Oscar decided he felt well enough to talk.

'Edie would have loved all this,' he said, running his hand

round the curve of a bleached oak side-table and noting how precisely it slotted into the pale green leather of his seat.

'What's that?' Max shouted over his shoulder.

'Edie! She'd have loved this!'

Max reduced *Cilissa*'s speed until her engines no longer drowned out conversation. 'She'd hate it,' he said firmly. 'Your sister's a purist, she only likes old and original boats.'

'Actually you're quite right, she does, particularly ones that sink. Has she talked to you much about her thesis?'

'Not if I can avoid it. That girl can bore for England about *Titanic*.'

Oscar didn't laugh. As her twin, he could complain about Eds as much as he liked, but he was protective when anyone else did. 'I don't think she's boring,' he said evenly. 'She's just clever. Edie got all the brainy genes.'

'Don't worry about that.' Max let out a cheerful blast of the ship's horn. 'While you're working with me, all you need is a good memory. Talking of which, it's time I gave you a test.'

'OK,' Oscar shrugged. It would take his mind off that heaving beast outside, and he'd spent ages memorising the list of names and numbers his uncle had given him. 'I'll come over,' he said, but as he got to his feet *Cilissa* gave a sudden lurch and he tumbled back on to the pale leather seating. 'No, I'll have to stay here. I'm still feeling queasy.'

As Max turned to look at him, Oscar hoped he was only imagining the flash of contempt in his eyes. Certainly his uncle sounded as cheerful as ever as he called over his shoulder, 'Give me the names of three clients who are currently domiciled in Monaco and whose families have been banking with us for more than four generations.'

That wasn't hard. Four generations must mean at least a century, and he could remember the titles on the oldest of the Monegasque files. 'Marquesa d'Alenza di Grigorvani, Moise and Else Fischer. And Renzo Moravia,' he finished triumphantly.

'Good. Now tell me about Viktor Gutman-Berenbaum.'

'He lives near Hamburg, account number IK44NPJ.'

'Quite right,' Max said, 'though I've never understood why he needs us. Only one account, declares everything in it, pays tax on the whole lot.' He sounded quite offended by his client's probity. 'Prince Jerichau. Tell me about him.'

'One of the principal Jewish families in Genoa.' That was easy. Years ago, on a history-of-art trip, he'd seen the façade of Palazzo Jerichau and had never forgotten it. 'Quentance Bank clients for generations.' That had to be right, the file was a thick one. Now for the difficult bit. 'They've got accounts in Switzerland, numbers 47-46835 and 57-22904.'

'Correct so far.'

'Hang on a second, it's coming back to me.' He screwed his eyes shut and tried to visualise the list of numbers he'd written out over and over again. 'It's in Guernsey, isn't it? Number YRR7879.'

'Not good enough, it's 7978.' Max swivelled round in his chair. 'This is important, Oscar. Our clients trust me because nothing's ever written down. Every detail's kept up here.' He tapped his forehead. 'And next time, I'm going to ask you about Count von Gril unt Critchel. He's got seventeen accounts spread around eight separate offshore judiciaries.

They're each held under a different name and I'll expect you to know them all.'

Oscar hated the feeling that he'd let his uncle down. 'Just try me on one more from the list you gave me.'

There was a pause while Max did something with one of the instruments in front of him. When he swung round, his face was deadpan. 'The Earls of Ivybridge. What about them?'

Oscar stared at his uncle. He couldn't remember anything except that they were the local posh family back in Devon, and they had no money at all. He was going to fail the test. 'I'm sorry. I didn't even know they were clients.'

'Very well done,' Max laughed, 'they aren't. They banked with us years ago, though. In fact there was a close friend-ship between the two families.'

'Quentances and earls? I'd no idea we were ever that grand.'

'Oh yes. Kit and the fifteenth earl were thick as thieves. Hugo Ivybridge always stood by him over those stories about *Titanic*, and then when Hugo died, Kit looked after Miles like his own child. He was always sloping off to Brink Castle to see him.'

'Who was Miles?' At least this was one lot of names he wouldn't have to remember.

'Miles Ivybridge was the sixteenth earl, the father of the present one.'

'So if we were so chummy with the Ivybridge clan, why aren't we now?'

'Oh, that's very old news.' Max swung his chair round to face the bows. 'I can't remember what happened.'

From his place in the stern, Oscar stared at the back of his uncle's head. His memory was phenomenal, it was impossible that he should have forgotten. He must just have lost interest. As if to prove it, Max leaned over and pushed the spare helmsman's seat so that it spun on its chrome pivot. 'Come up here so I don't have to keep shouting. It's time I told you about Guernsey.' Oscar got up, creeping forwards until he could perch beside his uncle. 'First of all, it's an island, so I can get there by sea.'

'Because you don't like flying.' Watching the spray flooding across *Cilissa*'s windshield, Oscar found it hard to understand how anyone could enjoy boating either, but he wasn't going to say so.

'That's not the reason. A boat's such an easy way to move hard cash.'

'But isn't money all moved by computers these days?'

'Far too risky.' Max shook his head. 'Electronic transactions make dirty great footprints, and you can't afford to leave any tracks for the authorities to follow. And there's another thing about offshore islands.' There was a pause while he reached up to flip one of the switches on the control panel, bringing the radar screen to a mauve glow of life. 'They run what they call "favourable regimes", which make it simple to evade the tax hounds.'

Evade the tax hounds. There was something uncomfortable about the phrase, Oscar didn't mind straying close to the line of legality but he didn't want to end up in prison. 'Max,' he started, 'I'd just like to be sure that...' but the words dried in his throat as the radar started to ping loudly, while red dots spread like flea bites across its screen. A glance outside showed a line of ships looming towards them. 'Look out!' he shouted.

'It's quite all right.' Max's voice was unruffled. 'We just have to be a bit careful here, it's one of the busiest shipping lanes in the world. Some days, it feels like trying to cross the M25 on foot.'

'Oh my God!' They shot under the stern of a tanker which appeared not even to have noticed them.

'Calm down, for heaven's sake. We're perfectly safe with modern radar.' With a careless flap of the hand, Max indicated the screen with its rash of scarlet spots. 'This tells me the speed and course of anything within miles of us.'

'Edie wouldn't have a doctorate to write if they'd had one of those on *Titanic*,' Oscar said, trying to sound nonchalant, but Max seemed to be concentrating hard and didn't answer.

Oscar found he felt safer with his eyes shut. He tried to think about music until eventually his uncle reached across to nudge his arm. 'You can relax now, we're well south of the shipping lanes. Mind you,' he added, 'this would be a bleak place to get into trouble. Just thousands of miles of empty ocean till you hit America.'

'But supposing the engine cut out?'

'That'd be no problem on a modern boat like this. We've got computerised engine-management systems and every sort of safety device you can think of.' Max smiled across at him. 'But to be honest, I used to scare myself witless bringing *Cassandra* through these waters in a heavy sea.

Horrible rocks, horrible tides and no way of communicating except VHF ship-to-shore. *Cilissa*'s dull by comparison.'

'I'll take dull every time.'

The colour was draining out of the sky when the flat-topped bulk of Guernsey humped itself out of the sea like some primordial monolith. A few early lights winked from millionaires' houses concealed along its wooded cliffs, and as *Cilissa* nosed her way round a curve of the island, Oscar caught the brighter glow of St Peter Port. The process of negotiating *Cilissa* into her berth and mooring seemed to take for ever, but finally he was stepping on to the wooden ramp that led up to the dockside.

As he reached the solid rock of the harbour walls, Oscar had the peculiar feeling that his legs were sliding away from him. He reached out to steady himself on his uncle's shoulder, pretending he'd been going to take the briefcase dangling from his uncle's hand. 'Why don't I carry that for you?'

'This? Don't worry, it's not heavy.'

Oscar was rather relieved. Maybe his uncle thought the briefcase was some sort of fashion statement, but to him it looked like cheap plastic.

As they walked along the harbour wall towards the town, Max paused to slip an envelope into a yellow postbox. 'Customs form,' he said briefly.

'I didn't realise we had anything to declare.'

'We certainly wouldn't be declaring it if we had. Come on now, we've a hike ahead of us.' Saying this, his uncle strode off into the narrow streets of St Peter Port and Oscar had to hurry to keep up. Without warning, Max disappeared through a gap between two houses and Oscar found himself climbing a series of dimly lit, granite stairways hidden in the heart of the town. Their footsteps echoed as they clattered upwards, twisting between high walls so that it was impossible to see more than a few yards ahead. A lingering smell of cigarette smoke suggested that they weren't the only people using these passageways, but they met not a soul.

With one final blind turn, they passed from the alley into a broad street of white-painted villas. Max slowed to a more normal pace, which gave Oscar a chance to get his breath back and to admire the elegance of the houses. He noticed that whilst the area looked residential, many of the doorways displayed discreet little corporate brass plaques, and was trying to commit some of these to memory when Max stopped abruptly.

'There,' his uncle said reverently, '*that's* what I brought you up here to see. Take your time,' he added, 'I'll be back in a minute.' Without another word, Max vanished into the shadows of a nearby alleyway.

Oscar gazed obediently. It was indeed a wonderful view. Through a break between the line of buildings, all the rooftops of St Peter Port were laid out in a wide panorama below. Looking further, he could see masthead lights dancing in the dark waters of the harbour, while beyond the granite walls of the port stretched the sea, and further still, the bulk of some neighbouring island arched against the faint horizon. He stood there, entranced, until he heard footsteps behind him and his uncle's voice saying, 'I'm starving after all that ozone. Time for dinner.'

*

Oscar was half asleep in his comfortable bunk when it occurred to him. That plastic briefcase. Max hadn't been carrying it when they came back on board *Cilissa*. Surely he couldn't have left it somewhere by mistake?

A boat's such an easy way to move hard cash.

Of course he hadn't. His uncle knew exactly what he was doing.

EIGHT

Edie gazed out of the library window. The sun was shining, but in her mind's eye all was dark. She was no longer breathing book leather and beeswax, but the tang of salt on icy air. Instead of sitting at a desk, she was standing on the bridge in that freezing night. She could almost feel the low vibration of the engines beneath her feet as she watched *Titanic*'s bow slicing through the ocean.

Next to her imaginary self stood First Officer Murdoch, nearing forty and a hugely experienced sailor. On such a dark night and with the threat of ice, he'd have been keeping an especially anxious watch, particularly since *Titanic* was making the equivalent of thirty land-miles per hour, and had a stopping distance measurable in miles too. Yet despite the speed, the dead calm and the lack of a moon, Murdoch would unquestionably have believed he'd have time to take avoiding action if ice were sighted.

No one knew what had gone wrong. William Murdoch had died that night, and whilst he'd certainly have justified his actions to his two superior officers, both Captain Smith and Chief Officer Wilde had also gone down with the ship. If only Murdoch had explained those vital moments before the collision to just one of *Titanic*'s survivors, she'd have the answer to that most basic question: why didn't an officer as skilled as Murdoch manage to avoid an iceberg large enough to sink his ship?

She bent over the wreck commissioner's summary, open on the desk in front of her.

> IN THE MATTER OF the Formal Investigation ... into the circumstances attending the loss of the steamship 'Titanic', of Liverpool, and the loss of 1,490 lives in the North Atlantic Ocean, in lat. 41.46' N., long. 50.14' W. on the 15th April last ... The Court finds ... that the loss of the said ship was due to collision with an iceberg, brought about by the excessive speed at which the ship was being navigated.
>
> Dated this 30th day of July, 1912

Perhaps their conclusion was right. Maybe *Titanic* did sink simply because she was going too fast. But why, in such dangerous conditions?

Pushing the report aside, she fingered a patch where the green leather covering the top of the library desk had begun to disintegrate. Her great-grandfather might have worked in this very chair. Perhaps he'd also sat here ruminating about *Titanic*? There was one crucial difference, though. She could only guess what had happened, while he'd actually been there. But Kit had died before she was born, he'd left no memoir to help her, and she must stop wool-gathering. It was late July, she'd be starting work at the bank in a couple of weeks, and that would put an end to these leisurely hours of study.

Edie returned to her notes, shuffling through them until she found the photograph of *Titanic*'s captain. Looking at the frank intelligence of that bearded face, she couldn't believe he'd wanted to set a new speed record for the Atlantic crossing. E. J. Smith would never take such a risk with his ship. He must surely have been given a direct order by *Titanic*'s owners.

She flipped on through her papers until she found another grainy photograph. Frowning, she stared into the big-nosed, angry-eyed face of J. P. Morgan. Rich and ruthless, he represented everything she despised about bankers and, worse, as proprietor of International Mercantile Marine he owned the White Star Line and hence *Titanic* itself. Pierpont Morgan would have wanted *Titanic* to chase the trans-Atlantic speed record. He was fighting for a monopoly of the North Atlantic passenger route and to win he had to beat his competitor, the Cunard Line.

Nothing changes, Edie thought, lifting her gaze to the fat, green hills on the far side of the Dart. The battle for the North Atlantic crossing was as vicious today as it had been a century ago, the only difference being that it was no longer steamship companies doing the fighting, but airlines. Bending over the desk, she scribbled, *To what do you not drive human hearts, cursed craving for gold?* She'd like to fit Virgil's sententious sentiment into her D.Phil. somewhere.

Turning back to Pierpont Morgan's face, she concentrated on the known facts about the American's role in the tragedy. J. P. Morgan was originally due to travel on *Titanic*'s maiden voyage, but he pulled out at the last minute and vanished to Aix-les-Bains with his French mistress. That in itself was an interesting fact, and so was the story of his first-class suite. After Morgan's cancellation, this was booked by Mr and Mrs Horace Harding, a hugely rich couple whom White Star Line would have been delighted to have captured. But then the Hardings changed their minds and decided to travel on *Mauretania* instead, their reason being that the Cunard ship would get them to New York faster than *Titanic*.

Edie made a note on her writing-block. *High-profile defection of Hardings must have infuriated J. P. Morgan, quite possibly to the point of insisting* Titanic's *maiden voyage had to be a record breaker.* If that was indeed the case, she could see how everything else might have followed. Bruce Ismay, the chairman of the White Star Line, ended up with the suite, and was also one of the few male passengers on *Titanic* who managed to worm his way to the safety of a lifeboat. It seemed to Edie to be entirely conceivable that Ismay, acting on Morgan's orders, might have encouraged Captain Smith to keep *Titanic* running on full steam, despite the conditions.

Facts, Edie! This is all just theory. She could almost hear her Oxford supervisor's scolding, but at least there was plenty of proof of *Titanic*'s speed. Picking up the report of the initial inquiry held in New York, she flicked through to Day 18 and the evidence of Leading Stoker Barrett. As head of the stokeholds and boilers in the bow section of *Titanic*, his evidence was invaluable.

'There was twenty-four boilers lit and five without. Fires were lighted in three boilers for the first time Sunday ...'

The only reason to light more boilers was to go faster, and Sunday was the fatal night.

'And that was the first time during the voyage that the twenty-four boilers were running?'

'Yes.'

Edie liked the sound of Frederick Barrett. He gave his evidence in such a straightforward way that it was easy to believe he was telling the truth.

She turned to the testimony of Quartermaster Hitchins. Unlike Leading Stoker Barrett, he was one of the witnesses whose evidence she was inclined to mistrust, but Robert Hitchins couldn't be ignored. He'd been in charge of the wheel.

'You have told us according to the Cherub log that the speed was 45 knots in two hours?'

'Yes.'

When Murdoch took over the watch at ten, *Titanic* was making twenty-two knots dead, but Hitchins' calculation of forty-five knots per two hours was the equivalent of twenty-two and a half knots per hour. So on a pitch-dark night, in an area of reported icebergs, the ship, already going dangerously fast, was putting on steam. No one could have made that decision except *Titanic*'s owners, driven by their mad desire for money.

A passage from Commander Lightoller's autobiography came into her head. He'd been talking about the lack of lifeboats, but his conclusion was the same. 'I'm afraid as far as life-saving equipment was concerned,' he'd written, 'it was just so much theory, concocted ashore with a keen eye to dividends.' Disheartened by this evidence of corporate greed, Edie stood up and stretched. The summer sunshine was irresistible. She'd go for a walk along the coast to see if a good blast of sea air might help her to think clearly.

She wondered briefly about going by bicycle, but it would take her a good hour to cycle to the coast, so instead she decided to take the Series One Land Rover. Max and her father almost always used the Bentley when they were at Dartleap, but Alec kept the old car to show off. When they had important people staying, he'd drive it round the estate to pretend his rural credentials, but for the rest of the time it sat unused in one of the garages.

Fortunately, she found that it had been left with fuel in the tank, and having fired up the engine, Edie headed off through the high-banked lanes of the South Hams, enjoying the feeling of every minor bump in the road through the car's rigid suspension. Once she'd reached the coast, Edie parked near a line of low cliffs where stands of scrubby trees scrambled down to the sea. She paused to admire the screaming flight of seabirds, then set off westwards along a rough coastal track.

She climbed fast as the path led her up on to the thin grassland that rolled back from the cliff edges. Scrambling to the top of a headland, she stopped to gaze at the great seascape of Start Bay. An onshore wind was crashing queues of white-capped breakers down on the rocky foreshore, and even though she was so high above the water, the sea-breeze whipped through her hair, carrying the bittersweet scent of seaweed. Far out in the bay, a coaster was ploughing through the sea, and Edie felt a sudden longing to be out there, to hear the roar of water surging against the ship's sides, to feel the deck bucking under her feet. Shrugging her shoulders, she turned away. She'd better get used to the fact that it was a desk she was going to be driving, not a boat.

Stuffing her hands into the pockets of her much-mended tracksuit, Edie set off in a loping walk along the clifftop. It was beautiful up here, with the bay to her left and the scrubby grassland stretching for miles to her right. An unexpected wave of happiness washed through her and she broke into a trot. She was young, she was fit, she could run for ever.

DANGER. KEEP OUT. She'd been watching the seagulls, and almost jogged into the sign before she saw it. A double line of barbed wire diverted her inland, away from the wildness of the coast. She'd always walked along these cliffs. Dismissing whichever health-and-safety busybody had blocked the path, she decided to ignore the notice.

A struggle with the fence added another rip to her tracksuit, but then she was through the wire and free. Striding onwards, Edie glanced inland to where the battlements of Brink Castle emerged over the top of a hill. It was a romantic sight, with enough of the ruined walls remaining to conceal the eighteenth-century house that had been built inside them, and there was the Ivybridge flag flapping on its pole. While she was eyeing this aristocratic symbol, a tussock of dead broom caught at her foot and she fell to her knees, one hand landing right in a scatter of fresh rabbit droppings.

By the time she'd cursed a couple of times and wiped the mess off her hand, she was no longer alone on the cliff-top. Someone was coming towards her from the direction of Brink Castle. There was something about his height, something about the length of his stride. As Edie realised who it was and whose land she was on, she looked round awkwardly, but there was nowhere to hide on that barren cliff and to run away would look ridiculous. She would just have to brazen it out.

'Edie Quentance. What a nice surprise.' Squinting up into John Tamar's face, she noticed that his eyes were endearingly mismatched, one blue and the other hazel. 'Didn't you see the signs?'

Taking in his clean T-shirt and chinos, Edie was uncomfortably aware of her dirty hands, untidy hair and unflattering old tracksuit. Using anger to hide her embarrassment, she said, 'I don't see why this land should be private just because it's yours. I bet it belonged to ordinary people like me before your ancestors got hold of it.'

'Now *that's* rather the pot calling the kettle black.' Tamar's face lit up in amusement. 'When it comes to how they got their land, the Quentance family aren't exactly beacons of purity.'

Not understanding what he meant, Edie was silenced, until she caught the sound of gunfire coming from somewhere close by. 'At least we don't use our land for slaughtering birds.'

For a moment he didn't respond, but as she was thinking that his half-smile was really quite attractive, it vanished. 'You're very welcome to walk here,' he said, 'but be careful. The shooting is because I let the Navy use this area for training exercises.' As he was turning away from her he added, 'They always used to train in the woods at Dartleap, too. That was until your family lost any vestige of a conscience.' Without another word, he left her and walked rapidly off towards Brink Castle.

Edie stared after his retreating back. She felt oddly ruffled. As she hurried back to where she'd left the car, she found herself going over their brief conversation. Why ever had she been so aggressive?

NINE

Although it was nearly dusk, the heat of the setting sun still radiated from the baked-clay walls. It seemed like hours since Max had ordered a drink, but what could you expect in a place like this? His limbs ached and his throat felt gritty, parched by the desiccated air of the filthy little town. He looked longingly down over the jumble of flat roofs towards the burnished plate of the Mediterranean, but there wasn't even a whisper of a sea-breeze. The north coast of Africa was an absurd place to be in August, and he'd never have dreamed of coming here if the invitation hadn't had too many possibilities to refuse. But at least when the party was over, he could hurry back to *Cilissa* and escape. He pitied the poor people who had no choice but to live in a hell-hole like this.

Peering over the parapet of the hotel's rooftop oasis, Max could see veiled women slapping along the narrow streets, their slippers kicking trails of fine dust as they shopped for the evening meal. As he watched, the first throaty call to prayer wavered from a nearby minaret and was picked up by other muezzins until the whole world seemed subsumed in an eerie evening chorus.

'Your *pastis*, Monsieur Quentance.' Because of the unearthly noise of the *adhan*, he hadn't heard the waiter's approach until he caught the rattle of ice cubes against the side of a glass. For a moment, he was tempted to send the drink back. When he'd given his order, he'd specifically asked for no ice, but there it was anyway, misting the sides of the tumbler with a tempting promise of coolness. The water was sure to be dodgy, but he hadn't the willpower to refuse it. Reaching out, he took a gulp of the aniseed-flavoured spirit.

'This has come for you, also, monsieur.' The waiter was still at his elbow, holding out an envelope.

'What? Oh, thank you.' Max passed over a handful of change while he pulled out a heavily engraved card.

Pour mémoire
*Tom and Bunty are looking forward to seeing you
at the souk tonight!
Dinner & Dancing & Decadence
Ten till late   Dress: Villainous*

A party in a souk. He knew just what that would be like. An absurd extravagance of food, drink and entertainment would have been hauled into this armpit of a town which his host and hostess would claim to have 'discovered'. Actually, the place would have been sourced by a party organiser whose main criterion would have been to find somewhere with a harbour deep enough to moor a fleet of super-yachts. Though at least with all the resulting security, *Cilissa* would be safe down at her mooring. He'd be sailing her straight on up to Monaco and she was carrying some valuable ballast.

Max frowned as his eye ran down to the bottom of the card. Villainous. He'd wear a pair of dark glasses out of politeness, but otherwise he was going in his normal clothes, he hated dressing-up. He'd never have accepted the invitation in the first place if his host hadn't inherited a fortune when a pile-up killed his father and elder brother. Max hoped to get a slug of Tom's money into the safe-keeping of Quentance Bank before the whole lot was frittered away.

The raw *pastis* had given him a headache, and he was fiercely hungry by the time he found himself following Tom and Bunty's guide away from the warm stench of the souk and into a maze of dark alleys. For five minutes or more, they jinked and back-tracked into the heart of the town's Moorish quarter, and Max had lost his bearings entirely by the time they halted in front of a low doorway. The guide held his flare high, nodded towards an intricately carved door, then turned and vanished back down the quiet alleyways.

At Max's push, the door swung open, releasing a roar of sound. Looking in on the raucous party, he saw bandits with harlots, vampires with cat-burglars – and then he remembered. Villainous. And he hadn't even brought his sunglasses. For a moment he was tempted to go straight back to the hotel, except he'd never be able to find the way, and besides, there was money in front of him. Taking a deep breath, he ducked inside.

He found himself in a two-storey courtyard, open to the

sky and lit by fire-baskets which threw eerie shadows high on to the clay walls. The courtyard was crammed with petal-strewn tables laid for dinner, while the party itself was going on in the encircling rooms and alcoves. He threaded his way between the guests, hoping to find his host before some other banker nobbled him.

'Tom? Naah, haven't seen him all evening,' said a Hitler, his moustache slipping in the heat. 'Here, d'you want a snort of devil's dandruff?'

'Sorry, darling.' A Cruella de Vil with over-large pupils pushed her face close to his. 'I caught a glimpse of Bunty, but I don't think Tom's here at all.'

Max squeezed himself on from group to group, getting hotter and crosser until eventually he had to abandon the hunt for his host. He was hungry, he had a headache, and he needed a break. A place like this was sure to have a private hammam, and by squirming between crowd and walls he finally reached it. The mosaic-walled room was a paradise of soft towels, scented air and running water, and after locking himself in, Max ignored the occasional thumping on the door while he spent a peaceful half-hour recovering his equilibrium.

He didn't emerge from the hammam until he heard the throb of a gong, and he was caught up in a surge of humanity sweeping hungrily into the central courtyard. By a lucky chance he stopped right by a place-card with MAX painted across it, and sank into a silk-draped chair. The table was already filling up, but as yet there was no one sitting on either side of him. He glanced at his neighbours' names. Zita. Scheherazade. He'd no idea who either of them might be.

He was nodding hello to a Captain Hook taking the seat just beyond the unknown Zita's when his eye was caught by a woman weaving her way towards him. She held her head erect, moving languidly as a dancer. From a thick, gold torque round her neck, chains of golden droplets trickled down over a clinging, vest-shaped dress. This dress was embroidered with flows of crystals, so that in the semi-darkness it seemed as if she was wearing water. She looked too fragile to be carrying such a weight of stone and metal, but as she came nearer, Max saw that there was a lot of defined muscle on those elegant arms and shoulders.

He was still staring when the woman paused beside him. He stood up and found himself examining the top of a head covered with waves of dark brown hair. The way she carried herself must have concealed it, but now he could see that she was tiny, scarcely more than five feet tall. She tilted her head, and Max looked appreciatively down into a round face, huge eyes and a cherub's mouth. It was the face of a pretty doll, though perhaps not quite such a young doll as he'd first imagined.

The woman leaned over to check his name card. 'Max. Good.' As she glanced at him again, he was struck by the extraordinary colour of her eyes. It was hard to be sure in such soft lighting, but they seemed to be a deep, velvety mauve. 'I'd heard you were gorgeous,' she gave him a wide smile, showing perfect little teeth, 'so I rearranged the *place-ment* to make us neighbours.' Her voice was teasing and he wasn't quite sure he believed her. 'I'm Zita Fitz.'

As she held out a hand, Max saw that the gold swinging from her wrists was interspersed with teardrops of diamonds and emeralds. He couldn't help making a mental calculation of their value, and it was a moment before he was aware that Zita was trying to disentangle her hand from his. 'I don't suppose you've managed to track down our host and hostess, have you?' he said lightly, holding her chair out for her.

'I'm not sure they've even bothered to turn up,' she said as he took his place beside her. 'The recently rich can be amazingly rude.' She paused, fingering the precious stones at her wrists. 'But isn't it easy to help them spend their money?'

Max gave a shout of laughter and poured them champagne from one of several opened bottles on their table. The evening was definitely looking up. 'So is that what you do?' he asked, raising his glass in a silent toast. 'Spend other people's money?'

'Not at all!' She widened her eyes in mock-horror. 'I only said I help them.'

'I'm lost.' Max was mesmerised by her face, lovely in the dim light of the flares. 'You'll have to explain.'

'Now that's not polite.' She was like a chameleon. One moment all smiles, the next grave and formal. 'You should tell me about yourself first.'

'Of course.' Max adjusted his features to mirror her serious expression. 'My brother and I run our family's private bank. He heads the English side and I look after our European clients.'

'You mean Quentance Bank? I've heard of it, obviously, but tell me more.'

'We give a very discreet service, high-end only,' he started evasively. But then Zita leaned close enough for him to catch the heady vanilla sweetness of her scent and he felt a childish urge to boast. 'My speciality's in keeping no unnecessary records. I rely entirely on memory.' Max stopped. Was he imagining it or had her eyes narrowed? He knew nothing at all about her. Supposing she was a nark for some tax authority? Recovering himself, he said quickly, 'So how about you?'

'I play in the high-end food chain as well.' She blinked once, very slowly, like a cat in a sunbeam. 'I help my friends smooth out the odd financial annoyance, and they drop me scraps from their tables in return.'

'Only scraps?' Max didn't believe her for a moment.

'Oh, I manage to pick a living wage off their gnawed bones.'

Her eyes were still on him, and as she stroked the chains of gold that dangled from her neck, Max understood. 'Provenance?' he asked quietly.

'Exactly.'

'Thank goodness for that.' This seductive woman was a pirate, just like he was. 'Are we talking yellow metal?'

'Gold-washing's so simple, isn't it?' she said easily. 'Pure and lovely, even though it comes from grubby old toms and druggies.'

Max nodded. He never thought about the less pleasant side of the business if he could avoid it. 'The end product's flawless,' he said, eyeing the fat, golden torque around her neck. 'How long do you wear it for?'

'A couple of months.' She picked up her champagne glass and peered at him over the rim. 'Long enough to be photographed a few times to show the world it's legit.' Max watched the movement of her neck as she drank. 'After that, it's whipped away and melted down into ingots.'

'Have you ever done anything except give provenance to major pieces?'

Max was hoping to get a bit more of Zita's background, but now he was afraid he'd made her cross. 'Me? D'you mean piling on a load of shoddily made necklaces and carting them off to some godforsaken gold-souk? No thank you! I'd never dream of being a mule. Mind you,' she added in a softer voice, 'I've worked with horses a few times. You'd be amazed how often a decent-looking cob can change hands during one of the big fairs. And always for cash.' Max was astonished. Here was someone who knew things about the business that even he'd missed.

So caught up was he with Zita that it was only when the food arrived that he realised how rude he'd been to the woman on his other side. He hadn't even introduced himself. To boisterous cheers, huge tanks were being carried in full of rock lobsters, all staring mournfully out at their Armageddon. Each guest had to choose their own, after which the little animals were to be whisked away to have their spines split and their flesh grilled. Zita selected hers and immediately turned to chat to Captain Hook on her other side, while Max switched on an apologetic grin for the neighbour he'd ignored.

Scheherazade turned out to be a great deal less exotic than her name. Over the lobsters, Max had a perfectly pleasant conversation about her houses, her children and her husband's money, but he couldn't help wishing he was still talking to the lovely Miss Fitz. Scheherazade must have guessed this, because at one point she broke off from a description of some property her husband had invested in to say sharply, 'Zita's like quicksilver, you know. Here today, gone tomorrow.' He caught the glint of envy as she added, 'And do be careful. She keeps a brain the size of Kent in that little gnat's body.'

Max turned from Scheherazade the moment the next course arrived, and found Zita examining a mélange of chocolate, meringue, cream and exotic fruits, over the top of which were scattered fragile leaves of gold. 'Money on a plate,' she said. 'Tasteless in both senses of the word, don't you think?'

Max took his fork and prodded an underripe lychee. 'You could eat twice as well for half the cost in Paris.'

'Is that where you live?'

'In the *septième*,' Max nodded, 'just off rue de Varenne. You know Paris well?'

'I'm there on and off. Do you have a base in England?'

'No need. I always stay with my brother when I'm in London. Alec has a flat above our branch in St James's Square.'

'Tell me about him.' She seemed genuinely interested. 'Is he married?'

'Separated.' Max felt the usual sadness. Alec alone in London, Clio alone in Bath, still bearing her grief like an albatross round her neck.

'Do they have children?'

'Twenty-five-year-old twins, both at the bank. Edie's just started in the London office, and Oscar's come to work with me. And I must say, he's turning out to be—' He broke off suddenly. 'I'm sorry, this must be terribly boring for you.'

'Not at all.' Zita speared a few wild strawberries and sucked them off her fork. 'I'm intrigued by other people's families.'

'Don't you have one of your own?'

Studying her plate, she said coolly, 'None to speak of.' But a moment later, her eyes were back on his. 'So your brother just has two children, does he?'

'There was another daughter.' That intent stare was immensely flattering, drawing confidences from him. 'She was only five when she died, poor little Ianthe.'

'Ianthe,' Zita repeated. 'Daughter of Oceanus and Tethys.'

'You know the Greek myths a lot better than I do.' A brain the size of Kent. Scheherazade had been right. 'All I know is that Clio got the idea from some book in the Dartleap library.'

'Dart Leap. Does that mean leaping darts or darting leaps?'

'The Dart's a river in Devon. The Quentance family have had a house there for generations.' He wanted to go on talking, but his words were subsumed into a drumbeat, starting low but quickly rising to a crescendo which made further speech impossible. Max saw that a space had been made in the centre of the courtyard and the floor scattered with fine white sand. Incense hissed from the flares as two giants slipped into the cleared area like shadows from a forest, their ebony bodies shining with oil. Both were naked apart from narrow leather loincloths and a row of amulets tied with string around their knees.

He heard Zita whisper, 'Senegalese,' close to his ear while, as graceful as panthers, the pair glided around each other, occasionally pausing to scoop sand up from the floor and throw it over their backs, where it stuck to the oil in white streaks. Scented smoke curled through the hot air, a tom-tom began to rap out a syncopation to the pounding drums, and the strange dance went on and on, its movements fluid, menacing and enigmatic.

The weaving lasted until one of the wrestlers saw an opening. The drumbeat pulsed furiously as the two giants slapped together in sudden violence, gripped, swayed, and it was all over, with one fighter pinned down by his shoulders on the sand while the other bent in triumph over him. The pair stayed completely still, as if frozen into a tableau, until the winner held out a hand to help his defeated rival to his feet and they stalked silently away.

'I've never seen anything like it,' Max breathed.

'It was a mystical battle to invoke an ancient magic. If you wish for something now, you'll get it.'

Max glanced from her face down to her bare arms and the curve of her bosom. It was far too early for him to say what he was wishing, but he hoped she'd guess.

'Be careful.' It was nothing like the flirtation he'd expected. 'Human desires can be misinterpreted by the spirits.' Max was starting to get used to her sudden changes of mood, and a moment later she yawned widely and extended both arms high above her head. 'Sorry. Flying's exhausting, isn't it?'

'I wouldn't know.' Max was finding it hard to drag his mind back from the expanse of golden flesh her vest-dress had exposed when she stretched. 'Where did you fly from?'

'Lake Como.'

'There's an airfield in the Italian lakes?'

'You'll find a few runways tucked between the slopes if you know where to look. A friend flew me over.'

Max felt the nip of jealousy. 'This friend,' he asked. 'Is he taking you back?'

'Oh no, he's flying on south to the diamond mines.' Raising her wineglass, Zita drained it, then pushed her chair back as if she was about to stand up.

'Can I give you a lift home?' He suddenly couldn't bear the thought of this woman disappearing from his life. 'I've got a fast boat down in the harbour.'

'Sweet of you, Max, but I've already got a berth.' Zita surprised him with a wink. 'On a frightfully vulgar yacht. There's a swimming pool and a helipad; it's even got a barbecue area on one of the aft decks. For all the movement you feel underfoot, you might as well not be at sea at all.'

'You like boats?'

'Proper ones, yes. They make me feel free.' Zita made a wide, graceful gesture like a bird opening its wings. 'I'm pretty handy at sea. I've crewed in the Fastnet, though what I really want to do is sail a Swan 45 in the Sardinia Cup. Then I could prove I'm just as much of a sailor as any man.'

Max saw his chance. 'If you like real boats, you should come out on *Cassandra*. She's nearly a century old. In fact,' he added, as if it was an afterthought, 'why don't you come and stay with me at Dartleap? That's where she's berthed.'

'It's a tempting idea, but I hardly know you.'

'I'll get my nephew Oscar to come down and play chaperon.'

'Perfect.' There was a whirl of gold, a rush of sweet vanilla and he felt a soft mouth against his cheek. 'I've got to slip over to England next weekend. How about then?'

He was taken aback by such rapid success. 'How can I get hold of you?' She whispered her number into his ear, and he felt his fingers fumbling with a childish excitement as he punched it into his phone.

TEN

'Where the hell've you got to?' Edie muttered, scrabbling through the cascade of documents in front of her until she unearthed her buzzing mobile from between two Land Registry reports. **Text received. Oscar mob. Read now?** Edie smiled. Before he went to Paris they'd talked all the time, but now it felt like an age since she'd heard from her twin and she missed him. Leaning back in her creaky wooden chair, she pressed the OK button. **Buy a hat. I hear wedding bells.**

Edie stared across the dusty cabinets of the basement room to the ceiling-high shelves of box files that lined its walls. Marriage? Surely Oscar was gay? She'd never push him to tell her, but one day he'd come out. It was obvious. Or was it? He certainly flirted with girls, so maybe he was bi? Or perhaps she'd got him completely wrong and he was as straight as he pretended to be. Either way, his message needed a neutral reply.

Can I be your best man? She re-read the sentence to make sure she'd written nothing that could upset her brother, then clicked Send.

There was no immediate answer, so she went back to her dreary new job. It involved checking the paperwork for every mortgage and secured loan, then sifting through the old-fashioned card index until she'd found where to lodge each item in the Records Room's labyrinthine filing system. The mortgage work was painfully dull, though the secured loans were occasionally quite interesting. It was fun to see which landowners had had to raise money against their Titians and their Raphaels.

There was another buzz from her mobile. Not me, you numpty, Max.

Edie laughed as she read Oscar's text. Partly it was incredulity at the idea that any woman could pin her uncle down, but mainly it was relief that nobody was stealing her twin away. Have you met her? she texted back.

Oscar's reply came almost immediately. Not yet. Umpiring lovers' tryst at Dartleap next weekend.

I'll come down too, OK? She needed another walk on the cliffs, and this time she'd be better dressed. She might even try a bit of lipstick.

No go, Eds. Just me and them.

It was irrational to be disappointed, but Edie couldn't bring herself to text some cheerful reply. Instead, she turned back to the heap of papers sliding across the desk and set herself to checking, cross-referencing and filing with a furious energy. She was still working a couple of hours later when a clerk appeared with a mug of tea and a plate of biscuits.

'Elevenses, Miss Edith. Good gracious!' He was gazing at the almost bare desktop where she'd been working. 'I've not seen the place so tidy since before Mr Oscar joined us.'

'He's dreadfully messy,' Edie smiled. 'I can't imagine he did much filing when he was here.'

'Not a lot,' the clerk nodded in agreement. 'But your brother was a real laugh. Had us all creased up with his jokes.'

She could just imagine him lolling around here in Records and Archives, luring the bank's clerks down to bask in the sunshine of his eternal good humour. Edie felt a sudden longing to hear his voice, and as soon as she was alone again, she slid open her mobile. **Fancy a chat?**

She was finishing her tea when Oscar's reply came. **Later maybe. Busy, busy, busy!**

Edie re-read the text then deleted it. She ought to be glad that her twin was throwing himself into his new role in Paris, because he must have been bored silly slaving away down here. She had a disloyal thought that it would be a lot more fun working with Max than with someone as austere as Dad.

Glancing up at the black hands of the wall clock, she saw that they were only just jerking past eleven. Another six hours before she could go home to the empty mews. Suddenly, the thought of spending months in this subterranean pit seemed insupportable. She needed to get promoted upstairs as soon as possible. Reaching for the internal phone, Edie dialled a number.

'Chairman's office.'

'Oh hi, Janet. It's Edie here.'

'Miss Edith, how can I help you?'

'Can I pop up for a chat with Dad sometime today?'

'Of course. Your father could see you in his office between noon and twelve-thirty.'

With less than an hour to wait, she simply couldn't face any more filing. Leaning down to her briefcase, Edie hauled out the largest of her *Titanic* folders, the one with *Collision* inked down its spine. She took out a copy of the helmsman's cross-examination and spread it in front of her.

Evidence of Quartermaster Hitchins

'I am in the wheelhouse and of course I couldn't see anything ... I might as well be locked in a cell. The only thing I could see was my compass.'

Stuck in the dingy Records Room, she could sympathise with Robert Hitchins. That cramped cabin tucked down behind *Titanic*'s bridge must have seemed depressingly claustrophobic when all the helmsman could do was to sit before the wheel and react to orders. On that particular night, he knew what speed *Titanic* was making, and he'd be aware of the threat of ice, so maybe he was feeling a bit jumpy as well?

'The only thing I could see was my compass.' She stared down at Hitchins' words as if they could tell her something about the man himself, one of the many enigmatic figures swirling round the heart of the *Titanic* mystery. A thirty-year-old master mariner, he'd served as quartermaster on the India route, and also round the Baltic and up the Danube. *Titanic* was his first experience at the wheel in the North Atlantic, and given how carefully White Star had hand-picked the crew, he'd have been highly regarded both as a sailor and as a steersman.

He'd survived the disaster, but suffered a mauling in the

witness stand of the British inquiry. After that, his respectable life had crumbled away into drunkenness and destitution, culminating in a failed murder attempt, imprisonment and a couple of tries at suicide. Robert Hitchins eventually died in poverty while working on a common cargo steamer. Poor man. What an end for someone who'd been helmsman of the most luxurious ship in the world.

'You have told us what happened. First of all, the signal of the three bells, then the telephone message, then that message was repeated to the First Officer, "Iceberg right ahead". Then the First Officer went to the telegraph to give an order to the engine-room and gave you the order, "Hard a Starboard"?'

'Yes.'

'Hard a-starboard'. The words reminded Edie that *Titanic* was operating under Tiller Orders, a fact she should make clear in her D.Phil. She scribbled a memo to herself. *Need to add footnote explaining why 'Hard a-starboard' moved bow to port and vice versa.* Then, putting down her pencil, she gazed vacantly at Robert Hitchins' words as she tried to picture the scene on the bridge.

Alert to the possible danger, First Officer Murdoch would be staring ahead, with nothing to distract him except for the occasional order and the steady rumble of *Titanic*'s engines as she powered through the ocean. With his lower angle of vision, he'd surely have sighted the iceberg before the three bells signal clanged from the crow's nest. Object dead ahead.

Edie knew the calculation as well as Murdoch would have done. In the conditions that night, he'd see anything big enough to damage the ship at around three thousand yards. With *Titanic* making over seven hundred yards per minute, that meant he had four minutes to steer her out of danger. And yet, if Hitchins was to be believed, Murdoch did nothing until he heard the three bells, and even then he waited politely for a telephone call from the crow's nest to be passed on to him. With the iceberg coming closer every second, he next went over to the telegraph and sent an order down to the engine room. Only *then* did he tell the man at the wheel to hard a-starboard. There was no getting away from it. Hitchins' evidence didn't make any sense at all.

She flicked on through the report until she found the testimony of Lookout Frederick Fleet. From his position at the wheel, Hitchins couldn't see anything, but Fleet was up in the crow's nest. He'd certainly had a good view of what happened.

Evidence of Lookout Fleet

'Did you notice how quickly they turned the course of the boat after you sounded the three bells?'

'They did not do it until after I went to the telephone.'

'How long were you at the telephone?'

'I suppose half a minute.'

'When you turned from the telephone. . . she just started to go to port?'

'Yes, Sir.'

So Fleet said the same thing as Hitchins. If their evidence was to be believed, Murdoch had wasted the first of those four minutes he had in which to save the ship. It seemed impossible, and there was conflicting evidence from the second officer, who'd questioned Fleet while they were still on *Carpathia*. She flicked on through the inquiry until she found the page she was looking for.

Evidence of Lookout Fleet

'Do you remember any conversation with Second Officer Lightoller about the lookout and seeing the berg? Just let me read out what Mr Lightoller said: "I asked Fleet what he knew about the accident and induced him to explain the circumstances ... I particularly wanted to know how long after he struck the bell the ship's head moved. He informed me that practically at the same time that he struck the bell, he noticed the ship's head moving under the helm ... I gathered from him the distinct impression that the helm was put over before and not after the report from the lookout." That is what Mr Lightoller said, Mr Fleet.'

'Well I am not going to tell him my business.'

'You really do not understand. That gentleman is not trying to get round you at all.'

'But some of them are, though ...'

So who was telling the truth? Had Lookout Fleet really told his senior officer that *Titanic*'s bow was turning even before he'd seen the iceberg from the crow's nest? If so, why did he later change his evidence to fit Hitchins' story?

And Fleet's last comment, 'But some of them are, though'. What could that have meant?

Edie was so absorbed that she didn't hear the clerk walking up behind her. His tap on her shoulder had her jumping to her feet.

'Sorry, Miss Edith, I didn't mean to surprise you. Mr Alec's running fifteen minutes late. His office will call down when he's free.'

'OK, thanks.' She sat back in her chair and waited for her heart to stop pounding. Fifteen minutes. Just time to skim through another piece of the puzzle.

Evidence of Fourth Officer Boxhall

'The Captain said, "What have we struck?" Mr Murdoch, the First Officer, said, "We have struck an iceberg. I intended to Port Around it but she hit before I could do anything more."'

On her notepad, Edie sketched the simple C-shaped movement of a port around. *Titanic*'s bow would first have been turned to port to pull the ship out to the left of the iceberg, and then the bow would be put to starboard to curve round it. She'd no doubt it was the best manoeuvre for Murdoch to have made, provided he had time to complete it. But if there was any risk at all that he couldn't do a full port around, Murdoch would surely have chosen a head-on collision. A direct hit to *Titanic*'s bow would be a thousand times safer than risking a gash along her side.

Edie had got to this point so many times before that she felt like screaming with frustration. *Why* was there that delay between sighting the iceberg and making the turn to port? *Why* did the lookout change his evidence on the timing of when the bow began to move? *Why* did such an experienced sailor as Murdoch start a port around manoeuvre if he didn't have time to complete it?

Her thoughts were interrupted by the internal phone. 'It's Janet Bishop here. Mr Alec will see you now.'

'I'm on my way,' she said, tugging on her jacket.

Although her father's office was in the building above her, there was no access to it from the basement. To get to the front entrance of the bank's Restoration townhouse, Edie had to go outside and climb the metal staircase to the pavement of St James's Square. Turning left, she hurried along to the main door, barely glancing at the soaring eagle that hovered over the central pediment, giving the false impression that the property had belonged to the family for centuries.

'Ah, Miss Edith!' She got a small bow from the porter-cum-security-guard. 'Come to see Mr Alec, have you?' Edie passed him with a nod and a smile. 'Up you go then,' she heard him say to her retreating back.

As she mounted the shallow treads, she eyed the gallimaufry of Quentance ancestors climbing the walls alongside her. The painted stares that followed her might be gentian, or cornflower, or even periwinkle, the lilac-blue most similar to her own eye colour, but none strayed beyond the blue spectrum. It was the same with their hair, which, though ranging from ash to straw to tawny, was uniformly fair. Out of the whole lot of them, Edie was the sole dark-haired misfit.

She bounded up the last few stairs and stepped straight on to the sprung boards of the house's former ballroom, which ran the entire five-windowed length of the first floor. Edie liked to imagine those eighteenth-century blades and their eager partners who must have flirted and waltzed here, though now it was just used as a grandiose corridor, leading past a run of meeting rooms to her father's office. Before she'd even reached his mahogany door at the far end, it swung open.

'Hi, Janet.'

'Miss Edith, I thought I heard you. Mr Alec is free for you now.'

ELEVEN

With a squeal of wheels on metal and a waft of diesel fumes, the 09:06 out of Paddington came to a gradual halt in front of them. 'There you are.' His uncle tapped his watch. 'Totnes Station at eleven-fifty-three on the dot. I told you this train was reliable.'

Being a frequent rail traveller, Max had known exactly where the first-class carriage would pull up, and he and Oscar stood side by side as the door opened. A pale leather suitcase appeared, followed by a pair of tanned legs beneath a plain white shirt-dress.

'Zita!' Max exclaimed. 'Welcome!' In one swift movement she was down on the platform.

'Max, how lovely, and you must be Oscar. I can't tell you how excited I've been about meeting you.' A moment later she had tucked one slim palm under his arm, the other under Max's, and he found himself carrying a surprisingly heavy suitcase with his free hand while Zita tripped along the platform between them.

Out in the station car park, the Bentley shone from the buffing it had been given earlier that morning. In exchange for dragging Oscar down to Devon to act as chaperon, Max had agreed to let him drive, and he settled himself happily at the wheel while Max tucked Zita carefully into the front seat as if she were a china doll.

Oscar concentrated on sliding the big car out of Totnes while Zita and Max chattered about the party they'd met at, but as the rounded hills of the South Hams bunched up along the road beside them he said, 'How d'you like the scenery, Zita?'

'Surprising. I'd imagined it would be flatter.'

'Seriously?' His uncle gave a snort of laughter. 'You mean you've never been to Devon?'

'Never.'

Oscar gave her a quick glance and saw that her smile had become a stony stare out of the windscreen. 'Dartleap's right on top of a hill,' he said brightly. 'It has grand views.'

'Grand. Oh really?' There was a sharp note in Zita's voice, though he couldn't see why. '*Elle est élevée?*'

'*Elle est très bien élevée,*' Max replied from the back. '*Comme toute ma famille.*'

Now he was working in Paris, Oscar's French was improving daily, but it wasn't yet up to a *double entendre*. For the rest of the short journey, he only half listened while Max and Zita showed off their fluency to each other, concentrating instead on avoiding the Saturday sailors on their way to Dartmouth, and the occasional farmer determined to squeeze his John Deere through the high-banked, car-crammed lanes and not minding whose paintwork he scraped on the way.

Zita was laughing at some story of Max's when Oscar

slowed down. 'Here we are,' he called as he swung carefully between the gates.

Max explained the landscape as they weaved up the long loops of the drive. 'It's high summer now, so you can't see a thing through the woods, but even in the dead of winter you don't get a glimpse of Dartleap till you're almost on top of it.' He paused, but Zita didn't make any comment and a moment later Max was off again, pointing out the river coiling far below them. 'We've got our own quay on the Dart. I'll take you down there this afternoon so you can see *Cassandra*.'

They passed through Dartleap's sheltering crescent of trees and after they'd pulled up in front of the house Oscar hurried round to open Zita's door. She'd taken her sunglasses off for the first time since he'd met her, and as she climbed out into the sunlight he felt vaguely disturbed by her eyes, which were so large that they hovered on the borderline between beauty and freakishness. Her irises, too, were extraordinary. They were black-rimmed, and as the sunshine struck them they seemed to vary in colour from violet to mauve to a lilac-shot grey. But what Oscar found most disconcerting was their expression. As Zita stood on the gravel and stared up at the five-storeyed façade, she looked almost afraid. He wondered what someone as sophisticated as Zita Fitz might have to fear, but even as he asked himself the question, he had the answer. She must find the grandeur of the house overwhelming, though to him Dartleap was just a big and rather boring old pile.

Max hurried on ahead of them, and when they got inside he turned round, a huge smile on his face. 'Welcome to

Dartleap,' he said, flinging his arms theatrically wide, 'ancestral home of the Quentance family.' Without pausing for a reply, he walked backwards, his eyes on Zita's as she and Oscar followed him along the hallway to where the double-helix staircase spun upwards through the heart of the house. 'What do you think?'

'It's lovely.' She stared up at the vertex of the glass dome. 'I bet you have your Christmas tree right here.'

'We do, as a matter of fact.' Max moved closer until he was almost touching her. 'What a clever guess.'

You're moving too fast, Oscar wanted to warn his uncle, but Zita didn't look at all put out. She patted Max's cheek gently, then twirled away towards the staircase, calling over her shoulder, 'I want to see every inch of this house.'

'Of course.' Max hurried after her. 'Let me show you which room you're in first.'

As Oscar trailed upstairs with Zita's suitcase he heard his uncle say, 'I'm tempted to ring my brother and see if he can get away from London this weekend. I know Alec would love to meet you.'

'He's a couple of years older than you, didn't you say?' Zita was replying as he caught up with them outside her bedroom door. 'Let's think about it when I've unpacked.' But Oscar and Max had hardly got to the foot of the staircase when they heard her calling down, 'We'd be mad to spend such a lovely day indoors. I think we should go and see *Cassandra* straight away.'

'Great idea! We'll have a picnic on board.' Judging by the way his uncle was staring up at her, Oscar thought he'd have agreed to anything. 'And if you want to, I'll take you out on *Cilissa* afterwards.'

'Lovely,' she smiled over the banisters. 'I hope you're coming too, Oscar?'

'I like the idea of lunch on *Cassandra*, but I think I'll pass on *Cilissa* and the sea trip.'

'Hey, I just got the connection! *Cassandra*, *Cilissa*, they're both characters from the *Oresteia*.'

'That's right.' Oscar was impressed. 'Edie thought of *Cilissa*. She's into ancient history.'

'Your twin?'

'Yup. She's the brains of the family.'

'Then I want to know all about her,' Zita called, vanishing into her bedroom.

Half an hour later, Oscar was standing guard over a picnic hamper in the hallway. How could Zita possibly be taking so long to slip into a pair of trousers? Edie would have done it in about three minutes. Even his uncle was starting to look irritated by the time they heard footsteps on the staircase, but any hint of annoyance on Max's face was erased when he saw her.

'*Mon Dieu! Tu me coupes le souffle!*'

To Oscar, Zita Fitz was no more than a pretty little doll with money, but judging by his expression, his uncle was well on the way to being smitten. It wouldn't last, of course, Max's love affairs never did, but for the moment he was standing, mouth open, staring at Zita as if she were some kind of divine apparition.

'And what do you think, Oscar?' she asked. 'Presentable?'

He took in the perfect fit of her navy dungarees. The legs were cut loose, like old-fashioned sailors' bell-bottoms, but further up they clung to her hips and were cinched in at the waist by a webbing belt which looked as if it had been spun out of gold. The top was backless while the front, though perfectly decent, had been cut to make it look as if her bosom might spill out at any moment. An articulated collar of gold ringed her neck like a fat anaconda, and a man-size watch emphasised the narrowness of her arms and wrists.

'You look like . . .' Oscar struggled to find the best way to describe her. 'You look like a statuette of every man's dream *matelot.*'

A throaty laugh told him he'd said the right thing.

Despite the weight of the basket, Oscar enjoyed walking down through the meadow. A cool breeze fanned his face, bringing with it the hot scents of baked earth and wild herbs, but when he passed under the edge of the woods, the atmosphere changed. There was no wind to stir the oppressive air, stagnant with the smells of rotting wood and overheated leaf-mould. Flies buzzed around his sweating forehead, and he could feel the nipping itch of midges in his hair. Apart from the occasional cracking of a branch where Max and Zita had gone ahead of him, the woods were profoundly quiet. Even the birds had stopped singing in the heat.

As Oscar plodded on down towards the river, he wondered about Zita. Was it marriage she was after? Max was certainly handsome, with more than enough money to make him a decent catch, and maybe she'd produce a Quentance son to continue the line. It would really take the pressure off Oscar if she did, but then she might be too old. In those sunglasses, she could have passed for thirty, but when she'd taken them off in front of the house, he realised he'd misread her age. From the lines round her eyes, Zita was more likely to be in her mid-forties, and he'd no idea if that was too late for babies.

At the bottom of the hill, Oscar emerged from the gloom of the woods and out on to the riverbank to find it empty, disturbed only by the rustle of willows drooping into the slow-moving water. Somewhere to his left, Max's loud laugh broke the silence, and Oscar followed the noise to the Dartleap quay. He found Zita and Max standing there, apparently engrossed by *Cassandra*. Switching the picnic basket from one hand to the other, he strolled over the concrete nose of the jetty to join them.

'Beautiful, isn't she?' he heard Max say. 'Larchwood hung on an oak frame, and hardly touched since she was built nearly a century ago.'

'Doesn't that mean her galley's pretty spartan?' Zita asked.

'Goodness no, I'm not that fanatical. I had a new one fitted as soon as I got hold of *Cassandra*, and a proper bathroom down in the stern as well. Come aboard and see.'

'But what about the picnic?' Oscar was hungry and wanted his lunch.

'Bring the basket with you, we'll eat in the saloon.' Max offered an arm to Zita, but she ignored it, hopping on to *Cassandra* and revealing flashes of brown leg as she flung herself over the guard-rails. A moment later his uncle vaulted after her, leaving Oscar to straddle the gap between the quay and the deck while he heaved the basket over *Cassandra*'s rail before hauling himself after it.

Once Oscar had carried their picnic through the wheel-house and down the few stairs to the boat's main living-room, Zita took charge, laying everything out in swift, neat movements which made him think that hidden under that doll-like exterior lived a practical and well-organised woman.

'This is delicious Moselle,' Max said a few minutes later. 'Sure you don't want a glass?'

'Go on, Oscar, have some, it's lovely.' Zita ran the tip of her tongue over her upper lip.

'No thanks, I try not to drink at lunchtime.' Oscar didn't add that he was worried about a muffin of fat on his hips and had decided to cut right back on the booze till he got rid of it.

Zita seemed to have no worries about her figure and tucked into beans, potatoes and a pair of enormous, herb-crusted lamb chops, occasionally pausing to suck her fingers or to reach for more wine. Inevitably the conversation revolved round the arcane world of boats, and Oscar could only listen while Max and Zita chatted about foc'sles, bunt-lines and other mysteries.

As the talk drifted to millionaires' yachts and their races, Oscar's eyes wandered idly round the varnished walls of *Cassandra*'s saloon until they were caught by a series of pairs of tiny holes. Intrigued by the thought that they'd been made by picture hooks, he interrupted a debate about rigging to say, 'Max, do you ever hang paintings in here?'

His uncle silenced him with a scowl, and even as Zita was getting up to take a closer look, said quickly, 'If you want to see *Cilissa* as well as *Cassandra*, we'd better hurry.' A moment later Max was urging her ahead of him up to the wheelhouse and saying, 'Actually, I've had a great idea. We'll go down to Dartmouth in *Cassandra*, then we can swap on to *Cilissa* and go out to sea. Oscar?' His uncle called down the steps. 'You don't mind walking back up to Dartleap with the picnic basket, do you?'

Night was falling, and in the deep valley below Dartleap the river had turned from gold, through silver, to black. Oscar stood on the front doorstep, peering down the drive. He was hungry, he was tired and he was bored after spending the whole afternoon and half the evening on his own.

He'd had a phone call from his uncle a couple of hours ago, only to have to listen to him raving about Zita. 'I don't think there's anything about boats she doesn't know, and for such a scrap of a thing, she's amazingly strong. And those eyes! Like the ocean at dusk.'

There'd been quite a lot more in the same vein before Oscar had managed to ask, 'When are you getting back?'

'In plenty of time for dinner.'

As it grew later, he'd tried to call Max several times, but there'd been no answer, and Oscar decided that if they weren't home in half an hour, he'd go ahead and eat by himself. He turned to go back into the house, and at last his mobile rang. 'Where are you?' he began, but his uncle interrupted him.

'I can't talk for long because Zita will be back in a minute, so just listen, will you? She's agreed to go back to Paris with me on *Cassandra* tomorrow.'

'That's terrific.' Oscar tried to sound enthusiastic. 'But are you coming back to Dartleap soon? I'm starving.'

'Sorry,' Max laughed, 'that's why I rang. Zita wants to eat by the sea, so don't wait up. Oh, and another thing.' Oscar caught the murmur of Zita's voice in the background. 'We're aiming to catch the early tide tomorrow. I doubt if we'll see you in the morning.'

'But Zita's hardly seen anything of Dartleap.' Oscar was annoyed that he'd been dragged all the way to Devon when he'd had plenty of things he could have been doing in Paris that weekend.

'Don't worry about that,' Max said. 'I think she prefers boats to houses. Here, she wants a word with you.'

He caught a whisper and a fumbling of the handset, and then Zita's voice. 'Dear Oscar, I'm so sorry to abandon you like this, but I'm dying to try *Cassandra* at sea. One of the Dunkirk Little Ships is a big deal for me. You'll forgive me, won't you?'

'Don't be silly, there's nothing to forgive.' He swallowed his irritation with as good a grace as he could manage. 'Maybe I'll see you in Paris?'

'I'll make sure you do.'

TWELVE

Edie's weekend had begun on a wave of self-doubt. Her father's words had stung, and they'd taken her completely by surprise.

It had started so well, and Dad had seemed really pleased to see her when she'd been ushered into his office. He'd been sitting very upright in that uncomfortable-looking chair of his, and as usual the polished desk in front of him had been empty apart from the old inkstand he'd used ever since she could remember and his black telephone which must have dated back at least half a century.

He'd given her a glass of sherry, and then told her how well she was doing in Records and Archives. She'd asked about her chances of promotion, and they'd talked about when she might be ready to meet some of the bank's clients. Edie could remember his next words exactly. She'd been looking down from his window at the old stables to the rear of the bank, and had idly asked why she and Oscar had never been allowed to play there when they were children, and then he'd said it. 'I couldn't dream of letting you meet any of our clients when you wear such extraordinarily unsuitable clothes.'

For a few moments she'd been silenced completely. Eventually she'd recovered, and had tried to get the conversation back on track by asking when she could visit his Investments Department. All she knew was that it was where the Adamantine Fund was run from, and that it was the core of Alec's financial success. When she'd said this, her father had smiled his thanks, but then that wretched phone on his desk had rung. He'd answered it, saying to the caller, 'Can you just hang on a moment, please?' while he waved her out of his office.

Extraordinarily unsuitable clothes. When she'd got home to the flat that evening, several honest minutes in front of the mirror in Oscar's bedroom had told her Dad was right. A shape-concealing top and trousers in murky colours really wasn't a good look at all, and something to disguise the pallor of her face might be an improvement, too. The trouble was, Oscar would be down in Dartleap all weekend and there was no one else to advise her. It was years since anyone had tried to get her to change her appearance. Even Clio had almost given up nagging, and none of her friends was interested. At her comprehensive only the thick girls were vain, and it had been the same at Oxford. Make-up and fashion were for lightweights.

Her reflection shrugged its shoulders at her. Other women bought clothes all the time. It couldn't be that difficult.

When she got down to her basement office on Monday morning, for the first time ever, Edie made straight for the mirror. As it was too small to show more than her face, she couldn't check that the long, narrow trousers of her new suit were really as flattering as they'd seemed when she'd put them on that morning, but the lipstick was definitely a success. 'Rose Madder' was a soft pink which somehow made her lips look attractively plump rather than fatly bee-stung. She'd certainly be wearing it the next time she strolled along the cliffs near Brink Castle.

Catching the soppy grin creeping across her face, Edie turned away from the mirror. She was daydreaming like a teenager. She needed some hard work to distract her, but now she'd got the backlog of filing sorted, there was really nothing else to do. Slumping down at her desk, it occurred to her that in many ways she might still be researching in her Oxford college library. Records and Archives had just that same smell of dust and old leather masked by an overlay of polish, those same scuffed wooden cabinets full of documents, and the same ceiling-high shelves heaped with musty books and yellowing papers.

In the thick silence of the basement, the only sound was the wall clock clicking the day away. Time! She sat upright in her chair as an idea struck her. Timing was the key. If she could unravel what was behind the discrepancies on the night *Titanic* sank, surely she'd get to the heart of what happened. That extraordinary delay between the 'Object dead ahead' warning and the order to turn the bow wasn't the only anomaly. There were other pieces of survivors' evidence that looked equally peculiar. Glancing guiltily up at the clock, she decided she'd just make a few notes. It wouldn't take long.

She took the shipwreck commissioners' report out of her case, picked up her pencil and flipped through the pages till she found Quartermaster Hitchins' record of the orders he'd been given immediately after the collision. Within moments, she was engrossed.

Evidence of Quartermaster Hitchins
'How long did you remain at the wheel?'
'Until twenty-three minutes past twelve.'
'And who relieved you?'
'Quartermaster Perkis.'

It was annoying that, whilst Walter Perkis had given evidence at the US inquiry, no one had asked him about his time at the helm, and he hadn't even appeared before the UK inquiry. There was nowhere to turn but Hitchins, and if he was to be believed, he'd been kept in his place at the wheel for three-quarters of an hour after they'd struck the iceberg. Why keep anyone at the wheel of a stationary ship on a calm night? The answer was obvious. *Titanic* wasn't stationary. She flicked on through the pages of the report to remind herself what one of the men in the engine rooms had to say.

Evidence of Greaser Frederick Scott
'You were employed in the turbine engine room, starboard side?'
'Starboard side.'
'You felt something; what was it?'
'I felt a shock and I thought it was something in the main engine room which had gone wrong. Then the telegraphs rang, "Stop".'

'Was that before or after the shock?'

'After the shock.'

Edie looked up. '*After* the shock,' she said aloud. So Murdoch hadn't even tried to reduce *Titanic*'s speed before the iceberg had been struck. Yet another piece of evidence that he believed he had time to avoid it. In which case, *why* delay turning the wheel? She shook her head. No point following that dead-end again. She must concentrate on what happened after the damage had been done, and Greaser Scott had more to say about the messages sent down from the bridge.

She read his testimony through twice, then pulled her notepad out to list the orders Scott had received.

11.40	*Iceberg struck*
11.40–11.55	*'Stop'*
11.55–12.05	*'Slow Ahead'*
12.05–12.10	*'Stop'*
12.10–12.15	*'Slow Astern'*
12.15	*'Stop', engines shut down*

After a few moments' thought, she added another line:

12.23	*Hitchins relieved from wheel*

Leaning back in her chair until the frame gave a warning creak, Edie linked her hands behind her head and gazed up at the ceiling. For a maximum of a quarter of an hour after the collision, *Titanic* had stopped powering forwards while she was inspected for damage. In a ship of that size, a fifteen-minute survey would have been cursory indeed. Surely it would have needed a couple of hours at the very least before Captain Smith could be sure it was safe to get under way again? After all, he had personally told the chairman of the White Star Line that *Titanic* was seriously damaged.

Evidence of Bruce Ismay

'You were awakened by the impact?'

'Yes.'

'Did you then get up?'

'I stayed in bed a little time, and then I got up. I went along the passageway and I asked a steward what had happened, but he did not know.'

'Then what did you do?'

'I went back to my room and I put a coat on, then I went up on to the bridge and asked Captain Smith what had happened.'

'And what did he tell you?'

'He told me we had struck ice.'

'Did you ask him anything further?'

'I asked him whether he thought the damage was serious, and he said he thought it was.'

Timings again. Edie found herself holding her breath as a terrible idea struck her. She looked from Greaser Scott's timetable to Ismay's evidence and back again, then she exhaled in a long whistle as the implications of what she was reading became clearer.

At eleven-forty, Bruce Ismay was woken up by the collision. The ship remained at 'stop' for fifteen minutes, during which time, by his own admission, Ismay was wondering whether to get up, then talking to the steward, then going to get his coat, then going up on deck. He might well have reached the bridge at eleven-fifty-five. Supposing he'd taken in what had happened, then immediately insisted on that slow-ahead order being sent to the engine room? Bruce Ismay would be fearful of the reputational damage to White Star Line and to his boss, J. Pierpont Morgan, if their luxurious flagship was allowed to wallow in the North Atlantic until some lesser boat towed her to safety. Supposing Ismay had preferred to take the risk of damaging *Titanic* further rather than put their investment in jeopardy?

Edie could easily imagine the fatal result of that 'Slow ahead'. The forward propulsion would have put extra pressure on the pierced keel, forcing the sea in and over the bulkheads, to flood compartment after compartment until the ship was doomed. If only she'd stayed still. Without that inrush of seawater, her pumping system would have stood a real chance of keeping *Titanic* afloat till everyone on board could be taken off safely.

'Here you are, Miss Edith.' The clerk's voice made her jump. 'I've brought you a cup of tea.'

'Thanks so much. Great.' Guiltily, she pulled some blank sheets of paper on top of the wreck commissioners' report. 'And couldn't you just call me Edie? Edith's a ghastly name and the Miss thing's practically feudal.'

'Of course, Miss Edith.' The door closed gently behind his retreating back, but Edie was worried that he'd come back with the inevitable biscuits and she didn't want to be caught skiving with *Titanic* again if he did. Instead, while she sipped her tea, she decided to ring Oscar and find out how his weekend with Max and the new woman had gone.

'Hi, babes, are you busy?'

'Busy? I've only just made it into the office! All the flights were delayed and I've had a ten-hour bloody nightmare getting here from Dartleap.'

'I bet Max was glad to have his plane-hate confirmed. Presumably he arrived on time and by train?'

'By boat, actually. He brought his new bird back to Paris on *Cassandra*.'

'That man moves fast. What's she called?'

'Zita, Zita Fitz. You'll like her, Eds. Amazing looks, and she's as dotty about boats as you are.'

Edie felt slightly put out. It sounded as if Zita Fitz had seduced her twin as well as her uncle. 'And does she just swan about on them,' she asked, 'or has she got a proper job?'

'I don't really know.' There was a pause. 'Honestly.'

'Something's up, isn't it?' When Oscar said 'honestly', it meant he was fibbing.

'Don't be silly, Eds, everything's fine.'

Edie frowned into her mobile. Since Oscar had gone to Paris, he'd been telling her much less about what was going on in his life than he used to. 'Is it Max?' she guessed. 'Is this woman bad news?'

'Zita? Heavens, no. If I sound worried, it's because Max keeps making me do tests. He expects me to remember strings of names and numbers, which is pretty bloody impossible if you haven't got a memory like his.'

'Is that all? Why don't you write everything down?'

'Max won't let me.'

'That's ridiculous. Make a note of everything but just don't tell him.'

'It's not as simple as that, Eds. But listen, I'd better go, there's a pile of work waiting.' A moment later he'd hung up, and she was left staring at the blank face of her phone. For the first time in her life, she had no idea what Oscar was feeling.

One thing that was certain was that Edie herself wasn't as busy as Oscar seemed to be, but as she drained her mug of tea an idea came to her. She'd go and have a poke around in the archives. It had been right to concentrate on records since it dealt with all the current lending business, but it was about time she checked on the other half of her department and had a look at where the details of bygone loans and mortgages were stored. Maybe the filing system in there needed updating? At least it would give her something to do.

The Archives store ran parallel to Records, but there was a fire door in between that was always kept locked and she had to open a safe to get the key. Edie cursed the obsessive separation between departments that her father insisted on while she struggled with the combination needed to get into the safe, and then with getting the key to turn, but eventually, she managed to open the door.

The walls were lined with shelves, each of them stacked with box-files with the names of archived clients written down their spines in thick ink. As she wandered down the long room, trying to decide where to start, a name caught her eye. IVYBRIDGE. Some words of John Tamar's leapt into her head. *When it comes to how they got their land, the Quentance family aren't exactly beacons of purity.* She'd had no idea what he was talking about, but perhaps the Ivybridge archive would explain it? Turning on her heel, Edie hurried off to fetch the rickety library ladder.

Fifteen minutes later, the stepladder rocked alarmingly as she stretched to put the file back in its place. Her legs felt shaky as she climbed down and walked slowly back between the dusty shelves and through the door to her desk. After a hasty fumble through the drawers to find her mobile, Edie stabbed out a number.

THIRTEEN

'That horse is such a bilious colour.' Clio felt almost offended by Stubbs's palette. 'A real chestnut stallion would never be so orange.'

'I've never liked it much either. I only suggested meeting here because the National Gallery's central and *Whistlejacket*'s easy to find.' Her daughter swivelled round on the bench to face her. 'It's so nice of you to come to London at such short notice, Mum. I didn't mean you to drop everything when I rang.'

Of course she'd come straight away. What else did Edie think her mother would do when she got a phone call like that? 'You said you needed me,' Clio said quietly, 'so here I am.'

'You look terrific, Mum. I really like the dress.'

Clio stared at her daughter in astonishment, her flowery shirt-waister was the kind of thing Edie normally loathed. 'Thank you, darling. And you're looking good too,' she said, taking in the suit, the rose-coloured top and the near-matching lipstick. Something must have happened for Edie to make such an effort, but she wouldn't risk sending her daughter back inside her prickly shell by probing. Instead, she stood up and said brightly, 'Come on. Let's look at the pictures while you tell me what's up.'

They wandered across the gallery to *The Fighting Temeraire*, and as Edie seemed to have fallen silent, Clio said, 'Amazing paintwork, isn't it? Just look at that sunset, and the way he's caught the quality of light on wet sand.'

'I suppose it is nice.' Her daughter was frowning at the picture. 'Though I can't understand why such a high-masted ship's being tugged up a channel that's obviously way too shallow for its keel.'

'Is that all you can say about one of England's greatest masterpieces?' Clio shook her head at the contrast between Oscar's love of art and Edie's lack of interest. 'I suppose I should be grateful that at least one of my children appreciates paintings.' As there was no answer from her daughter, Clio waited quietly until whatever was worrying her came out.

'Mum?' Edie said eventually. 'There's something I need to ask you.'

Clio nodded, her eyes still on Turner's ghost ship.

'The thing is, I was going through one of the old files at the bank yesterday and – well, I was quite surprised by what I found and I wanted to check whether it was true. I thought you might know.'

'Go on.'

'I found a letter from Kit Quentance to the sixteenth Earl of Ivybridge.'

'Miles.'

'What was that, Mum?'

'Miles,' Clio repeated. 'He was the sixteenth earl. John Tamar will be the eighteenth earl in due course.'

Clio half expected a tirade against the upper classes, but all Edie said was, 'I found these in the archives. Will you tell me what you think?'

'Of course, darling.' Moving aside so that other visitors could see *The Fighting Temeraire*, she took three letters from her daughter, seeing at once that they were all written on the heavily crested Dartleap writing-paper. The first was dated 1961, and was addressed to the sixteenth Earl of Ivybridge at Brink Castle.

'*My dear Miles,*' she read, recognising Kit Quentance's black italic.

Your father's funeral was a deeply moving affair, and on occasions like yesterday I am almost tempted by the comforting rites of the Roman Catholic Church. You conducted yourself perfectly, and I know that my dear friend Hugo would have been immensely proud of the way in which his son laid him to rest.

Yesterday was not the appropriate time to talk business, but as you will be taking over the Ivybridge estates, there is one thing of which I would like to assure you. You may be aware that in the difficult years since the war, Quentance Bank has lent money to your family, secured against mortgages which we hold against your land. When those loans were first extended I told Hugo just what I am telling you now, which is that whatever the financial circumstances you may find yourself in from time to time – for example, you will now have significant death duties to pay – while it is

not in my power to waive the mortgages completely, I give
you my word that I will not allow Quentance Bank to fore-
close on them.

I do hope that this will set your mind at rest on this one
issue at least,

With every good wish,

Kit Quentance

'Kit was a decent man, whatever they say about him,' Edie
was looking questioningly at her. 'Don't you think so, Mum?'

Clio shrugged her shoulders. She'd respected the old man
while he was alive, but she'd heard the *Titanic* cowardice
story so often that she wasn't sure what to believe. Without
answering, she unfolded the second letter. It was recognisably Kit's handwriting, but the script was much shakier.
Looking at the date, she saw that it had been written in
1980, just two years before he died. The letter was addressed
to Crispin, the seventeenth and current Earl of Ivybridge,
and as she skimmed through it, Clio saw that it covered
much the same ground as the first one.

My dear Crispin

It was with great sadness that I heard of your father's
death. How tragic to lose such a good man so suddenly, and
at the relatively young age of fifty-five. I have long thought
of Miles as if he were my son, and I hope you will allow me
to continue thinking of you as fondly as if you were my own
grandson. I will, of course, be attending the funeral next week,
but in the meantime I wanted to reassure you on one point
in relation to your family's financial affairs.

For many years now, Quentance Bank has been pleased to act as banker to the Ivybridge estates, and as part of our service, we have extended loans which have been backed by the security of mortgages on your land. Some years ago, I assured your father that our holding of these mortgages was a matter of policy only, and while I was unable to give a formal guarantee, I gave Miles my word that Quentance Bank would not foreclose on your property in any conceivable circumstances.

The purpose of this letter is simply to reiterate that my word continues to stand in this matter.

With my fondest good wishes to you at this most difficult time,

Kit Quentance

The third letter was from Alec. As she saw his handwriting, Clio glanced up and caught Edie looking at her, and if she hadn't known how rarely her daughter cried, she'd have thought there were tears in her eyes. 'Go on, Mum,' she muttered, 'please read it.'

Clio looked at top of the letter and saw that it had been written in 1983 and was also addressed to Crispin, the current earl.

Dear Lord Ivybridge,

Thank you for your kind letter of condolence on the death of my father. It has been a sad shock, coming as it does only a year after the death of my grandfather Kit, who was, I know, a close friend to your family.

Following our father's death, my brother Max and I will

be taking over the management of Quentance Bank, and while I am writing, I should inform you that in these difficult times we will have to make changes to the lax policies that were in effect during my father's and grandfather's tenures as chairmen of our bank.

I note, in particular, that in respect of loans that have been extended to the Ivybridge estate, both principal and interest payments have fallen into arrears. Since you are now in default on these mortgages, Quentance Bank will unfortunately have no alternative but to foreclose and take possession of your lands unless you agree to repay our capital immediately.

I look forward to hearing from you at your earliest convenience.

Yours sincerely

Alec Quentance

'Is it true?' Edie was staring at Clio as she finished reading Alec's letter. 'Did Dad really grab the Ivybridge land?'

Clio couldn't understand why her daughter seemed so upset by this particular foreclosure. After all, once they'd taken over Quentance Bank's reins, both Alec and Max had been ferocious about repossessing land, houses, paintings or whatever else the bank's money had been secured against. Perhaps the Ivybridge estate was simply the first example Edie had come across?

'It's just how your father does business,' she said, trying to sound neutral. 'Most banks repossess if they've got a problem loan.'

'So that's why there's such a big estate at Dartleap.' There was a tremble in her daughter's voice. 'Dad foreclosed on the Ivybridge land the year Oscar and I were born, didn't he?'

And the year Ianthe died. Her attempt to be objective about Alec's banking practices was crushed by a sudden fury. 'Yes he did,' Clio said coldly. 'I can remember him boasting about it.' She could see him now, only days after Richard's funeral, swinging a proprietary arm around the bulbous green hills near Dartleap, then waving grandly to where the slopes mounted one upon another towards the grey haunches of Dartmoor. 'Your father even seemed to think he'd done something decent by leaving them Brink Castle and all the coastal property,' she added, then, ignoring any other art lovers who might be trying to examine the picture, Clio moved till she was standing four-square in front of *The Fighting Temeraire*.

'So it was Dad's idea to take the land, was it? Just him, not Max as well?'

Without turning from the picture, Clio said, 'You see that stippled figure crouching on the foreshore? I've no idea what he meant to Turner, but he reminds me of your father. A bit menacing, rather mysterious, and yet he's somehow so magnetic that your eyes keep getting drawn back to him. That's how Alec is. For all his charm and his brilliant memory, Max is weak. It's your father who has all the willpower.' Feeling suddenly tired, she went back to sit on the central bench, and after a moment Edie came and perched beside her.

'Thanks for telling me, Mum.' A hand crept over and slipped into hers, taking Clio by surprise. They sat in silence for a while until Edie said, 'You know what you were just saying about the difference between Dad and Max?'

'Uh-huh,' Clio nodded.

'I was wondering about Ianthe. Did Max try to persuade Dad to pay the ransom?'

'What an odd question.' Clio felt her hand closing convulsively on her daughter's.

'Sorry, Mum.' Edie withdrew her hand and sat rubbing her fingers. 'I just wanted to know if you think Max is a better person than Dad.'

'When Ianthe vanished, they were one as bad as the other. The kidnapper wanted five million pounds, which was a vast sum of money in those days. Alec was too terrified of poverty to pay up, and Max was too dependent on his brother's love to argue. Though to be fair,' Clio added, 'I think if it wasn't for Alec, Max would have been prepared to give up everything.'

Clio closed her eyes, remembering how Max and she had gone down to the quay together, searching. They'd got there at low tide, and he'd been peering down at the scrape of a hull mark in the mud. 'Some little boat must have moored here and slipped away just before the tide fell too far for it to float off,' he'd said crossly. 'It's perfectly obvious to anyone that this is private land. Cheeky trippers. If I ever catch them at it, I'll make them pay.' She remembered the word, because that was when she'd broken down, begging Max to pay whatever was needed to rescue Ianthe from the horrible, dark place where Clio knew she was being held. 'Of course we will,' he'd said as he'd half carried her hugely pregnant self back up the hill. 'If we need to, we'll sell Dartleap, the bank, everything to get Ianthe back. I'll talk to Alec.'

'So what happened, Mum?' she heard her daughter asking. 'Didn't they at least try to raise the money?'

'Oh, they tried all right. They came up with some idea which involved borrowing the money from one of their clients' funds.'

'I don't see how that would have worked.' Edie had shifted round to face her. 'It would all have to be paid back at the end of each accounting period.'

'They had some clever answer for that.' Clio tried to recall the details. 'I think what they were going to do was get a flow of new investments coming in to replace the money they took out. Alec thought that if they were careful how they kept the records, it'd be impossible to see that any cash had been siphoned off.'

'Sounds completely illegal to me.'

'And far, far too late. But the thing that hurt the most,' Clio went on, half to herself, 'was that I begged Alec to forget his complicated schemes and just sell up. I knew how much he loved me, and if he couldn't bring himself to be poor for Ianthe, I thought he'd do it for me.' She shook her head. Any minute now, she'd embarrass her daughter by bursting into tears. 'Come on.' She stood up. 'Let's go and get some lunch.'

Down in the National Gallery's café, Clio felt brighter after a large glass of house white and a prawn sandwich. 'How are you enjoying London, darling?' She tossed her hair back off her face, remembering the days when a chorale of wolf-whistles would follow her all the way along the King's Road. 'When I was your age, I used to dance all night and still have enough energy to study for my art degree during the day.'

'Well I wish I'd inherited your vigour, Mum. After a day in the basement, it's all I can do to drag myself out for a run in the evenings.' Seeing her daughter picking at a salad, Clio was about to point out that she'd have more energy if she exercised less and ate more when Edie said abruptly, 'Do you happen to know if the Navy ever used the land around Dartleap for training?'

'The Navy? Now you ask, I do remember Alec telling some story about how he and Max were chased down through the woods by men with guns when they were children. They ended up hiding on *Cassandra*.' Clio raised an eyebrow. 'But why ever do you want to know that?'

'No reason. It's something John Tamar mentioned to me, that's all.'

'You see him, do you?' Clio couldn't quite believe what she'd heard. Edie with an aristocrat!

Her dream of being the mother of a countess only lasted an instant. 'Of course I don't *see* him, Mum. I wouldn't go out with a toff like John Tamar if he was the last man on earth. And besides, why would he be interested in me? I bet he only dates pretty little debs.'

'He's not such a toff as all that. I think he works as a chartered accountant. And anyway, there's no reason why you shouldn't be pretty too. You've got good cheekbones, you've got great skin, and your mouth looks a lot better with that lipstick.'

'I have been trying. I bought all these new clothes.'

'Then you just need to try a bit harder, darling. Anyone

can change how they look if they make enough of an effort.'

To Clio's surprise, her daughter pushed her chair back from the table and said quietly, 'This is just how I am, Mum, and men are never going to pursue me the way they used to run after you. Thanks for coming all this way to see me,' she said, standing up. 'I ought get back to work.'

With a quick peck on the cheek, she vanished out towards Trafalgar Square, leaving Clio to wonder yet again why Edie had always been such a difficult child to get on with.

FOURTEEN

'So tell me about Miss Zita Fitz.' Jerichau's hooded brown eyes were fixed on him. 'She is your *inamorata*?'

'If only.' Max toyed with his wineglass and wondered how much he should say. After all, the man was his client, not his friend. Eventually he decided to make a joke of it. 'I tell you, Isaiah, I'm losing my touch. I had her to myself on *Cassandra* the whole way over from Devon, but when we anchored to get some sleep, she just locked herself in my cabin. I had to bunk down in the saloon and wash in the galley.'

'*Brava!* What a woman, to hold out against the charm of Max Quentance! Or maybe it's the *letto nuziale* she's after.'

The words were followed by a sigh, and Max decided it was time to change the subject. Isaiah Jerichau was a recent widower, and how embarrassing it would be if he took it into his head to pour out his feelings about his dead wife. He glanced at the scene around them. 'Isn't it good when the restaurants open again after the summer break?'

'And how original of you to take a table up here. Your Zita will like the view.'

They were sitting in one of those Parisian restaurants where the best places were naturally kept back for the French, and being both English and untitled Max had been seated at one of the raised tables just beyond the inner circle. He knew it was a socially inferior position and he didn't need to have it pointed out by one of Prince Jerichau's barbed observations.

He was struggling to find a suitable put-down when he saw Zita slipping between the tables. Max felt a frisson of jealous pride as he saw how many heads turned to watch her pass by. He heard Jerichau's muttered '*Che bellezza*,' and a moment later she was beside him.

'Max. How are you?'

'Zita.' He wished he had the courage to touch her jaw so that his kiss would land on her mouth rather than her cheek, but he contented himself with stroking her upper arms just at the point where they emerged from her silky slip of a dress. He felt her right arm flexing away as she extended a hand beyond his back.

'You must be Prince Jerichau,' she said over his shoulder. 'How lovely to meet you.'

'Call me Isaiah, I beg you.'

Was it his imagination or was the Italian holding on to that hand for rather longer than necessary? 'Come and sit on either side of me,' Max said, but although he managed to separate them, the conversation went on as if he wasn't there.

'Isaiah, then,' Zita smiled. 'Max has told me nothing except that you live in Genoa. Whereabouts is your house?'

'Palazzo Jerichau is on le Strade Nuove – the oldest streets in Genoa, obviously. And you, *incantatrice*, where do you live?'

Although he was annoyed by Jerichau's oily compliments, Max was keen to hear what Zita would say because he hadn't managed to get a clear answer to the question himself. She seemed to have an entirely peripatetic existence, moving between the spare room of a friend in Paris, a *pied à terre* in Geneva and an unspecified space in Milan.

'Me?' She seemed to hesitate, and before she said anything further their conversation was interrupted by the arrival of waiters and menus.

Max was forced to sit through a recital of *plats du jour*, followed by a lengthy debate over whether or not they could manage the seven-course *menu dégustation*, but he was determined that Isaiah's question shouldn't be forgotten. 'Remind me, Zita,' he said the moment their orders had been given, 'whose house do you share in Paris?'

'Remind you? I don't think I ever told you in the first place.'

'And if you wish it to be secret, so it should be, *cara*,' Jerichau interrupted, making Max feel he'd been reprimanded for his nosiness.

'Of course I'll tell you, Max,' Zita patted his arm. 'It's rather sensitive, that's all. I rent a couple of rooms from a friend. It suits me, and it helps him out, but Edouard-St Jean would rather the world doesn't know he's short of money.'

Jerichau was looking astonished. 'You surely don't mean Edouard-St Jean de Culot?'

'Unwise investments. The poor lamb's had to take a job. In a shop.'

Max made no comment. Quentance Bank had never broken into the highest echelons of French society. The de Culot family and others like them would have looked down their ducal noses at him, and frankly he didn't give a toss if they lost their ancient fortunes or not. Not, that was, until he heard Jerichau asking, 'Do the de Culot paintings still hang on the walls, Zita? Perhaps Max told you that I deal in Old Masters.'

'Isaiah will give you a commission if you recommend him to Edouard-St Jean,' Max said, putting a protective hand on Zita's wrist.

'An excellent idea.' Her warm palm closed on top of his. 'OK with you, Isaiah?'

'*Va bene*, if you can get him to sell.' Isaiah shrugged his shoulders. 'I expect Max will want his cut, too. You have the old boat here?'

Catching Zita's questioning look, Max hesitated.

'Perhaps I should pay a tactful trip to the ladies',' she suggested, but as he looked into those angelic eyes, he felt certain that he could trust her.

'There's absolutely no need for you to leave. What Isaiah means is that *Cassandra*'s saloon has a lot of bulkhead space and I've never known even the nosiest customs officer to take any interest in what happens to be hanging there.'

'Good God, Max! They *were* picture-hook holes!'

Zita was still laughing when an *amuse-bouche* of multi-coloured carrots arrived, and the conversation drifted back to the *ancien régime* and their fortunes. Having little interest in people who would never trust their money to him, Max listened in silence, idly wondering how Zita had managed to break into the *salons* of the old French aristocracy.

He had crunched his way through most of the carrots when Isaiah said, 'And what of Philippe and Marie-Alexandrine? Their daughter is to marry an Austrian. Rudy Ginsburg, he's called.' Max sat up at the name of one of his clients. 'A commoner.'

'Rudy's the son of a very successful industrialist,' Max cut in briskly. 'He may have no title to give her but *la petite princesse* will have anything else she wants.'

'So you know him?' Zita asked.

This time, Max didn't hesitate. He'd already trusted her with how he shifted Isaiah's pictures, so there wasn't much point in being secretive about how he moved cash. And besides, having a woman on board during a drop would be perfect camouflage. 'The Ginsburg family have been clients of ours for generations,' he said. 'Unfortunately, they live in a part of Austria that's been endlessly fought over, so we've got rather good at moving their money to safety whenever someone unsavoury tries to get hold of it.'

'Like the taxman?' Zita's head was tilted in the graceful gesture that Max found so irresistible.

'Most recently, yes. And if you want to see what capital flight really means, I'll take you out on *Cassandra* and show you. If you can use a winch, that is.'

'Absurd!' Jerichau interrupted. 'She is too fragile.'

'Oh I don't think so.' Zita smiled sweetly. 'I'll go out with Max and we'll see if I can use a winch or not.'

Max was delighted. 'I can get everything fixed for the day after tomorrow. Does that suit you?'

'Impossible.' Zita blinked once, very slowly. 'I have to be in Italy.'

There was something so definite in her voice that Max was silenced, but Isaiah said immediately, 'You are in Italy? Then you must come to Genoa.'

'Not this trip, sorry.'

'But why not?'

'Because I can't. I have to go to Lake Como.'

Even Jerichau seemed to pick up the finality in her voice and they chatted about other things until their first courses arrived. Under cover of the noise of the waiters and the ceremonial lifting of silver domes, Zita murmured to Max, 'As soon as I'm back from Como, I'll come out on *Cassandra* with you.' Digging her spoon into the centre of a cube of truffled jelly, she watched the yolk of an egg oozing out. 'And who knows,' she added softly, 'maybe we'll have cash in the hold and some nice pictures in the cabin?'

FIFTEEN

For once, Edie ignored the dinghies bobbing in the scummy waters of the Boat Float and the larger boats idling at anchor out beyond the marina. She'd slipped down to Dartmouth intending to spend a happy hour watching the river, but for the first time in her life she found herself staring into the shop windows instead. It being a Sunday, they were mainly closed, but she could get a clear reflection of herself in their plate-glass doors while she tried to decide whether or not she looked all right.

The problem wasn't from the waist down, the jeans were definitely great. But the upper half she was less sure about. Her new T-shirt was lilac blue and pretty much the same colour as her eyes, but it was really tight, showing the flat outline of her abdomen and her small bosom jutting embarrassingly clearly above it. Edie moved on, then stopped again, this time in front of a lingerie shop which had a full-length mirror just beyond its window. Perhaps the top might have looked less provocative with one of her old bras instead of the new, silky push-up she was wearing?

As she stared at herself, a couple passing behind her were

reflected briefly in the shop's mirror. The tall, lanky frame of John Tamar was unmistakable, as was the attention he was paying to the auburn-haired woman beside him. Edie swung round and watched them sauntering away from her towards the quay. The woman was walking very close to him, one hand tucked into his arm, her head tilted so that she could look up into his face. It was obviously his girl-friend.

She was gazing after them when John suddenly turned his head. For a second, they stared at each other, then he bent to say something to his companion and they swung round and walked back towards her. Edie had only a moment to take in the woman's wide, grey eyes and pretty face and to think, Well, at least he's got good taste, when the pair stopped in front of her.

'Edie, how nice!' He smiled down at her. 'This is my cousin, Mary Kersey.' He turned to the woman beside him, saying, 'This is Edie Quentance, Mary,' but Edie scarcely heard him. His cousin. She felt quite dizzy with relief. 'Mary's staying at Brink Castle for a few days,' John added.

'And I'm having a great time, though my daughter's whining about leaving her pony and my husband's grum-bling about leaving Suffolk. I keep telling them it's only fair that we come to see my family *occasionally*.'

'Are you a cousin on the Ivybridge side?' Edie asked care-fully.

'That's right. The earl is my mother's brother.' Mary's voice was curious. 'But why do you ask?'

Edie stared down at her hands. 'Because it means I need to apologise to both of you.' In the silence that followed, she had an odd feeling that the three of them were quite alone in the middle of the Dartmouth bustle. 'The thing is, back in the 1980s, Quentance Bank reneged on promises my great-grandfather had made to your family. We fore-closed on our mortgages, and took over most of the Ivybridge estate.' She was feeling better now she'd got the worst of it out, but she couldn't look at either of them till she'd finished. 'The bank should never have gone back on Kit's word, and I'd have apologised long ago if I'd known. I only found all this out when I started working for the bank myself.'

'You work for Quentance Bank, do you?' Dragging her gaze away from her hands, Edie looked up and caught the pair exchanging a look that she didn't understand.

'I have to. I don't have any money of my own and I couldn't get anyone to pay for me to stay on at Oxford.'

'That's a shame,' said Mary Kersey gently, 'and it was sweet of you to want to explain about the land, but let's forget it now. It's all in the past.'

'Mary's quite right, it's history,' John added. 'And my stomach's telling me it's lunchtime. Coming?'

He guided them briskly along Higher Street, and rather than the smart restaurant Edie assumed he'd choose, they stopped outside the Cherub, an unpretentious pub used mainly by Dartmouth locals.

'You two go on upstairs and grab a table while I order. Sunday roast, extra chips and a pint?' Without waiting for an answer, he ducked his head and vanished into the bar, leaving Edie to follow Mary up the narrow stairs to the first floor.

'John's a nightmare with food,' Mary said as they found

a corner table. 'He eats like a horse and he always expects everyone else to be as hungry as he is. Mind you, I'm starving myself after the endless sermon we got at Mass this morning.'

Edie hunted for a safe reply. There'd been very little religion in her upbringing, and what there was had been Church of England. 'What was the sermon about?'

Mary rubbed her chin and smiled ruefully. 'I'm afraid I can't remember a word of it. I probably listened to the first sentence or two but then my mind wandered. Here's John.' Her smile widened. 'Let's ask him.'

'Ask me what?' John put a jug of beer and three glasses down on the table, then folded his long legs around the chair next to Edie.

'The gist of today's sermon.'

'It was about forgiving your enemies, you idle sinner. I can't believe you've forgotten already.'

'Ignore him, Edie, he's just showing off.' Mary reached across the table to give her cousin a friendly thump. 'My trouble is, I'm spoiled by having the best parish priest in the entire world. Peter Cromwell never preaches for more than five minutes.'

'I wish some of my tutors at Oxford were the same.'

Beside her, John stretched an arm out along the back of her chair so that Edie could feel the warmth of his hand, hanging inches from her shoulder. 'Three roasts?' She didn't realise she'd been holding her breath until it came out in a great rush as the waitress put their food down on the table.

Edie was about to pick up her knife and fork when John stopped her by saying, 'Grace first.' She threw a horrified glance across at Mary, but she'd already inclined her head over her hands, so Edie pressed her own palms together above her plate, relieved that there was no one she knew in the Cherub to see her.

'Let us pray,' John began, 'that those people who love us will go on loving us and that those who don't love us will come to love us.' Above her clasped hands, Mary was smiling but Edie kept her face straight. It seemed an odd sort of grace, but then Catholics were an odd sort of people. After a pause, John went on blandly, 'And that those people who don't love us and never will love us all break their ankles so we may recognise them by their limping.'

Edie couldn't help laughing, and Mary joined in while John sat grinning smugly over the success of his grace. After that, Edie began to feel happier and more relaxed than she'd been for ages. Mary chatted away about life in Suffolk with her pony-mad daughter and her academic husband, while John told silly jokes in between swallowing mouthfuls of roast beef and gravy.

Once the plates had been cleared away, and despite protests from Mary, he ordered treacle tart and custard for the three of them, after which he turned to Edie. 'Now come on, Miss Quentance. It's about time you told us all your sins.'

'I haven't got time for any,' she said. 'Every moment I'm not slaving in the bank I spend trying to finish my doctorate. It's supposed to unravel the secrets around *Titanic*, but I haven't had a breakthrough yet.'

'Luxury ship, rich passengers, big iceberg. Isn't that pretty much it?'

'Well, there's more to it than that.' Edie hunted for something that might interest him. 'For instance there's the whole insurance question. *Titanic*'s policy had a limited liability provision, so her owners would only have had to pay for lost cargo.'

'Not lost lives?' asked Mary. 'There must have been a lot dead people whose next of kin would want to sue.'

'There were nearly fifteen hundred victims, not to mention the survivors who'd lost anything they brought with them on the ship.'

'Lucky owners, having limited liability,' Mary said.

'Ah, but you see they didn't!' Edie caught her voice rising in excitement. 'The insurance cover was invalid if there was any way the ship's owners could have influenced the captain's actions during the voyage. And Ismay himself was on her maiden trip.'

'Who's he?' queried Mary.

'Bruce Ismay was chairman of White Star Line, which owned *Titanic*.'

'So having him on board nullified their cover. That must have been painful.' John waved his half-empty beer glass in the air. 'Without insurance, the owners would presumably be sued for every penny they had.'

'That's exactly it,' Edie said, 'but only if the disaster was White Star's fault. So after *Titanic* sank, they pulled every string they could to prove it was an accident.'

'And *was* the company to blame?'

'Well, they certainly wanted *Titanic* to run at her full speed on that maiden trip, and I think Ismay was telling the captain to ignore the ice warnings and show what the ship could do.'

'You're an expert,' Mary smiled.

'And I can be extremely boring if you give me half a chance. Tell me what you do.'

'For starters, I go up five dress sizes if I eat this sort of thing.' Mary looked at the slab of hot treacle tart that had just been put in front of her. 'But mainly I work for the Treasury, trying to track down inside traders and other City scumbags. You'd be horrified by how much money some of them are making out of this financial crisis they got us into.'

With a spoonful of tart halfway to her mouth, Edie asked, 'So what are you working on right now?'

'For God's sake, John, take this away from me!' Mary pushed her plate over to her cousin before turning back to Edie. 'Right now, I'm trying to make sure a certain Russian oligarch loses some of the fortune he's got locked up in a particularly grubby hedge fund. I haven't got my hands on his cash pile yet, but I'm getting close.'

'Wouldn't it be like getting a tiger by the tail?' Edie said, thinking of radioactive drinks and lethal pellets in umbrella spikes.

'More like a crocodile.' John shot an anxious look across the table. 'Faster, fatter and a lot scalier.'

'Oh, I'll be all right.' Mary laughed at her cousin before turning her attention back to Edie. 'And John's not as innocent as he looks either, he's a forensic accountant. It may sound dull but he's involved in even seamier things than I am.'

'Like what?' Edie saw that, having wolfed down his own pudding, he was now starting on Mary's. He certainly didn't *look* like some high-flying investigator.

'Mary's exaggerating,' he said, pouring more custard on to his plate. 'I just sit at my computer screen and worry about illicit cash movements.' He waved a hand in the air. 'All far too dreary for a Sunday lunchtime. How long are you down here for?'

Edie noted the smooth change of subject and was rather glad he wasn't one of those men who want to talk about their work all the time. 'I've got to go back to London tonight, and I really hate leaving Devon when the weather's like this.'

'I know what you mean. I've got to make a guilt-trip across Dartmoor to see my parents this afternoon,' Mary grumbled. 'Letty's promised to keep Guy amused while I'm gone. Letty's my sister,' she explained to Edie.

'You're very trusting to leave her alone with your husband,' John laughed. 'I've never been sure she's entirely straight about the eighth commandment.'

'I think you mean the seventh,' Mary said.

'That one too,' he nodded.

Edie counted on her fingers and tried to remember which rule was which. 'Theft and adultery? She sounds like an exciting woman.'

'Troublesome's a better description,' Mary said. 'Have you got a sister?'

'Not any more.' Edie fiddled with the edge of the table. 'But I've got a twin brother.'

'And how's your mother?' John asked. 'I liked her when we talked at your party. A very attractive woman.'

'I wish she could hear you say that. Anything to cheer her up.'

John stopped mopping up the last crumbs of Mary's treacle tart and looked at her. 'I'm sorry, has something happened?'

'Oh no, it's a very old story.'

'Tell me.'

He looked so concerned that Edie found herself telling him about Ianthe's death, ending by saying, 'It happened twenty-five years ago, but Mum's never got over it.'

'And how do you and your mother get on?' Mary asked.

Edie shrugged. 'With difficulty.'

'I'm not surprised,' Mary said gently. 'You were born the very day your mother found her first child dead, so she never had time to grieve for Ianthe before another daughter came to take her place.' Her hand slid across the table to cover Edie's. 'No wonder she couldn't bond with you.'

Mary Kersey's words hit Edie hard. All her life she'd felt unloved and had resented her mother for it, but she'd never thought about the relationship from Clio's point of view. She felt John Tamar's arm slipping along the back of her chair until he wrapped it round her and gave her a squeeze. Finding it strangely difficult to turn and meet his eyes, she looked across at Mary instead and said, 'Thank you. You've no idea how much happier that makes me.' And it was true. Mary's words and John's hug had made her feel terrific.

'I'm glad.' Mary Kersey glanced down at her watch and leapt up from her chair. 'Good God! My parents will be furious if I'm not there in time for tea, and I've got to drop you off first, John. Can we rush?'

Removing his arm from round her shoulders, John stood up too. 'If it helps,' Edie said, 'I've got a car. I can easily give you a lift back to Brink Castle.'

'That's brilliant,' Mary answered for him. 'You're an angel!' Blowing a hurried kiss, she rushed off down the narrow stairs.

'Which one's yours?' John asked as they strolled into the marina car park a few minutes later.

Edie's heart sank as she remembered. The old Land Rover wouldn't start that morning. 'It's that Bentley.' She pointed to the hateful car, squatting smugly in the September sunshine. He'd think she was a terrible show-off. Maybe he'd think she'd been lying about having no money of her own? 'It's not mine,' she rushed to explain. 'I don't even own a car. I go everywhere by bike.'

'There's no need to apologise to me.' His expression was unreadable. 'I'm all in favour of bankers getting their just rewards.'

The big car was a nightmare to navigate through the twisting side streets that led out of Dartmouth towards the coast, and Edie had to concentrate too hard to talk. Beside her, John seemed quite happy to sit humming to himself, but once she'd successfully got them out of the town, he burst into song.

'Hail, Queen of heav'n, the ocean star, guide of the
    wand'rer here below;
Thrown on life's surge, we claim thy care, save us
    from peril and from woe.
Mother of Christ, star of the sea,
Pray for the sinner, pray for me.'

His voice was such an unexpectedly deep bass that Edie was surprised into laughing.

'Now that's not very polite, is it? Don't you like being sung to?'

'No, I do, my twin does it all the time. It's the religious tone I'm not so used to.'

'Then it's about time you were. Come on, sing with me.' He started the next verse of the hymn and she joined in the chorus, tentatively at first, gaining confidence as the road snaked up on to the high, coastal downland, and by the time they arrived at the turning to Brink Castle, Edie was belting out the words with him.

'Mother of Christ, star of the sea,
Pray for the sinner, pray for me.'

Having steered the Bentley between the turreted remnants of a gatehouse which straddled the ruins of the castle's curtain wall, she glanced across and caught John watching her. 'You've never been here before, have you?' he said.

'Never been invited, and it's not really surprising, given the history.' Edie made a rueful face at her passenger as she pulled into a wide courtyard.

'Mind out!'

With a wild swerve, she just managed to avoid a low, circular stone wall and came to a jerky halt beside it. 'Sorry about that. How odd having a well so far from the house.'

'Not really, it's eighteenth-century.' He nodded towards the pleasant, four-square building ahead of them. 'One of my ancestors decided the castle was too much for him, so he put up something more manageable on the site of the original keep.'

'So the well pre-dates the house?'

'It's ancient. Come and have a look.'

Once they were standing over it, Edie found that there wasn't a lot of the well to see as its top was completely covered by a weather-worn wooden lid that had been padlocked and bolted into its old stones.

'There's supposed to be a priest-hole hidden somewhere down in the shaft, but I've never had a chance to check.' John perched on the well's low wall. 'This cover's been on all my life, and I don't suppose anyone even knows where the key is. Come and sit next to me, I want to ask you something.' Obediently she squatted down beside him, close but not quite touching. 'You said you'd found out about Quentance Bank foreclosing on our land and that you thought your family had behaved badly over it. I need to know if there's anything more recent you're concerned about.'

'What sort of thing?'

He leaned so close to her, she could feel his breath on her forehead. 'I was wondering about money-laundering.'

She couldn't believe it. He'd put his arm round her in the pub, he'd made her sing with him in the car, and now he thought he had the right to grill her about her family. 'I don't know anything about that,' she said coolly. 'And what's so bad about it anyway?'

'It depends how you feel about the drugs trade and people-trafficking. And let's not forget funding terrorists.' He stood up slowly, unfolding his long body until he was towering over her. 'Are you quite sure there isn't anything worrying you?'

Edie got up, but she didn't meet his eyes. 'You sound as if you're accusing me of something.'

There was no reply, and when she finally tilted her head to look at him, she saw nothing beyond a slight, formal smile.

'Thanks for the lift. You know where I am if you ever want to talk.'

As John walked off towards the house, Edie stared at his retreating back. She could see now that his shoulders were actually quite broad, it was just his height that had made him seem narrower than he was. She didn't move until she saw him vanishing into the house, but he never once turned his head to look back at her.

Edie climbed into the Bentley. Work tomorrow. More dreary hours down in the bank's basement, and only this miserable weekend to look back on. By the time she'd turned the car in between Dartleap's gates, Edie had made up her mind. She was going to do some investigating. She'd enjoy proving to John Tamar that he was wrong.

SIXTEEN

'Good-morning, Miss Edith. You're an early riser.'

'Morning! Very shiny buttons today.' Edie smiled.

'The wife polishes my little eagles for me every Sunday night. She'll be pleased you noticed,' Quentance Bank's porter called after her as she sped across the marble floor to the main staircase.

Edie gave herself a quick check in one of the gilt-framed mirrors on the first floor. Her hair was brushed, her lipstick was in place and her trouser suit looked respectable. She hurried the length of the old ballroom, her feet bouncing off the sprung floorboards in her rush to get to her father's office. After a night disturbed by dreams of John Tamar bawling accusing songs at her, she'd woken at dawn, determined to prove he had no right to be suspicious about her family's business. As a first step, she was going to insist that Dad show her the bank's accounts.

The outer office was deserted. She hadn't expected her father's assistant to be there at eight-fifteen, but Edie was surprised not to get an answer when she tapped on Alec's door, since he was usually there by eight at the latest. As

Edie hung around beside his PA's desk, she noticed that the brass desk calendar was still set for the previous Friday, so she turned the little knob on the side until it showed the correct date, Monday 15 September 2008. After waiting for several minutes, she wandered back to Alec's door and tried the handle. She'd expected it to be locked after the weekend, but it opened straight away. That meant her father must be around somewhere, so Edie decided to sit in his office until he came back.

A sheet of writing-paper lay on Alec's desk where normally there was nothing but his inkstand and telephone. For a while, Edie forced herself to stare out of the window at the courtyard and the low run of deserted stables at its far end, but eventually the lure of that open letter became irresistible. Moving over to her father's desk, she leaned down to read it.

Dear Mr Quentance,

I am writing to you on behalf of my clients, Mr Peter, Mr Nicholas and Mr Edward Coverley-Kissing, being the children of Mrs Flora May Angela Coverley-Kissing.

Glancing at the top of the page, Edie saw that it had come from some grand-sounding firm of solicitors in Lincoln's Inn Fields.

Mrs Coverley-Kissing has informed her sons that she recently invested £28 million, being the sum total of her inheritance from the estate of her late husband, into a fund known as 'Adamantine' of which I understand you to be the sole manager.

You will, I am sure, appreciate my clients' concern that

their mother, a vulnerable and elderly lady, should have placed all of her very considerable fortune into one single investment, with all the risks that such a strategy entails.

Twenty-eight million quid, all in one pot! Dad might be a brilliant investor, but all the same, Mrs Coverley-Kissing's children had a point. Edie sat down in her father's chair and shuffled her feet forwards under his desk.

The Bakelite phone rang, making her jump. She reached out a hand, but when she answered it, there was no sound at all from the receiver. The line seemed to be completely dead. Putting the phone back in its cradle, she returned to the letter.

Whilst my clients are not suggesting that undue influence was brought to bear, you appear to be Mrs Coverley-Kissing's sole financial adviser, and as such you would be expected to be cognisant of the need for her to spread her monies rather more widely than into one single fund. Furthermore, my clients are unable to understand your claims to achieve consistent and exceptional returns from Quentance Bank's Adamantine Fund, particularly given the present state of the financial markets.

In the circumstances, I am sure that you will concur with my clients' request that you contact Mrs Coverley-Kissing suggesting that a significant proportion of her funds be withdrawn from your Adamantine Fund and spread across other investment vehicles in order to mitigate the current risk. You are doubtless aware that the relevant authorities might be expected to express their concern if this proposal is not followed.

'Relevant authorities'? 'Concern'? Surely this couldn't be all John Tamar had been asking about? Dad might have a ton of bureaucrats coming down on his head if he wasn't careful, but it didn't exactly feel wrong, and it certainly wasn't money-laundering.

As Edie shifted her feet under the desk, she nudged some irregularity in the carpet. Immediately the Bakelite phone rang again. Frowning, she leaned forward to answer it, but just as before, the line was dead. She shuffled her foot, and again the phone rang. It took her a moment to realise that it was a dummy, an ideal way to get rid of unwanted visitors. She remembered the last time she was in this office, when she'd been asking Dad some questions about the bank. That fake phone had rung and her father had waved her out, pretending to be taking a real call. He'd done that to his own daughter! In a sudden fury, she stamped on the concealed button, making the bell ring again and again.

There was a rush of footsteps and a door banged. Edie just had time to get up from her father's desk when the handle of his office door was wrenched open with a shout of 'What the hell's going on in here?' and then her uncle was standing in the doorway, blocking her exit.

Edie watched his eyes moving from her face to the letter on Alec's desk and back again, while she tried to show neither guilt nor an unexpected flutter of fear. 'What a nice surprise to see you.' To Edie, her voice sounded a mere whisper, but it must have been louder than she thought because a moment later a brighter blond head than Max's pushed itself into the doorway.

'So it was you playing musical phones in here, I might have guessed.' Edie caught her uncle flicking his expression from mistrust to benevolence as Oscar slipped past him. 'What an improvement! I love the lipstick, Eds.'

'Do you really?' She felt suddenly happy. Life was so much better when Oscar was around. 'I wish it didn't keep rubbing off, though. How do other girls manage?'

'Oh, we have our little secrets.'

Edie laughed, relieved that Oscar's camp voice had made Max smile too. Hoping he'd decided to ignore anything he might have seen her doing, she slipped across to give her uncle a kiss. 'When did you get here?'

'Only this morning. I wanted to give Alec a surprise, so I forced your hydrophobic twin to come over with me on *Cilissa*. We slipped her into a touristy marina down on the south coast and got the train up to London. By the way,' Max added, 'where *is* my brother?'

Edie was about to explain she'd been waiting to see Dad herself when she heard the soft creak of leather shoes as her father slipped into the room. His thin face was expressionless and he showed no sign of surprise at seeing them all. 'Max,' he said quietly, 'I'm glad you're here. Have you heard the news?'

Taking Oscar's arm, Edie pulled him out of the way as their father advanced like an automaton towards his desk. As he sat down one of the drawers slid open, but instead of the files and papers she expected to see, a computer emerged, rising automatically to the height of the desktop. She watched in surprise as the father she'd only ever seen with a fountain pen tapped in a password. The screen powered up to show red numbers flickering down page after page of stock-market prices.

'Lehman Brothers,' Alec said softly to Max, who was leaning over his shoulder and staring at the screen. 'They've filed for Chapter Eleven bankruptcy protection.'

Edie could see now that her father's apparent unconcern was actually a reaction to shock. His face had gone as white as his hair, and there was a tremor in his hands. Max went across the office to fetch one of the visitors' chairs, collapsing into it like an old man. Neither Edie nor Oscar said a word. Silently, they stood staring at the screen as the scarlet flood of tumbling values rippled over the financial world.

Edie had no idea how long their hiatus lasted, or for how much longer they might have stayed, frozen in that uncomfortable tableau, if they hadn't been disturbed by a tap at the door. 'Mr Alec? May I come in?'

'Janet, of course, good-morning.' Her father pulled himself to his feet, and Edie felt something close to awe as she saw him take control of his features. He smiled as his PA gave him a sheaf of papers, but once she'd returned to the outer office Alec went straight back to his screen.

Edie couldn't wait any longer to find out what was going on. 'Dad?' He showed no sign of having heard her, so in a louder voice she said, 'Dad! You've got to tell Oscar and me what's happening.' Max eyed her in silence, but Alec still didn't turn round so she went on talking to the back of his head. 'We're shareholders too, Dad, we've got a right to know how safe the bank is. And I'm worried about that letter on your desk,' she added fiercely. 'The one about Mrs Coverley-Kissing and the Adamantine Fund.'

There was a soft click as the computer vanished back inside her father's desk. Very slowly, he turned until he was facing Edie and Oscar. His expression was one she recognised from her childhood, a combination of indifference and incomprehension.

'Edie.' How did he get such a world of boredom into one word? 'Quentance Bank is extremely conservative in all its policies. Your uncle and I have worked very hard to build up a business that we can hand on proudly to future generations. The question I suggest you and Oscar should be asking yourselves . . .' he paused to give both of them his pale, blue stare, 'is whether you're keeping your side of the bargain.'

As Alec fell silent, Max took over. 'What your father means is there's not a lot of point in our slaving away to grow the bank and keep it safe if neither of you is going to have any children to pass it on to.'

Edie thought her uncle looked awkward, but he didn't make any effort to stop Alec's sudden rush of venom. 'For God's sake, Edie, that suit makes you look like a man. It's no wonder you never have any boyfriends. And you, Oscar!' He rounded on her twin. 'You don't even have the excuse of being unattractive. It's about time you got married and gave me an heir. Now get out, both of you.' He turned his back on them. 'Max and I have work to do.'

Her father's words seemed so cruel that Edie felt she simply couldn't move. Oscar came to her rescue, propelling her through Alec's door, past Janet and out into the old ballroom. 'Don't listen to Dad,' he said, guiding her over to the long line of windows. 'You look lovely.' He led her gently until they were standing side by side, looking out at the trim gardens in the centre of St James's Square. 'He's right to be worried about one thing, though.' Oscar bent and breathed the words into her ear. 'It's been hell to come to terms with, but I won't be marrying any girls.'

In an instant the sting of her father's words was forgotten. She stroked his arm and said, 'I'm so relieved you've told me.'

'You're not shocked?' Edie shook her head, but was prevented from saying anything else as her brother took her into his arms and held her tight. 'I've found someone, Eds,' he muttered into her hair. 'He's helped me accept I'm gay.'

'But that's wonderful.' Pulling back from Oscar's arms, she looked into his face. 'Have I met him?'

'D'you remember Yves de la Châtaigne?'

Edie's heart sank. Of course she remembered Yves, with his high-pitched voice and his sharp tongue. But if Oscar loved him, she'd have to try to do so too. After the briefest of pauses, she said, 'He's not someone you'd forget easily.'

'He's not, is he?' Oscar was gazing beyond her and out of the window. 'Yves makes me feel I'm at home in my skin for the first time in my life.'

A door banged and they both spun round to see their uncle hurrying towards them. 'Twins, I'm glad I caught you. Your father didn't mean what he said, it's just he's had a shock. This Lehman's crisis is hitting the markets hard and he's going to have to concentrate on keeping his investors calm. We don't want anyone pulling cash out of the Adamantine Fund, so don't distract your dad, will you?'

Whilst he seemed to be talking to both of them, Edie felt as if Max was aiming his words at her in particular. An unpleasant thought jumped into her head. Had her father been vile just so as to divert her from asking questions? Surely not. The idea was absurd, and anyway Dad would need support, not mistrust. 'Will you be here for a while?' she asked. 'It's great having you around to keep us calm.'

'I daren't stay. I've run out of legal days and the bloody taxman's cracking down on non-residents.' Edie turned her head, afraid of showing her disapproval. 'Be ready to leave at two, Oscar,' Max went on cheerfully. 'Zita's promised to crew for me on *Cassandra* and I'll need time to get everything ready.'

Edie felt a sudden longing to be away from London and out on the clean, wide seas herself. She hadn't been on *Cassandra* for months, though there was no point in moaning about it while Max was in the middle of one of his love affairs. 'I'd really like to meet Zita,' was all she said. 'Oscar told me she's the new woman in your life.'

'I'd be a bloody sight happier if she was in my bed as well as my life,' he muttered.

Edie decided she must have misheard. Max had always been irresistible to women. With a brief wave at her uncle as he strolled off towards the stairs, she took hold of Oscar's arm and gave it a friendly tug. 'Come on, babes. I want to show you how tidy Records and Archives are after the disaster zone you left me.'

'Sorry Eds, another time.' Her twin disentangled himself and smoothed down his sleeve where she'd rumpled it.

'There are things I need to do as well.' With a quick hug, he was striding off down the ballroom to catch up with their uncle.

SEVENTEEN

There was a strong sea running up from Brittany, and in the wheelhouse Max was having to work hard to hold the old boat steady so that her bow faced into the oncoming waves and pitched smoothly over them. During a brief lull in the weather, he threw a glance over his shoulder and was relieved to see that Zita was safely in place out on the aft deck.

Turning back to face the bow, he spotted a twin-seated helicopter flying fast and low across the water, straight to where *Cassandra* was waiting. 'Here it comes, Zita,' he bellowed over the noise of the wind. 'Are you ready?' Max certainly hoped she was. He'd explained everything clearly enough once they'd got out into the English Channel.

'I don't believe it!' She'd thrown her head back and laughed when he'd told her what was going to happen. 'It's just too simple to be credible.'

Peering out through the spray lashing against the wheel-house windows, Max had pretended to be offended. 'It may be simple, but it's foolproof. My clients get their cash flown out of anywhere in Euroland. They drop it down to us, we haul it into the boat and push straight on to the Channel Islands, where the money vanishes into an offshore account.'

She'd looked at him with something like awe. 'You're mad, do you know that? Stark staring lunatic mad.'

He'd taken her smile for an invitation and had put his arms round her waist while *Cassandra*'s wheel spun madly beside him. He'd had to let her go again when he felt her spine arching away from him. Fighting to get the boat's helm under control again, he'd said, 'I'm not mad, Zita, I'm brilliant.'

The thudding of rotor blades overhead brought Max's mind sharply back to the present. It was a perfect pass. The helicopter hovered above them, a door opened and a water-tight suitcase attached to a float splashed down into the surging, grey-flecked waves, only yards from *Cassandra*'s stern. Immediately the helicopter swung round and vanished back towards the French coast.

For the next few minutes, all Max's attention was given to looking aft as he steered *Cassandra* astern, guided by Zita's hand movements. It was only when she'd got hold of the float with the boat-hook and had completed the delicate task of roping it to the winch that he looked ahead again. A small boat was bounding over the sea towards them. Someone else had seen the helicopter.

Max gave a horrified shout. 'Zita! Coastguard!' She waved a hand to show she'd understood, and immediately he saw her stamping down on the footswitch to start the winch. It sparked into life and began its slow job of reeling float and suitcase in.

Max felt his heart pounding as he alternated between

peering aft at Zita and staring anxiously forward through the wheelhouse windscreen. The coastguard's boat was less than half a mile away and was bearing down on them fast. Max gauged that despite the heavy swell it couldn't be more than a couple of minutes before the boat was close enough for its occupant to work out exactly what Zita was doing.

There was no time to be lost, and he acted quickly, swinging the wheel hard to starboard. *Cassandra* lurched round ninety degrees and was soon facing due west so that her entire length formed a barrier between the coastguard and the winch with its cargo. But now, instead of riding head-on to the waves, *Cassandra* was being hit broadside and immediately began to roll ponderously from side to side.

'For God's sake, hurry!' Max saw Zita glance up at him just as the boat wallowed down the side of a large wave. 'Mind your left hand!' he pointed frantically, realising that he'd broken her concentration. 'Zita, your hand! It's too close to the winch!' he bellowed, but the wind whipped his voice away.

As *Cassandra* shifted heavily to starboard he saw the rope slackening. Unable to leave the wheel, Max watched helplessly as *Cassandra* rolled back in the other direction and the rope snapped taut again, trapping one of Zita's fingers between the dead weight of the boat and the opposing pull of a capstan winch. Over the shrill keening of the wind Max heard one high scream, then *Cassandra* lurched to starboard again, the rope slackened off and Zita was free.

Forgetting the wheel, he was out on deck beside her in an instant, but already there was so much blood spurting from her hand that he couldn't see what damage had been done. 'The case, Max,' she groaned, and he saw that the waterproof suitcase was already out of the sea, and dangling only inches from the stern rail.

A moment later *Cassandra* heeled over to windward and they both almost lost their footing as the deck lurched away from them. 'Can you manage to hold her steady while I get this hauled in?' Max asked, watching her face anxiously. To his relief Zita nodded, then, gingerly tucking her wounded hand inside the cream corduroy gilet she was wearing, she staggered back to the wheelhouse.

Once he'd seen her take control of the helm, Max heaved the dripping suitcase up and on to the deck, then slipped the float back overboard. Hurrying past Zita with a murmured 'Just a moment longer,' he lugged the case down into the saloon and slid it into the hidden locker under the companionway.

As he was leaping the few steps back up to the wheel-house, he heard the scrape of the coastguard's rubberised boat against *Cassandra*'s side. Zita was standing at the helm, struggling to keep the wheel steady with her undamaged hand, but when she turned towards him, Max was horrified to see the bright red stain seeping across the pale material of her waistcoat.

'Zita! Oh my God, oh no!' He rushed to her side.

'He's out on deck behind you,' she breathed, and let go of the wheel.

'*Eh! Monsieur!*' Just as the bearded face of a French coastguard loomed through the wheelhouse door, Zita crumpled into Max's arms. For a brief moment, he was overwhelmed. She felt tiny and fragile, and yet she was so strong, it was like holding an injured swan. '*Mon dieu!*' The coastguard cut across his brief reverie. In two steps he was close beside Max, peering at Zita's blanched face and the spreading patch of blood. '*Madame est blessée. Allons-y!*'

'You go ahead, I'll follow.' Despite his shock, Max managed to maintain his chosen persona of innocent English amateur sailor. The coastguard stared at him suspiciously, and Max was afraid it would only be a matter of moments before the man noticed the betraying trail of seawater that had dripped from the suitcase as he'd shifted it down the companionway to its hiding-place.

He was saved by a moan from Zita. 'Max!' She drew out her damaged hand. 'It hurts.'

Perhaps it was by accident that her fingers fluttered so close to the coastguard's face, but he recoiled in horror at the bloody mess. '*Ahem. Monsieur.*' The Frenchman pulled the wheelhouse door open and leaned against it, looking as if he might be sick.

'Go on ahead of us to St Malo!' Max was relieved to hear how authoritatively his own voice rang in his ears. 'We'll follow once I've done some first aid.'

'*Comment?*' The coastguard seemed to be struggling between duty and nausea.

'*Premiers soins,*' Zita groaned.

'*Bien, bien.*' The man backed out on to the deck. '*St Malo. Suivez-moi.*'

It was not until they heard the roar of a fast engine retreating south towards the French coast that either of them spoke.

'I'm badly hurt, Max. I need a hospital.'

'Of course you do. As soon as he's out of sight we'll head straight for the Channel Islands.'

'That's too far,' Zita groaned. 'The pain's unbearable. Take me to France. It's so much closer.'

Max looked at Zita in an agony of indecision. She looked miserable, and yet he could see some colour returning to her cheeks. It was a ghastly choice, but it had to be made. 'France is impossible,' he said gently. 'We'd be searched the moment we touched land, and there's a million euros in that suitcase. It'd mean prison for both of us.'

'Oh shit! I think I've lost half my little finger. It's agony.'

'I've got painkillers in the galley.' Max forced himself to smile. 'And when we get back to Paris, I'll buy you a thousand pairs of gloves.'

'Bastard,' she said faintly. 'They'll have to be *couture*, understood? Lanvin, Givenchy, Chanel. And I'll want them diamond-studded, fur-lined, satin-trimmed, leather-laced, the works.'

'I'd give you anything to stay out of a French nick.'

'Anything?' Her voice sharpened. 'I'll need to think about that. A bloody great whisky would do for starters.'

'The moment we've agreed *Cassandra*'s course,' said Max, pulling the first-aid box from its locker and taking out gauze and bandages.

Zita slumped down beside the chart table and eyed her blood-covered hand. 'Channel Islands then,' she said. 'But it'll cost you.'

Much of Zita's whisky slopped over the wheelhouse floor as *Cassandra* fought her way westwards into a rising gale and Max struggled to keep the wheel steady. Horizontal rain crashed against the windscreen like bucketfuls of gravel, while waves exploded against the bow, throwing up towers of green water which tumbled on to the decks. Everything that wasn't safely battened down was washed away, but Max didn't mind. The swelling rage of the storm would make it impossible for them to be followed by even the most determined of coastguards. He settled down at the helm and prepared himself for a long battle.

When he was able to take his eyes from the sea and his muscle-sapping fight against wind and wave, he peered back to check on Zita. She lay quite still, her face as innocent as a child's. He closed his eyes briefly to fix an image of her in his brain, and as he opened them again he was surprised by a rush of love. The future seemed very simple as he turned to resume his fight with the storm.

Zita was still lying in exactly the same position when Max eventually felt a slackening of the sea. The mountainous waves relaxed down into mild undulations, while overhead the scudding clouds dispersed to allow a few pale rays of light to break through. He slowly unclenched his hands from the wheel, rolling his neck to ease his tense shoulders, then, climbing down from his stool, he stepped over to Zita. 'How are you feeling?' he asked as her eyes fluttered open.

'Aching like buggery. And I've been mulling over what you said about giving me anything to make up for this.' She slid her injured hand towards him so that Max could see it, the bandaged finger blood-caked and trembling.

'Poor hurt little thing.' He touched her hair softly. 'Were you thinking of something in particular?'

'Yes I was.' Zita pushed herself upright. 'I'd like half your share of Quentance Bank. I've got great contacts and I can help you build up the European business.'

Without a moment's hesitation, Max crouched down on the wheelhouse floor and took hold of her undamaged hand. 'Live with me and you can have it all.'

He bent forward to kiss her but she pulled her head away, saying simply, 'I can't.'

He sat back on his heels, more astonished than upset. 'Of course you can.' All his adult life, women had been chasing him, and he'd always assumed that once he finally invited one of them to share his house, she'd move in straight away.

'I can't.' Zita's voice weakened. 'Not now, not with this.'

Seeing how she winced as she moved her injured hand, Max kicked himself for his insensitivity. Of course she couldn't think about committing to a relationship when she was in so much pain. 'Forgive me. I'm a callous idiot.'

'Just a bit impetuous. How much longer till we make shore?'

'Half an hour.' Max stood up and peered out of one of the wheelhouse windows. 'Or maybe less, the sea's like glass now. More painkillers?'

'No thanks, I'm rattling already.'

Max turned back to the wheel, and in the long silence that followed he assumed she'd gone to sleep. He was tired himself after that long battle through the gale, and there was something soporific about the rhythmic beat of *Cassandra*'s engine. He had to force himself to concentrate on the vague opalescence of the horizon. Jersey's dark rump would be looming up through that veil of mist any minute now.

'Max?' Her voice so soft, he wasn't sure he'd heard it. 'Is

it true there's a secret hoard of gold at Dartleap?' It occurred to him that her mind might be wandering after so much whisky and painkillers, until she said more loudly, 'Tell me, Max, is it true?'

'How d'you know that old story?' he asked, bending to check the compass yet again. Surely Jersey should be in sight by now – unless he'd made some dreadful mistake in plotting his course?

'Oh, everyone knows it. If there's a tale going round about secret treasure, you can be sure it's going to get told in Geneva.'

A softening of the mist became a shadow, gaining definition to become a shape and then a clear lump of land. Max let out a low whistle of relief. 'I can see Jersey! We'll have you in a hospital in no time.' He glanced round and saw that her eyes were shadowed with pain. She'd been astonishingly brave, bearing the agony of that finger with so little complaint. He longed to sit beside her and whisper words of encouragement, but he daren't take his eyes off their course as *Cassandra* slipped in amongst the sharp-rocked waters of the islands. He'd entertain her with the myth of Dartleap's hidden gold instead.

'The rumour began with my grandfather, Kit Quentance,' he said over his shoulder. 'He skipped off *Titanic* in questionable circumstances and a tale grew up that he'd taken stolen gold on to the lifeboat with him. My father certainly believed it. He made one hell of a mess digging up the Dartleap cellars after Kit died, though he never found a thing.'

'So was that it?' The disappointment in Zita's voice was almost tangible. 'No gold?'

'Not quite. It's a long time ago now, but I once found a bar of gold in *Cassandra*'s ballast.'

It had been shortly after Kit died. Neither his father nor Alec had been remotely interested in boats, so he'd taken *Cassandra* for himself, and it had been while he'd been checking the hull for soundness that he'd chanced on a lump of ballast with a deep dent. He could see himself, sitting back on his heels above the bilges and holding the heavy block in his hands. He'd thought what an exceptionally hard knock it would take to dent pig-iron, and as he'd turned the piece of ballast over, he'd seen the thin, gold scratches that had told him it wasn't pig-iron at all.

'That's amazing!' Zita's voice cut through the memory playing in his head. 'Did it have a hallmark?'

'Not a hallmark exactly, there was just an eagle stamped into it.' Max eased back the throttle as he spotted the tell-tale swirl of water suggesting submerged rocks away to starboard. 'Alec and I guessed that Kit had it done as a stylised version of the Quentance crest, but it was hard to see. The gold was high-carat and very soft, and I'm afraid I scratched it when I scraped the paint off.'

'This bar, what happened to it?'

'We've kept it hidden away ever since.' Max laughed as he remembered what Alec had said when he first held it. *This thing's far too heavy for Kit to have hauled off* Titanic. *I'll bet that priggish old bastard was up to his neck in gold-running for his clients.* 'The gold bar's a sort of talisman,' he told Zita. 'It reminds us that, despite appearances, every Quentance is a buccaneer at heart.'

'And did you find any more of it?'

'Sadly not. I crawled through the entire ton and a half of ballast in *Cassandra*'s bilges and found nothing but innocent pig-iron.'

'Then I don't see why you're grinning like the Cheshire Cat.' Zita's voice sounded flat, and with another quick look back from the windshield, he saw that she'd closed her eyes. Poor thing, she needed distracting from her pain. He'd already told her half the story, now he'd trust her with the rest.

'I'm only smiling because painting gold to look like pig-iron was an idea of genius. It's been worth a fortune, and the risk's one hell of a lot lower than being a conventional banker. I've had the occasional customs man take a peek in the bilges, but my ballast always looks completely normal.'

'You move gold.' It was a statement more than a question.

'I do,' he said. 'Today's euro-running is just a sideline. Shifting gold's what I love to do.' There was a footstep behind him, and suddenly she was beside him, clutching her wounded hand, her breath coming hard and fast. Thinking how much she must be suffering, he said sharply, 'What's up? Is the pain bad?'

'Bearable.' She took a step backwards and he couldn't see her face any more. 'I was thinking about *Cassandra* and the busy life she's had. Gold-running, Dunkirk, suitcases stuffed with euros.'

'And don't forget the paintings. That was Kit's idea too,' Max couldn't help adding. 'There were picture hooks in the saloon bulkheads when I inherited *Cassandra*.'

'Convenient for Isaiah.'

'Convenient for all my clients. Between *Cassandra* and *Cilissa*, I can shift paintings, gold and cash to pretty much any coast in Europe and North Africa.'

'Max?' Zita murmured, even though there was no one for miles around to hear them. 'I know a Russian in Geneva. He had to leave England sharpish a couple of years ago over some story about a murdered banker, but he's been tipped the wink it's safe to slip back now. I've heard he wants to move some of his gold to London secretly.'

They were crawling down a mist-drifted channel, and as Max sounded a warning on *Cassandra*'s horn the noise echoed mournfully back to them. 'So this Russian,' he said. 'What's his name?'

'You'll find out if I manage to introduce you.'

'Should I go to Geneva to see him?'

'Certainly not!' Max wondered what had brought that note of fear to her voice. 'Only people he trusts completely go to his house. He's not a nice man at all, Max.' She sounded almost flustered. 'Actually, I wish I hadn't mentioned him.'

He felt touched that she should be afraid for him, but the thought of having one of those boundlessly rich oligarchs as a client was more than tempting. 'I'm a grown-up, Zita. I want to meet him.'

'Well, if you're sure.' She hesitated again. 'If you're *absolutely* sure, I know he'll be in Genoa for Isaiah's party.'

'What party? Has that oily creep been sucking up to you behind my back?'

'Don't be silly. I'll call Isaiah to make sure you and Oscar are both invited. But listen, if you're serious about moving his gold, you can't run any risks.' She moved her uninjured hand to his shoulder and squeezed it hard. '*Cassandra* will have been compromised. That coastguard had a pretty good look, so you must get rid of her.'

Max stared out at *Cassandra*'s foredeck as she nosed her way through the silent sea. He'd restored every inch of her forty elegant feet to their original condition, allowing nothing modern to distract from her purity of line. Zita was right, of course. His long run of luck with *Cassandra* had finally run out, but how could he bear to pass her on to strangers?

As if she'd read his thoughts, Zita said softly, 'Is there someone in your family you could pass her on to? Someone trustworthy, who'd never want to use her for anything unusual?'

A screen seemed to flash in his brain, showing his niece, shock-haired, upright, puritanical. He saw Edie standing by that Coverley-Kissing letter on Alec's desk. He heard her pushing the dummy phone. He watched her clever, inquisitive face as she questioned the bank's ability to survive a market collapse.

'You're a genius,' he laughed softly. 'I'll give the boat to my niece. It'll take her mind off anything else, and the best thing is that she'll berth *Cassandra* down at Dartleap. I can keep an eye on both of them.'

EIGHTEEN

'Welcome on board the ten-thirty service to Bristol Temple Meads. This train will call at Reading, Didcot Parkway, Swindon, Chippenham and Bath Spa, due to arrive at Bristol Temple Meads at twelve-fifteen.'

Edie peered along the compartment as the train jolted into motion and began to crawl out of Paddington Station. She'd managed to keep the place next to her for Oscar, but there was no sign of him, and with passengers crowding down the carriage she couldn't hang on to his seat for much longer. Maybe he'd missed the train altogether? She checked her mobile but there was no message from him.

'Excuse me, but is that seat taken?'

'Well yes. That is, I'm expecting my brother.'

'The train's full, if you hadn't noticed, and I want to sit down.'

Edie was about to give up and shift across to the place she'd been saving when she caught sight of Oscar's head almost brushing the grubby ceiling of the carriage as he squeezed his way towards her. 'Here he comes, sorry.' She smiled up into the face of her would-be neighbour, who moved on reluctantly, and a few minutes later her twin lowered himself down beside her.

'This seat's ridiculously small. Why the hell are we sitting in steerage?'

'Because I can't afford to travel first-class. And with the amount you seem to spend on suits these days,' she added, taking in a sharp, navy pinstripe, 'I don't see how you can either.'

'Max and I always go first,' Oscar said. 'It doesn't cost a thing because he sets it off against tax.'

'Visiting our mother's hardly a business expense.'

'For heaven's sake, Edie, don't be so dreary.'

Even a month ago, after an insult like that they'd have had a punch-up and made friends again with a joke, but today it would have felt awkwardly childish. Maybe it was Yves, or maybe it was success at the bank, but Oscar seemed to be getting too grown up for silliness and teasing, and sometimes Edie thought she ought to be the same. And yet she couldn't get comfortable with the career that had been forced on her. That letter in Dad's office, for example. The idea that he was encouraging elderly investors to take such risks felt wrong. But then she knew so little about the world of business. Maybe what her father was doing was just normal banking practice. And perhaps being punctilious about expenses *was* dreary. Unsure of her ground, Edie changed the subject. 'Did Mum say why she needed to see us so urgently?'

'Not a hint. All I got was a frantic message in Paris, saying we had to go to Bath straight away. I'm betting she invested in Lehman's and now she's lost all her money.'

'She hasn't got any to lose.' Edie gazed at the landscape rattling past the window and thought about their mother. 'Oscar,' she said, turning back to her twin. 'About Mum. You know she's never liked me?'

'That's going a bit far. What's not to like about you?'

'That's not the point. It's just that I understand Mum now.' Edie smiled as she thought of Mary Kersey explaining everything.

'How do you mean?'

'It's obvious when you think about it. We were born so soon after Ianthe died that Mum had no time to grieve. I suppose she took to you because you were a boy, but I can see why I'd have been a problem. A new daughter demanding attention, when all she wanted to think about was the one she'd lost.'

'Eds, listen to me.' It was a while since Oscar had looked at her like that. 'Mum adores you. She may not realise it now, but one day she will. And when she does,' he added quietly, 'let's hope you still love her enough to care.'

Leaning over, Edie planted a grateful kiss on her brother's jaw.

As the train gathered speed the heating came on, and with Oscar crammed beside her Edie started to feel uncomfortably hot. She couldn't bear the thought of getting sweatmarks on the close-fitting jacket she'd bought after much dithering over the price, so she tugged it off and folded it carefully on her knee.

'Very nice.' Oscar touched the dove-grey velvet, then shifted sideways to look more closely at her. 'And your hair's a lot better, much softer than the old spiky look.'

He paused, then said casually, 'You're not in love, are you?'

'Don't be ridiculous. Whatever makes you say that?'

'It's obvious. Everyone looks better when they're in love. I know I do.'

Edie waited to see if he'd tell her more about his love life, but as he didn't say anything else she asked about their uncle's instead. 'Why are you and Max keeping this Zita Fitz such a big secret?'

'She's not a secret, more of an enigma.' There was a pause. 'Which makes her an ideal partner for Max, I guess.' Oscar was looking down at his hands, a crease visible between his eyebrows.

'What's up?' Edie had a sudden, irrational fear that he knew something catastrophic about the bank.

'Nothing's up.' Oscar's frown vanished. 'Except Father Christmas is coming early.'

'What *are* you talking about? It's October.'

'Max doesn't want to keep *Cassandra* since Zita's accident. He's going to give the boat to you.'

'I don't believe it!' Every other thought vanished from her head, and for a while Edie could only grin inanely at her brother. 'That's wonderful! *Cassandra*, for me! It's incredible!'

Eventually Oscar interrupted her. 'Don't tell Max I told you. He wants it to be a surprise, but I know you hate surprises. Unlike me, and I didn't get one.'

Catching a touch of envy in her twin's voice, she hurried to soothe him. 'You wouldn't have wanted *Cassandra*, you hate boats. Anyway, I'm stuck in the basement while you get to swan around Europe living a glamorous life on expenses.'

'It's not glamorous at all, more like a non-stop mental-arith-metic test.' Oscar's voice tightened. 'For heaven's sake keep this to yourself, but I simply can't remember all the different account names and numbers that Max thinks I should keep in my head. I've started to write the whole lot down.'

Her twin looked vulnerable, as if his veneer of sophisti-cation had crumbled, leaving the real Oscar beside her again. Without speaking, Edie slipped a hand into his as they watched the countryside flashing past the train windows.

When they arrived at Bath Spa, an autumnal sun was soft-ening the stones of the Georgian houses, while leaves the colour of new pennies spotted the crowns of the turning trees. 'What a heavenly day.' Edie stood outside the station and gazed at the city spread out in front of them. 'Let's walk to Mum's and get up an appetite.'

'I've got one already,' Oscar said, pulling her towards the taxi rank. 'Besides, it's much too far, we'd be late for lunch.'

In the taxi, Oscar pulled out his mobile. 'Hi, Mum,' he started brightly. 'With you in five minutes.' He listened for a moment then added gently, 'It's OK, we'll be as quick as we can. Don't worry.'

'What's up with her?' Edie asked.

'I don't know, but it doesn't sound good. I think she's crying.'

Oscar was right, as was clear the moment they found their mother waiting for them at the door to her basement flat. Her eyes were red, and streaks of mascara chased tears down her face.

'Mum,' the twins said in unison, both trying to kiss her in the narrow doorway.

'Thank you, darlings, thank you for coming.' Clio's voice sounded rusty, as if she'd been weeping for hours. Exchanging a brief glance, Edie and Oscar followed her as she walked down the long central corridor and into the kitchen. Despite the fine day, the blinds were drawn over the bank of windows, shutting out the garden beyond. Dozens of scented candles had spread their musty haze through the room, and in their light the painting of Ianthe glowed eerily.

Clio motioned towards a bottle of wine open on the table. 'Help yourselves.' Watching her mother sipping from a large glass, Edie wondered if all this misery wasn't merely the result of too much alcohol too early in the day, but then she said, 'A man called Inspector Howland's been in touch. He's the head of a police department that looks at old, unsolved cases.' Not just the wine then. Edie sat up and concentrated. 'He'd like to reopen the investigation into Ianthe's death.' Clio ground to a halt, and immediately Oscar was there, hugging her.

'Whatever for?' Edie asked. 'It was so long ago.'

'That's the point,' her mother said. 'It was 1983, before DNA testing. This inspector's job is to revisit cases like Ianthe's and see if they can get a result with modern methods.'

'But Mum,' Oscar said gently, 'surely Ianthe's been buried for far too long to . . .'

His voice tailed off, and there was an uncomfortable silence until Clio said gently, 'It's all right, I know what you mean. Inspector Howland's interested because they're still holding the strands of hair I found on Ianthe's body. They were blond hairs, and at the time the police just assumed they must be mine or your father's, but now they want to run DNA tests on them. They'll need blood from all of us to make sure they're not just innocent hairs from a member of the family.'

'They can have as much of my blood as they like,' Edie said, and was rewarded by a faint smile from her mother. 'We'll do whatever we can to help, won't we, Oscar?'

'Of course. But are you really sure you want to go through with this, Mum?'

Instead of answering, Clio pulled out a much-folded piece of paper and pushed it over for them to read.

CORONER'S REPORT

Name:	Quentance, Ianthe Ruth
Age:	5 years
Summary finding:	Death by natural causes

POST-MORTEM EXAMINATION

External examination: Well nourished, evidence of proper care and attention, no marks of restraint

Internal examination: Atrial septal defect; pulmonary valve stenosis; other internal organs normal

Cause of death: Cardiac arrest

Comments: This child suffered from an undiagnosed heart disorder. Any sudden exertion could have caused the cardiac event that led to her death. It is impossible to establish whether cardiac arrest was triggered by shock

'We knew she died of natural causes, didn't we, Oscar?' Edie said. 'But not that she had such a weak heart.'

'Her heart was fine,' her mother said firmly. 'Ianthe sometimes told me she could feel a butterfly in her chest, so of course we took her to see a heart specialist, but he told us she just had an "innocent murmur".' A tear trickled down her face, but Clio's voice was steady. 'The kidnapper shut Ianthe up in some dark place, and it was the shock and the terror that killed her. I'd give anything to catch her murderer.'

'And you know we'll do anything we can to help, Mum.' Oscar stood up. 'Shall I play us something soothing?'

'Bless you, darling, off you go,' Clio said, and in a few moments, Oscar's sweet tenor floated to them from the formal sitting-room just along the corridor from the kitchen.

'I am your eyes now, you'll see in the dark,
You'll be forever in my beating heart.
I am an artist, you're my midnight blue,
I'll paint the whole world and give it to you.'

Edie had always liked to hear her twin sing, but as his voice wove around her she began to wonder whether he might not have a serious talent that ought to be developed properly.

'Your singing voice is pretty too.' Clio cut through her thoughts. 'Or at least it always was. But you were such a stroppy teenager, and one day you just refused to have any more music lessons.'

'Sorry, Mum.' Across the sound of Oscar's composition,

the hymn she'd sung with John Tamar came back to her. *Mother of Christ, star of the sea.*

The memory was interrupted by her mother saying, 'This sounds like a love song. Has Oscar found a girl at last?'

'I'm sure he'll tell you if he has.' Edie made her voice as non-committal as she could. She was certain that her twin was pouring out his new-found passion for Yves de la Châtaigne, but it was up to Oscar whether he told Clio. In the meantime, Edie had to protect him, which meant a quick change of subject. 'I'm a bit worried about the bank.' She blurted out the first thing that came to mind. 'Lehman's are bust, every other bank in the world is suffering, but Dad seems to think that Quentance Bank is going to sail through unscathed.'

'Are you afraid there'll be a run on the bank? Investors pulling all their funds out?'

'That's exactly it. You sound like a banker yourself.'

'Just because I'm artistic, it doesn't mean I'm thick, Edie. Is there anything specific that's bothering you?'

'Well, yes. You won't approve, but I read a letter Dad left lying on his desk.' She looked up, but Clio didn't seem concerned by her breach of good manners. 'It was from a family lawyer, threatening to cause trouble if we didn't hand back an elderly client's investments, and it was a lot of millions of pounds.' Edie glanced up again and caught her mother staring at her. 'This lawyer can't be the only person feeling nervous, and if Dad's investors take their money out of the Adamantine Fund, we'll still need cash for the outstanding mortgages.'

'And now the banks have stopped lending to each other, your father couldn't just go out and borrow it...'

'So Quentance Bank would go bust,' Edie finished quietly.

They sipped their wine while the tentative notes of a new tune floated in from the piano next door. Eventually Clio said, 'I wouldn't care what happened to the bank if your futures weren't at stake.'

'To be honest, Mum, I couldn't care less about our inheritance, and I hate my job.'

'Don't be unrealistic.'

Edie pinched her forearm sharply to remind herself not to get cross.

'You may think you don't need a proper income, but what about your brother? Have you asked him what he feels?'

'Not yet, he's got other things to think about.' She kept her voice low. 'And besides, I'm talking about selling the bank, not handing it over for nothing.'

'But Oscar seems to love being a banker, and I've heard he's doing very well.'

'Quentance Bank isn't going to make him happy in the long run, Mum. Oscar doesn't realise it himself yet, but he'd have a better life making music than making money.' As if on cue, her twin raised his voice in a joyful crescendo.

'You're certainly right about his voice,' Clio said softly as the last words died away. 'But tell me, what did you mean about selling the bank? I wouldn't have thought it was possible.'

'I think it might be. We'd only need a simple majority in favour, and we know who holds the shares.'

Clio nodded. 'Alec and Max have thirty each, and so do you and Oscar. So if you could get hold of the other twenty shares, you twins would have a straight majority.'

'Teddy.'

'Teddy,' Clio agreed, 'assuming he's still alive. I wonder how we could find out?'

'I've got an idea.' Edie tried to keep her voice neutral. 'John Tamar's some sort of investigative accountant and I think he might be able to help.'

'So you *are* seeing him?' Clio leaned forwards, her eyes bright with excitement.

'No I'm not,' she snapped. 'Sorry. It's just I'm not dating him, if that's what you mean. And by the way, I'm starving.' She stood up and moved to the kitchen door. 'I'll tell Oscar it's lunchtime or he'll go on playing all day.'

NINETEEN

As Oscar followed his uncle into Palazzo Jerichau's frescoed arcade, he was struck by a roar of noise. It poured from a pair of double doors at the far end of the loggia and reverberated back off the high walls of a formal garden, just visible through the arched colonnade to their left. Oscar would have liked a moment to compose himself before diving into the mass of strangers, but his uncle urged him onwards. As soon as they were inside, Max said, 'You're taller than me. I'll stay here while you see if you can spot Zita.'

While his uncle watched the entrance like a gaze-hound, Oscar stared around the *salone da ballo*, trying to make out Zita's tiny body among the crowd. But as it was clearly going to be impossible to tell which out of a multitude of dark-haired heads might be hers, he gave up in favour of admiring the baroque extravagance around him. From where he was standing he could see the entire length of the ballroom, and as he looked along a succession of silver sconces and mirrored panels, the last conversation he'd had with Yves jumped into his head.

'But I can't possibly take you,' he'd said, 'you haven't been invited. I've only been asked myself because Prince Jerichau's a client of my uncle's.'

'Why are you being so pathetically bourgeois?' Yves had stopped stroking his thigh and gave him a sharp slap instead.

He'd bent forward to kiss Yves' lips, pouting sulkily below that curling cavalier's moustache, but Yves had turned away, saying, 'Every host wants to have lovely people at their parties. Take me with you and you'll see I'm right.' A ghastly row had followed, and as Oscar looked at Jerichau's guests, he thought sadly that Yves would have fitted in perfectly.

'Have you spotted her yet?' Max had come over to stand next to him but was still staring at the doorway. 'It's bizarre at my age, but I'm feeling as excited as a child about seeing Zita. You've no idea how brave she was on *Cassandra*, and she's been so sweet about it ever since.'

Oscar knew exactly how brave Zita had been. Although the accident had happened back in September, his uncle was still talking about Zita's courage, and Oscar was pretty certain that Max was falling in love with her.

Love. He felt his face relaxing into a smile. Looking beyond Max, Oscar spotted a plump man wearing an ornate tourmaline ring, and thought how much better it would have looked on Yves' slim fingers. The jewel gave him an idea. He'd buy Yves something extravagant to make up for his cowardice. Because, if he was honest with himself, the reason he hadn't brought his lover to this party had little to do with the lack of a formal invitation. It was more that he hadn't the courage to tell Max he was gay. Telling Edie had been one thing. She was his twin and he'd guessed she'd be fine about it. But explaining it to his uncle, who'd be sure to tell Dad, that was something else entirely.

'There she is!' He heard Max's voice above the noise of the party and turned towards the entrance.

Zita was glowing in the doorway, and at first glance she looked entirely naked. Oscar looked again and saw that, whilst she gave the impression of bareness, she was actually perfectly decent in a dress of flesh-coloured tulle. Swirls of embroidered velvet were strategically sewn into the near-transparent silk to conceal her bosom and hips, and to pour down her spine and onwards to give weight to a little fish-tail of material that swept the ground behind her. It was a piece of extraordinary *trompe l'oeil*, an artful pretence of nudity.

His uncle hurried over to claim Zita, and a moment later she was beside him, holding her face up to be kissed. As Oscar bent down to her cheek, his eyes were caught by her evening gloves. They were an identical colour to her dress, and were seeded with pearls up as far as her elbows. 'Stunning gloves!' He spoke close to her ear.

'Aren't they just?' Zita's eyes sparkled. 'If I'd known how generous Max was going to be, I'd have slipped the other hand into the winch as well. This dress cost him a fortune, and if I wore all the stones he's given me, I'd look like a mobile jewellery store.'

'And then everyone would want to shop in you and I'd be madly jealous.' Max caressed Zita's jaw with the back of his hand. 'Doesn't she look lovely?'

'Very,' Oscar agreed, though he wasn't sure she looked entirely comfortable. His uncle seemed unable to stop touching her and he couldn't help noticing how Zita slid away every time he did so. He was wondering if perhaps this was just her way of flirting when there was a flurry of noise and their host thrust through his party towards them.

'How enchanting to see you here in my house!' Isaiah Jerichau bent his dark head low over Zita's hand. '*Perfezione*,' he murmured reverently as he straightened up and eyed her. Oscar thought the prince looked pretty perfect himself. He'd love to be slim enough to wear such a tightly cut smoking jacket, and that maroon velvet was a perfect contrast to Jerichau's café-au-lait colouring.

'You're sweet to have invited me.' Zita beamed up into his face. 'And our Quentance friends too, of course.'

'But of course.' Their host's eyes looked welcoming enough as they swept over Oscar, but there was a hint of ice when they reached Max, and Jerichau gave his uncle only a slight nod of recognition before turning all his attention to Zita. 'I have told many of my guests about your beauty, *cara*, and now you must come with me so that they can see it for themselves.'

'For heaven's sake, Isaiah,' Max cut in. 'You can't go dragging her all over the place. She's only just recovered from a serious injury.'

'Sustained on your boat, no? At least with *me* she is safe.'

Oscar could see his uncle's colour deepen, while Jerichau's lips narrowed into a thin line. How ridiculous for two grown men to behave like jealous teenagers, but it was clearly time for him to distract their attention. Zita had been watching quietly, her expression unreadable, and he turned to her, saying loudly, 'Have you noticed poor Marsyas being flayed alive over our heads?'

Zita obediently followed his pointing finger to the ceiling. 'Good God,' she chuckled, 'what a lot of gore. What's it about?'

'You see the hairy guy with the Pan pipes?' Oscar said, rather pleased to get a chance to show off his knowledge. 'That's Marsyas, the satyr who challenged Apollo to a flute-playing competition.'

'And who are the lovelies in the next one?' Zita was standing very close to him, her neck curving backwards as she stared up at the triptych of paintings.

'Those are the Muses crowning Apollo as victor. And d'you see poor old Marsyas watching from the reed-bed? He knows what's coming to him.' Oscar glanced sideways and saw that Max and Jerichau had stopped trading insults and were listening to him. 'His skin's going to be stripped from his muscle.'

'Oscar, for God's sake, that's enough blood,' Max said suddenly, putting an arm round Zita's shoulders.

'I'm fine, honestly.' Her smile was as sweet as ever, but Oscar caught the impatience in Zita's voice as she shrugged off his uncle's encircling hold. 'Go on, Oscar, I was enjoying it. What's your lookalike doing in the next one?'

Oscar smiled up at a glorious Apollo, all naked flesh and bulging brawn. 'He's nailing the satyr's flayed skin to a pine tree, though it looks more like a shaggy red rug from here. It's an allegory of hubris.'

'Amazing!' Zita took his arm and squeezed it. 'However did you know all that?'

'Just stories I picked up from Mum. She's an artist.'

'She has a valuable collection?' Jerichau was looking at him in sudden interest.

'Hands off, Isaiah,' Max interrupted. 'Clio's a talented painter, but not a commercial one, isn't that right, Oscar?'

'Exactly.' He nodded politely towards his host. 'Prince Jerichau's the one with value on his walls.'

'Indeed,' Jerichau inclined his head, 'but I must explain something to Zita.' He put a hand on the thin silk covering her shoulder. '*Cara.*'

'Yes, Isaiah?' Oscar waited for her to shift away from Jerichau's touch, but she let his hand stay where it was. He hoped Max didn't notice.

'Oscar is right to say I have value on my walls, but like every Italian family I also have a *tesoretto.*'

'A what? I thought my Italian was faultless.'

'And it is,' Max pushed closer to her, 'though I can't place your accent. Where did you learn to speak it?'

'Here and there,' Zita shrugged, casting off Prince Jerichau's hand as she did so. 'But I want to know what a *tesoretto* is.'

'A *tesoretto, carina,* is—'

'Nothing remotely exciting.' Max cut across their host before he could finish. 'It's just a bit of money kept squirrelled away from the Italian authorities.'

'Dearest Max.' Zita touched one of his lapels. 'Do you think you could find me some brandy? You know how it's the only thing that helps when my finger throbs.'

Instantly Max was all concern. 'Of course! Just wait here.'

A moment later he had vanished into the heaving heart of the party.

As he watched him going, Oscar's eye was caught by a particularly beautiful young man who reminded him of Yves, and he only half heard Prince Jerichau saying to Zita, 'Squirrellings indeed! As you are my very special guest, I'm going to show you what a *tesoretto* really is. Oscar, will you excuse us?'

'What? Yes, of course.'

When he looked again, the young man had vanished, so Oscar turned back to watch Jerichau and Zita. They had managed to move no more than a couple of feet away from him, and he heard quite clearly when Zita said, 'Tell me something, Isaiah. In the war, how did a Jewish family like yours keep their fortune safe from the Germans?'

It was an interesting question, and Oscar took a step after them to catch Jerichau's reply. 'We were helped, *carina*, by a good and brave man. You will be surprised when I tell you who it was.' Oscar tried to push closer to listen, but a waiter stopped just in front of him with a tray of cocktails. He grabbed the glass nearest to him, but by the time he could move again, Zita and their host had vanished.

The drink was bittersweet and delicious, so for want of anything else to do he caught up with the waiter and asked what it was. '*Come si chiama questo?*'

'*Negroni, signore.* Campari, gin, *vermut*, with peel of *arancia*.'

Oscar had downed two negronis and was gazing vaguely along the *salone da ballo* and when he heard his uncle's voice at his shoulder. 'This brandy was the devil to find. Where's Zita?'

'She slipped off somewhere with Isaiah, but I'm sure she'll be back in a minute.'

'That man thinks he's some sort of Casanova,' Max grumbled. 'Good heavens! Look over there!'

Following his uncle's gaze, Oscar saw a strange thing happening. The Genovan *bel mondo* were shrinking back from a quartet of black-clad minders who were clearing a path through the party. Coming along it was a short, square-shouldered man, with Zita on his arm.

'Whatever's she doing with Platon Dyengi?' Oscar heard his uncle say.

'Who?' He'd heard the name before, but couldn't place it.

'He's one of those astonishingly rich Russians,' Max said, his eyes still fixed on the approaching couple, 'though the word on the street is he's lost quite a bit of money recently.'

'Subprime mortgages?'

'Oh no.' Max gave a half-laugh. 'Dyengi's far too cunning to follow the Gadarene swine, it was something completely different. Apparently the UK Treasury cracked down hard on a hedge fund he was invested in, and I take my hat off to them. It's a brave person who gets on the wrong side of a thug like him.'

As the Russian came up to them, Oscar could see just what Max meant. Dyengi was a man to be feared. It might have been the expression in his black eyes, or some hidden menace in the way he carried himself, but he could see that Zita was afraid of him too. 'This is Max Quentance, Platon,' she said. 'He's a magician with gold. He can move it anywhere, and he'll wash it on the way, won't you, Max?'

How absurd. Oscar waited for his uncle to deny having anything to do with laundering, but instead, Max nodded. 'Yes,' he said, 'that's exactly right.'

Oscar grabbed another negroni from a passing waiter's tray. He was shocked by what he'd heard, and furious that Max had kept it from him. Platon Dyengi, on the other hand, seemed delighted. He laughed, showing a set of neatly crowned teeth, then said, 'Dirty gold disappear from one place, clean gold come in another place, *prikrasny*!'

'Yes it *is* beautiful, isn't it?'

'You speak Russian?' Dyengi stared at Max as if he was assessing him.

'Hardly at all. I only know *prikrasny* because it's what I say to all the girls.'

Since his uncle spoke excellent Russian, Oscar was surprised to hear this, but then he understood. Max must be lying about the language for a good reason, and the other thing would be untrue as well.

'Tell me how you do your magic,' Dyengi said in his heavily accented English, and Oscar leaned closer to make sure he heard the answer.

'Magicians have to have their secrets,' his uncle smiled, 'but you can be sure my methods are foolproof. I've been cleaning up my clients' gold for decades and I've never had a single problem.'

So Max wasn't pretending. Oscar felt a complete fool. He'd trusted his uncle, hero-worshipped him almost, and in return Max had lied to him. Suddenly Oscar felt he couldn't be close to him for another moment, and would have stormed off if he hadn't felt Zita's hand taking hold of his arm. In the crush, he couldn't see whether it was the damaged one and didn't dare pull away in case he hurt her.

He heard Dyengi asking, 'So if I have gold to be moved, what do we do?'

'Well, let me see.' Max rubbed his chin as if he was thinking deeply. 'You have a yacht?'

'*Da.* Moored in Antibes.'

'Well then, that's very convenient because my boat's down in Marseilles.' Max grinned at Dyengi as if he'd suddenly come up with an idea. 'So if your gold were to be on your yacht and if it happened to pass close to *Cilissa* somewhere out at sea, then life would be very easy.'

There was no answering smile from the Russian. 'We do it immediately. My assistant will contact you.' Without another word, Dyengi spun round, and with his minders again clearing the way, he vanished back into the party.

As the crowd closed behind him, Zita regained her voice. 'Oh God! I'd no idea Platon would want to move so fast. I wish I hadn't brought you here to meet him.' Her eyes flicked from Max's face to Oscar's and back again. 'You will take care, both of you?'

'I don't think I'm involved, am I?' Oscar looked accusingly at his uncle. 'Capital flight's one thing, but cleaning drug money's something entirely different.'

'Oh, do grow up,' Max said crossly. 'The money's not necessarily criminal. Quite often, it's just an innocent variant on tax evasion.'

'And that's a good thing, is it?'

'How many cocktails have you had, Oscar?' Zita put in gently. 'You know it's only the little people who pay tax.'

'And that's unfair!' He was feeling quite belligerent now.

'That's as maybe, sweetheart,' he felt Zita's hand on his arm, urging him towards the door, 'but it's why they're little.'

Three hours later Oscar woke up. His parched mouth and pounding head proved that Zita had been right about one thing at least. He'd had far too many negronis. A mug of tap water and a couple of aspirins made things marginally better but, try as he might, he couldn't get back to sleep. When he moved he felt dizzy, and when he sat up he felt sick. Worst of all, he had the feeling that he'd come to a decision point in his life, but in his muddled state it was hard to pin down.

An image of Dyengi's cold eyes floated into his head. The Russian had probably been brought up in some Siberian shit-hole where the only moral compass was the one that pointed to survival, and that was the code he'd stick to. Max, on the other hand, didn't seem to have a moral code at all, and Oscar had an inkling that the thing he'd admired most about his uncle was just that lack of scruple. Max loved having money, he spent it freely, and he didn't seem to care how he got hold of it. But Oscar didn't have either excuse. Clio had taught him right from wrong, and what Max did was definitely wrong. He should hand in his resignation tomorrow.

He pushed himself upright to get some more water, feeling his stomach churn as he switched on the bedside light. Sinking back against the pillows after a long drink, he stared weakly round his bedroom. Brocade curtains, tapestry wall-hangings, *Belle Époque* comfort, it had everything you'd expect in Genoa's most expensive hotel, and yet he'd already got so used to luxury that he'd hardly noticed.

Oscar thumped his pile of pillows and turned off the light, but he couldn't switch his brain off. Maybe he was being naïve in assuming that bankers should constrain themselves with ethics? After all, he could always give his bonus to charity if he felt like it. Thinking he'd come to a decision, Oscar lay back and closed his eyes, but in the thick silence of the hotel bedroom, guilt buzzed round his brain like a troublesome wasp. After nearly an hour of tossing and turning, he switched the light on again and reached for his mobile. Although she'd be fast asleep by now, he might feel better if he was in contact with his twin.

Thumbs poised above the buttons, Oscar toyed with the idea of telling her what their uncle got up to, but decided he needed to give it more thought first. He'd keep the message crisp and short.

Ravishing palazzo, he typed. Max has new oligarch client.

Having pressed the Send button he waited, just in case Edie was still awake wherever she was, but his phone stayed silent. With a sigh, Oscar switched off the light and flung himself back against the pillows. He'd have to try counting sheep.

TWENTY

Max has new oligarch client. Edie scrolled back to re-read Oscar's message before tucking her mobile into the netting above her head. Hands linked behind her neck, she lay back in her narrow bunk and worried. She'd read about those oligarchs, and not much of it had been nice. Supposing it was some Moscow mafia hood who'd end up dragging Quentance Bank's name into the mud and taking her own reputation with it?

The *put-put-put* of a marine engine drifted through the open porthole, and when the boat passed by, its wash set *Cassandra* rocking. The eerie quacking of disturbed mallard floated across the water, followed by the splash of paddling feet and the clap of wings as they took off into the night. Calmed by these familiar river sounds, Edie thought again about Oscar's message.

Rather than a threat, it might be very good news. A single Russian billionaire could deposit enough to balance all the outflows from nervous investors in her father's Adamantine Fund, and then she wouldn't need to think about tracking down Teddy's shares and selling the bank.

And that meant John's trip out to *Cassandra* would be a waste of time. Her eyes flew open at the thought. Oligarch or no oligarch, she was going to have to ask John about finding Teddy. It would be dreadful to have lured him out on the pretence that she needed help and then to say there was no problem after all.

Shivering, Edie pulled the duvet up around her ears. Although the night was cold, she couldn't bear to close the porthole and shut herself in with the stuffy boat smells of old wood and brass polish. Instead she lay breathing in the scents of salt and weed that rose off the river while she tried not to get agitated about the morning. She hadn't seen him since that Sunday in Dartmouth. It had started so well, but in the end he'd just wanted to know about her family's business. Supposing it was the same this time?

'I'm being a drip!' Edie said to the empty boat. 'He wouldn't have agreed to come if he didn't like me.'

Flicking the overhead light on, she hopped down on to the floor and went over to the mirror on the far side of the cabin. It was different when she was being compared to Oscar, but on her own she wasn't at all bad-looking. She fingered her dark hair thoughtfully. She'd had it in those aggressive spikes for so long, she'd almost forgotten it wasn't straight, and it looked a lot softer since she'd let it grow. In fact it was almost pretty, with those feathery little waves curling round her jawbone. She gave herself a wide smile then shut her mouth again. Maybe that gap between her front teeth wasn't such a good look. She'd have to practise smiling with her lips closed.

Edie glanced at the clothes hanging from the front of

the built-in wardrobe. Instead of her standard boat uniform of baggy shorts with a fleece, she was going to wear tight white jeans, black trainers and a close-fitting jumper. She'd bought yet another new bra and matching pants – not, she told herself hurriedly, that she was expecting anyone to want to see them.

She woke to a perfect morning. It was very cold, but as Edie poked her head out of the cabin porthole she caught her breath at the beauty of the low autumn sun, sparkling the river into bright shards. A single-masted sloop passed by on its way down to the sea, its outboard chugging quietly until it could catch enough wind to fill its mainsail. Looking over towards the Dartmouth steps, she saw that there were already people moving about, climbing in and out of dinghies, and there was the water taxi puttering its way towards the marina. The water taxi? If it was already working, it must be far later than she thought. Pulling her head back inside, she slammed the porthole shut and jumped down off the bunk.

Twenty minutes later she was washed, dressed and out on deck, sipping a mug of strong tea while trying to work out when John Tamar might arrive. He'd have to drive over from Brink Castle and find somewhere to park in Dartmouth's crowded streets. And since she'd had to moor *Cassandra* midstream, he'd need to phone for the water taxi and then he'd probably have a chilly wait down on the pontoon until it came to pick him up. A cheerful round of church bells echoed over the Dart and reminded her that it was a Sunday. He'd go to Mass first. It was far too early to expect him.

Collecting up her mug, Edie slid down the companionway and into the comfortable saloon-cum-galley that Max had created. At least she could get the coffee ready for when he arrived. Clean mugs, spoons and milk were all to hand; there was even a packet of biscuits she'd bought the previous afternoon, but she couldn't find the sugar anywhere. She glanced out of the galley porthole in search of inspiration and saw him immediately. John was standing on the pontoon and squinting against the low sunshine, his height making him unmissable. As she stared, she saw the water taxi pulling in alongside him. He'd be with her in minutes.

Edie checked her face in the galley mirror. 'Don't look over-eager,' she told her reflection, but then she caught the rumble of an engine and hurried back on deck as the little taxi chugged alongside.

'Here we are then,' the boatman's voice floated up to her. 'The butter-coloured boat.'

He was there, and as he climbed the little wooden ladder the sun caught his face, lighting up his eyes. 'What a beautiful boat,' John said, stepping through the guard-rail gate and on to *Cassandra*'s deck. 'I love all this wood.'

Seeing his smile, Edie relaxed. 'I was on my knees all day yesterday.' She couldn't help looking proudly along the curving lines of *Cassandra*'s deck, glad she'd spent so much time scouring it to that uniform dove-grey colour.

'Praying?'

'Scrubbing.' She glanced back into his face, but he'd moved slightly and now the sun was behind his head, blinding her so she couldn't see his expression. 'Thanks very much for coming. I hope you didn't think it was an imposition, me asking?'

'Of course I came, Edie.'

Just then, a disembodied voice called from the water taxi. 'Shall I collect you later?'

Edie had a sudden, mad idea that he might say he was staying, but he called back, 'Yes please, I'll phone when I'm ready.'

The little boat puttered away, leaving a faint smell of diesel hanging in the crisp air. Alone with him in the middle of the river, Edie felt suddenly at a loss. She couldn't dive straight into the unwholesome story of Teddy Quentance, but like an idiot, she couldn't think of anything else to say. Apparently perfectly relaxed, John stood quietly, one long hand resting on the guard-rail while he waited for her to speak.

'Shall I show you over *Cassandra*?'

'I'd like that.' He gave her a lazy grin, and she was rather comforted to see that one of his front teeth was crooked, something she hadn't noticed before. Maybe he'd also been a stroppy teenager and had refused to see an orthodontist?

Her self-possession recovered as she saw how cautiously he moved past the sail lockers, grabbing every available hand-hold even though the boat was quite still. 'You're not really a sailor, are you?'

'Certainly not, I hate being on water! I like to feel good solid land under my feet.' As she passed ahead of him towards the wheelhouse, Edie smiled. Even though he didn't like boats, he'd come out on the river when she'd asked.

'Well this is a lot more civilised than I'd expected,' John

said as he followed her inside. 'Can I try the driving seat?' Without waiting for an answer, he stepped across to the helm and perched himself there, idly stroking the smooth wood of the wheel. But while he seemed relaxed, something in the stillness of his position made Edie think that he was taking everything in.

Pleased by his interest, she pointed out the old-fashioned chart table and *Cassandra*'s original ship's bell, both of which had survived with the boat ever since she'd been built. Edie moved closer to show him the rolling brass compass set into the surface just beside the helm. 'This should be a collector's piece, but we still use it. Max always wanted to keep *Cassandra* original so he refused to put in any modern instruments.'

'Does your uncle manage the boat alone, or does it need two of you to go out to sea?'

'Oh no, I can manage perfectly well on my own.'

He swung round on the stool and stared at her. 'That sounds risky. I hope you've got a life-raft.'

'Of course I have. It's in that box hanging from the stern guard-rails.'

He got up and peered over to where she was pointing. 'That white thing? It looks like a suitcase.'

'The life-raft's inside. You just chuck it into the sea and it inflates automatically. The only thing you have to remember is to cut the rope attaching the raft to the guard-rails. If you didn't, you'd get pulled under when your boat sank.'

'And suppose you don't have a knife?'

She moved the few steps away from him to unhook a sturdy leather satchel from its place on the wall above the chart table. 'I keep everything I might need in this grab-bag,' she said, tipping out its contents.

As he came to look, she was distracted by his closeness, but he only seemed interested in fingering the things spread over the table. 'Fishing line and hook. Very sensible if you like raw fish. And here's the knife.' He tested the blade against his thumb. 'I suppose these are sick bags? And what's this?' He held up a mirror and turned to her, grinning. 'I've misread you entirely, Edie. I'd no idea you were so vain.'

His eyes were teasing, one eyebrow raised, and Edie felt herself blushing like an idiot. 'It's a signalling mirror.' She stuffed everything back into her grab-bag then stepped away from him to hang it in its normal place. 'Shall I show you over the rest of the boat?'

'Please do.'

He was still smiling as they went down the few steps of the wooden companionway, but as they emerged into *Cassandra*'s forward quarters Edie had the odd feeling that he was withdrawing into himself. 'Did your uncle put in a lot of storage space?'

She'd no idea why he was asking, but the answer was straightforward. 'Of course he did. In a boat this size you use every inch from the hull upwards.' Pulling a long cushion off one of the bench seats, she lifted a lid to show the compartment below, stuffed with spare pillows and towels. 'See what I mean?' she said, before hopping over to the old mahogany cabinet built into a corner of the saloon. Bending down, she touched the concealed handle and felt the drawer behind it sliding out smoothly. 'Clever, isn't it? I keep my passport and foreign currency in here.'

She'd expected some sort of reaction to this beautiful piece of carpentry, but when she turned round she caught him watching her, a frown creasing his forehead. Having no idea what was wrong, Edie said brightly, 'Shall I show you the other cabin? We'll have to go through the engine room.'

She went ahead of him down the few steps and into the narrow space that ran past *Cassandra*'s fuel tank and engine, with its familiar smells of diesel and motor oil. 'Careful you don't trip on one of the struts,' she called over her shoulder, 'we're walking right on *Cassandra*'s skin here. The rest of the boat's got floorboards laid over bilges, but the engine sits on the hull so it can take water direct from the sea to cool it down.'

'You mean seawater comes right into the boat? Aren't you afraid of leaks?'

'Oh, it's quite safe.' Edie led him up the few steps from the engine room into the sleeping-quarters in *Cassandra*'s stern. 'There are sea-cocks to keep the water out. I can show you one if you like. Look.' She crouched down to point out the sea-cock just inside her cabin door. It was never used now, having served the old-fashioned heads before Max had a more practical bathroom installed down in the stern, but at least she could show him how it worked.

Edie turned the tap on and off, but John showed no interest in it at all. Instead, he asked, 'Do you see much of your uncle?'

'Max? Not a lot, he's based in Paris. Much loved by me since he gave me *Cassandra*.'

The flicker of a grin lifted the corners of his mouth. 'This boat's yours? I didn't realise.' The nascent smile vanished as he went on, 'But presumably you help your uncle out on his sea trips?'

'I certainly don't.' She was beginning to get annoyed by these questions and mood changes. 'I wouldn't be seen dead on a ghastly gin palace like *Cilissa*, and I can't think when Max and I were last out on *Cassandra* together. Why do you ask, anyway?'

'No reason.'

Now he'd made her irritable, he was suddenly smiling. 'Do you think I'd fit into a bunk like this?' He took a step closer. 'Edie,' he murmured, bending towards her, but it was as far as he got. There was a roar of a powerful engine, and *Cassandra* began to rock violently in the wash of some big boat, speeding downriver. Trying to regain his balance, John stood upright too fast and crashed his head against the cabin's low ceiling.

For a moment, Edie was afraid he might be concussed. Eyes closed, he swayed like a reed while she stared at him, trying to think what she ought to do. Eventually, his eyes opened and he reached a tentative hand up to feel the top of his head. '*Now* I know why I don't like boats. They're made for midgets.'

Hearing him speak normally, Edie breathed a sigh of relief. 'Come on,' she said urgently, 'let's go outside where there's no ceiling.' Without waiting for an answer, she led him back through the boat and up to *Cassandra*'s stern deck, where she made him sit on one of the sail lockers. She left him rubbing his head while she slipped down to the galley to make two mugs of strong coffee.

When she came out on deck again, Edie was relieved to

find him standing by the rails and gazing out over the river. John turned to her and smiled. 'I was thinking how lovely Dartmouth looks from out here. If it wasn't for the death-traps down below, I think I'd quite like this boat.' He moved over to take one of the coffee mugs from her. 'Maybe you'd take me on a nice gentle trip upriver to Dartleap one day? I scarcely know your family.'

Family. The word made her start, though John didn't seem to notice. His odd-coloured eyes were gentle. Any minute now, he'd put down that coffee and kiss her. Maybe he'd risk *Cassandra*'s low ceilings again. And afterwards, would she tell him about Teddy? Supposing he was disgusted?

With a shiver of horror at the thought, Edie sat down. 'There's something I must ask you. The reason I rang to see if you'd meet me here. I wouldn't want you to think ...' Edie looked up, realising she was sounding ridiculous. 'I'm not making much sense, am I?'

'Not a lot.' He crossed the deck to sit beside her. 'But I'm in no hurry. Why don't you start again?'

Edie took a gulp of coffee. One of his long legs was pressing against hers, making it hard to concentrate. 'It's compli-cated, very complicated.' She took a deep breath. Better get on with it. 'I need to track down a long-lost relative and I thought you might be able to help. Or maybe your cousin Mary would know how to find him.'

'Who is he?' She glanced up, but John was staring out across the river. Then he turned his head and she saw that his eyes were bright and intent. 'Go on. Who is he?'

Edie closed her eyes. It would be easier if she wasn't distracted by looking to see how he was taking her story.

'My grandfather Richard was married to Eve, my grand-mother, obviously. All the pictures of her were thrown away, but Dad remembers her as being very beautiful, even though she had dark hair.' Edie couldn't help adding wryly, 'It must be where I get mine from. Every other Quentance is blond as a buttercup, lucky beggars.'

She opened her eyes and found him smiling at her. 'I'm glad you're not blonde, Edie,' he said. 'So, about Richard and Eve?'

'My grandfather had a younger brother. Teddy was hand-some as sin and could charm the birds off the trees, and one day he ran away with Eve. I'm sorry, it's not a very salu-brious story.'

'Don't worry.'

He certainly didn't sound shocked, so Edie went on, 'My great-grandfather Kit was horrified. He disinherited Teddy, but he couldn't take back what his younger son had already been given. Teddy's got twenty shares in Quentance Bank,' she finished. 'That's why I want to find him.'

'And how do you know he's still alive?'

'I don't, though he'd be in his mid-seventies now. But even if Teddy's dead, the shares must have gone somewhere.'

Beside her, John nodded thoughtfully. 'And who are the other shareholders?'

Edie could see no reason why she shouldn't tell him. 'Dad, Max, Oscar and I each have thirty shares. So if Oscar and I ever wanted to, we could force a sale of the bank, just as long as we had Teddy's shares to give us a majority.'

'Is it Oscar who wants to sell up? He's working for your uncle now, isn't he?'

Edie couldn't remember telling him that, but when she looked at him, something in his expression persuaded her to confide in him. 'I know Oscar's anxious,' she said slowly, 'though it's not about the bank.'

'About what, then?'

'He's gay.' She stared out across the cold waters of the river. 'I think he dreads telling our parents.'

In the silence that followed, she realised she'd put another nail into the coffin of her family's reputation. 'I shouldn't have told you. You Catholics think homosexuality's a sin, don't you?'

He startled her by giving a great shout of laughter. 'Well I certainly don't. Christ never said a thing against gays, and if He didn't mind, I don't see why anyone else should.' He took her hand, his thumb stroking her palm as if he was soothing a nervous animal. 'But now you've started, you might as well finish. You *are* anxious about your family's bank, aren't you?'

Edie was glad of his patience. It was impossible to explain her anxiety without making her father sound either crooked or incompetent. 'It's my innate sense of caution, I suppose,' she said eventually. 'I'd feel safer knowing where all the shares are, just in case.'

'Just in case what, Edie?'

'Oh, nothing really.' She kept her voice nonchalant. 'I suppose every banker's worried about panicky investors pulling their funds out. And besides,' she added, remembering Oscar's text message, 'Max just picked up a grossly rich Russian client, so I guess we'll be fine.'

His hand tightened around hers as he said, 'This Russian, what's his name?'

'I don't know.'

Abruptly, John dropped her hand and stood up. 'If you think I'm going to believe you haven't grasped what's going on, you must take me for a fool.'

Edie stared at him in surprise. 'I've no idea what you're talking about.'

'Do I really have to spell it out? Your uncle Max is a highly efficient money launderer.'

'You must be mad! I'd know if he was.'

'Be quiet and listen.' He sat down again, but this time he didn't take her hand. 'I've heard about this new client from other sources, and I hope your uncle knows what he's getting himself into. He's messing in the big league now. You should warn that twin of yours as well.'

'What do you mean? What about Oscar?'

'He's in it too, isn't he?'

'In what? Oscar wouldn't dream of doing anything crooked.'

John got up and went to lean on *Cassandra*'s guard-rail. She wondered if he'd chosen that particular place on purpose because it was just where the sun was directly behind him, dazzling Edie so she couldn't even look at him.

'Why can't you be honest? Just tell me who Max shifts money for and I'll do the rest.'

'I can't see why it's any of your business.' She tried to hide how upset she was. 'If there's anything to know, I'll find it out myself.'

'I really wouldn't advise that. Leave it to the professionals.'

Edie could feel a tear rolling down her cheek and turned away from him. She'd be damned if she let him see her cry.

In the silence that fell between them, the noises from the river seemed disproportionately loud. When eventually he spoke again, John's words were politely formal. 'Thanks for the coffee, Edie, and I'll see what I can do about tracking down your missing relation. I'd better get going now.'

'Fine.' Edie kept her head down as she collected their coffee mugs and took them down to the galley.

While she waited for the hot water to run, she stared at her face in the little mirror above the sink. Her lipstick was smudged and her hair was all over the place, but she no longer cared. How *dare* he accuse Max like that?

John's voice floated down the companionway. 'Is that the water taxi? Can you collect me from *Cassandra*? . . . Yes, the butter-coloured boat . . . As soon as possible, please.'

After the call was over, she heard him moving about in the wheelhouse. Edie thought she heard the scrape of her grab-bag against the wall and then the shuffle of maps on the chart table, but she wasn't going to go up and check. If he wanted to see her, he'd have to come down and find her. No way was she going to make the first move.

Edie washed the mugs, and had just started drying them when she heard the thump of fenders against *Cassandra*'s side. The situation suddenly felt ridiculous. Here was the water taxi, and they hadn't even said goodbye. Dropping her cloth, Edie was hurrying across the saloon when she heard her phone tweet from the galley. She was tempted to ignore it, but couldn't quite bring herself to do so in case the message was urgent. Nipping back to the shelf where she'd left it, she slid her mobile open and read **143**. For three thudding beats of her heart, Edie stared at the little screen. 143 was their private emergency code. One letter, four letters, three letters: I Need You. It must be that Russian oligarch. Her twin was in danger. Feverishly, she punched out Oscar's number, but the call diverted straight to answerphone. She'd have to go to Paris.

As she stood in the galley trying to work out how quickly she could get there, Edie caught the cough of the water taxi's motor as it accelerated away. Dropping her mobile, she rushed up to the wheelhouse, but by the time she got on deck, all she could see was the back of John's head as the taxi puttered off towards the shore.

Her legs felt like lead as she stumbled down to her cabin. Like an automaton she stuffed what she'd need into an overnight bag and went back up to the wheelhouse. Edie paused at the door. That 143 message meant that Oscar needed her urgently, so there was no time to take the boat's key all the way back to Dartleap. After a moment's thought, she decided to leave it under the lip of the foc'sle hatch. Her uncle always used to put it there when *Cassandra* was moored up at Dartleap, and surely it'd be perfectly safe. Only Max and the few people who'd stayed with him on the boat would know where it was hidden.

TWENTY-ONE

The departures board still showed WAIT AT GATE, and when Edie checked her mobile, her most recent message winked back, unanswered like all the others. **Flying from Bristol, landing CDG 7.50 p.m. How are you? PLEASE text me.**

Something dreadful must have happened, though at least worrying about Oscar took her mind off that miserable parting from John Tamar. She glanced round at the other waiting passengers, but everywhere she looked there were happy couples. It was over before it had started, and he'd never even kissed her.

She jumped when her phone bleeped. Sliding it open, she felt a rush of relief. **Miserable. Need you.** At least he was alive. There was a cough from the airport loudspeakers. 'Calling all passengers for Air France flight number 1673 to Paris Charles de Gaulle. Will all passengers please make their way to gate number seven, where their flight is now ready for boarding.' Hoisting her overnight bag on to one shoulder, Edie leapt up to join the queue that was already milling round the gate.

*

As the plane shuddered its way up into the night sky, Edie found her brain running a hamster-like circuit between Oscar and John, but by the time the flight levelled off she'd decided that a bit of work on *Titanic* would be more productive. Feeling under the seat for her bag, she pulled out a notebook, pencil and copies of the ice warnings that had been received during the course of the ship's final day. After adjusting the light above her seat, she settled down to a serious attempt at drawing conclusions.

The first message had come from SS *Caronia* at about midday. She was a Cunarder travelling from New York to Europe and had sent out an alert to all ships within range. WESTBOUND STEAMERS REPORT BERGS, GROWLERS AND FIELD ICE IN 42 DEGREES N FROM 49 TO 51 W. The ice was in precisely the area of sea where *Titanic* was headed, and as was normal, SS *Caronia*'s warning was immediately posted on the bridge so that the officer of the watch was aware of the potential danger ahead. Mysteriously, the next telegram to come through was not.

SS *Baltic*'s alert was handed to Captain Smith at lunchtime. It read, HAVE HAD MODERATE, VARIABLE WINDS AND CLEAR, FINE WEATHER SINCE LEAVING. GREEK STEAMER *ATHINAI* REPORTS PASSING ICEBERGS AND LARGE QUANTITY OF FIELD ICE TODAY IN LATITUDE 41.51'N, LONGITUDE 49.52'W. As with *Caronia*, this ice warning related to the exact direction in which *Titanic* was heading, and given this fact, Captain Smith's subsequent action was incomprehensible. Instead of having *Baltic*'s message sent straight to the bridge, Smith gave it to Bruce Ismay, who put it into his pocket and didn't give it back for several hours. In his evidence, Ismay claimed that Captain Smith had simply handed him the message then gone away. Edie stared down at her copy of the signal. It seemed unbelievable, but then Smith hadn't survived to give his own side of the story.

By the early evening, when *Baltic*'s telegram finally made it to the bridge, other ice warnings were arriving. A message from SS *Amerika* came through with a terse AMERIKA PASSED TWO LARGE ICEBERGS IN 41.27N, 50.8W ON THE 14TH OF APRIL, followed shortly afterwards by SS *Californian* with LATITUDE 42.3N, LONGITUDE 49.9W. THREE LARGE BERGS FIVE MILES TO SOUTHWARD OF US. And then there was the signal from SS *Mesaba*. ICE REPORT IN LAT 42 TO 41.25'N. LONG 49 TO 50.30'W. SAW MUCH HEAVY PACK ICE AND GREAT NUMBER LARGE ICEBERGS. ALSO FIELD ICE. That one arrived less than two hours before the disaster, and never got further than *Titanic*'s wireless room.

Edie gazed out of the plane window, catching the flash of the wing lights against the dark sky. As a hypothesis formed in her head, she bent over her notebook. *Three key errors*, she wrote. *1) Hubris: Despite warnings, there was no reduction of speed because they were so confident they'd see any ice in time to avoid it.* She paused to search for a good word to describe what Ismay had done. Rapacity? Avarice? After a moment, it came to her. *2) Cupidity: Ismay pocketed Baltic message because if it was seen on bridge, order might be given to abandon speed trial and hence affect value of White Star Line's investment.* The third one was the easiest. *3) Blunder: Wireless operator put Mesaba's warning under a paperweight and forgot it.*

Pride, greed and a cock-up. It was such a common

combination of human failings, and quite as applicable to a banking collapse in 2008 as it was to a tragedy at sea nearly a century before. She was about to jot this down when she was interrupted by an air hostess at her shoulder. 'Can I get you anything to drink?'

'Yes please.' She never normally drank spirits, but it had been a trying day and she still had Oscar's troubles ahead of her. 'Can I have a large gin and tonic?'

'This Beaujolais is fine, Eds,' Oscar said as she filled his glass. 'I don't really care what we have as long as there's a lot of it.'

'Ditto,' Edie said, pouring some of the wine for herself. 'I was so worried about you, I've been knocking back gin on the flight over.'

The bistro Oscar had chosen was of the dark-curtained, candle-lit sort, but even so she could see that he'd been crying. 'You're an angel to have come. Is everything OK with you?'

Edie thought of John Tamar, his sharp questions and their frosty parting. Everything wasn't at all OK with her, but despite this she nodded. 'I'm fine, just worried about you. Why the one-four-three?'

'I got this e-mail.' Without looking at her, he pushed the latest piece of mobile technology across the table.

'These things cost a fortune!' Edie was momentarily distracted. 'However much is Max paying you?'

'Just belt up and look at it, can't you?'

Edie touched the screen and began to read.

To: Yves de la Châtaigne
From: Daniel@cock.com
Subject: Bugger off

Basically I didn't call you because it's over. I've no idea what you see in
Oscar Quentance, but if you want him, you can keep your hands off my
pepper pot. I'm a one-man boy.

Puzzled, she shook her head when she got to the end.
'So Yves has broken up with his ex. What's the problem?'
'Scroll on and you'll see.'
An artificial cough didn't quite disguise the wobble in
his voice, and Edie put her hand over his while she read
the next message.

To: Oscar Quentance
From: Daniel@cock.com
Subject: Fw: Bugger off

To: Daniel@cock.com
From: Yves de la Châtaigne
Subject: Bugger off

Of course I won't bugger off. Oscar means less than nothing to me. Or
at least, I like his money, but I love your poivrière.

Edie's hand tightened on Oscar's. 'What a bitch! He must
have forwarded it to you on purpose.'
'He did. Look at the next one.'
She stroked the oblong screen until the final e-mail in
the chain appeared.

To: Oscar Quentance

From: Daniel@cock.com

Subject: Fw: Bugger off

Sorry, big boy. Fat-thumbed this to you by mistake. Oops!

Edie couldn't decide which of Yves and Daniel she hated more. 'What a vile little shit. That was no mistake.'

'Whatever, it's over.' Oscar was trying to smile. 'Though it's a bit much Daniel calling me "big boy". His arse is so vast, you could see it from outer space.'

'Whereas you're getting way too thin,' said Edie, letting go of his hand to reach for the menu. 'Comfort food's what you need.'

'*Vous avez choisi?*' A waitress ambled over to their table.

'Yes, we have.' Edie assumed the girl would understand English. 'Another bottle of Beaujolais and a plate of charcuterie to start with, please, and then we'll both have steak tartare with salad, mayonnaise and a mountain of chips.'

She turned from giving their order to find her brother staring at her.

'Tell me what to do, Eds. I'm heartbroken.'

'Don't be.' Edie searched for the right words to cheer him up. 'You're beautiful, you've got a stunning voice and everyone loves you.'

'Yves doesn't.'

'Well then he's a fool, and you should try to forget about him. And vast-arsed Daniel as well,' she added, getting a flicker of a smile in return.

'*Une charcuterie, un vin. Voilà.*' An oval plate piled with smoked ham, pâté, *saucisson*, butter, cornichons and olives was plonked down on their table, together with an opened bottle of wine and a basket of *pain de campagne.*

'Shall I tell you what I think?' Edie asked. Her brother nodded as he spiked a couple of olives and a slice of ham on his fork and started to eat. 'It's time you came out.'

Oscar swallowed his mouthful in one gulp and shook his head. 'Dad.'

Her twin was right, of course. Alec's reaction would be pitiless, particularly given his hunger for a grandson to continue the Quentance line. 'You should get Mum on side first,' she said firmly. 'She can handle Dad. I'll come with you if you like.'

There was a long silence. Edie picked at the pâté with the point of her knife while she watched Oscar down a glass of Beaujolais and pour himself another. Eventually, he looked across at her with one of his brave smiles. 'You're right, Eds, we'll go to Bath and see Mum.'

'Good, and don't worry, she'll be fine. She adores you, you know that.' As she said the words, Edie was surprised not to feel a twinge of jealousy over Clio's preference for her brother. Maybe she'd finally learned not to mind.

She was so taken by this idea that it was a few moments before she realised that Oscar was talking. 'The thing is, Eds,' she heard him saying, 'we always think about Mum and how she feels, don't we? But have you noticed how we only ever discuss Dad as if he's a machine, not a real person at all?'

'His charm's real enough. He gets perfectly sane people to pour their entire fortunes into his Adamantine Fund.'

'That's true,' Oscar conceded, 'but it's just a façade to get everyone to do what he wants. Most of the time he doesn't *look* real, either. Even at weekends, he's in perfectly ironed shirts with cufflinks.'

'He does twist them when he's agitated, that's human.'

'It's often the only sign he's alive.'

'*C'est terminé?*'

'*Oui. Merci.*'

Ignoring the clatter made by the waitress as she cleared the *charcuterie* away, Oscar went on, 'The point is, I've no idea what Dad really feels or why he feels it, and I think that's unusual.'

Edie waited until the waitress had gone before she replied. 'Unusual's a good word for the bank as a whole, don't you think?' Although there was plenty of noise around them and no one seemed to be listening, she leaned across the table and went on quietly, 'I mean, I've no idea what really goes on in London because I'm kept shut away in the basement. For instance, I've never even seen the people who work on the top floor because Dad's so obsessive about keeping his investment strategies a secret.' Bending even closer towards her twin, she asked, 'Did you ever go up to Investments?'

Oscar shook his head. 'Never even tried.'

'So didn't you ever think—' Before Edie could go any further, the waitress was at her elbow with their steak tartare and it was a while before she could get back to the family bank. Once they were alone again, Edie said, 'The truth is, Oscar, I can't think of any bit of our London business I'm *not* worried about.'

'And there's something else, isn't there?'

Edie almost smiled at how well her twin could read her. As she paused to drink her wine, John Tamar's words rang in her head. *Your uncle's messing in the big league now. You should warn that twin of yours.* She put her empty glass down hard on the table. 'This new Russian client of Max's, who is he? I think he might hurt you if things went wrong.'

'He certainly looks rough. He's called Dyengi, Platon Dyengi. He's rich as Croesus and Max is going to shift some of his money for him.' Her twin's eyes flicked away, and when they turned back to her she read something like shame in them. 'Actually, there's more to it than that. I should have told you straight away.'

'Told me what?'

'Max and Dyengi were talking at that party I went to in Genoa.' It was Oscar's turn to lean over the table and lower his voice. 'I was right beside them when Max admitted it quite openly. No, he was almost boasting about it.'

'About what?' Edie whispered, her throat dry.

'Our uncle specialises in cleaning dirty money, gold in particular. Apparently he's been doing it for years.'

Not Max. She couldn't believe it. Oscar had to be wrong. But even as she was thinking this, she remembered the library at Dartleap, a solid gold bar, Max's uncharacteristic anger when she'd found it. This must be why John had turned so cold. She'd denied that Quentance Bank had any involvement in money-laundering and he'd thought she was lying.

'We can't just talk about this,' she said abruptly. 'We've got to stop it. And you can start by giving me the details of all Max's clients. You told me you write them down.'

'I'd lose my job. I daren't.'

'You must! You've got the list on you, haven't you?'

It was a lucky guess. Oscar reached in his pocket and brought out a small, leather-bound notebook which he put on the table beside him. 'What would you do with it?'

'Max uses Guernsey, doesn't he? I'll take it over there and see what I can find out.'

Edie saw her twin brightening. 'I suppose that's not such a daft idea,' he said. 'I've heard the Guernsey authorities are shit-hot, so they'd be bound to help if you went to them with evidence. But you've got to understand one thing, Eds. It'd be the end of Max's business. What he does is all based on secrecy and trust, and the moment those are gone, his clients will vanish.'

'Surely Max's clients can't all be crooks? There are families who've been with our bank for generations.'

'Like the Jerichaus.'

And the Earls of Ivybridge. 'We'll only know how much clean business the bank's got once we've cleared out the dirty stuff. That's why I must go to Guernsey and find out what's straight and what isn't.'

'*Vous voulez quelque chose?*' The waitress was there again, clearing away the half-eaten detritus on the table.

Edie just wanted a mint tea, but Oscar said, 'I'll have a double espresso and a *crème brulée*. It doesn't matter if I get grossly fat now.'

'You're hardly going to get fat on one *crème brulée*,' Edie said briskly, determined not to be sidetracked. 'So that notebook. Are you going to let me have it?'

'Promise you won't show the names to a soul apart from the authorities on Guernsey?'

Edie hesitated. She longed to show the lists to John, because doing so might just possibly persuade him that he could trust her after all.

'Promise me,' Oscar repeated urgently. 'I can't afford to get the sack.'

'I promise.'

'Here you are then, and for God's sake look after it.' Oscar pushed the notebook across, and Edie slipped it into her pocket.

'*Un thé menthe, un café, une crème brulée.*'

After the waitress had gone, Edie smiled across at her brother. 'Thanks. It's nice to know someone trusts me.'

'Of course I trust you.' Oscar looked surprised. 'But listen, I was a bit pissed when Max was with Dyengi, and I haven't had a chance to talk to him since. Before you go haring off to Guernsey, don't you think we should give him a chance to clean up his own act?'

'I suppose that would be fair.' Edie shrugged. 'I'll ring Max and find out if we can see him tomorrow.' She looked across at her twin and smiled. 'Our uncle can come clean and you can come out.'

At eight the next morning, Edie and Oscar were walking down the rain-soaked pavements of rue de Varenne, occasionally leaping to avoid being splashed by the cars of Monday commuters. It was bitterly cold, and neither of them spoke until they turned through a carriageway between a pair of eighteenth-century houses.

'Don't you love these secret bits of Paris?' Oscar asked as they hurried across the courtyard to Max's house.

'No. I hate secrets.' Edie went up the grey marble steps to their uncle's front door and pressed the bell. Rain dripped from an ornamental balcony above their heads and they had to huddle for shelter under the wooden carvings of fruit and flowers that swagged the door's architrave.

Fortunately it wasn't long before they heard Max calling, '*J'arrive!*', followed by footsteps thudding on a wooden floor and the sound of a bolt being shot back. 'Twins! Come on through.' He led the way to the cosy kitchen-cum-dining-room at the back of the villa, saying over his shoulder, 'I'm glad you got here early, I've a busy day ahead. I'm finally getting some blood taken for Clio's policeman to do his DNA tests on, and then I have to catch a train down to Marseilles.'

Oscar strolled over to the window to admire Max's garden, but Edie could think of nothing but the reason why they had come, and felt tongue-tied and embarrassed. This was made worse by her uncle's charm, which he turned on at full blast. 'What a lovely surprise to see you, Edie, I've never seen you looking prettier. Now let me get you a delicious *café crème*.' While he bustled about grinding coffee and heating milk, Max went on cheerfully, 'And how's *Cassandra*? Have you taken her out to sea much?'

As Edie found herself drawn into talking about her beloved boat and how grateful she was, the idea of challenging her uncle became more and more difficult. Oscar didn't help by coming away from the windows with some comment about a new rill that was being dug in Max's garden, and this took them on to planting and landscape architecture, and even further from where she wanted it to be. If she let the conversation drift on like this, they'd have finished their coffee and be back out on the street again before she'd had the chance to say why they'd come.

'Can I ask you something?' It came out more abruptly than she'd meant, but at least Max stopped chattering to look at her.

'But of course you can.'

'I've heard rumours that you launder gold, and I want to know the truth.' There. She'd said it.

'I've absolutely no idea what you're talking about.'

Edie took a deep breath. 'If you don't stop, we'll sell the bank.'

There wasn't a flicker of an expression on her uncle's face. Pouring himself another cup of coffee, he went over to her twin, walking around Edie as if she wasn't there. 'Oscar, my boy,' he said, 'take your sister away, for God's sake.'

For a long moment, Oscar stayed still. Then he came slowly across the room until he was so close that his arm pressed against her shoulder. 'If Eds thinks we should sell the bank,' he said, 'then I'll back her.' He slipped his hand into hers and Edie clung on to it as if they were children again.

'Don't be ridiculous, you don't have enough shares.' There was an edge to Max's voice. 'Your father and I would vote you down every time.'

'You should check the register,' Edie said quietly. 'There's twenty shares floating around which would give us a majority.'

'You can't mean the ones Teddy had?' Max's laugh sounded quite genuine, and he astonished Edie by winking at her, as if everything was completely normal again between them. 'Don't be daft, he hasn't been seen since before you twins were born.' Max was still looking straight at Edie, but his eyes seemed out of focus and she guessed he was riffling through his memory. 'It was the day we buried your grandfather. Very hot it was.' Max closed his eyes. 'I saw Teddy at the back of the church, though he'd gone by the end of the funeral. But later he drove some old rattletrap up to Dartleap, said he was our long-lost uncle and claimed a share of our money.'

Beside her, Oscar asked, 'Did you give him any?'

'Christ no, the silly bugger was just trying it on. Your father sent him packing, and we've neither seen nor heard of him since.' Still smiling, he turned back to Edie. 'And by the way, if the bank was sold, what do you imagine you and Oscar would live on?'

'At least we'd be able to live with our consciences. We wouldn't have to spend our lives looking over our shoulders for Russians with bad reputations either.'

'What rubbish you do talk.'

'I saw John Tamar at the weekend. He warned me.'

'And what does that etiolated throwback know about my business?'

'He's not an etiolated throwback, and it's not just he who knows. John has a cousin called Mary Kersey who works for the Treasury, and if you're helping some dodgy oligarch to launder his gold, can you imagine what'll happen when they catch up with you?'

'I dare say you're going to tell me anyway.'

'Quentance Bank's accounts will be frozen, your clients' cash will melt away, and our reputation will be mud. So if you don't stop what you're doing, I'll go over to Guernsey and talk to the authorities there. *Cassandra* could do with a good run, and I bet she'll jog a few memories.'

'*Cassandra*? Guernsey?' All pretence of disinterest vanished as her uncle gave a roar of anger. 'You filthy little tramp! Don't you dare!'

Max strode across the room, one hand raised, but before Edie could move Oscar had stepped in front of her. 'Time to go, Eds.'

Leaving their uncle, they walked out of the kitchen and were crossing the hall when the front doorbell rang. They heard footsteps behind them, and then Max pushed past to open the door. Outside, a female voice said, 'Good, you're still here. I thought you might have left for Marseilles already. Oh! What's up?'

The voice broke off suddenly as Max said, 'Oscar's here with his sister. They're just going.'

'Then they must change their minds.' In the doorway appeared a cap of dark hair above a smiling face. 'Oscar, hello. And you must be Edie.' The woman extended a small, black-gloved hand which Edie took politely, finding herself looking into a pair of disproportionately large eyes. 'I'm Zita Fitz.' Still clasping her hand, Zita was examining her carefully. 'You've a wonderful bone structure, and just look at the length of those legs! You will come back inside, won't you?'

Upset by the row with her uncle, and now embarrassed by this stranger's flattery, all Edie wanted to do was to get away. 'I'm sorry, we can't.' She pulled her hand free and turned to leave.

As she and Oscar were going down the front steps, Edie heard Zita say, 'Did I sense a bit of tension there?'

Before the door closed behind them, she caught her uncle's reply, 'Too bloody right you did. I'll tell you about it later.'

TWENTY-TWO

Max had to slew the heavy car right across to the outside lane to overtake a gritter which was crawling along spewing salt-stones along the motorway. 'Damnation,' he muttered as he heard the light rattle spattering against his bodywork. The car-hire firm would be sure to charge him extra for any scratches on their Range Rover. Distance gradually extinguished the lorry's revolving orange glare from his rear-view mirror, leaving him to drive on in a solitary darkness that was penetrated only by the car's headlights and an occasional patch of luminescence where a thin moonlight reflected off ice in the fields beyond the road.

Only once he was sure there was nothing apart from a faint glow of headlights approaching from far behind him did Max move cautiously back into the inside lane. Despite the near-empty motorway, he was steering with extreme care and didn't dare push the Range Rover much over fifty. He'd never carried anything like this much gold before and was worried that the car's suspension might roll suspiciously at a higher speed. He was also concerned that there was too much weight for it to stop fast, particularly when there was ice about. A skid, a crash and the resulting police search wouldn't bear thinking about.

After a few more monotonous miles, the road bent eastwards around the dark haunch of a hill and Max caught the faintest tinge of gold on the horizon, an auspiciously coloured dawn. Feeling suddenly brighter, he gave himself up to remembering the last few days. It would be as good a way of staying awake as any.

Monday's train down to Marseilles had been a joy. A comfortable seat in a quiet carriage and no hold-ups on the line. He smiled at the thought of that wonderful moment somewhere around Avignon when he'd looked out of the window to see the first olive trees flashing past and had known that he was in the south. After that, it hadn't been long till the train slowed for its long pull through graffiti-scribbled suburbs. Arriving on time at Gare St-Charles, he'd taken a cab down to the port, and then there'd been the elation of going up the gangway to feel the fluid movement of *Cilissa*'s hull under his feet.

It was while he was trying to recall the leather-and-laminate smell of *Cilissa's* wheelhouse that the scene with Edie crept into his head. He could still hardly believe it, but he'd been so outraged, he'd raised his fist to her. Glancing down he saw his hands, white-knuckled on the steering wheel as he relived his fury, and then the speedometer caught his eye. It had crept up to well over seventy. 'Shit! Shit! Shit!' he said aloud, taking his foot right off the accelerator. Because of the weight of the car, he didn't dare brake, and his gaze moved anxiously between the dials and the road until he was back down to fifty. As soon as he felt safe,

Max flicked on the Range-Rover's automatic speed control. He wasn't going to risk letting himself be caught out like that again.

With both feet off the pedals and the dark road ahead still clear, his mind went back to his niece. What was it about Edie that made her so difficult? Sometimes she didn't seem to be a Quentance at all, and it wasn't only the dark hair that made him think that. For one thing, she took everything so seriously. He couldn't remember her ever getting totally pissed, or having fits of falling-about laughter like Oscar did. And then she was so boringly, scrupulously honest, with not a drop of pirate blood in her. Max tapped his fingers on the steering wheel.

Even Zita hadn't been much help. He'd explained everything to her, about Teddy and the missing shares, about Edie's threat to track him down and sell the bank, and about her planned trip to Guernsey to shaft him with the authorities. Zita had been sitting down when he'd told her, and for most of the time Max had talked to the top of her shiny dark head. When she'd finally looked up, he'd been surprised by how anxious she was about Edie.

'You can't possibly let her take *Cassandra* to Guernsey. It's far too dangerous.'

Thinking she'd meant it would put the bank in danger, Max had said his niece knew nothing and couldn't do any harm, but Zita had gone on fretting. It was a difficult journey for anyone. Edie was far too inexperienced to do it alone. If Max couldn't prevent her from going, someone else would have to.

'It's sweet of you to care,' he'd said eventually, genuinely touched, 'but Edie won't change her mind once it's made up. There's no point even trying, Zita, so stop worrying.'

Dear Zita. She'd arrived in Marseilles late on Monday afternoon, looking so glad to see him. They'd cast off at sunset, pottering out of the harbour as if they were on a pleasure trip. With her help, everything had gone perfectly. The meeting out at sea, the careful shifting of unmarked gold bars from Dyengi's hideous super-yacht on to *Cilissa*. And then there'd been the roar of engines as he'd accelerated southwards and that feeling of wild freedom as his boat reared out of the water. They'd bounced off south-westwards, slicing through the waves towards Spain, Gibraltar and then the wide Atlantic Ocean.

'Annoying twerp!' Max said as he was forced to concentrate on driving. The Range Rover's speed control was keeping him at a steady fifty, but now an irritating little van which had just overtaken him going downhill had slowed as the road climbed upwards, forcing Max to overtake. Easing the overladen car carefully into the middle lane, he drove past, making sure he was a safe distance in front of the van before he pulled back into the slow lane.

The sea trip from Marseilles had been perfect, or almost. The one blot had been Zita's continued refusal to sleep with him, but he'd seen signs that eventually she would. After all, she'd behaved like a real partner over introducing Dyengi, and she'd often hinted about having a share in Quentance Bank. On *Cilissa* too she'd been wonderful, crewing efficiently despite her damaged hand, and insisting on sharing the helm so that they could keep going through the night. Cruising at thirty-three knots, with occasional bursts at

Cilissa's maximum thirty-seven knots when the water was calm enough, they'd managed to outrun the storms forecast for the Bay of Biscay, and despite having to stop to refuel they'd made the south coast of England after only five nights at sea, slipping into harbour at just after one that morning.

The hire-car had been there waiting, and Max had tried to persuade Zita to drive to London with him. 'Please,' he'd begged. 'I so want you to meet my brother, I know you'd like him.'

But Zita had been adamant. 'I can't, Max. There's something else I have to do.'

Briefly, he'd been annoyed, but he could never stay cross with anyone for long, let alone Zita. Like him, she'd had no sleep, but she'd insisted on helping him shift the gold from *Cilissa* into the Range Rover, making sure they spread the weight evenly across the floors, under the footwells and in the car's boot. Zita was a brick. A twenty-four-carat-gold brick.

He saw a pair of feeble headlights crawling by his window. They were on a long, downhill stretch, and that wretched van was pulling past him again. Max was tempted to reduce his speed so it could get far enough ahead not to bother him again, but he needed to drive as fast as he safely could if he was going to get this gold shifted into the bank's vault before anyone was about to see him.

The final climb was a long one, and again he had to overtake the slowing van. As he breasted the hill and looked down towards the great bowl of the Thames valley, Max saw the orange glow of London flushing the skyline. Although there was more traffic around, it was still early. He'd be at the bank in no time, and Alec would be there, calm as ever. He hadn't turned a hair when Max had rung to say he was bringing a load of Russian gold to store in the vault.

Reaching forward, he pressed a number into the car's telephone system.

'Yes?' The familiar voice sounded tired, but then his brother was never very bright in the early morning.

'I'm about half an hour away and in dire need of coffee. I'll drive straight round to the vaults.'

'I'll be there.'

Max turned into a narrow cul de sac behind St James's Square. He'd been expecting to find Alec waiting for him, but the street was empty, with no sign of life from behind the high walls that ran down either side. Three-quarters of the way along, he pulled up beside an anonymous door set deep in a border of dirty bricks. After a careful check in his rear-view mirror, Max turned off the engine and eased his tired body down from the Range Rover. There wasn't a soul about, so after making sure he'd locked the car he went over to the door in the wall and punched the bank's entry code into a keypad concealed in the brickwork. The door clicked open, and with a glance over his shoulder, Max pushed his way straight into the old stables at the end of the bank's rear courtyard.

He peered past the musty straw and the skeins of greying cobwebs that draped the long-empty stalls, but there was still no sign of Alec, so Max bent over and started shifting an old tarpaulin, heaving at it until he uncovered the entrance to the bank's vault. As he was staring down at the smooth circle of polished steel, he heard footsteps behind him and felt his heart gave a bound of fear. Trying to adjust his face to an expression of innocence, Max turned slowly round, but it was only Alec, holding two paper cups full of coffee.

There was something wrong. Max could see it instantly from a certain blankness on his brother's face, and the rigid set of his thin shoulders. 'Whatever is it?' Max felt himself swaying with tiredness and had to put a hand out to support himself against a splintered pillar.

'I need to talk to you.'

'Of course we can talk. But we have to get the gold shifted in here while there's no one around.'

'We need to talk first. It won't take long.'

'All right then, but there's a fortune in that Range Rover. We'll have to sit out there to guard it.'

Although he'd only recently been driving, the car had already got cold, so once they'd climbed up into the seats and found cup holders for their coffee, Max switched the engine on to warm them both up. There was a murmur beside him, but with the noise of the turning ignition, he thought he must have misheard his brother. As soon as the motor was running smoothly, he turned to face him. 'Sorry, Alec, I didn't quite catch that.'

His brother was silent, apparently concentrating on flicking specks of imaginary dust off his jacket, but then with a glance at Max he said, 'I've been running a Ponzi scheme.'

At first Max just gaped. What was Alec talking about?

Surely Ponzi had been some American crook who'd ripped off his investors? His brother had to be joking. Alec had turned his head and was gazing calmly into the empty street, so Max searched his brother's profile. It was pale, stern, patrician as always, and with absolutely no sign that he'd meant to be funny. Max blurted out words which sounded foolish even as he said them. 'Are you sure?'

'Of course I'm sure!' Alec gave a short, barking laugh. With the remnants of a smile still lifting the corners of his mouth, he said, 'I've been running the Adamantine Fund as a Ponzi scheme for years, and not a soul's guessed, not even you.' He crinkled the corners of his eyes at Max. 'It's been so easy,' he went on, his voice as cool as if they'd been discussing the weather. 'Investments come in, and out they go as dividends. Everyone's thrilled that I give such consistently high returns. It makes me rich, and as long as there's always new money pouring into the fund, everything's plain sailing.'

'But, Alec.' Max felt himself stumbling over his words. 'I thought you actually *did* invest the cash in the Adamantine Fund. I mean, what about your Investment Department? What does that do?'

'It doesn't exist.' Alec's face was tranquil. 'It's just a blank door.'

Max felt his throat go dry as the truth began to sink into his tired brain. His brilliant, beloved brother had been running a giant fraud for years and he'd never had the first idea about it. 'So why are you telling me this now?'

'While there's cash coming in, a Ponzi scheme's straightforward. As fresh investors join up, their money flows straight out to earlier investors.' Alec began to fiddle with his cufflinks. 'But I've hit a problem. This crunch has made my clients nervous. Some of them want to pull out, but just at the moment it's hard to drum up new funds.'

'My God! Are you telling me there's nothing left in the Adamantine Fund? That mountain of money invested with you has all been paid out?'

'Exactly.' Given what he'd just said, it seemed bizarre when Alec gave him a broad smile. 'Do you know something, Max? All this has made me rather proud of my daughter. Edie guessed this might happen even before I did.'

'So what are you going to do?' What with his own lack of sleep and his brother's unnatural composure, Max had the feeling that he'd stepped into some strange, parallel universe.

Alec reinforced this by replying gently, 'It's quite simple. I just need to borrow this lot.' With the polished black toe of his shoe, he flipped back the rubber mat to reveal the dull gleam of gold in the footwell. 'I'm sure there's enough in this car to tide me over till the cash starts rolling in again.'

'But you can't have it.' Max shook his head, trying to get rid of a growing sense of unreality. 'I couldn't possibly let you.'

Ignoring him, Alec went on talking as if he were explaining things to a child. 'You see, I don't only need to be able to repay my clients' original investments the moment they ask for them. I'll have to keep paying out dividends as well or confidence in me would vanish. You do understand, don't you?'

Max didn't answer straight away. In the rear-view mirror, he'd caught sight of a man pausing to stare at his car before slowly crossing the road at the end of the cul de sac. Even after the man had vanished, Max felt irrationally ruffled. The lack of sleep was really getting to him. 'I'm sorry, Alec, but it's impossible. It's Platon Dyengi's gold. He'd *kill* me if he found out!'

'But why ever should he find out?' Alec raised an eyebrow in surprise. 'You told me yourself the gold was likely to sit in our vaults for months before your Russian decides what he wants done with it. We'll have it back here long before then. And look on the bright side.' Alec tapped his arm playfully. 'All you need to do is ring one of our banker friends right now and say we've got this lot as surety for a loan. You can drive it straight on to their vaults and I'm sure they'll be happy to unload all these gold bars for you. It'll save you a lot of effort.'

Max was silent, staring blindly ahead through the Range Rover's windscreen. 'Max?' With an effort, he turned his head to look at his brother. 'I need you to help me. I couldn't bear it if . . .' As Alec's voice tailed off, Max caught the fear in his eyes and understood the fragility behind it. His brother's need for respect was at the core of his personality, and to be exposed as a common fraud might break him. 'And besides,' Alec added gently, 'I'd do it for you.'

If Max hadn't already been persuaded by the need to protect his brother's ego, those last few words would have made his mind up. Flicking through their past, he saw Alec taking a thrashing from their father for him, comforting him when he was sent away to school, protecting him from the terrors of an unhappy childhood. Then, as adults, he saw Alec fighting shoulder to shoulder with him, praising his successes as they struggled to build up the bank, celebrating together as they became rich.

Max bowed his head over the steering wheel. 'Of course I'll do it.'

There was no hug, no emotional outburst, but the warmth of Alec's 'Thank you' was enough. 'I could do with having the cash in the Adamantine account as soon as possible,' he added. 'Why don't you make that call now?'

Max half hoped that he wouldn't be able to track down anyone who could do the deal, but it turned out to be all too easy. The first banker he called was at home, would go straight to his office to get the paperwork sorted, and was happy to have his vault opened to take the gold as soon as Max could get there. 'All done, Alec,' he said when he'd finished. 'You'll have your cash in a couple of days.'

With a brief touch on his shoulder, his brother slipped down out of the car.

As there was no turning space, Max had to reverse the gold-laden Range Rover all the way along the cul de sac. When he finally reached the main road, he looked back to wave, but Alec had already vanished.

TWENTY-THREE

How near Bath are you?

Crawling through the outskirts. You?

On the train. Edie frowned as she added, Low carbon footprint.

It wasn't that she resented Max giving her twin a brand-new Audi TT, rather the timing of it. Coming so soon after that confrontation in Paris, it looked like a bribe, and she had the uncomfortable feeling that it was working. Oscar had been so supportive at first, handing over his notebook, backing her over selling the bank, but now she was afraid he was having second thoughts. He loved his job and the lifestyle that went with it, and he was nowhere near as angry as she was about the laundry business.

As if to confirm her unease, another text came through from her twin. Is notebook safe? Not sure I should have given it to you.

She patted the pocket of a new, putty-coloured skirt until she felt the little book's hard corner. Ignoring Oscar's second sentence, she typed back, Absolutely safe. Got it on me.

You haven't told anyone? The answer came so quickly that she guessed he must be sitting in a traffic jam.

I promised. Remember? Having sent her reply, Edie scrolled back through their messages. *Not sure I should have given it to you.* She'd better get herself and Max's client list over to Guernsey as soon as possible, or Oscar might change his mind.

With a shake of her head, she returned to the book she was reading. Commander Lightoller's autobiography, *Titanic and Other Ships*, was published in 1935 and there were inconsistencies with his testimony to the 1912 inquiries. One in particular was troubling her a great deal.

In his book, Lightoller's description of what happened while they were loading passengers into the lifeboats couldn't have been clearer. 'It was about this time that the Chief Officer came over from the starboard side and asked, did I know where the firearms were?' she read. 'I told the Chief Officer, "Yes, I know where they are. Come along and I'll get them for you," and into the First Officer's cabin we went – the Chief, Murdoch, the Captain and myself – where I hauled them out, still in all their pristine newness and grease.'

From everything she'd read about Charles Lightoller, he'd been an admirable man. He'd sunk U-boats in World War I, and he'd taken his own motor yacht to the Dunkirk evacuation in World War II. He'd even undertaken spying missions against the Germans while he and his wife pretended to be an innocent elderly couple enjoying a cruise along the Dutch coastline. So why had a man of his calibre never mentioned the conversation in Murdoch's cabin to either inquiry? And it was more than a simple omission. When asked, he'd specifically denied that any such meeting had taken place.

Edie pulled out a sheaf of notes and riffled through to where one of the senators conducting the US inquiry in 1912 was asking Lightoller about his last words with the First Officer.

Senator SMITH.	Did you see Mr. Murdoch after handing over the Watch?
Mr. LIGHTOLLER.	I saw him when I came out of my quarters after the impact.
Senator SMITH.	Where was he?
Mr. LIGHTOLLER.	On the bridge.
Senator SMITH.	He was with the captain?
Mr. LIGHTOLLER.	Yes sir.
Senator SMITH.	Did you speak to him after that?
Mr. LIGHTOLLER.	No, sir.
Senator SMITH.	I mean after he took the Watch?
Mr. LIGHTOLLER.	No, sir.
Senator SMITH.	You never spoke to him again?
Mr. LIGHTOLLER.	No, sir.
Senator SMITH.	You were not together when finally parted from the ship?
Mr. LIGHTOLLER.	No, sir.

Edie stared out of the train window. Lightoller had handed the watch to Murdoch at ten o'clock, and in his sworn evidence to the inquiry, he'd absolutely denied that he'd ever spoken to him again. Yet in his autobiography

Lightoller described how they'd been together in Murdoch's cabin far later on during that fatal night, and that the captain and the chief officer had been there too. In that brief time alone, *Titanic*'s captain and his three senior officers would surely have talked about what went wrong, about why the berg hadn't been avoided, about those last few minutes before *Titanic* was holed. So why should a man of Lightoller's integrity have concealed such a crucial meeting?

Her concentration was broken as she noticed the train slowing down, and a moment later a message from Oscar came through on her mobile. Just arriving, where are you?

Edie got up and tugged on her coat before replying, Pulling in to Bath Spa.

Walking seemed like a good idea when she left the station, but after ten minutes she started to regret it. Edie was learning to like the way men now eyed her as she passed by, but there were disadvantages to being better dressed, and the worst was the discomfort of heels.

Pausing in Milsom Street to massage an ankle, Edie noticed a clock in a shop window. Eleven-thirty on a Saturday morning was a perfectly respectable time to make a phone call. Without giving herself time to change her mind, she pulled out her mobile and clicked on a contact.

He replied after only one ring. 'John Tamar.'

Hearing his voice, Edie had a nervous urge to flip her phone shut. Realising how silly that would be since he'd see that the call had come from her mobile, she said, 'It's Edie Quentance here.'

'Edie! That's a really nice surprise.' He did sound pleased, but just as he went on to say something else, a tourist group passed by, exclaiming so loudly at Bath's beauties that Edie couldn't hear a word he was saying.

'Hang on,' she shouted over the noise, 'I'll just nip into Quiet Street.'

'Very appropriate,' she heard him laugh. 'Can you hear me now?'

'Much better.' She leaned against a convenient doorframe. 'Sorry, I didn't catch what you just said.'

'I said I was going to ring you. I think I've found Edward Quentance.'

'You're a genius!'

'Not really, I've got friends who track down missing people.'

'Well then they must be brilliant. Teddy's still alive, is he?'

'Alive, but very frail and living in an expensive nursing home on Lake Como. I've got his address on my mobile, shall I forward it to you?'

'Yes please.' She glanced down at her feet and wondered what he'd think of her open-toed boots.

'Was that why you rang me, or did you just feel like a chat?'

His words brought her up with a start. 'Not at all. I mean it's nice to chat, obviously, but there's something I need to tell you.' There was silence from the other end, so she stumbled on, 'It's about my uncle. I'm sorry I didn't believe you, but the fact is, you were right and I was wrong. Max *is* laundering money and he seems to have been doing it for a long time.'

John said something so quietly she wasn't quite sure she'd heard it right. It sounded like 'Thank God.'

As he didn't add anything else, Edie thought she should tell him her other bit of news. 'And also, I've found out the name of my uncle's new Russian client. He's called—'

'Not now!' The urgency in his voice stopped her. 'Not over the phone.'

'Should I come to Brink Castle later today and tell you?' Edie tried to sound casual. 'It's no problem as long as you don't mind picking me up from Totnes Station.'

'Sorry, I'm nowhere near Devon, and I can guess who it is.'

'Then you don't need me to tell you.'

John surprised her with a laugh. 'I wish I could see you today, but not because I need to know anything. That is, unless ...' The teasing edge vanished from his voice. 'Have you found out who Max's clients are?' Edie could feel the notebook in her pocket, but she'd made a promise. 'Are you still there? Can you give me any names?'

'Not now,' she said slowly. 'I'll be taking *Cassandra* out to sea in the next day or so. Maybe I'll be able to tell you something when I get back.'

'You're not still trying to find out what's going on by yourself, are you? These people aren't nice, they're dangerous!'

'I'm sorry, but I've made up my mind. It's something I have to do.'

There was a pause, and when he spoke again his voice sounded gentle, almost pleading. 'Edie, listen to me. Just don't take any risks.'

'I won't, I promise.' A pair of men sauntering hand in hand down Quiet Street reminded her why she'd come to Bath. 'I'd really better go now, my mother's expecting me.'

As she flipped her phone shut, an empty taxi came down the street towards her. With her new boots rubbing her feet, the temptation was too great to resist. Holding her hand out, Edie flagged it down.

Her phone buzzed almost before she was in her seat. Edward Quentance, Ospizio della Trinità, Lago di Como.

TWENTY-FOUR

'Do you still love me, Mum?'

'How could anything make me stop loving you?'

Oscar was sitting on the kitchen floor, his head against her knees, and Clio was glad he couldn't see her face. Her reply had been instinctive, but it was a struggle not to cry after such a shock. He was gay. How *could* he be gay? Her darling boy, her only son. Was there something wrong in the way she'd brought him up? Had she been too happy to encourage his artistic side? Or maybe not strict enough? She'd dreamed of having grandchildren as beautiful as he was, and now that would never happen.

'I've been so nervous about telling you,' Oscar murmured into her leg. 'You've no idea how lonely it's been, keeping the most important thing in my life to myself.'

Hearing the catch in his voice, she looked down at the back of his neck. It was a long time since they'd sat like this, but she remembered how he was always burying his head in her lap when he was small. He'd been a sensitive child, and when Edie wasn't around to fight his battles for him, Oscar had often been teased about his mop of blond curls. Maybe that was where she'd gone wrong? If she'd insisted on a more manly haircut for her little boy, would he have grown up straight? With one finger, Clio traced the soft indentation just below the bulge of his skull, following it down to the top of his spine. Some vulnerability in the way he was leaning on her suddenly caught at her throat. What gays did was dangerous. He might catch something.

'I'm glad you've told me, darling,' she said gently. 'All I'm worried about is whether you might have got AIDS.'

'Well I definitely haven't.' Oscar sat back and looked up at her. 'When you asked me to give blood for Ianthe's DNA test, I thought I might as well get checked for HIV at the same time. It came back all clear.'

A loud, 'Thank heavens for that!' from the doorway made them both jump.

'Hello, darling. Your brother's been so brave.' Resting a protective hand on Oscar's head, Clio realised that even in such a short time she'd come to terms with his gayness. Her son loved her and he needed her. That was more than many mothers had. Seeing how nicely her daughter was dressed, she smiled across the kitchen at her. 'You look very pretty.'

'*Very* pretty, Eds,' Oscar echoed. 'I told you mascara would be good on you.'

Clio stood up and clapped her hands. 'Champagne time, don't you think? Get us a bottle from the fridge, will you, Oscar?'

'By the way, Mum,' Edie said as she got three glasses out for them. 'I've just heard something interesting from John Tamar.'

The sigh of gas escaping round the champagne cork echoed Clio's 'Oh!' of surprise. Perhaps there *was* something going on between those two. Holding a glass out to be filled, she said to Oscar, 'You do know Edie's got very friendly with John Tamar, don't you?' Her son looked blank. '*You* know, darling, Viscount Tamar. He's heir to the Earl of Ivybridge.'

Oscar had stopped pouring champagne and was looking at his twin in surprise. 'Hob-nobbing with the snobbery are you? I thought you despised them.'

'And I do. John's only been helping me find Teddy's shares. Apparently there's an Edward Quentance living on Lake Como and he's the right age to be Teddy.'

'Teddy? How extraordinary.' Clio pulled out a chair and sat down. 'What do you think we should do?'

Edie seemed about to say something, but Oscar cut in first. 'I don't think we should do anything in a hurry. We don't want to risk disrupting things at the bank, particularly during this credit crisis.'

His words sounded quite sensible to Clio, but for some reason they made her daughter furious. 'Oscar! You don't want to risk losing your fat salary and your nice new car,' she said fiercely. 'That's what you really mean, isn't it?'

Clio wasn't having the day ruined by one of Edie's tiresome arguments. 'You've got a new car, have you, Oscar? You must be doing well.' She was about to suggest that they all go out and admire it when a thought struck her. 'Just a minute – if this old man really is Teddy, he's close family.' Her eyes drifted to her painting of Ianthe, then back to Edie, who was still looking cross. 'If you give me his address, I'll pass it on to Inspector Howland right now.'

'You don't need to do it today, Mum, surely,' Oscar said. 'He'll hardly be working on a Saturday.'

'Don't you think so?' Now she'd had the idea, Clio was keen to get on with it. Even the tiniest lead might help trace the sadist who'd kept her beloved child shut up in the dark. 'Inspector Howland said I could call any time if it was important.'

'Of course you should, and I've got Teddy's address right here.' Edie pulled out her mobile. 'I'll forward it to you.'

As soon as she'd received her daughter's text, Clio began pushing buttons on her own phone. 'There we are,' she said when she'd finished. 'I've told the inspector where Teddy lives. Let's hope it's some help, though if I'm perfectly honest,' she added, 'I can't see this DNA testing getting us very far after all this time.'

'Don't say that!' Oscar drained his glass. 'D'you mean I gave them that armful of my blood for nothing?'

'You big weed.'

Watching Edie ruffle her brother's hair, Clio couldn't help smiling at the abrupt way the twins abandoned their quarrels.

Oscar was just pouring out the remains of the champagne when Clio's phone made a noise. Flipping it open, she read the message then looked up with a triumphant smile. 'I told you the inspector was keen to help. It says here that he's going to fly out to see Teddy straight away. Today! What d'you think of that?'

'Probably fancies a weekend on expenses and some cheap Italian booze,' Oscar said cheerfully. 'Talking of which, let's open another bottle. By the way, Mum,' he said over his shoulder as he went to the fridge, 'can I stay here till tomorrow?'

'I'd be furious if you didn't,' Clio smiled. 'How about you, Edie?'

'Sorry, I'm taking *Cassandra* out on a trip.'

Catching the sharp look that flashed between the twins, Clio guessed there was an argument that had been simmering for some time. When they were younger, their squabbles had sometimes dragged on for days, flaring up, vanishing with a hug or a joke, only to burst out again over some triviality. If that was the mood they were in, she was glad Edie was going away. Besides, it would be a treat to have her son to herself for a bit.

TWENTY-FIVE

Edie groaned when her alarm went off. Five o'clock in the bloody morning. She forced herself to sit up in her bunk, but there was nothing to see beyond *Cassandra*'s porthole except the star-flecked darkness of the river. Falling back against her pillows, she was tempted to give the trip to Guernsey a miss. Her head ached from all that champagne with Mum and Oscar, and though she was certain she was doing the right thing, she hated leaving in the middle of an unresolved quarrel with her twin.

Life felt a lot better once she'd got dressed and had some hot food inside her. Going out on deck, Edie looked west over the river to the silent town of Dartmouth, and then eastwards to Kingswear and the dark halo of hills rising behind it. The night sky was marred by the glow of street-lights, but she thought she could already see the faintest smudge of dawn tipping the cliffs on the south-eastern horizon. If she was to make Guernsey by mid-afternoon, she'd better get moving.

The safety drill before going out to sea was automatic, and something Edie never skimped on. She started by going right round the deck, testing ropes and making sure the hatches were all firmly closed. Next she went over to the stern rails, where *Cassandra*'s life-raft hung, undoing the padlock that kept it safe from thieves and tugging the raft's mooring line to make sure it was securely attached to *Cassandra*'s stern cleats.

It was chilly outside, and once she'd checked everything on deck Edie was glad to get into the warmth of the wheel-house. She looked around carefully. There was the grab-bag, hanging in its normal place. Three small bottles of fresh water were on the chart table, and together with a large bar of emergency chocolate they were holding down the corners of her planned course to Guernsey. Her eyes moved across to her life-jacket over by the door. Edie gave it a guilty glance but left it where it was. She knew she ought to wear it when she was going out to sea alone, but she hated the feeling of being constricted.

As she bent to check *Cassandra*'s instruments, Edie felt Oscar's notebook in the pocket of her jeans. She'd put it there for safety, but its sharp corners were distracting. Pulling it out, she slipped the notebook into the grab-bag before turning to see that the hand-held VHF radio and a torch were in the safety netting as usual, within easy reach of the wheel. Having made sure that their batteries were fully charged, she slipped down below.

With the same care that she'd taken on deck and in the wheelhouse, Edie ran a full inspection of the engine, checking that the fuel lines were clear and the sea-cocks were turned to their correct positions. She then went through her cabin and down to the stern to double-check that she'd closed the sea-cock in the heads. Only when she was happy that everything was safely in order did Edie skip back up to the wheelhouse and switch on *Cassandra*'s ignition.

As usual, the engine sputtered fitfully before starting. Knowing that it would be a good five minutes before it settled into its steady *poketa-poketa-poketa* rhythm, Edie used the time to make sure that the main VHF radio was working properly. Then, after a final check of the various gauges, she hurried out on deck to cast off from the fore and aft mooring buoys, rushing back inside to take the wheel before the tide could swing *Cassandra* broadside to the stream. Once the helm was safely under control, Edie headed her boat down along the estuary and began to relax.

From the Dartmouth side of the river, she caught the faint sound of church bells tolling across the water and remembered that it was a Sunday. She thought of John Tamar getting ready to go to Mass, until a slight change in the putter of the engine caught her attention. With a quick adjustment to the throttle, the motor settled back into its normal rhythm, after which Edie checked the compass, moved the helm three points to the east and concentrated on where she was steering.

As *Cassandra* slipped between the twin castles of One Gun Point, the sea opened up before her. It lay supine, without even the whisper of a breeze to ripple its surface. Over beyond Start Point, the westerly horizon was indigo and punctured by stars, but these had all vanished from the eastern sky, wiped out by the nascent glow of a new day. Suddenly elated, she swung the wheel on to the first leg of her journey.

*

Edie had been going for hours. She'd crossed the shipping lanes, and was now in that desolate area of ocean extending down to the Channel Islands and the French coast. During the entire voyage, it had seemed as if the sea just hadn't the energy to heave itself from the horizontal. There was something almost artificial about the flatness of the water. She'd felt none of the usual lifting of her boat underneath her, there'd been no break in the steady swish of the wash parting from *Cassandra*'s sides, and she'd seen nothing but the gentlest of ruffles to stir the sea from its languor. When she'd gone out on deck it had been the same. The air felt too thin to carry any warmth from the wintry sun, too still even to whip up the droplets which would normally rime her lips with the taste of salt.

After a careful look round the empty horizon, Edie went back into the wheelhouse and checked her course and compass. Everything was boringly normal, and there was an uncomfortable rumbling in her empty stomach. She was still some way from the rock-sown waters of the Channel Islands, so this would be a good time to grab a hot drink and something to eat.

Edie was just putting the kettle on down in the galley when she realised she'd left both the handheld radio and her emergency torch in the wheelhouse. She paused for a moment, undecided. It was against all her safety rules to come below without them, but on the other hand she could feel from the steadiness under her feet that *Cassandra*'s movement over the calm sea was entirely unchanged. Suddenly realising she needed to pee, Edie decided to take the risk. She scuttled down the saloon companionway, along the engine room and up through her cabin to the heads.

By the time she got back to the galley, the kettle had boiled. Edie made herself a mug of strong tea, opened a packet of sandwiches and went back up to the wheelhouse where a quick check told her that everything was fine. The wheel was steady, the compass showed that *Cassandra* was still bang on course, and there was no sign of any other ship between her and the horizon. Settling down at the helm, she began to eat.

It was while she was finishing the last crumbs of her sandwich that Edie noticed a slight alteration in the sea. It still stretched slack and unmoving, but instead of reflecting back dancing flashes of light, the surface was now a dull pewter. She went out on deck and gasped at the drop in temperature. The air was icy cold, and so still that it felt as if the atmosphere itself was holding its breath. Edie was about to go back into the warmth of the wheelhouse when she spotted a wisp of cloud rising in the north-east like a distant bonfire. Even as she watched, the cloud grew, obscuring the horizon around it. Through the soles of her sailing shoes, she felt *Cassandra* lifting herself gently to rise over the first of a long series of waves which seemed to be rolling directly from that remote blur. It was as if, far away, a stone had been dropped into the water. Edie knew what was coming. She paused on deck only for a few more moments, the time it took for a hand of cloud to reach out from the darkening horizon, growing till it covered first the sun and then the entire sky.

When the squall hit, Edie thought she was ready, but its

violence and direction took her by surprise. Instead of meeting the oncoming seas bow-on, *Cassandra* heeled right over as waves coursed down her port side. Immediately Edie flung the wheel round, trying to get *Cassandra*'s nose turned to the storm. The compass spun wildly, and she realised she might be driven off her planned course, but there was no choice in a gale like this. She'd just have to ride the waves till the wind blew itself out.

Edie had expected the squall to be typically violent and short-lived, but after nearly an hour there was no lessening in its fury. *Cassandra* kept going bravely, surging over the huge seas like a steeplechaser, but Edie's hands and arms were tiring from the fight to keep the wheel steady. At first she'd tried to keep an eye on the compass to give her a vague idea of her boat's position, but she'd had to give that up to concentrate all her attention on the helm. As another huge wave surged down on her, Edie had a moment of despair. She was becoming exhausted, and worse than that, she was lost. For all she knew, she could already have been carried far out into the Atlantic. Despair turned to panic as she realised she might be out of radio contact as well. *Cassandra*'s VHF radio would reach a maximum of twenty-five miles in the right atmospheric conditions, but these conditions didn't feel right at all.

Although it was still afternoon, the sky was dark as night, so Edie missed the wave that came hurtling down broad-side until it broke, and a mountainous sea thundered over the decks. *Cassandra* paused in a deep trough, shuddered, then fought her way upwards again, but not before Edie had seen the trickle of water coming under the wheelhouse door. A few more waves like that would swamp her. She wished now that she'd put her lifejacket on but she didn't dare take her hands off the wheel and risk losing control of the helm, even for an instant.

The wind was shrieking round the wheelhouse when *Cassandra* began to buck wildly under her feet. It was several moments before she realised that her poor boat was caught in cross-waves which were tossing her up and down, pounding her hull and sides relentlessly. Quite suddenly, Edie had the horrible feeling of leaving her stomach behind her as *Cassandra* was thrown right up out of the water. When the boat tumbled back down again, the colossal smack of hull on sea threw her right across the wheelhouse. Edie staggered and fell. Her forehead hit a sharp corner of the chart table, momentarily stunning her.

When her brain had steadied and she'd wiped her eyes clear of the trickle of blood running down from her brow, Edie saw that the wheel wasn't spinning uncontrollably as she'd expected. Instead, there was something sluggish about the way it veered from port to starboard and back again. She struggled to her feet and felt a change in the way *Cassandra* was moving. It was as if the boat was wallowing through the waves rather than rising over them, like a horse too tired to jump any more. Outside, the wind seemed to be quietening, and over its slackening howl Edie was able to hear a far more frightening sound. It was the whine of *Cassandra*'s bilge alarm and the rumbling cough of the automatic pumps starting up in the engine room. Water must be coming into the hull.

Automatically, her safety drill kicked in. The first rule

was to stay calm, and Edie felt momentarily proud to see that her hands were quite steady as she switched her radio to Channel 16. She listened, but there was nothing. She pushed the Press To Speak button and as evenly as she could manage said, 'Mayday, Mayday, Mayday. Over.' She bent towards the receiver but heard only silence, although she did notice that there was far less noise coming in from outside. Maybe the storm really was dying away. Unfortunately, this meant that the sound of the bilge alarm now seemed much louder and more urgent, and when she again pushed the Press To Speak button, there was a definite tremble in her fingers.

'Mayday. This is *Cassandra*. This is *Cassandra*. This is *Cassandra*. Mayday. Over.' There was still no answering call, but this could be for a number of reasons. A ship might already be steaming over to help her. No. She pressed her lips together to hold back a sob of fear. No ship could find her unless it knew her boat's position, and she didn't know it herself.

Edie took a deep breath and told herself to keep calm. She'd just have to guess. 'Mayday. This is *Cassandra*. Fifteen to twenty miles west-north-west of Guernsey.' She felt a lurching roll under her feet and her voice rose to a shout. 'MAYDAY! This is *Cassandra*. I need IMMEDIATE assistance! Over.' Again she bent forwards to listen; again there was nothing. Edie felt her breath coming faster. She'd have to go down below and see what could be done.

Grabbing the hand-held VHF radio and the torch from their safety netting, she stuffed one into each of the front pockets of her jeans. Down the first companionway, the saloon and the galley looked normal, but as she turned to climb down to the engine room, Edie gave a moan of fear. There was water in there, and when she stepped down onto the engine-room floor, she found that it was already up to her ankles. Heart thudding, she forced herself to stop and think. The first thing she must do was to check the fore and aft bilges. If they were dry, if the bulkheads between them and the engine room were watertight, and if it was only the hull below the engine room that had been damaged, then *Cassandra* should stay afloat for hours.

Even in the few moments while Edie was working this out, the incoming water had crept up to her shins. She sloshed on through the engine room and climbed up the companionway to her sleeping-cabin. The floor in there was dry, and with any luck the space below would be dry too. Looping a finger into a brass ring set into the floorboards, she lifted the hatch and stared down into the aft bilges. Water was slopping around the ballast. It was seawater, and rising. Edie's breath came in shallow gasps as she took in what this meant. *Cassandra* was sinking. She must get help immediately. Feeling deep into her jeans pocket, she pulled out the hand-held radio, but as she did so *Cassandra* wallowed heavily to port, throwing Edie off balance. She put an arm out to save herself and the radio fell with a little plop into the open hatch at her feet.

She had to retrieve it. Under the bright cabin lights, she could see that the water level in the bilges was rising steadily. There was no time to be lost. She *had* to send another Mayday signal, and straight away. Without a second's thought, Edie dropped to her knees, tugged up her sleeve and reached down into the bilge to recover the radio. After a moment's fumbling in the freezing water, she'd just got her hand round it when in one terrible, tumbling movement, *Cassandra* lurched so far to starboard that it felt as if she was standing on her beam-ends. The extreme degree of the roll dislodged the boat's ballast, and before Edie could do anything at all, she was trapped to the wrist by cubes of solid pig-iron.

'Panic kills,' she whispered, making herself move gently as she tried to wriggle her hand free. She could feel *Cassandra* settling back to the upright and hoped that the ballast might shift too, but the iron blocks wouldn't budge. The icy water in the bilge was creeping up her arm, and suddenly all Edie's self-control deserted her. She flung her body flat on the floorboards and struggled until the pig-iron had cut deep gashes across her wrist, but her right hand was still completely stuck.

A new noise made her open her eyes wide in fear. There was a long, whining sigh from the engine room, and then quite suddenly the bilge alarm fell silent, the automatic pumps stopped and all the lights went out. *Cassandra*'s main diesel motor was spluttering unevenly, but at least it was still running. Edie froze, listening in the darkness. The engine coughed on for a while before it let out a gentle wheeze and stopped. She lay like a dead thing, flat on the floor of her cabin, while she tried to grasp what had happened. Incoming seawater must have reached the boat's main batteries and shorted them. Now Edie had no lights, no power and no engine.

The realisation made her spring back to life. She had to get her hand free or she'd drown, and she *had* to recover the hand-held radio because the main one would never work now *Cassandra*'s batteries were dead. A thin beam of sunlight was shining in through the porthole, bringing Edie the faintest flicker of hope. At least the blackness of the storm had finally passed over.

The daylight was too feeble to illuminate the bilge where she was trapped, so with extreme care Edie fumbled, left-handed, for her torch. Once she'd extracted it from her pocket, she lifted it up over her head before moving the switch with her thumb. To her relief, its narrow beam came on immediately. She shone it down into the bilge and almost wished she hadn't. The water was now only an inch or two below the floorboards, and given the way her hand was caught, it wouldn't be long before the sea crept over her face.

Something swam slowly into the torch-lit circle of water. Edie screamed, the high sound echoing round the wooden walls of the cabin as her fear of a slow drowning was over-taken by a more immediate terror. The bloated body of a rat, a huge, green, decomposing rat, was floating in the bilges just below her nose. Wildly, she tugged her trapped hand against the sharp-edged ballast as the corpse drifted closer to slap its fat, leathery softness against her arm. Edie felt the boat spin around her. She was going to faint, and then she was going to drown.

There was a long groan from *Cassandra*'s hull. The boat reeled slackly beneath her, the ballast shifted, and suddenly she was free. Without a thought for the radio, Edie snatched her icy arm away from that horror in the bilges and leapt to her feet. Clutching the torch, she fumbled her way back down the dark companionway, gasping as she plunged up to her thighs into the freezing, oily water that was flooding the engine room.

Terrified of falling and losing the only light she had, Edie had to wade at a nightmarishly slow pace towards the far steps. The seawater clung to her jeans, holding her back. At every moment she expected to feel that last, sickening lurch before *Cassandra* sank, taking Edie down, trapped in this smelly blackness until her lungs burst and she was forced to take the water-logged breath that would drown her. With a gasp of relief, she made it across the engine room and dragged her soaking legs up into the saloon. The floor there was already sodden, and strewn with things that had been displaced by the boat's exaggerated rolls. Ignoring the mess, Edie squelched as fast as she could through the saloon and pulled herself up the final few steps to the wheelhouse.

After her ordeal down below, she was surprised to find everything there looking quite normal. The helm was steady, the compass had stopped spinning, and the only really notice-able change was the lack of noise from either the engine or the wind. She bent down to retrieve the water bottles from where the storm had thrown them, then took a glance forward through the windscreen. She put a hand to her mouth and stared out in disbelief. In the aftermath of the storm, waves were still slapping against *Cassandra*'s sides, but now they were also washing over the deck. It was less than a foot above the surface of the sea.

Again, she heard the words Max had dinned into her. *Panic kills!* Edie made herself stand quietly and take a couple of deep breaths. She'd have to abandon her boat for the life-raft, and as quickly as possible.

Knowing what had to be done, Edie moved fast. Pulling her lifejacket from its hook, she slipped it over her head and tied the tapes round her middle, then in two paces she was by the chart table, lifting down her grab-bag. She forced herself to take an extra moment to put the strap diagonally across her body so that it couldn't slip off, then stuffed her three water bottles in under the satchel's flap. *Cassandra* settled leadenly under her feet. Not daring to pause for even a moment to double-check that she hadn't forgotten anything, Edie scurried out through the wheelhouse door.

The cold air whipped through her sodden jeans, and she started to shiver violently as she went over to where the life-raft hung from the stern guard-rails. The water was now only inches below the deck and Edie found she had to paddle through the waves that were constantly flowing over it. Any minute now, the sea would flood right over the surface, forcing its way into the hatches, and *Cassandra* would go down like a stone. Terror gave her strength, and in one movement Edie lifted the life-raft's case up off its mounting and threw it over the side, where it bobbed at the end of its mooring line. Grabbing this rope, she gave it a firm tug, letting out a yelp of relief as the casing flew open. A moment later she heard the comforting sound of the raft's black buoyancy floats as they automatically inflated, and then the enclosed orange oblong of the shelter slowly rose above them.

Edie pulled the raft as close to the stern rails as she could. She knew she must make the leap from *Cassandra*'s side to the small flap in that orange tent, but it was hard to gauge the distance with the waves lifting and tugging the life-raft away from the boat's side. With a last, despairing turn of her head, Edie scanned the horizon. Perhaps even at this, the very last minute, a rescue ship might be in sight? She searched for as long as she dared, but there was nothing. No boats, no land, nothing but the dome of a cold sky above her and the grey-green immensity of water below. She was lost somewhere out in the ocean, and if she didn't move she'd soon be at the bottom of it.

A prolonged, creaking groan from beneath her feet made the final decision for her. She took a wild leap over *Cassandra*'s rail and tumbled, half in, half out of the life-raft. She managed to find a proper grip for her hands, but her legs flailed in the sea as she searched for a foothold on the canvas boarding-ladder. Quite a bit of water sloshed in with her when Edie finally made it inside the shelter, but she couldn't stop to bail out. If she didn't manage to slice through the rope attaching life-raft to boat, she'd be dragged under, raft and all, when *Cassandra* sank.

With hands numbed by the cold, Edie fumbled in the grab-bag until she found her penknife. She could already feel the life-raft being drawn closer by the pull of her sinking boat and began to saw fiercely at the connecting line. The rope was wet, and it was with a horrible slowness that the fibres gradually parted. The little raft started to bounce and bob at the end of its line as *Cassandra* settled further into the water, and this helped by increasing the tension on the rope. Edie could feel blisters rising on the palms of her wet hands as she worked the knife until there was only a thin strand left. Just as she felt herself being tugged downwards, the remaining threads gave way. The life-raft leapt free and then began to revolve slowly, high on the surface of the waves.

At the first turn, Edie saw *Cassandra*'s wheelhouse squatting incongruously on the sea, with no deck left visible. The life-raft continued its gentle spin, and when her boat came into sight again all she could see was a couple of feet of stubby mast poking up out of the waters. Before the turning raft hid it from view, Edie caught a final image of the tip of the VHF aerial as it vanished below the waves.

TWENTY-SIX

Oscar was sitting in a café by Pulteney Bridge, drinking black coffee and trying to summon the energy for the uphill walk to collect his overnight bag. He was feeling distinctly uneasy, though he wasn't quite sure if it was a rational anxiety about Edie or an irrational postscript to a weekend of drunken carousing with his old friends in Bath. He checked his watch for the umpteenth time that afternoon. Ten-past five, and the last Paris flight out of Bristol on a Sunday took off at seven. If he didn't make a move now, he'd never get to the airport in time. He frowned at the rainbow sign on the café's window and at the growing darkness beyond. It was going to rain, damn it, and he hadn't brought a coat. He hurried outside and set off towards Clio's flat.

It had been a perfect day, or rather two perfect days. Mum had been nicer than he could have dreamed of when he'd told her he was gay. She'd almost made it feel like something to celebrate. After they'd had champagne at her flat, she'd taken him and Edie out to a long, boozy lunch and he didn't feel as if he'd stopped drinking since. He'd been so relieved, he'd even taken a bottle of beer with him when he'd gone to Bath Spa Station to see Edie off.

Edie. Oscar walked faster, feeling the first heavy drops of rain on his head. He simply didn't understand why she refused to see both sides of the argument. Of course money-laundering was wrong. He'd given her his notebook, hadn't he? But there was no need to rush off like this, surely? If they'd waited a bit, he might have found a way to resolve everything without risking his own career. Oscar swore as he splashed through a puddle and shot dirty water up the legs of his trousers. He thought she was being selfishly impulsive. She thought he was being plain selfish, and they'd gone on quarrelling till she'd slammed the train door in his face and vanished into the carriage.

Seeing a shop awning ahead, Oscar dived under it and pulled out his phone. He checked the screen, but there were no messages and no missed calls. He'd not heard a word from Edie since they parted, and he was starting to feel very unhappy. He should never have let his twin go off alone like that, in the middle of an argument. And *why* hadn't she rung?

She'd promised to call before she got in touch with the Guernsey authorities, and had said she'd be near enough to the Channel Islands to be in range of a mobile network by three at the latest. That was over two hours ago, but he hadn't heard a thing from her and whenever he called her number he got the 'unobtainable' signal. Maybe her mobile wasn't working? But even so, she should be safely moored in the harbour at St Peter Port by now and would have called him from the town. Oscar felt his breath coming faster.

Leaving the shelter of the awning, he broke into a fast trot up through the rainy streets of Bath.

'Mum?' he called as he pushed his way into Clio's flat. 'Edie hasn't rung here, has she?'

'No, darling.' His mother came out of the kitchen, wiping her hands on a piece of cloth. 'Were you expecting her to? And hadn't you better get going?' she added, coming up the hall towards him. 'It's gone half-past five, you know. You'll miss that flight if you don't hurry.'

There might be some perfectly simple reason why his twin hadn't called. He didn't want to worry their mother unnecessarily, and besides, if he did say something to Mum, there'd be awkward questions about why Edie had taken *Cassandra* all the way to Guernsey on her own. Supposing the whole story came out and it got back to Max? He knew what his uncle would say if he found out Oscar had given Edie those client details. There'd be an unbelievable fuss, after which he'd have no job and no money. He decided to let things be.

Having made up his mind, Oscar started off down the hall to collect his luggage, but he paused as his eye was caught by one of Clio's paintings. It was a portrait Edie loathed because it made her hands and feet look enormous. As he looked up into his twin's eyes, a shiver ran through him, and quite suddenly he was swamped by a wave of desolation. He was standing safely in his own mother's hallway, and yet he felt fearful, lost and alone. Unable to stop himself, Oscar turned to Clio and groaned, 'Oh God, Mum. I can't bear it.'

'Bear what?' Her arms were round him in a moment.

'Darling, you're shivering.' She hurried him down the hall to the kitchen. 'Now sit here and tell me what's wrong.'

'It's Edie. I think she's lost.'

'Lost?' His mother was looking at him blankly. 'How do you mean?'

Oscar buried his head in his hands. 'Could I have a cup of tea?'

'Of course, but have you got time? What about your flight?'

'You don't understand, Mum,' he said, churning his fingers through his hair. 'I'll have to stay here tonight. I can't go anywhere till I know Edie's safe.'

'Safe? You don't mean she's—' Clio broke off and sat down heavily on one of the kitchen chairs. 'Tell me calmly, Oscar!' Her voice rose as she spoke. 'What's happened to her?'

'I wish I knew. She was going off on *Cassandra* this morning and she promised she'd ring me by three.' He glanced up at the kitchen clock. 'It's nearly twenty to six, and I haven't heard a word.'

As her face moved from disbelief, through shock, to tears, it occurred to Oscar that if his twin could see Clio now, she'd never again doubt that their mother loved her. 'Edie,' she groaned. 'Oh, my poor little girl!'

Oscar tried to calm her down. 'It's all right, she really hasn't been missing that long. I'm sure she'll turn up. She'll come back to us, Mum.'

His mother looked up at him from streaming eyes. 'I've lost her. I've lost both my girls.' Burying her head in her hands, Clio abandoned herself to weeping.

Oscar stood up and began to walk round the kitchen. His mother was clearly going to be no help, so it was up to him to work out what to do. He glanced at the phone, and kicked himself for not having thought of it straight away. Not wanting to upset Clio even more, he took the receiver down to the far end of the flat before dialling 999. As soon as he was put through to the coastguard emergency service, he said, 'I need help! My sister's gone missing.'

'I'm sorry to hear that,' a calm voice came from the other end of the line. 'I'll need to ask you for a few details before we can start to look for her.'

As Oscar ran through a description of *Cassandra*'s size, age and appearance, he found himself settling into a soothing rhythm of question and answer.

'Does your sister's boat have satellite, or ship-to-shore radio, or both?'

'I'm pretty sure it's just ship-to-shore, but Edie's very safety-conscious.'

'And you say she left Dartmouth for St Peter Port, Guernsey?'

'That's what she told me she was going to do.'

'Have you got a copy of the course your sister planned to take?'

'I'm afraid not, no. Does that matter?'

'Not necessarily. We should be able to plot her where-abouts from the tides, just as long as you can tell me exactly what time she left Dartmouth?'

'I can't!' Oscar felt his throat tightening in anxiety. 'Edie told me she meant to leave early this morning, but that's all I know.' He glanced at his watch. 'Except that she said she'd be there by three and now it's nearly six. Please find her!'

'We'll certainly do our best. I'll alert all ships in the area where your sister might be, though I can assure you we haven't heard of any distress calls.' The voice remained comfortingly steady. 'As a matter of fact, there was a nasty little storm reported heading for the Atlantic this afternoon. I'd say the chances are that *Cassandra*'s been driven right off course, and quite likely she's gone out of VHF-radio range as well.' Oscar's heart began to hammer at the thought of his twin lost on the ocean, but the coastguard didn't seem too concerned. 'If that's what's happened, I've no doubt your sister will turn up safe and sound. We'll let you know when we hear anything, and in the meantime, try not to worry.'

Try not to worry! That was a lot easier said than done.

His mother seemed calmer when he went back to the kitchen, and he felt a bit better himself once they'd shared a bottle of wine, but the wait was endless. His eyes switched constantly between his mother's phone and his own mobile, but both stayed silent. After he'd fidgeted round the flat for nearly an hour, Clio sent him off to get a takeaway. Fresh air and a brisk walk made him feel hopeful, but when he got back there was still no news.

For a while he and his mother pecked at their food in silence, but then she dropped her fork and moaned, 'I can't *bear* this. Edie!'

His twin's name brought back a rush of the fear and isolation that had struck him earlier. 'We *can't* just sit here and wait for the coastguard to call.' He leapt to his feet. 'We've got to do something.'

'What about asking John Tamar? I got his number when Edie forwarded that text message.'

'Worth a try, Mum. He found Teddy's address, didn't he?'

Moments later, Clio was clutching the phone to her ear. 'It's Clio Quentance here. I'm so sorry to bother you, but Edie's disappeared out at sea somewhere and we're at our wits' end ... Would you really? Would you? We're in Bath.'

When the conversation was over, Clio looked at him, damp-eyed. 'He's been in Cheltenham all day and he's in his car now, quite close by, and he's coming straight here. We can't see him in the kitchen.' She stood up. 'Let's go into the sitting-room.'

'I'll get it,' Oscar said when the doorbell rang. He'd only seen John Tamar a couple of times, and then only from a distance, so it was a surprise when he found that despite his own height he had to look quite a long way up to meet his eyes. Odd eyes they were too, one blue and one hazel. As they shook hands, Oscar realised he was a lot younger than he'd assumed, clearly not much more than thirty, and then he was caught by something in Tamar's expression. There was a thoughtfulness there, a lightness, and some-thing else that he couldn't quite make out. Whatever it was, Oscar felt that here was a man he was going to get on with.

This impression was borne out when he saw how kind John Tamar was to Clio. As soon as they were sitting down he reached out and engulfed one of Clio's small hands in his own large one. 'I can't tell you how glad I am that you rang me. I'll do everything I can to help find Edie, but at the moment all I know is that she's missing.' Still holding Clio's hand, he looked over to where Oscar was sitting. 'Could someone tell me what's happened?'

'She went off alone on *Cassandra* this morning,' Oscar said, 'and she hasn't been seen since.'

'I see.' Tamar nodded slowly. 'And where was she going?'

'I don't even know,' Clio groaned.

'It's all right, Mum.' Putting his arms round her, Oscar spoke into her hair. 'Why don't you go and lie down while we see what can be done?'

To his relief, Clio took the hint. As soon as she'd gone off to her bedroom, Oscar said, 'This room's freezing.' He led their guest next door into the kitchen, saying, 'It was so kind of you to come here, Lord Tamar. Do you think you can help?'

'As long as you call me John,' he laughed. 'Too much respect goes to my head.'

'John then.' Oscar managed a grin as they sat down at the table.

'So can you tell me everything you know?'

'Edie left Dartmouth in *Cassandra* this morning.'

'What time?'

'The coastguard keeps asking me that, and I wish I knew. She's usually up at some revolting hour to go for a run, so she might well have left around dawn. But on the other hand, it could have been later.'

'Where was she going?'

Oscar hesitated. So far, he'd told no one but the coastguard where Edie had gone. She had his notebook. He couldn't risk Max finding out what she was planning. Oscar took a deep breath. His job wasn't everything, he could get another one. He couldn't get another twin though. 'Guernsey,' he said.

'Do you know why she was going there?' As Oscar stared into those odd-coloured eyes, he recognised the look he hadn't quite been able to interpret earlier. It was integrity. This was a man he could trust.

'I gave her a list of all my uncle's clients. Names, aliases and account numbers. Max moves and cleans money,' he went on baldly. 'He uses Guernsey for some of his offshore accounts, and Edie was going to show my list to the authorities over there.'

John's reaction astonished him. He thumped his fist on the wooden table and said, 'Why the hell didn't she tell *me* she had that client list? Was Edie covering up for your uncle?'

'Of course not! She didn't tell anyone because she promised me she wouldn't.'

'Why ever would she make a promise like that?'

'I asked her to.' Oscar looked away, ashamed to meet John's eyes. 'Max would chuck me out on my ear if he even knew I'd been writing down details of his clients, let alone passing them on to Edie.'

'I've been a fool,' John said quietly, 'a suspicious fool. It's my job not to trust people, but I should have seen that your sister's as straight as a die.'

'I'd trust Edie with my life. I just pray she's still alive.'

'Dear God, so do I.' He felt John's hand touch his shoulder. 'What are the coastguards saying?'

'When I first called them, they thought she'd just turn up. There was a storm this afternoon and they guessed she'd been blown off course. They're taking it seriously now, but the trouble is, we've no idea where to look.' That terrible, choking feeling of fear and loneliness rose in his throat.

'No Mayday call's been picked up, in fact she's not been in radio contact at all. And there've been no distress rockets seen. They've widened the search right out into the Atlantic, but *Cassandra* just seems to have vanished.'

'I've an idea!' John got up suddenly. 'I wish I'd trusted Edie, but because I didn't, there's a chance I may be able to help track that boat of hers down.' His rapid footsteps retreated off down the corridor.

Left alone in his mother's kitchen, Oscar pulled out his phone. Automatically, he called Edie, but all he could hear was the 'unobtainable' sound. With a sigh, he dialled another number. It was time Dad knew what was happening.

TWENTY-SEVEN

Max groaned as a beam of wintry sunlight lanced through a gap in the curtains and struck his eyes. He rolled over on his pile of pillows to peer at his bedside clock. Twelve-thirty. He'd slept till nearly lunchtime and, even worse, it was a Monday. He was always in his office by nine after a weekend, and Claudine would have no way of finding out what he was up to because his mobile was disconnected. His mind worked slowly as he struggled to wake up.

He remembered switching his handset off at six that morning because he just had to get some sleep. His brother had started ringing late the previous evening, and had bombarded him with contradictory calls throughout the night. Edie had vanished without telling anyone what the hell she was up to. She'd taken *Cassandra* – she might have drowned! Did Max really think the wretched girl would try to sell the bank? Not even a distress call from his poor little Edie – the waiting was unbearable! She'd been going to Guernsey. If Max's business was damaged by her snooping they'd be in one hell of a mess. The coastguard had called off the search for the rest of the night – it was outrageous!

Max was suddenly wide awake. At some points during that long night, Alec had sounded quite close to collapse, and now he must be wondering why his brother had stopped answering his phone. But before he rang Alec, he'd better call Clio's flat to find out the latest news. Surely Edie would have turned up by now.

He switched his phone back on and selected the Bath number. After a couple of rings, a sleepy voice answered, 'Hello.'

'Oscar? Is that you?'

'Yes, Max.' His nephew sounded muted, but that might just be exhaustion.

'Any news?' he said eagerly. 'Has Edie been found?'

'I'm afraid not. They've been out searching since dawn, but *Cassandra* could be anywhere in a massive radius by now.'

Max felt his shoulders sag, but he knew how important it was to stay optimistic. Trying to keep his voice bright, he asked, 'How's Clio?'

'There's no sound from her, so I hope she's asleep.'

'Well, tell her I'm thinking of her when she wakes up, will you? And let me know the moment there's any news.'

'Will do.' Max heard his nephew drop the receiver with a clatter. Poor Oscar must be just as exhausted and anxious as the rest of them.

No, he corrected himself. Not as anxious. No one could have as much to worry about as he had. For once, his innate cheerfulness deserted him as his gaze roamed bleakly round his bedroom walls. A Largillière, two Chardins, a Watteau. He closed his eyes. They were the fruits of some of Alec's

most profitable foreclosures, but even his brother's presents couldn't lift his mood when there was so much to
make him miserable.

Edie was missing on some unspecified trip to Guernsey,
one of his favourite places for depositing his clients' cash.
That thought alone would be enough to upset him, but
there was far, far worse. He could still hardly believe it, but
he'd taken Platon Dyengi's gold, and he'd deposited it with
another bank in return for a loan to shore up Alec's Ponzi
scheme. The fraud was massive. How long would his brother
need to be bailed out for? Max's mind moved feverishly on
to the Russian. Supposing he suddenly wanted his gold back?
As an image of Dyengi's dark eyes flashed through his brain,
Max reached for the phone.

'Is that you, Max?' Alec was talking before he'd even had
the chance to say hello. 'Have you heard any news about
Edie?'

'Still nothing. I've just come off the phone to Oscar.' There
was no answer from his brother, so Max went on, 'Are you
all right? Do you want me to come over to London?'

'Not today. I'm going to Bath to see Clio, but I'll have to
get back to the bank tomorrow morning. Will you come
then?'

Max didn't hesitate. 'Of course I will.' He called the
Eurostar timetable up in his memory. 'If I get the seven-
minutes-past-eight train tomorrow morning, I'll be with you
by ten.'

'I'll be able to cope if you're with me.'

Touched by his words, Max decided not to ask his brother
about raising the funds to buy back Dyengi's gold. It could

wait till the next day. 'Take care of yourself,' he said gently, 'and I'll see you in St James's Square tomorrow.'

As Max stumbled downstairs to cook himself a lonely brunch, depression wrapped him like a damp cloud. While he was eating he tried to read a newspaper, but it was impossible to concentrate. His mind moved to Zita. He imagined that he was looking at her, but as his eyes travelled down the curves of her body, dejection hit him again. They'd never even had a proper kiss. Every time he approached her, she seemed to slide away.

Pushing his half-eaten food aside, Max tried to comfort himself by riffling through the images of Zita stored in his memory, but quite unexpectedly Isaiah Jerichau's face interposed itself. He saw himself and Isaiah sitting in a restaurant together, waiting for Zita to arrive. Jerichau's lips were moving, and a moment later, the words followed. *Maybe it's the* letto nuziale *she's after.* Could that be the answer? He got up and hurried off to get his coat. There was a jeweller he knew in the Marais. Zita would like things done the old-fashioned way.

An hour later he was unlocking his front door again, his head buzzing with dreams of Miss Zita Fitz becoming Mrs Maximilian Quentance. While he was out, he'd called Oscar again to be told that there was no news, and he'd also taken a moment to chase a recalcitrant client as he waited for his card transaction to go through, but he wouldn't ring Zita till he was on his own. But once in the hallway, he couldn't even wait to take off his overcoat before he called her. It took several rings before she answered her mobile, and Max fondly imagined her scrabbling for it in one of her fashionably voluminous handbags.

'Hi, Max,' he heard her voice at last. '*Tout va bien?*'

'Not *bien* at all. Edie's gone missing on *Cassandra*.'

'Impossible!' He heard the sudden tapping of high heels on a pavement. 'I'm coming straight over.' She cut him off before he had a chance to say why he was ringing.

No more than ten minutes later, she arrived on his doorstep. Instead of being perfectly groomed, Max was touched to see Zita looking red-faced and almost dishevelled, as if she'd been running. What an angel she was to care about his niece's safety when she'd scarcely even met her.

'Tell me what's happened,' she said as soon as he'd closed the door behind her. 'Edie can't be lost!'

'She is, but I'm sure she'll turn up. There's a full search going on, and you know what a sound boat *Cassandra* is. Why don't we talk upstairs?'

Max took Zita's arm and guided her up to his first-floor *salon*. What he had to say needed a certain formality, and he'd already put a bottle of champagne and a couple of glasses on one of the side tables. She didn't seem to notice them as he led her into the room, perching herself on one half of his double-sided *duchesse* chair while he sat on the other half.

'Tell me everything!' Zita said, her eyes wide.

He looked at her dear face, at her hair blown into untidy strands as she'd rushed to see him. This was the woman he loved. Of course he'd tell her everything. 'I'm terribly worried, and not just about Edie.' Holding her eyes with his, he said, 'My brother's been running a Ponzi scheme from London. His investors have started asking for their money back and I've let him use Dyengi's gold to pay them.'

'No,' she whispered. 'I don't believe you've done that.'

'It's true.' His heart started thumping as her fear infected him.

'He'll kill you! I swear to you, Max, you're a dead man if he finds out!'

'He's not going to find out.' Max spoke as confidently as he could. 'Alec's promised he can lure in new investors, and Platon Dyengi's gold will be back in our vaults in no time.'

'If only I'd never introduced you to him.' Zita reached over to touch his arm. 'I couldn't bear it if anything happened to you.'

There was no possible doubt about that look in her eyes. In one easy movement, Max had pulled the little box out and slid down on to one knee in front of her. He lifted the rose cluster of diamonds out of its velvet bed and laid it in the palm of her gloved hand.

'My darling—' he started, but she pulled back with a little cry.

'No!' She wasn't looking at him, but at the glittering jewel.

Assuming she was just hesitant as he'd heard women being proposed to always were, he went on, 'I adore you, Zita. Will you marry me?'

'No, Max.' She rose to her feet. 'I can't.'

'Don't you love me?' he asked, getting up off his knees. This must be some sort of a game that women played.

Zita walked away from him towards one of the floor-length windows, her back straight as a ruler. 'I do love you,

Max,' she said to the wintry garden below. 'Just not in the way you want me to.' She revolved on the ball of one foot until she was facing him again. 'And I never will.'

'I see.' Max put the empty box back in his pocket. 'I'm going over to London first thing in the morning.' His voice didn't sound very steady but it was the best he could manage. 'I may not see you for a while.'

'Max?' Squeezing his hands into tight fists in his pockets, he turned his back so he wouldn't have to look at her. 'Will you let me know when Edie's found?'

'Of course,' he said, but he didn't turn round.

'And Max?' This time he made no sign that he'd heard her. 'For God's sake be careful with that gold.' Her voice sank. 'I'm so sorry.'

'Please, Zita. Just go.'

She lingered for a long time, but he managed to keep completely still. Eventually, he heard her footsteps moving away across the *salon*, then her heels clicked down the stairs and across the hall. Max didn't move until he heard the front door close behind her.

TWENTY-EIGHT

When Edie woke up, she found herself curled into a ball against one side of the life-raft. Her head was pounding, and as she stared into the darkness around her the uncontrollable shivering started. Occasionally during the day, in between bouts of seasickness, she'd felt the thin sunshine penetrating through the sides of her shelter, but it hadn't been warm enough to dry her jeans, and now she had another freezing night in damp clothes to get through. Why had no one found her? She put a hand to her mouth and tried to blow some warmth into her icy fingers while she counted how long she'd been here. Sunday afternoon, Sunday night, all day Monday, and now she was facing a second night alone. How could she bear it?

'Don't be a tit!' Edie admonished herself out loud. 'Pull yourself together!' She struggled to sit up but was overcome by dizziness. She closed her eyes and felt her confined world spin madly around her. Eventually, the giddiness passed off and she forced herself upright. If she was going to survive, she couldn't afford to abandon herself to despair again.

After watching *Cassandra* sink and bailing out the life-raft, she'd simply given up, collapsing in a huddle on the wet, black floor where she'd finally cried herself to sleep. When she'd woken up, it had been pitch dark outside and she'd no idea whether it was still Sunday night or the early hours of Monday morning. At least the sleep must have restored some of her strength, because she'd been able to think quite rationally. She'd known she must get something to eat straight away. Chocolate would help drive out the cold and it would raise her flagging spirits.

Edie remembered how she'd scrabbled through her grab-bag in the dark, but her numbed fingers hadn't been able to feel the emergency bar of chocolate. She had managed to find her torch, and with the help of its light she'd made a careful search right through her satchel. The first thing she'd pulled out had been the emergency flares. There were the handheld ones to guide a rescue ship towards her at night-time, but the distress flare was an orange smoke rocket. It could only be seen in daylight, so it was useless to fire it now. She'd wasted the whole of Sunday afternoon either sobbing or sleeping when she might have been signalling for help!

In the torchlight she'd checked every single thing in the grab-bag. She'd found Oscar's notebook, and there was a pen in the bag as well. She'd stared at it, sure she hadn't put it there herself. Then she'd pulled out the fishing line, the signalling mirror, a twenty-four-hour supply of seasickness pills, everything she'd expected except the chocolate. It had taken her a while to realise what had happened. In her panicky rush to leave her sinking boat, she'd picked up the water bottles from where they'd been rolling on the floor, but she hadn't spotted the chocolate. By now it was at the bottom of the sea, along with her beloved *Cassandra*.

With nothing at all to eat, Edie had thought things couldn't get any worse, until she felt the heave of the life-raft beneath her. The torch had begun to flicker, and after making sure she could reach the water bottles and seasickness pills, she'd switched it off. For the rest of that night and during the whole of Monday she'd been sicker than she could have dreamed possible. As the sea had got up, the black floor of the life-raft had surged under her, sliding up and down over the waves like a giant water-bed. Almost worse, the raft had begun to spin, and the combined lifting and whirling movements had been like some nightmare fairground ride. The anti-nausea pills couldn't cope at all.

At one point during the day the sea had calmed enough for her to be able to undo the zip and fire off the orange smoke signal, only for the wind to whip it horizontally away along the surface of the sea where no one could see it. After that the waves had risen again, and Edie had been thrown about inside the life-raft, too weak to hold herself still, too sick to do more than surrender to an endless cycle of sipping water and throwing it up again. As the day had dragged towards evening, she'd known she was getting through the water too fast, but the constant vomiting had only added to her thirst. Not until dark had fallen did the sea began to slacken, by which time she was too exhausted to care. Her head thumping painfully in time with her heartbeat, she'd felt herself drifting into unconsciousness.

Now that she was awake again, Edie rested against the side of the life-raft and tried to concentrate. It was frustrating, but every time she focused on anything, a haze seemed to drift inside her throbbing head and confuse her. She set herself the task of working out how to get drinking water. Dehydration would kill her long before cold and hunger. Was that true? She'd read it somewhere. Could she collect rainwater in the bailer? That was a good idea. If it rained. Mustn't drink seawater, it drove you mad. Seawater stayed static, Max had told her. The water inside a wave didn't flow along with it. Funny thing, that. Each drop of water orbited within the wave then returned to its original position. Not really very funny.

Realising that she'd slumped down towards the floor, Edie pushed herself back upright and buried her aching head in her hands. She was fed up with the dark. Should she leave her torch on all night? If there was a boat passing near by, it might see the light shining out from her life-raft. But then the battery would go flat and she'd have no light in an emergency. Lights on the masthead. Red over white, fishing tonight. No. Much better to be coming into harbour. White over red, safe home to bed.

When she came to, one side of her face was in a sick-smelling puddle in the bottom of the raft. She couldn't see a thing in the pitch darkness, but as she tried to get her tired arms to push her body upright, she let out a cry of horror. That green thing she'd seen in the bilges, it had come after her. She'd felt it, floating against her face. The thing was in the raft, waiting to nip her. With a whimper, she made herself as small as she could. Lying pressed against the rubbery walls, her brain cleared suddenly. Was she hallucinating?

Was this nightmare-filled terror how it felt when you were about to die?

Mother of Christ. Where'd that come from? She said the words out loud. 'Mother of Christ.' She must have learned it somewhere, and she was glad because it felt very comforting. 'Mother of Christ.' No, wait, there was more. 'Mother of Christ, star of the sea.' With an effort, Edie struggled once more into a sitting position, then, leaning her head back against the canvas walls of her shelter, she repeated the words over and over again. 'Mother of Christ, star of the sea. Mother of Christ, star of the sea.' A bloated green rat's body drifted before her eyes, but the name of the Star drove it right away. 'Mother of Christ, star of the sea.'

There was a roaring noise from outside and then a great brightness shone through the orange fabric. Relief flooded through her. It was the star of the sea, come to rescue her. But the noise grew louder. There was too much light. The star would devour her! Edie cowered in terror as she watched the life-raft's zip slide open. But it wasn't the blazing star of the sea whose head came in. It was a black seal, dripping wet. She froze into utter stillness as the seal goggled at her.

'Hello there,' it croaked. 'Anyone alive in here?'

Edie felt she'd been cruelly deceived. It wasn't the star, it wasn't even a seal. 'Fuck off, froggy,' she muttered crossly.

The frog gave a gulping noise which might have been a laugh and called over its shoulder, 'She's alive all right.'

TWENTY-NINE

As the early-morning Eurostar shot into a tunnel on the outskirts of Paris, Max caught a glimpse of his face reflected in the sudden darkness of the window and felt a fleeting relief that Zita couldn't see him. His hair was dishevelled, his cheeks had sagged and there were deep rings under his eyes. Not really surprising, he thought, as the train flashed out into a grey daylight, he'd hardly slept at all. There was an unwashed taste in his mouth though he was sure he'd remembered to clean his teeth before he left, and when he looked down at his hands he saw that he'd put on non-matching cufflinks. He switched his gaze back to the window, where the flat fields of northern France were shrugging off the Parisian suburbs, and wondered if he'd ever be happy again.

The train flashed over a level crossing and he caught a glimpse of a young couple on bicycles, snatching a kiss while they waited for the barriers to open. Why wouldn't Zita let him kiss her like that? He'd been so hurt that he hadn't even taken the trouble to ask. Max turned from the window and as he gazed vaguely down the grey velour seats of business class he caught the eye of a dark-haired man who was shifting his shoulders uncomfortably in a suit that seemed far too tight. Normally Max would have flashed him a friendly smile, but he was too unhappy to do more than nod before turning to stare out at the drab ploughland again.

He should never have let Zita go like that. A decent man would have tried to understand what was wrong rather than driving the woman he adored out into the dismal Paris rain. Her last words to him had shown how much she cared. She'd warned him about Platon Dyengi's gold, as if she'd been truly frightened for him. 'I'm so sorry,' she'd said. And he hadn't even bothered to ask why.

'Would you like some coffee?' The stewardess's voice interrupted his miserable self-reproach.

'Yes please,' he said, though he knew he wouldn't touch Eurostar's undrinkable coffee.

'I'll be back shortly with breakfast,' the woman said brightly, and as she moved off down the aisle, something in her height and angularity reminded him of his niece.

When he hadn't been agonising over Zita, the remainder of Max's night had been spent worrying about Edie. It was Tuesday morning now, and she'd been missing since Sunday. He'd checked with Alec just before he went to bed, but there'd been no news, just a catch in his brother's voice as he'd begged him to get the earliest possible train to London. So here he was on the 08:07 and dreading the day ahead of him. He'd have to try to support Alec while keeping quiet about his own heartbreak.

Max checked his watch. It would be seven-forty-five in

England. His brother should be on his way back to London by now. He picked up his mobile, but before he'd had time to dial the phone started to ring.

'Edie's safe!' Alec's voice bellowed in his ear. 'It's the most extraordinary story! She was picked up by the Royal Marines a couple of hours before dawn. She was in a life-raft, right out in the middle of the ocean.'

'That's brilliant news! Brilliant! However did they find her?'

'I've absolutely no idea. All I know is she's safe. Where are you?'

'I'm on my way to London.' Noticing that the young man in the over-tight suit was staring at him, Max lowered his voice. 'I'm thrilled about Edie, but since I'm already on the train, I'll come and see you anyway.' As he rang off, Max felt a wave of relief. Now his niece had been found, he'd be free to pour his own misery into his brother's ear. And just as importantly, Alec would be able to concentrate on pulling new investors into the Adamantine Fund so Max could stop fretting over the Russian's gold.

While the train flew northwards through the Pas de Calais, Max toyed with an omelette and tried to read his paper, but he found it hard to concentrate. Maybe it was just his general upset, or the fact that he'd had no sleep, but he was beginning to get the feeling that he was being watched. The dark-haired young man had struggled out of his jacket to reveal a sweat-stained shirt and a very broad pair of shoulders. He had a laptop open in front of him, but every time Max glanced at him, he seemed to catch his eye. There was someone else too. An older man, also wearing a suit but with an incongruous pair of grey trainers on his feet, seemed to pass up and down through the carriage rather too frequently.

As he was trying to persuade himself that he was imagining things, there was a screech of brakes. The train jolted, slowed down, then came to a halt. There was a long silence while Max stared blankly out at the dismal view of Flanders fields stretching away to a flat horizon, until eventually that most depressing of announcements came. '*Mesdames, messieurs, votre attention, s'il vous plaît. En raison d'un accident de personnes …*' Max stopped listening. Wretched train, it was an absolute magnet for death-jumpers.

The man in grey trainers came padding back along the compartment towards him. There was a soft cough as the stranger passed his seat, and Max had the uncomfortable sense that he'd paused just behind him. Could it be a disgruntled client? Some nosy authority? A Russian, even? He felt a prickle of fear. If anyone really was trying to get at him, they'd do it in the darkness of the Channel Tunnel. He needed to be off the train before then. He'd get a hire-car to pick him up at Calais and take him right through to St James's Square.

Max dialled his secretary's number and as soon as she answered he said urgently, '*J'ai besoin d'une voiture à Calais.*'

'*D'accord, Max.*' Claudine's easy competence calmed him as he dictated his instructions.

The train pulled in to the Gare de Calais Frethun nearly an hour late, by which time Max was beginning to feel that his panicky change of plan had been foolish. The broad-shouldered young man was still in his seat, but for ages he'd scarcely taken his nose from his laptop, while the older one with the trainers seemed to have vanished completely. Still, the car would be outside waiting for him by now, and it was far too late to change his mind. Gathering up his brief-case and his overnight bag, Max stepped off the train into the concrete, metal and glass structure that was Frethun Station.

It was an uncomfortable place, an anonymous outpost of the Channel Tunnel which had been dropped on to this isolated spot to the south of Calais and was surrounded by nothing but derelict farm buildings and empty fields. A cold wind whipped round the pylons supporting an arch-modernist roof, and Max shivered as he hurried towards the *sortie*. With a murmur of gratitude for Claudine's effi-ciency, he spotted a large M. QUENTANCE card and walked briskly over to the man holding it.

'*Monsieur Quentance, c'est vous?*'

'*Oui, c'est moi.*'

Taking his overnight bag with a polite smile, the driver said, '*Suivez-moi, monsieur. La voiture vous attende dehors.*'

As the man led him out to a big, black-windowed Mercedes, Max decided he'd get a present for Claudine while he was in London. She really had done very well to organise some-thing so comfortable at such short notice.

'*Tout va bien, monsieur?*' His chauffeur glanced at him in the driving-mirror as the car accelerated away from the station. Max feared that if he gave him any encouragement, the man might expect to chat all the way to London.

'*Assez bien, merci,*' he said, before opening his briefcase and noisily pulling out some papers.

There was no further comment from the front, and after a while Max looked up from the handful of dull memoranda he'd brought with him and stared out through the car's blacked-out window. The dark glass made the dreary flatlands round Calais seem even more sombre, and he was glad when they joined the A16 and began to pass retail parks and other signs of humanity. He was still gazing outside when he noticed they were coming up to Junction 42 and a sign indicating, TUNNEL SOUS LA MANCHE. The driver was speeding along the outside lane of the *autoroute* and swept past the junction without appearing to have noticed it.

Max leaned forwards, exclaiming, '*Mais vous avez loupé la sortie!*'

'*Déviation, monsieur.*'

Max hadn't seen any sign of it, but presumably the man knew what he was doing. He had just settled back in his seat when the chauffeur swerved across to the inside lane and shot down the exit road for Calais St-Pierre.

'*Mais pourquoi va-t'on ici?*'

'*C'est plus vite par là.*'

Max didn't know Calais well enough to argue, but he peered out of the window, searching for any signs to the Channel Tunnel. They were passing through a bleak area of industrial estates, empty of anything but wind-blown posters and a few rusting cars when, with a loud squealing of tyres, the driver pulled the Mercedes to a halt. Before he realised what was happening, the door beside Max opened and a stranger pushed his way into the back seat next to him.

Something was terribly wrong. Max slid over to the other side of the car and tried to open the door. It took him a few moments of tugging at the handle before he realised that it was locked. 'What's going on?' he roared. 'Let me out!'

'*C'est un copain*,' the driver said calmly, making a racing start away from the kerb.

Max eyed the man beside him, taking in high cheekbones, slanting eyes and a square chin. 'Who the hell are you?' He'd tried to keep his voice firm, but his words came out in a squeaky shout.

His wrist was grasped in such an agonising grip that he could feel his bones crunching together. '*Tiho, a to etoi zhe vot rukoi tebe sheyu skruchu!*' Max wished he hadn't understood. He'd said that he'd twist his head off if he didn't shut up.

The man was built like a heavyweight boxer and there was no way he could fight him. Instead, Max shrank as far into his own corner as he could and stared out of the window. After a while, he saw that they were joining the A16 again and a bit of his normal optimism crept back. Surely nothing much could happen to him on a motorway? As they swept through a tunnel, he caught a brief flash of his shadowy reflection in the darkened glass. He adjusted his features from their look of abject terror and relaxed his hunched shoulders. Maybe this was all someone's ghastly idea of a practical joke?

Or maybe not. They were nearing another turn-off, Junction 49, and the driver was pulling across to the inside lane. Max felt his pulse hammering in his throat as he read the sign. AÉRODROME DE MARCK. Sweat trickled from his armpits as they hurtled off down the slip road. *Aérodrome.* Even the word filled him with fear.

As if not wanting to draw undue attention to the Mercedes, the chauffeur slowed right down through the village of Marck and Max stared hopelessly at bleak lines of single-storey whitewashed houses and deserted pavements, which soon petered out as they drove on into an area of flat, marshy countryside. Max could see nothing alive apart from a few scruffy horses grazing the thin coastal grasses, their tails turned to the sharp winter wind. He'd seen no more signs to the aerodrome and was beginning to hope that it wasn't where they were headed when they passed a tattered wind-sock, swinging and tugging against its pole. A moment later, the car juddered across an area of uneven concrete, and then they came to a halt in front of a line of low buildings.

As the driver came round to open his door, Max had a brief idea of struggling and running until the big Russian wrenched his arm up into the small of his back.

'Vnyeh!'

Max had no choice. He climbed out of the car, and because of the angle he was being held at, he was forced to shuffle forwards across the rough concrete slabs, bent over like an old man.

As they came up to a door the hold on his wrist relaxed a little, allowing Max to stand upright. He peered at a wind-torn notice nailed to the entrance. Written in both French and English, it read FLYING SCHOOL. TOURIST FLIGHTS AVAILABLE IN SEASON. Just below it a handwritten sign had been stuck. FERMÉ. There was no explanation, no indication of how long the place was going to be closed, but there was no doubt that it was deserted. Whatever he was facing, he'd have to face it alone.

Through the dirty glass of the door, he saw a figure. The man was standing in the shadows so that his face was impossible to make out through the grimy pane, but Max knew who it was. Platon Dyengi was waiting for him.

THIRTY

Edie opened her eyes. The room was dim, though light seeping through the curtains showed that it was daytime. Her hands moved over a strange bed. Sheets, blankets, the silky plumpness of an old-fashioned eiderdown. And on the walls a muddle of photographs, watercolours and pen-and-ink drawings hung in every available space. The floor was cluttered, too. Ties, socks, piles of books. A masculine room, but whose? Closing her eyes, she tried to collect her fragmented memories.

There'd been lights, a noise, then she'd been hauled out of the life-raft. The rescue boat had smelled strange, a mixture of carbon fibre, rubber and gunpowder, and she'd glimpsed sailors, armed sailors. And wasn't there a paramedic who'd said she was dehydrated? Edie ran a finger down her wrist and felt a plaster where the drip had gone in. So that bit was true. She was sure someone had taken her clothes off and helped her to get clean. And hadn't they wrapped her in a blanket and put her in a bunk? The rest of the night was a haze. She had a notion she'd seen John when she was being brought ashore, but that didn't seem right. She must have dreamed that bit.

Edie ran her tongue over her teeth, aware of a filthy taste in her mouth. She'd spotted a white porcelain basin in one corner of the room, so at least she could have a good rinse. It took her a moment to struggle out from under the bedclothes, then she tested the floor with a cautious foot, feeling wooden boards and a rough bedside rug. Her legs were wobbly, but otherwise she felt fine as she went over to the window. She opened the curtains to find herself staring down on an unfamiliar wilderness of orchard and grass. Wherever she might be, she certainly wasn't looking at the sterile perfection of Dartleap's lawns.

Someone had left a toothbrush and toothpaste in a mug by the basin and she felt much better once she'd scrubbed the taste of sick out of her mouth. Catching sight of a mirror propped against one of the walls, she went over to look at herself. Her hair was wild, and there was a big bruise over one eyebrow. She glanced down at her legs and saw that she'd cut one of her knees. She also noticed that she was wearing a large, man's shirt.

Hearing footsteps outside, Edie swung round just as the door opened, and to her amazement John Tamar walked in, carrying a mug and a plate and bringing the delicious smell of Marmite toast. 'It's actually lunchtime,' he said cheerfully, 'but I thought you ought to have breakfast first. And I'm glad to see you in front of a mirror as usual.'

Uncomfortably aware that she was naked under the cotton shirt, Edie went back to the shelter of the bedclothes. 'What are you doing here?'

'I don't really see why I shouldn't be,' he said calmly. 'You've been sleeping in my bed and that's my shirt you're wearing.'

'Oh,' Edie said. 'Does that mean . . .'

'It's all right,' he said, passing her the mug and the plate. 'The paramedic looked after you, and as this was the only bed made up I slept on the sofa downstairs.' He sat down beside her. 'I dare say you want to thank me.'

'Thank you?' Edie looked at him suspiciously. 'What for?'

'Did you notice the pen in your grab-bag?' Edie nodded and waited for him to go on. 'There was a tracking device hidden in it. I slipped it inside that satchel of yours when I thought you might be using *Cassandra* for gold-running.'

'You thought *I* was gold-running?'

Ignoring the question, he said, 'That tracker saved your life. When I heard you'd gone missing, I got in touch with the people who use my coastal land for training. They contacted their mates in the Royal Marines, who managed to pick up a signal. They found you bobbing about on the Atlantic, miles off the main shipping lanes, dehydrated but otherwise fine. It seemed easiest for them to bring you to Brink Castle and so here you are.' He leaned forwards and took her mug. 'How are you feeling?'

'Stronger.' Edie reached for the last piece of toast, but John whisked the plate away. He bent forwards and brushed her bruised forehead with his lips, then he kissed her once, very gently, on her mouth.

'Now, about this shirt of mine,' he said, and started to undo the buttons.

*

He was asleep, flat on his back beside her, when Edie woke up. For a while she lay immobile, looking at his firm profile, his neck, the muscle on his chest and abdomen. His breathing went on, calm and regular, until suddenly she couldn't resist touching him. As she put a tentative hand on his shoulder, John's eyes flew open and he turned his head to smile at her. Then he rolled towards her lazily, his warm hand closing on her right breast. 'Hungry?' he asked.

'Ravenous!' She reached up to his face, running her finger down along his cheekbones and nose and on to his lips. 'I haven't had anything proper to eat since I was on *Cassandra*.' Edie pulled her hand back and pressed it over her mouth. Saying the name of her poor boat had opened a flood of memories.

'It's all right.' John stroked her back. 'You're safe now.'

'But *Cassandra* shouldn't just have sunk like that!'

She shivered, and felt him pulling the blankets up to cover her shoulders. 'So what do you think happened?'

'She must have been deliberately holed.' Edie could remember the sinking with increasing clarity. 'Her hull smacked down on a cross-wave and I felt her flooding almost immediately. I could understand it if she'd hit a rock or something, but we were right out in the ocean. It must have been a decent-sized hole, as well. The water was streaming into the bilges when I went down to look.' She squeezed her eyes shut as she remembered. 'I dropped my emergency radio, and when I reached down to get it, I got trapped by the ballast. I thought I was going to drown.'

'But you didn't. Come on, lazybones, let's get some food.'

Although she was hungry, Edie didn't want him to let go of her. 'You can't get up yet. I haven't told you the worst thing.' She pressed herself close against his long body. 'When my hand was stuck in the bilges, there was a horrible great green thing slapping against my arm. It must have been a dead rat.'

'Rats are brown, not green.' He began kissing her.

'I thought you were starving, and besides, I must look hideous.'

'That's true,' he said, laughing down into her face, 'but you've got a beautiful soul.'

'I'd rather you thought I had a beautiful body.'

'I haven't had the chance to tell yet.' He peeled back the bedclothes. 'I'd better have a proper look.'

Afterwards, Edie was half inclined to go back to sleep again, but John wouldn't let her.

'Your poor mother's waiting for you at Dartleap. She's longing to nurse you and I promised I'd get you over there this afternoon. Tell you what,' he flung his legs over the side of the bed, 'there's half a roast chicken in the fridge and I've got a couple of ripe mangoes as well. I'll pop down-stairs and fetch them, then you can eat them while you're having a bath.'

'A bath, that would be heaven.' Edie reached out a hand so that he could pull her upright. 'Lead me to it.'

The bathroom was as endearingly scruffy as John's bedroom. There were water-stained prints all over the walls, and yet more piles of books and old magazines on the floor. John wrapped her in a towel and sat her in an armchair by the window while he turned on the taps, pouring in a whole cupful of lavender-scented bath salts. Then he went off to collect the promised food while she eased herself carefully down into the hot water.

Stretching out luxuriously, Edie smiled as a thought struck her. Despite her arty mannerisms, Clio had always been insistent that the twins behaved in a way that she described as 'proper'. Wandering around with no clothes on and eating roast chicken and mangoes in the bath would hardly have fitted her mother's idea of propriety, but to Edie, John's lack of inhibition was a joy.

He came back into the bathroom with a couple of plates, then, still naked, he collapsed into the armchair and chatted while they ate. Afterwards, he gently scrubbed her back for her, then lent her his shampoo. When he'd finally persuaded her to get out of the cooling water, he wrapped the towel round her and hugged her to him. 'Edie,' he murmured into her damp hair. 'Thank the Good Lord you're safe.'

After he'd had a quick bath himself, they had to hunt around for something for her to wear, as everything she'd worn on *Cassandra* had vanished. Eventually, half drowned in one of his jerseys and a pair of extra-long man's socks, Edie looked at herself in John's bedroom mirror. 'Oh God, I look ghastly.'

'You look lovely to me.' He came up behind her and began kissing the back of her neck. 'Irresistible.' It was nearly an hour before they were finally inside his car and driving towards Dartleap.

THIRTY-ONE

As Max stood blinking through the dirty glass of the Aérodrome de Marck's main building, Platon Dyengi nodded once in his direction, and immediately the door creaked open. Max felt a shove in the small of his back and was propelled forwards, almost stumbling to his knees in front of the hard-eyed Russian. Dyengi watched as he recovered his balance, and while Max was still scrambling for words he said, 'Mr Quentance. I want to talk to you.'

You're a dead man if he finds out! Zita's warning sang in his ears. Dyengi must have guessed about the missing gold. Feeling as if his legs were about to give way, he looked around for a chair, but the entrance hall they were standing in was quite empty of furniture.

'Yes, Mr Quentance. I have a problem.' Dyengi's voice was harsh. 'Your English authorities are sniffing round my affairs. Who could have told them? You promised me nothing is ever written down.'

So it *wasn't* about the gold. 'And it's true,' Max said, trying to keep the relief out of his voice. 'I write down nothing and talk to no one. I imagine it's the Treasury that's been bothering you.' A memory flickered in the back of his mind. 'Someone told me they've been sniffing round.'

'Who is sniffing?'

Max closed his eyes, and despite the remnants of fear, his brain didn't let him down. He saw Edie in his Paris house, asking about money-laundering, threatening him with the authorities. She'd mentioned John Tamar, but that had to be a joke. There was someone else she'd told him about though, a woman. The name came to him. 'Mary Kersey.'

Dyengi's reaction was immediate. 'Kersey? Mary Kersey? This woman I hate!' The Russian came so close that Max could smell the stale mixture of hair oil and tobacco that clung to him. 'And another thing. Where is my gold, Mr Quentance?' Having thought he was safe, the question stupefied Max. He stood in silence as Dyengi growled, 'You think I'm a fool? I check before I trust. I have you followed.'

Max rocked back on his heels as the memory hit him. He felt the lag in the steering of the overloaded Range-Rover as he drove towards London. He saw the sunrise on the motorway and the irritating van that kept passing and repassing him. What an idiot he'd been to think he could get away with it. He staggered, and would have fallen if someone hadn't come up behind him and grabbed him by the shoulders, preventing him from moving.

'So where is my gold?'

'It's fine, honestly, it's perfectly safe, absolutely, I'll tell you exactly where it is.' Hearing himself gabbling the details of the bank where Dyengi's gold was lodged, he tried to slow his speech. 'You'll get it all back, I swear.'

Platon Dyengi took a step backwards. Addressing whoever was behind Max, he said, '*Uvedite evo I ustroitye vse kak nado.*'

'Take me away where?' Max gasped. 'Do what?'

'Why did you tell me you don't speak Russian when you do?' Dyengi was eyeing him disdainfully. 'You lie very much, Max Quentance.'

Max tried to turn round, but the grip shifted, locking his elbows behind him so that his upper body was immobilised. 'Please! Let me go,' he begged as he found himself being shuffled forwards through the building, but the only answer was an increase in the pressure on his back and arms. A pair of glass doors appeared ahead, and beyond them a landing strip. At the sight of the small plane waiting on the runway, Max lost control. 'Not in an aeroplane,' he begged. 'No!' Despite a sudden agony in his left shoulder, he wrenched himself round so that he could scream at Dyengi, 'Joke over, for God's sake! I swear I'll get your gold back, but I must go to England.'

There was a brief silence while the Russian took a few steps towards him. 'No. You go flying.' A shout of laughter rang in Max's ears as Platon Dyengi spun on his heel and walked away.

THIRTY-TWO

'Rise and shine, Eds! Here's something to kill the morning breath.'

'Thanks, babe.' His twin rolled over in her bed and smiled at him. 'That's two mornings running I've had breakfast in bed.'

'I bet I'm a better cook than John Tamar. Don't tell me his bacon sarnies are anywhere near as nice as mine.'

'It was Marmite toast, actually. And later on we had roast chicken and mangoes in the bath.'

'No!' Oscar put the breakfast tray down with a crash. 'Don't tell me you two have been shagging?'

'You bet.'

'Good for you, Eds.' Oscar sat on the bed and took her hand. 'He rang a bit earlier, by the way. He's coming over to make sure you're OK.'

'Do you like him, Oscar? D'you think you can get on with him?'

'I *really* like him. Is it serious, Eds?'

'It is for me.'

She buried her face in the mug of tea he'd brought up,

but as she put it down again he noticed a tautness round her eyes. 'Did you sleep all right?'

'Not really. Nightmares.'

'*Cassandra* sinking?'

'More something I saw when my arm was trapped in the bilges. You know how I hate rats.' Oscar was about to say something soothing when the hand holding his tightened. 'But it can't have been! Rats don't have fingers.' She stared at him. 'It wasn't a rat at all. It was a glove, an olive-green leather glove! Whatever was it doing in *Cassandra*'s bilges?'

Oscar looked at his sister in silence. He could think of only one person who wore gloves.

THIRTY-THREE

'How was Edie, darling?' Clio called when she saw her son coming round the curve of the staircase. 'Oh sorry, I didn't realise you were on the phone.'

'Don't worry, there's no reply.' Oscar closed his mobile. 'I left Edie eating her breakfast and looking a lot brighter.'

Clio was about to slip upstairs to see her daughter for herself when the hall telephone rang. Never sure who might be calling the Dartleap number, she answered with a polite 'Good-morning.'

'It's Alec. I wondered how Edie was getting on.'

'I was just going to check.' Clio hesitated. Alec had come down to Bath as soon as he knew Edie had disappeared, and he'd stayed with her right through Monday night's vigil until they'd had the news that their daughter was safe. At the time, she'd been too concerned about her child to worry about her long-estranged husband, but now she thought about it, there'd been some vulnerability about him that she'd never seen before. 'How's everything with you?'

'Could be better.' She was right. He did sound tense. 'Some of my clients are so nervous about the crisis that they're pulling their cash out of the Adamantine Fund and stuffing it under their mattresses. I tell you, Clio,' he went on, 'I'm trying my damnedest, but I just can't find new investors to replace them.'

'I'm sorry to hear that.' It was the first time she could ever remember him sharing his business problems with her. 'Is this what you called to talk about?'

'Not particularly. I don't suppose Max has been in touch?'

'No, he hasn't. Why?'

'He was coming over yesterday morning, but he never turned up.'

'That's very unlike him.' Both brothers *always* knew where the other was. 'Does he know we found Edie?'

'I rang and told him while he was on the train but I haven't talked to him since.'

'And his office doesn't know where he's gone either?'

'They've no idea.' The wobble in his voice took Clio by surprise. 'After I'd spoken to Max, he apparently called Claudine and asked her to send a car to collect him off the Eurostar. She'd got it all arranged and the driver claims he was waiting for Max at Calais Frethun, but then he was told he wouldn't be needed after all.'

'Max has always been very fond of Edie,' Clio suggested. 'Perhaps when you told him she was safe, he decided to skip off on *Cilissa* and celebrate.'

'I bet that's it!' Alec's voice brightened. 'He's got what sounds like rather a serious girlfriend, and he's told me she loves the sea. Thanks for cheering me up.'

'Any time.' Clio found herself smiling into the receiver. 'Let me know when you find him, won't you?'

A few minutes later, she was arranging flowers for the drawing-room when the phone rang again. 'Good-morning.'

'Hello, Mrs Quentance, I'm glad I've tracked you down. It's Joel Howland here.' With everything else that had been going on, it took Clio a moment to remember. The cold-case review into Ianthe's death; the DNA tests against those hairs she'd found on the body. 'Mrs Quentance? I hope I'm not disturbing you too early?'

'Not at all, Inspector. Any news?'

'As a matter of fact, there is.' If she hadn't believed that his calm was unshakeable, Clio might have thought the police inspector was excited. 'Could I come over to see you? I'm not far away.'

'Of course.'

Half an hour later, Clio was checking her appearance in one of the sharp-bevelled mirrors hanging on the drawing-room walls when she caught sight of her daughter reflected in the doorway behind her.

'Edie!' She swung round to face her. 'You look lovely!'

'Thanks, Mum. John's coming over in a minute.'

'Inspector Howland's on his way to see me, too.' With her daughter restored to her and looking so beautiful, how could an extra visitor matter? 'The more the merrier.'

The doorbell rang, followed by a shout from Oscar in the hall – 'I'll get it!' –and shortly afterwards he came into the drawing-room, followed by Joel Howland.

Clio shook his hand before turning to her twins. 'Darlings, this is Inspector Howland. Can I get you some coffee,

Inspector? Biscuits?' Clio caught an underlying sense of excitement in his crisp refusal of anything to eat or drink, and it was only a few minutes before he was sitting beside her on a low-backed sofa while Edie and Oscar sat on a couple of armchairs.

'We've had something of a breakthrough,' the inspector started immediately. 'And it's all thanks to that tip you gave us about a Mr Edward Quentance living in the Italian lakes.'

'Did you manage to talk to him?' Clio leaned forwards eagerly. 'Is he still *compos mentis*?'

'Oh yes, he's still got his marbles. He's had something on his mind for a long time, and I think he was really quite relieved to talk. I've brought the recording of what he said.' Clio saw him glance at Edie and Oscar before turning back to face her. 'There's no easy way of saying this,' he said gently. 'The bald fact is that he's your kidnapper. It was Edward Quentance who took Ianthe away.'

'Teddy?' As she felt the room begin to spin, Clio reached out blindly in front of her. When she opened her eyes she found Oscar squatting at her feet.

'It's all right, Mum. You don't have to listen if you don't want to.'

'I think I need to know it all now, darling.' She turned to Joel Howland. 'Will you play the interview?'

He pulled a little machine out of his briefcase, and a moment later the husky voice of an old man filled the room. His sentences were short, with long pauses for breath in between. 'Bloody family drove me out of my home ... My own father banished me from Dartleap ... struck me out of his will, just for running off with my little Eve ... Quite wrong. Richard never loved her, used to beat her up ... My own Evie. She died, you know?'

Teddy's words ended in a confused splutter of coughing, and then the inspector's voice said, 'There's no hurry, Mr Quentance. Would you like some of this water?'

Over the noise from the tape, Clio caught a single ring on the doorbell. She looked up to see that Edie was already slipping out.

'Quentance gold. I'd heard about it for years. Not just when I was a kid in England, but in Europe too ... A mouth in a bar in Vienna, a tart in West Berlin ...' There was a sudden break, a hacking cough and then he went on, 'It was always the same story ... My father Kit had a fortune in gold hidden away somewhere ... Stolen off *Titanic*, was the rumour. I picked up other stories, too ... I bumped into an old couple in Rome once. Can't remember their names ... told them I was Teddy Quentance ... Was I related to Kit Quentance, they asked. I said yes, he was my bloody father ...'

In the prolonged coughing fit that followed, Clio looked across the room to see John Tamar coming in. He had one arm round Edie. Good!

'I thought they were going to kiss my feet. They said Kit was a bloody saint ... Some problem they'd had with the Nazis and a fourteenth-century triptych ... My father reframed it as three separate paintings and slipped them over to England hung in *Cassandra*'s saloon.' Clio thought Teddy was coughing again until she realised that it was laughter. 'Kit moved bullion for them too ... Bloody old Father, just the sort of crazy thing he would do ... But there it was. Smuggling. Hidden gold. I believed the rumours after that.' The old man's voice rose to a querulous shout. 'My family were sitting on a bloody great fortune at Dartleap, while there I was ... a Quentance, scrimping a living from cards and the odd grubby deal. Not fair,' the voice sank again. 'I was going after my share of the plunder.'

There was another pause. A prolonged, bubbling cough came from the tape, and then, 'I tracked them,' the old man went on. 'Kit died, so I followed my dear brother Richard instead ... Richard and his two sons ... swanking around in their fast cars, smarmy clients in Paris art galleries ... Thought I'd have some of that, then Richard died too ... I watched him buried, saw the child ... That gave me the idea.'

'Aaah!' Clio couldn't help crying. 'Teddy turned up at Richard's funeral! He asked for money afterwards, but Alec wouldn't give him any.' She dug around for a handkerchief. 'I'm sorry,' she sniffed, 'I'm all right now. Please keep playing the tape.' After an anxious glance at her, Howland moved a switch and the old voice filled the room again.

'In the end it was easy. I saw her, a little golden-haired girl ... playing in the sunshine on the edge of the terrace.' There was a pause. 'I grabbed the child, got a hand round her mouth and was off down the slope without a sound ... Hard work that was, running to the trees with the child struggling ... Hot day, too. Such a little thing, she was ... surprising how much energy she put into fighting me ... but not for long.'

Teddy made a peculiar, creaking noise in his throat, and then Inspector Howland's voice was asking him if he was all right. 'Got to get it all told now I've started.' He sounded weak but determined. 'I was carrying her, she was battling me, then she stopped ... just stopped ... Her little head fell against my shoulder ... I kept my hand over her mouth just in case. Didn't want her to wake up suddenly and scream ... I got to the quay on the Dart ... put her down ...' There was an interminable, choking cough and then a few more words. 'I saw she wasn't going to wake up again.'

With a click, the recording stopped. No one said a word until the inspector broke the silence. 'Mr Quentance became distressed at this point; he needed a bit of a rest. I had a further interview with him later the same day if you'd like to hear it?'

Clio managed a smile and nodded her head.

'You're sure, Mum?' Oscar got up from where he'd been squatting in front of her and stretched his legs. 'Sure you'll be OK?'

'I think so, darling,' she said firmly. 'I need to hear it all.'

They heard a crackle from the machine, and then the inspector's voice saying, 'So, Mr Quentance. You told us you'd carried the little girl – Ianthe, I think we should call her – you'd carried Ianthe down to the quay at Dartleap, and then you saw that she wasn't going to wake up again. How did you know that?'

'She was so still.' There was a new tremor in Teddy's voice. 'Her eyes were open, staring... big violet eyes she had, just like my Eve' s ... Her lips were blue ... I knew she was dead.'

The old man fell silent. There was the sound of his rasping breath and then the inspector's gentle encouragement: 'So you saw that Ianthe had died. What did you do then?'

'Only thing I could do,' Teddy started up again. 'I'd gone to the Dartleap quay in a little motor launch ... Put her body in the boat and slipped away downriver ... no nosy parkers about to peer into the cabin ... no one to see the bundle under a rug ... I was lucky, I suppose.' There was a sudden, hoarse laugh. 'Easier to handle a dead child than a live one ... Lucky, but not lucky enough ... Never dreamed they'd refuse to pay a ransom ... would have given my life for my own ...' The voice tailed off into another fit of coughing.

'And so you held on to Ianthe, but you could get no money for her,' Howland could be heard nudging Teddy along. 'What happened next?'

'My nerve broke.' There was a new note of anger coming from the tape. 'I left the child on my father's grave ... All Kit's fault for disowning me ... best place I could think of.'

There was a click as the tape finished. In the silence that followed, Clio felt suddenly unnerved. It had been so long ago. 'Is this true?' she whispered. 'He's not just making it all up?'

'It's true.' Howland's voice was quietly emphatic. 'I had a blood sample taken from Mr Quentance immediately after the interview. Those hairs you found on Ianthe's body were his. There's no doubt about it at all.'

'So ... so ...' Clio felt as if a light was spinning in her head. 'If she died while Teddy was carrying her down from the garden, that means Ianthe was never shut up in a box, doesn't it?'

'No boxes, no dark places,' Howland nodded. 'And there's another thing. We know from the original coroner's report that Ianthe's heart failure was catastrophic, don't we? Well then, I believe she'd have had a shock when Mr Quentance picked her up, but after that her death came fast. There was no time for Ianthe to be really afraid, or even much upset.'

THIRTY-FOUR

'Oscar, thank God! I saw your missed call and I've been trying to get through to you ever since.'

'Sorry, Zita, the police came over and I was—'

'The police?' Her voice cut across his. 'Was it about Edie?'

'Edie? Oh no. She was found two nights ago.'

'She's safe! Oh thank heaven!' Her scream of joy was so loud that Oscar had to hold the phone away from his ear.

'But didn't Max tell you?'

'I haven't seen him since Monday morning.'

There was a catch in her voice. Could she and Max have split up? Oscar was tempted to ask her, but there was something else he had to find out first. Feeling a need to sit down after the morning's drama, he crossed his bedroom to a chair by the window, knocking against one of Dartleap's many copies of the family tree as he did so.

'Zita,' he started awkwardly, 'there's something I need to talk to you about.'

'My poor Oscar.' Her voice was immediately sympathetic. 'You sound upset. Why don't you tell me about it?'

Suddenly feeling that he couldn't dive straight into Edie's near drowning, he grabbed the chance to talk about something else first. Zita listened to the entire story in silence. '... And so that's what happened,' he finished. 'Teddy Quentance was after our money and it ended up with my sister's death.'

'What proof do you have?'

It was a strange reaction, but Oscar gave her the answer. 'A perfect DNA match between Teddy and the hairs found on Ianthe's corpse.'

'I see.'

As she didn't say anything else, he decided he'd better get his question over and done with. 'Edie found an olive-green leather glove while *Cassandra* was sinking. Was it yours?'

'Yes.' Zita's voice sounded unnaturally calm. 'And after what I've just heard, I suppose I should tell you.'

Oscar's mouth went dry. 'What did you do?'

'It was simple.' Zita spoke as if she was telling a rather dull story. 'I didn't even have to break into the wheelhouse because Edie had left the key where Max always hid it. I opened one of the sea-cocks and stuffed my glove in. I was sure that as soon as *Cassandra* started to move, the pressure on the hull would force the glove out, then water would gush in and scupper the boat before she'd left Dartmouth.'

This all sounded completely wrong. She must be making it up. 'I don't know much about sea-cocks, but I know Edie checks everything on that boat before she goes anywhere.'

'She'd never have thought of the disused one where the heads used to be.' Zita seemed distant, as if she was talking to herself. 'Who'd have thought that glove would stay put for so long? I suppose the leather must have swollen as it got wet, and then it would have been smacked out during that storm she got caught in.'

'But why?' Oscar decided he must be in shock. His voice sounded so normal that he might have been asking for directions in a strange town. 'Why did you do it?'

'I had to stop Edie from getting to Guernsey and ruining the bank till I'd got my fair share.' It was extraordinary. She sounded quite angry. 'And I had to protect my father.'

'But I'd no idea you even had a father!' Zita had nearly murdered his sister, and yet they were having this surreal conversation about her parentage.

'Of course I have a father! Everything I did was for him. Max would take me on as a partner and give me a proper share of the bank, and then Papa and I would have what was rightfully ours.'

'But who *is* Papa?'

'I'm not Zita Fitz.'

'You're not Zita Fitz,' he echoed. 'So who are you?'

'My name's Zita FitzEdward Quentance. My papa is Edward Quentance.'

Stunned, Oscar turned in his seat and ran his eye down the bogus parchment version of the family tree that was hanging on the wall behind him.

QUENTANCE FAMILY TREE
The Twentieth Century

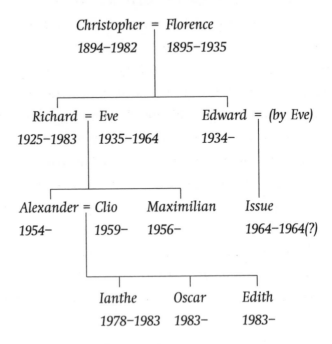

So Issue hadn't died after all.

'Teddy's your father,' he said slowly. 'The man who killed my sister.'

'He didn't kill her! You just told me she died of a heart attack!' Her voice softened. 'I'm sorry about Ianthe, I didn't know what Papa had done. But listen, Oscar. I'm your aunt.'

'I don't care.' What sort of aunt scuppered her niece's boat? Oscar suddenly longed to get her off the phone, but there was a question he ought to ask first. 'Does your father still have his Quentance Bank shares?'

'Yes of course.' There was a pause. 'I'll let you have them in exchange for half the Quentance gold.'

'Don't be ridiculous,' he snapped. 'There *is* no gold.'

'Of course there is. Isaiah Jerichau told me about it.' Oscar didn't want to have to listen to any more of her lies, but she was already talking. 'Isaiah's family have used Quentance Bank for generations, and it makes me proud to know what my grandfather did.' It took Oscar a moment to realise that the grandfather Zita was referring to was Kit, and it did nothing to soften his anger. 'When the Nazis started confiscating Jewish property, Kit took *Cassandra* on a series of trips to Europe. His clients trusted him, you see, and he smuggled their treasure back to England to keep it safe from the Germans. He was a brilliant man. He'd paint gold bars with red lead so they looked like pig-iron, and then he'd use them instead of ballast.'

'What's this got to do with secret hoards?'

'When the war ended, Kit returned what he could, but many of his Jewish clients didn't survive the Holocaust. If you seriously mean you haven't found it, there's a hell of a lot of gold hidden somewhere, and part of it's mine.'

'You can think about that when you're in prison for attempted murder.'

There was a long silence, which Zita eventually broke with a laugh. 'You have the glove then, do you?' When he didn't answer, she went on, 'Thought not. So unless you've been recording this conversation, it'd be your word against mine. And Max adores me. He'll stand by me through thick and thin. Especially when he knows he's my brother.'

'You should have told him straight away instead of leading him on. I'm sure Max is in love with you.'

'But I told you, Oscar. I had to protect Papa.'

Papa. Teddy. Ianthe's kidnapper. He couldn't listen to her voice any more.

Oscar hung up without another word and leaned his head back against his seat, trying to take in everything he'd heard. There were footsteps outside, his bedroom door swung open and Edie's white face appeared. 'Dad just called. Something's happened to Max.'

THIRTY-FIVE

The taxi driver who'd collected them from Le Touquet Airport had insisted on setting them down in this bleak area of industrial warehouses and mean-looking shops. He'd pointed them towards the police mortuary at the end of a no-through-road but refused to drive them all the way, explaining that he'd be unable to turn when he got there.

'Glad I didn't give him a tip,' Oscar muttered as they battled against an icy wind until eventually they reached a range of high walls, topped with rusting barbed wire.

Oscar was doing his best to stay cheerful, but he couldn't hold back a shudder as they came to a pair of metal gates and he got a glimpse of the grim encampment of concrete buildings beyond them. He and Clio were kept waiting in the biting cold while their passports were checked, but eventually they were taken across a desolate car park and into the morgue's reception area.

It was a profoundly depressing place, with austere seating and a few dusty French magazines, but at least it was warm. A female *gendarme* kept an eye on them from beyond a glass-panelled door, but otherwise they were left alone to wait. Oscar tried to flick through the pages of *Paris Match* but it was impossible to concentrate on anything except what they were there for. Throwing the paper aside, he said, 'Have the police got any news yet? Surely Max's body can't just have turned up on the beach without anyone noticing how it got there.'

'It seems to have drifted in on the tide.' Clio reached over to touch his hand. 'You know he was found near Cap Gris Nez?'

'But you don't imagine he jumped?' His laughing, bucca-neering uncle? It was unthinkable.

'It needn't have been suicide. Maybe he was just out walking and he fell. You can get strong winds up on the cliffs.'

Oscar closed his eyes on an involuntary image of Max screaming in terror as he tumbled through the air. 'Aren't you glad we didn't let Edie come with us?' he said, relieved that his sister had been spared this grim waiting-room and the ordeal ahead.

'I'm sure she's better off in rue de Varenne, though it's your father I'm more worried about.'

Unable to think of anything comforting to say, Oscar nodded. He was anxious about Dad, too. He seemed to have aged years since he'd heard about Max's death. His face was pinched, his eyes were dull, and his skin had taken on the quality of crumpled paper. All his self-possession seemed to have vanished as well. When they'd arrived at Max's house the previous day, Dad had gone straight upstairs, climbed into his dead brother's bed and refused to leave it.

'Poor Alec, he needs me now.' Clio sounded as if she was talking to herself. 'What a lot of years I've wasted being angry with him when even if he *had* paid Ianthe's ransom, it would have made no difference.'

Before Oscar could think of a reply, a grey-haired man wearing a white laboratory coat appeared in the doorway. '*La famille Quentance? Vous êtes prêts à voir le cadavre?*'

Oscar hesitated, but his mother stood up and said, 'As ready as we'll ever be.'

They followed the man through a pair of plastic swing-doors and into a white-tiled corridor which jinked through the building in a series of irregular angles. The smells of antiseptic and preservative combined unpleasantly as they walked along spotless grey linoleum, occasionally passing stainless-steel doors, through some of which came the vibrating hum of refrigeration units. Apart from this, the place was eerily quiet. Even the sound of their footsteps was muffled by the rubbery thickness of the flooring.

After several minutes of walking in silence, they stopped in front of yet another stainless-steel door. 'I speak to you in English?' their guide asked.

'Oh yes please,' Clio answered for both of them. 'That would be so much easier.'

'So, before we go in, I will explain.' The man put one hand on the anonymous door and turned to look at them. 'You are here to identify your relation and this is not so easy. His corpse came from the sea but he was not drowned. One head-side is broken, maybe as he hit the water, so we only show the *profil*, understand?'

Feeling Clio sag against him, Oscar forced out a brief, 'Yes. Thank you.'

'*Eh bien.*' Pushing open the door, he ushered them into a starkly lit, concrete-floored chamber.

Oscar took in the hip-level stainless steel table whose sides sloped inwards to a central drainage channel, and the body-sized aluminium trays stacked against one wall. An extractor fan whined dizzyingly overhead, and the cloying smells of bleach and formaldehyde were nauseating. He felt himself rocking and had to put a hand out to the cold metal of the autopsy table for support.

'*Ça va, monsieur?*'

'I'm fine.' Oscar pushed himself upright. His mother was clinging on to his arm. He must be strong.

After giving him a brief, assessing glance, their guide went over to a dully shining door set into one side of the clinical little room. He tugged against a vacuum until the door flew open, letting a cloud of frosty air roll out. As the man leaned forwards into the refrigerator, there was a click, and then a metal body-tray rolled out, its contents covered by a layer of plastic sheeting.

He folded one end back carefully, and as the icy mist from the fridge cleared away Oscar found himself looking down at the damply wrinkled skin of a recent corpse. The hair was matted, though recognisably blond, but the visible half of the face was hugely bloated so that the nose and jaw had all but vanished. He knew it was Max, though. His uncle's eye was half open, and the sea had done nothing to fade that sapphire stare.

His mother had buried her face in his shoulder, and Oscar

was about to turn away too when their guide asked, 'It is your relation?'

'Yes.' Oscar put a tentative hand towards the body, then pulled it back again. 'Yes, it's Max.'

THIRTY-SIX

It was nearly dark by the time Edie heard the taxi pull up in the courtyard outside Max's villa. 'You poor things, you must be exhausted,' she said, going down the steps to kiss her mother before Oscar folded her into one of his huge hugs.

'How's Alec?' Clio asked, already making her way up to the front door. 'I'd better go and check on him.'

'He's been sleeping off and on,' Edie called after her. 'I took him up a bottle of whisky and that seemed to help. But are you all right, Mum?'

'Of course I am. I'll be down again shortly.'

Edie stood leaning against her twin and watched anxiously as their mother stumbled off across the parquet of the entrance hall and up the crimson-carpeted staircase. 'Mum looks terrible,' she said as soon as she was sure Clio was out of earshot. 'It must have been ghastly.'

'It was definitely Max, and that's all you need to know.' There was a silence before Oscar went on, 'It's really made me think, though. Those great looks, all his energy, that astonishing memory, and yet the only thing Max has left behind is money. It's not what *I* want to be remembered for.' Afraid of saying the wrong thing, Edie made no answer apart from reaching up to kiss his cheek. 'And now I need a bloody great drink.'

'Lead me to it.'

As they went along to Max's kitchen, Oscar said, 'As if today wasn't bad enough, Zita rang just before we got here. She claimed she's got no money, Teddy can't be moved from his ridiculously expensive nursing home, and she was in a terrible state about Max.'

'Crocodile tears.'

'I hate her too, Eds, but to be fair, I think she was genuinely fond of him. The trouble is . . .'

Edie turned to look at him as his voice tailed off. 'Spit it out.'

'Apparently Max proposed to her, and now Zita thinks he committed suicide because she turned him down.'

'Good.' Edie couldn't feel sorry for a woman who'd nearly killed her. 'Let's hope she lives a lonely and miserable life.'

'I doubt that,' she heard Oscar mutter. 'Unless I'm wrong, she's already got Isaiah Jerichau buying her clothes.'

Once they got to the kitchen, Edie's legs went wobbly, as they still did sometimes, and she had to collapse on to one of the rococo chairs that Max had been so proud of. For a while she watched in silence as Oscar made coffee and found the brandy bottle, but then a thought struck her. 'Babes,' she started, 'I'm worried.'

'What's up? You're not getting one of those anxiety syndromes are you?'

'Hardly. It's just that while you were away I found something in Max's hall cupboard and I don't know what we should do with it. Will you go and have a look?'

He was back a few minutes later, struggling with a large canvas. Resting the picture on top of the kitchen counter, Oscar swivelled it round to face her. 'This is amazing, Eds, a bloody good take on a Winterhalter.'

It had been hard to see in the cupboard, but under the kitchen lights, Edie was torn between sorrow and admiration as she took in the sombre, cloudy background out of which Max seemed to leap like a joyful, living presence. The artist had caught every detail of how he looked when he was at his happiest. His curling hair glowed golden in a single, illuminating sunbeam, his tanned cheeks were flushed with health, and that huge grin lit up his entire face. Most startling of all was how the painter had caught those amazing deep-blue eyes, crinkled at the corners by his permanent smile-lines. Edie remembered how expressive they'd been, always ready to wink at a pretty girl, to narrow as he concentrated on some unusual feature of the sea, or to widen into a distant stare while he scanned his extraordinary memory. She was glad she hadn't seen his corpse.

'That's astonishing!' Edie hadn't heard her mother's footsteps, but as Clio came into the room, she was relieved to see her looking a lot stronger than when she'd come back from the morgue. 'Astonishing,' she repeated. 'It's Max to the life!'

'Max is dead.' The hoarse voice came as such a shock that Edie slopped coffee on to the table while Oscar swung round, open-mouthed. Only Clio remained calm. Turning to the doorway, she took her husband's hand and led him into the room. His footsteps were slow, like an old man's, and Edie saw how his eyes slid obliquely over the picture as if he was afraid of looking at it. 'My brother.' Tears leaked out of the corners of his eyes. 'My poor, dead brother.'

'A very nice portrait, isn't it, Alec?' Clio said calmly. 'And Oscar's quite right, it is in Winterhalter's style. I wonder where Max got the idea from?'

'There's some of his work in the Jacquemart-André.' The exaggerated brightness in her twin's voice told Edie that he was trying to help drag Dad out of his gloom. 'Max was forever nipping down there. It was one of his favourite places to meet clients.'

'And won't it be lovely having this picture to look at when we're in Bath?' Clio put out a hand to take Alec's.

Edie exchanged a glance with Oscar. Things *had* moved on. As her eyes went back to her father, she saw that his vague stare had switched to the lucidity she was used to. 'There's something else we need to take home.' Without another word, he walked over to the half-concealed door which led out to Max's private garden and pushed it open, letting in a bite of wintry air. The rest of them followed close behind as he clattered down the cast-iron staircase and out on to Max's cherished patch of Parisian lawn.

A series of security lights came on, illuminating the trenches and piles of soil where Max's landscaping was still uncompleted, while from the base of the staircase to the garden's further wall a double line of flagstones emerged from the gloom. Alec paced along this path before squatting down by what looked like a small irregularity in one of the flags.

'A nice idea of Max's,' Edie heard him mutter, 'but not secure.' Her father flexed his fingers. There was a grating sound, and one of the flagstones moved slightly. Grunting with the effort, Alec pushed it further to reveal a square, metal-lined hole of about the size to hold a dozen wine bottles. At first sight it appeared to be empty, but as Edie moved closer she saw her father lean right down into the hole, and a moment later he pulled himself upright again, grasping something wrapped in thick, dark material.

He unbundled it under the stark brightness of the lights, and as glints of gold began to show through the cloth, Edie guessed what it was. She'd seen one once before, in the library at Dartleap. Max had come in and grabbed it from her. He'd shouted that he was going to Paris. Maybe it was this very bar he'd taken with him?

As the last of the covering fell away, Alec stood up, holding the block of gold in his hands, and Edie saw that the blankness was back in his eyes. 'Max found this on *Cassandra*,' he said in an odd, sing-song voice. 'He was so excited when he showed it to me. "Look at the hallmark, Alec! An eagle! That means it's Quentance gold." We were so happy, Clio.' He turned to face her mother. 'We *were* happy, weren't we? Before we lost Ianthe, and everything went wrong.' His voice cracked, and his shoulders seemed to hunch over the weight in his hands. 'I'm sorry, so sorry.'

'Well don't be. We'll be happy again.' Clio looked across and caught Edie's eye. 'When *Cassandra* went missing, I learned to value what I've got more than what I've lost.'

Edie couldn't help herself. She went over to where her mother was standing and flung herself into her arms. 'Oh Mum,' she muttered into the top of Clio's head, 'do you mean that?'

'Of course I do, darling.' Letting Edie go, she said to Alec, 'It's getting rather chilly out here. What are you planning to do with that gold bar?'

There was no reply. Instead, her father raised the heavy block until he was holding it high up above his head. Its matt sides flared under the security lights as if it was an oblation to some ancient deity. 'Max died for gold,' he said. 'It's our inherited sin.' Then, like a priest casting down a sacrificial victim, Alec flung the lump on to the grass, where it landed with a thud, slicing a muddy gouge in Max's lawn. 'I murdered my brother!' he shouted, before collapsing face-down on the wet grass.

Clio was kneeling beside him in an instant. 'Don't be silly, Alec, we all know you didn't kill Max.'

'No! You don't know anything! I've been running a Ponzi scheme.'

Edie opened her mouth to cry out, but a kick from her twin turned it into a hiss of, 'That hurt!'

'Tell me about it some other time.' Edie was astonished that her mother managed to keep her voice so neutral, but it seemed to be effective.

Her father got up slowly, saying, 'I must tell you now. It's been one gigantic fraud.'

Clio took hold of his hand. 'Does anyone know about this?'

'Max knew. He borrowed the Russian's gold for me, and now he's dead.' Alec looked as if he might collapse again.

'Give me a hand, will you, Oscar?' Clio said. Taking hold of an arm each, the pair of them guided him slowly back up the staircase to the kitchen.

Left alone, Edie stared down at the gold bar. After a few moments' thought, she bent to pick it up.

Alec was unconscious, having been given a couple of strong sleeping-pills, and Clio and Oscar were slumped in front of Max's television trying to understand a French game show while drinking their way through a magnum of burgundy. Edie slipped off upstairs to make her phone call in private.

She climbed on to one of Max's extravagantly ornate spare beds before dialling the number, and felt relief flood through her as he answered almost straight away.

'Hello, my beauty, I've been thinking about you. How's it been going?'

Just the sound of his voice lifted Edie's spirits. 'Pretty grim. I'm ringing from Max's house in Paris.'

'I wish I was with you. Shall we go there in the spring-time when the chestnut blossom's out?'

As they chatted, Edie felt increasingly awkward about confessing to yet more crooked dealings in her family's bank. John must have sensed this because he suddenly broke off from some story he was telling her to say, 'I can hear something's bothering you. Tell me.'

'My father's been running a Ponzi scheme.'

'My poor darling.' There was no sharp intake of breath, no hint of disgust. 'None of us is to blame for what our relations get up to. Don't forget that for a moment, will you?'

'I won't, and thank you.'

'I mean it.' He blew a series of loud kisses down the line, but when he spoke next, his voice was serious. 'This Ponzi scheme. You're talking about his Adamantine Fund, are you?'

'I'm afraid so. He persuaded Max to raise cash for him.'

'Let me guess, he borrowed against his Russian client's gold.'

'Exactly. That's how much Max loved Dad.'

'Did they raise enough money to stabilise the fund?'

'I think so,' Edie said uncertainly, 'but I don't know how long for. I'm afraid my father's pretty vague at the moment, and in his present state he's not going to be getting any new investments in.' Her heart started thumping fearfully as she went on, 'Supposing someone comes after Dad for that gold?'

There was a short silence, then John said, 'Do you remember my cousin, Mary Kersey?'

'Of course I do.'

'Well, Mary might be able to help. She's already on our Russian friend's tail for dodgy hedge-fund dealing, and a few other things. I'll ask her to try and distract his attention by turning the heat up.'

Edie felt relief wash over her. 'Oh thank you, thank you so much!' Then, remembering something Oscar had told her, she went on, 'By the way, Quentance Bank may not be all bad. Oscar's sure there's still a lot of value in the European business. He thinks Max had plenty of perfectly solid clients, if only he could remember all their aliases and account numbers.'

'That would be handy.'

'All the details were in Oscar's notebook,' she went on

sadly, 'which was in my grab-bag. I had it with me on the life-raft, but I suppose it's at the bottom of the sea by now.'

'Not necessarily.' There was a cough from the other end of the line. 'I might have forgotten to tell you this, but your bag was passed over to me when the Marines landed you.'

'You monster!' Edie couldn't decide whether to be amused or furious. 'Why didn't you tell me before? Do you still not trust me?'

'Not trust you? My sweetest Edie, I'll never make that mistake again.' His voice was emphatic. 'I took it because there's been some serious stuff going on, and I *had* to have those client details. Since you'd promised Oscar to keep his notebook secret, it seemed easiest if you didn't know.'

'Well I suppose I'll have to forgive you, especially if it helps us to keep Max's good clients happy. As a matter of fact,' her voice brightened, 'we've a lot of UK clients who aren't invested in the Adamantine Fund and who've been doing perfectly legitimate business with the bank for generations.'

'The Ivybridge family, for example.'

'Oh please,' Edie groaned, 'I've had enough grief for one day.'

THIRTY-SEVEN

Edie hadn't appreciated quite how heavy a bar of gold was until she'd lugged her suitcase halfway across London to Paddington Station, and later had to haul it in and out of the taxi that took her from Totnes to Brink Castle. By the time she'd humped her case from the castle's curtain wall to the house, she was sure one arm was going to be permanently longer than the other.

'Edie! I didn't think you'd be here for hours!' John folded her into his arms. 'Why didn't you let me know you were coming this early? I'd have met you off the train.'

'I wanted to give you a surprise.' She pulled slightly away from him, taking in the strands of silver tinsel draped round his neck. 'And it looks as though I have.'

'You're the best surprise I've had all morning.' He bent his head to give her a kiss before reaching down to pick up her suitcase.

'Watch out, it's heavy,' Edie warned.

'It certainly is. I suppose you've stuffed it full of clothes and make-up?'

'Gold, actually.'

He dropped the suitcase at the bottom of the staircase. 'The mysterious gold bar! Let's have a look.'

'I wrapped it up in my underwear to keep it safe. Perhaps I'd better find it myself.'

'Much more fun if I help,' he said, and soon they were sitting on the stairs, draping each other with the contents of Edie's case. But as John reached under a pair of woolly socks and pulled out the gold bar, he fell silent. Weighing it in his hands, he said, 'If this is a standard four-hundred-ounce bar, it's worth over a quarter of a million pounds. That's a lot of money for your uncle to keep buried in a garden in Paris. Come on.' He stood up. 'Let's get a magnifying-glass and see if we can read the hallmark.' Leaving Edie's belongings littered all over the stairs, John led her to a large room running along the garden side of the house.

'This is lovely,' she breathed as they went in, taking in the books propped haphazardly on shelves around the walls, the shabby comfort of faded chintz-covered chairs and sofas, and the enormous, part-decorated Christmas tree in front of a pair of French windows.

'I'm glad you like it.' There was a smile in his eyes as he paused to look at her. Edie leaned back her head for a kiss, but he was already going across to a large desk in the far corner of the room.

Unlike every other surface she'd seen in the house, the desktop was bare, and when John pulled open one of its drawers she saw that everything inside it had been placed there with a military precision. Edie's own desk was exactly the same. She didn't mind a scruffy room, but she hated to work in a mess. As she thought how much they had in common, her heart seemed to turn over with love. If only she could be quite sure he felt the same way. She longed to touch him, but he'd already pulled out a magnifying-glass and was peering at Max's gold bar.

'This is annoying,' he said after a few minutes of concentration. 'The gold's so badly scratched, I can't make out what the hallmark is. It might be your family's eagle, but I'm really not sure. See what you think.'

Edie couldn't help herself. As she took the magnifying-glass, she brushed the corner of his mouth with her lips, and felt his hand closing round hers. 'If you do that again, I'll have to whisk you straight up to bed.' Abruptly, he took the glass from her hand and put both it and the gold bar inside his desk. 'As a matter of fact, there's a perfectly good sofa right here.'

'If you keep distracting me, I'm never going to get anything finished,' he said later, kissing her bare shoulder. 'I still haven't done the Christmas tree.'

'It won't take long with both of us.' She stretched happily against the worn cover of the sofa. 'I'll just nip upstairs and make myself presentable.'

'You look perfectly decent to me,' he said, running his fingers up and down her spine until the tickling became unbearable.

Laughing, Edie wriggled away from him and stood up. 'I'm not going anywhere near those pine needles without my clothes on.'

When she came down again, she found him fully dressed and surrounded by boxes, all overflowing with Christmas decorations. The tree was now completely covered, from the battered angel dangling from the top, right down to the sweets, miniature teddy bears, stars and miscellaneous trinkets dripping from its lowest branches. It was such a contrast to the Dartleap tree, with its immutably tasteful arrangement of maroon velvet bows and spun-glass balls, that Edie clapped her hands in delight. John turned from draping gold tinsel round the topmost branches and grinned at her. 'Do you like it?'

'I love it,' she said, moving close behind him and putting her arms round his waist. 'But you seem to have a lot more things than you've got tree to put them on.'

'These, you mean?' He nudged a nearby box with his toe. 'They've just accumulated over the years, I suppose, and what won't go on the tree gets draped all over the house. When I was a child, we used to have decorations for the entire twelve days of Christmas, right from a dozen porcelain lords a-leaping to a partridge with real feathers and its own tiny pear tree.' He bent and fumbled in another of the boxes, saying, 'Most of them got broken, but one of the maids a-milking survived, and the five gold rings are here somewhere.'

'Is all this decorating just for you,' Edie reached up to adjust a scarlet-nosed reindeer which had slipped upside-down on one of the branches, 'or does your family come here for Christmas?'

'Family, cousins, friends, I get a great crowd descending on Christmas Eve. They all hang around till New Year and clear out when they've drunk the house dry.' He looked up from his search in the box. 'You will come and help me, won't you? Apart from anything else, my parents are going to be thrilled to meet my future wife.'

Edie felt her heart skip a beat but she forced herself to sound cool. 'And who might she be?'

'Who do you think, you silly girl? Obviously you must marry me.' He wasn't even looking at her as he bent to sift through the box of decorations again.

'Is that a proposal?' Edie started laughing. 'Aren't you supposed to tell me you love me first?'

'Sorry, that wasn't very romantic, was it? I should have planned it better, but I've found what I was looking for.' He stood up and, before she realised what was happening, he'd got hold of her left hand and slipped a metal ring set with an enormous blue glass stone on to her finger. 'It's one of the five gold rings, and it'll have to do for the moment.' Pulling her into his arms, he murmured, 'My darling Edie, I love you. Please marry me.'

'Certainly not,' she spoke into his shoulder. 'It's against my principles to marry an aristocrat.'

'Don't be ridiculous,' he said into her hair. 'Think how happy your mother will be.'

'There is that,' Edie said consideringly. Pulling back from his arms, she twisted the bauble on her hand, but it wouldn't budge. 'Well I suppose I'd better say yes.' She stared up into his face. 'I can't get the bloody thing off my finger.'

They kissed for a long, long time and then, abandoning the decorations, John pulled her off to the kitchen where he unearthed a jar of *pâté de foie* and a bottle of champagne to celebrate. Edie was in a fog of happiness as they ate, drank and laughed together, but eventually their conversation turned to the gold bar, Quentance Bank and what should be done about it.

'It's Dad I'm really worried about,' Edie said, looking down at their entwined fingers. 'I know his Ponzi scheme was dreadful, but the more I think about it, the more I realise he only did it because he's so needy for esteem. He's used to being admired as a brilliant investor, but if the bank collapses and he's exposed as a fraud, I'm afraid the shame would break him.'

'Particularly after the shock of his brother's death. The problem is, you'll need a lot of cash to shore up the business. I agree with Oscar that there's value in Quentance Bank, but it'll take a year or more to sort out the bad bits and to get the good parts sold.'

'At least we won't need Teddy's shares for that,' Edie said mournfully. 'With Max dead, I don't think Dad would mind who bought the bank. Assuming there's anything left to sell, that is.'

'Well, we've also got a gold bar and a rumour about a hidden hoard of World War II treasure.' John squeezed her hand. 'If it's true that your great-grandfather transported the gold on *Cassandra*, he'd have landed it at the quay below Dartleap and taken it up to the house. Is there any way it could still be there?'

'I honestly don't think so.' Edie shook her head. 'My Grandfather Richard searched everywhere. He even ripped the cellars apart, but he never found a thing.'

'All right then. Let's try to think where else it might be hidden.'

Edie had no idea where to start. Instead, she found her

mind wandering to Christmas and to whether her first meeting with his parents would be embarrassing. It was awful that the families had fallen out over money. The Quentances had behaved so appallingly in foreclosing on the Ivybridge mortgages, it didn't seem likely that the old friendship could ever be renewed.

She was mulling this over when an idea struck her. 'Our families were very close, weren't they?'

'Yes they were.' John looked at her in surprise. 'Your great-grandfather Kit was thick as thieves with my own great-grandfather, Hugo.'

'So Kit would have been in and out of here all the time. Where do you hide things at Brink Castle?'

Scraping back his chair, John stood up. 'I know where they hid priests. Come on, we'll have to go shopping.'

The service at the ship's chandlery on the edge of Dartmouth was charming but slow. There was a lot of Your Lordshiping to John, and it took them an age to buy a rope ladder, metal-cutters and a big torch. Then, when they were finally back out in the car park, Edie made him go inside again to buy some separate coils of rope in case they needed them. Eventually they were back at Brink Castle and standing together beside the ancient well in the middle of the court-yard.

A north-easterly wind had got up, but Edie hardly felt the cold as she watched John sliding the metal-cutters through the padlock. Despite the strength of his arm muscles, it took a lot of effort before the bolt finally snapped open. Together, they lifted off the weather-worn lid and peered down into the depths of the well. Edie had been expecting an unpleasant, stagnant smell, but all she caught was a clean, mossy dampness.

'There must be fresh water down there,' John said. 'I wonder if we could use it.'

'I'm not letting you get close enough to find out!' Having seen how deep the well was, Edie was glad she'd sent him back for those extra coils of rope. Without giving him time to protest, she slipped a length round his waist and tied it with a reef knot, looping the other end twice round the base of the well. 'If we attach the top of the rope ladder to the car and leave it in gear, this should keep you safe,' she said, hauling out another length of line.

The biting wind chilled her hands and made her fingers slow as she carefully tied the rope ladder to the car's towbar. 'Come on, Edie.' John stamped his feet impatiently. 'I'm not climbing Everest.'

'I do know that, but I know about knots, too.' She looked up from where she was squatting over two lines of rope. 'Anyway, it's ready now, Spiderman. Down you go.'

There was a wide stone lip round the top of the well, and Edie slowly paid out the line round John's waist as he swung himself over and began a cautious climb down the swaying rope ladder. An icy squall whipped across the exposed court-yard, but she forced herself to stand still, carefully releasing the safety line as John disappeared into the darkness. When only his head was visible above the well's lip, he cried, 'Pass me that torch, will you? I can see something!' She handed the torch down to him, and heard him call, 'There's a line of big stones set into the brickwork here. I think they're meant to be used as steps.' There was a pause while she paid out more rope, and then a bellow echoed up round the walls of the well. 'Give me more of that line, Edie. Quickly! I've found the priest-hole!'

Edie peered nervously over the lip of the well, but all she could see was a faint light reflected off its old brick walls. There wasn't a sound except for the wind blowing in her ears, and she suddenly had a terrible thought that there might be another, parallel well and that he might have fallen down it. Without stopping for a second to think how unlikely this was, she leaned over as far as she dared and screamed, 'John! John! Are you all right?'

To her vast relief she saw his head pop out from the darkness below her. She couldn't make out his expression, but the excitement in his voice was enough. 'It's here, Edie! It's like a dragon's den! Hundreds of bars of gold, all stacked in a sort of cave dug into the side of the well. Just hang on a minute.' He vanished again and his voice came to her in a hollow boom. 'I'll put a couple of bars in my pockets and bring them up to show you.'

A moment later he reappeared, and Edie braced herself against the rope round his waist while he scrambled back up the wildly swinging ladder, threw one long leg over the top of the well, and was at last standing safely beside her. 'Quickly,' he said, 'let's get the cover back on the well, then I'm taking you inside to thaw out.'

Ten minutes later they were back in the warmth of the kitchen with the two bars of gold on the table in front of them. 'Have a look,' John said, passing her the magnifying-glass. 'The hallmark's an eagle all right, but it's not the Quentance version.'

She examined the sharp-beaked bird with its angular wings and averted head, then put down the glass, horrified. 'But this is the Nazi symbol! Does this mean Zita lied when she told Oscar that story about Kit and Jewish gold?'

'Not at all, I've seen other hallmarks like this. It's not the real thing. The talons are quite wrong, and so is the depth of the stamp.'

'So what is it then?'

'It's the best copy of the Nazi eagle they could manage. It was to make this gold look legitimate in case brave men like Kit were caught by the Germans while they were transporting it to safety.' He leaned forwards to take her left hand and kissed the ring he'd put there. 'And now you and I have millions of pounds' worth of untraceable gold hidden down the well, and we need to decide what to do with it.'

'I think,' Edie said slowly, 'that we should use it to prop up Quentance Bank for the time being, and then once the bank's been sold we should find some deserving causes and give the whole lot away.'

'That's exactly what I think we should do too. Your great-grandfather would have been proud of you.' John turned over her hand and planted a kiss on the inside of her wrist. 'Kit was a brave and good man.'

'I'm sure he was.' Edie smiled into the eyes she loved. 'I just wish I knew what he'd done on *Titanic*.'

2009

However often she shifted her position, Edie couldn't get comfortable. Either her stomach dug into the desktop, or she had to sit sideways-on and strain her shoulders. If it wasn't for fear that all her time would soon be eaten up by Christmas, and then by babies, she'd have given up trying to work and gone outdoors. Stretching her arms above her head, she let her eyes drift out to the garden beyond the French windows.

It was one of those freezing December days when, despite a sky of the clearest blue, the sun gave no warmth to the air. Edie smiled as she caught sight of John struggling to get a nest of artificial robins to stay put on a lichen-crusted branch. To celebrate their first married Christmas, he'd decided to decorate the outside as well as the inside of Brink Castle, but she wasn't at all sure that his orchard miscellany of birds, squirrels and streamers would survive the forecast snow and ice.

Ice. Icebergs. Edie's midriff bumped against the desk as she forced herself back to her D.Phil. *RMS* Titanic: *The Application of Historical Source Analysis to Maritime Myth.* Her supervisor liked the title, but he'd warned her that a rehash of the known facts wouldn't earn her a doctorate. For that, she'd need to come up with something truly original.

Her thesis had a section on greed, and she was pleased with the parallels she'd drawn between the careless avarice of bankers in 1912 and of those nearly a century later. The North Atlantic battles of Cunard and White Star seemed to her to be just like the struggle for scale that had tempted twenty-first-century banks into takeovers of spectacular foolishness. And between the Edwardian financiers in first-class luxury and the poverty-stricken emigrants down in third yawned the same gulf as between today's winners with their million-pound bonuses and the invisible underclass on benefits.

The parallels carried on into risk-taking, too. Bruce Ismay and J. P. Morgan had extended *Titanic*'s first-class promenade at the expense of space for lifeboats. After the tragedy, their excuse was that they'd stayed within the regulations, but the truth was that a promenade deck made money, whereas a lifeboat deck didn't. Edie was tempted to give the desk leg a good kicking when she thought how little had changed. Twenty-first-century bankers had used just the same excuse. They may have lost billions in reckless gambles, but they'd stayed within their regulators' guidelines.

Edie threw down her pencil. She was glad that John was out of the room because economics was the only thing they ever quarrelled about. She believed that governments should interfere more and that the authorities needed the power to investigate anything they wanted to. Her husband, on the other hand, thought businesses should be freed from red tape. John had the unfair advantage of knowing what he was talking about, and when her opinions got particularly passionate he'd roll out a few facts which contradicted everything she said. She stroked her swollen stomach and smiled. However furious she got, John always stayed calm. He actually seemed to enjoy their arguments, while she loved the way they made up afterwards.

With a sigh, Edie realised she'd let her mind wander again. She dragged her thoughts back to the conclusion of her D.Phil. and the problem she faced. Whilst she'd written a lot about greed and risk-taking, she'd added nothing at all to the core questions. Had they really been running a speed trial? Why did First Officer Murdoch take so long to turn the helm after the berg was sighted? Who took that slow-ahead decision so soon after the collision? And if *Titanic* was truly going too fast to avoid the iceberg, why didn't Murdoch take the safer option of hitting it head-on?

'Shouldn't you have your feet up?'

Edie swivelled round in her chair with a laugh. 'If I put my feet up, I'd topple over backwards with the weight of your twins. By the way, I forgot to ask if you got hold of Dad this morning?'

'Yes, I did.' John came over and began to rub her back. 'He's agreed to the sale of the bank's UK business. It's a good offer.'

'And how did he sound?'

'Much the same.' His fingers probed the stiff muscles between her shoulderblades. 'Quiet, distant, out of it.'

'Mum's a saint to put up with him.'

'Sensible woman, your mother.' Edie smiled at the unlikely

fondness that had sprung up between her husband and his mother-in-law. Using the balls of his thumbs, John began to massage the base of her neck. 'It would help if Alec could stop blaming himself for Max's death.'

'Does Mary still think Platon Dyengi was behind it?' Edie shifted in her chair so that he could reach down her spine.

'I don't think she can prove anything.' He stopped rubbing her back and rested his hands on her shoulders. 'To be honest, I hope she doesn't. He's a dangerous man.'

'She's very brave.' Edie put a protective arm over her bulging stomach as she thought of Mary Kersey being at risk. 'I know,' she said suddenly, leaning her head back so that she could smile up at her husband. 'Shall we ask her to be a godmother? And I do think Oscar would make a good godfather.'

'You think he's suitable, do you?' John slipped his hands down to the small of her back. 'He seems to be turning Dartleap into a mini-Glastonbury.'

'So what? We might have musical children.' That was as far as she got before he started to kiss her.

'Darling, the doorbell's ringing.' Edie was back at her desk and frowning down at a wad of notes.

'Ignore it,' John mumbled from the sofa.

'But it might be important.' Her face relaxed as she turned and saw how he was sprawled along the cushions, his long legs dangling over the armrest. 'And anyway, I bet you forgot to lock the front door.'

Footsteps out in the hall proved her right, and a moment

later her twin's bright head appeared round the door. 'Can I come in?'

'You seem to be in already.' She smiled at his happy, handsome face. 'What are you looking so pleased about?'

'He's guessed I've got a couple of bottles of '99 Potensac that need drinking.' John stood up and stretched. 'With my wife off the booze I thought I'd have them all to myself, but I suppose I can share one with you.' He reached over to give Oscar a friendly punch.

'We might need them both once I've shown you what I've got here.' Fishing around in the pocket of his jeans, Oscar pulled out a sheaf of papers. 'I just hope it doesn't over-excite Eds.'

'What *are* you talking about?' Edie pushed herself upright. 'This isn't some new song of yours, is it?'

'Even better than that,' he grinned. 'I think you should both sit down to hear it.'

Edie sank down on the sofa with John beside her, while Oscar pulled an armchair over to sit close by. 'And now,' he said, 'let me start with the letter which arrived this morning.' Unfolding the first sheet, he began to read.

Dear Mr Quentance,

I've recently been turning out some old family papers and came across the enclosed Dunkirk memoir written by my grandfather, the late Commander Charles Lightoller.

'Lightoller?' Edie said sharply. 'The one who was on *Titanic*?'

'Just listen, Eds, and you'll find out.' Oscar went back to his letter.

He writes of a conversation with Kit Quentance, and as your
surname is an unusual one, I'm assuming that you're a descen-
dent of his.

I hope you find it of interest.
Yours sincerely
Louise Patten

'Kit Quentance,' Edie said breathlessly, 'I don't believe it!'
Oscar seemed to be taking an age to shuffle the pages that
had come with the letter. 'For heaven's sake get a move on.
What does it say?'

'It starts with some boat gobbledegook, but I guess you'll
want to hear it. "M.Y. *SUNDOWNER*,"' Oscar read. 'Should
that be "My *Sundowner*"?'

'M.Y. stands for "motor yacht",' Edie said impatiently. 'Keep
going.'

'"Fifty-nine foot over all. Twelve foot beam. Five foot draft.
Six-cylinder Gleniffer Diesel giving a speed of ten knots."
Ten knots. What's that in English?'

'Around twelve miles per hour, which is about as fast as
you're reading. Darling, *please* will you take it from him?'

'We'd better indulge her,' John said, holding out his hand,
and a moment later his deep voice took up the story.

My eldest son, Roger Lightoller and I with an 18 year old Sea
Scout took Sundowner *out of her winter quarters at Cubitts*
Yacht Basin Chiswick on the 31st May at 11 a.m. and proceeded
according to instructions towards Southend. At 3.15am June 1st
we left Southend in company with five others. Arriving off
Ramsgate I asked for orders and was instructed Proceed to Dunkirk.

We left Ramsgate at 10 a.m. and half way across avoided a floating mine by a narrow margin. At 2.25pm we sighted and closed the 25ft Motor Cruiser Westerly, *broken down and badly on fire. As the crew of two (plus three naval ratings she had picked up in Dunkirk) wished to abandon ship – and quickly – I went alongside and took them aboard, thereby giving them the additional pleasure of once again facing the hell they had just left.*

We were subject to sporadic bombing and machine-gun fire but as the Sundowner *is exceptionally quick on her helm, by waiting till the last moment and then putting the helm hard over we easily avoided every attack – though sometimes near lifted out of the water.*

'This is amazing,' Edie couldn't help interrupting. 'We're listening to a first-hand account of one of the Little Ships being bombed by the Luftwaffe. Does Kit come into it soon, Oscar?'

'I think so, though I only flicked through this before I dashed over here.'

'Hang on.' John was skimming down the page. 'We're just getting to it, listen.'

It had been my intention to go right on to the Beaches, but those of the Westerly *informed me that the troops were all away from there, so I headed up for Dunkirk Piers. The difficulty of taking troops on board from the quay high above us was obvious, so I went alongside a destroyer,* Worcester *I think, where they were already embarking. I got hold of her captain and told him – with a certain degree of optimism –*

that I could take a hundred, though the most I had ever had
on board was 21. He, after consultation with the military C.O.,
said 'Go ahead. Take all you can.'

Shortly afterwards a cruiser, Cassandra, *came alongside.*

'*Cassandra!*' Edie cried. 'Just read that bit again, will you?'
'"Shortly afterwards a cruiser, *Cassandra*, came alongside,"'
John repeated.

Her skipper had had the same thought as me about the height
of the quay. He cast a line over and called that he could take
fifty. I was inclined to doubt this as his boat was no more
than 40ft but before I could say so he introduced himself. Kit
Quentance, last seen on Titanic. *I hadn't recognised him after*
nearly 30 years, but I remembered him well.

We had no time to exchange more than a word as troops
were starting to pour down off Worcester *and onto*
Cassandra *and* Sundowner. *Roger, as previously arranged,*
packed the troops in down below. At 50 I called down 'How
are you getting on?' receiving the cheery reply 'Oh plenty of
room yet.' Quentance called it a day at 45 and cast off. At 75
Roger admitted they were getting just a bit cramped.

'I've forgotten who Roger is,' Oscar interrupted.
'Do try and concentrate, it's Lightoller's son,' Edie said.
'Please keep going, darling.'
'Where was I?' John ran his finger down the page. 'Oh yes.'

At 75 Roger admitted they were getting just a bit cramped
so I told him to let it go at that and pack them on deck. By

the time we had 50 on deck, I could feel her getting distinctly tender, so took no more. Actually we had exactly 130 on board including 3 Sundowners and 5 Westerlys.

Casting off and backing out we again entered the Roads, where it was continuous and unmitigated hell. The troops were just splendid and of their own initiative, detailed look-outs ahead, astern and abeam for inquisitive planes as my attention was pretty well occupied watching the course and passing word to Roger at the wheel. Anytime an aircraft seemed inclined to try its hand on us, one of the look-outs would just call quietly, 'Look out for this bloke Skipper' at the same time pointing. One bomber that had been particularly offensive, itself came under the notice of one of our fighters and suddenly plunged vertically, hitting the sea at some 400 m.p.h., about 50 yards astern. It was a sight never to be forgotten. Incidentally it was the one and only time that any man on board ever raised his voice above a conversational tone, but as that big black bomber hit the deck they all raised an echoing cheer.

My youngest son Pilot Officer H. B. Lightoller – lost on the very day war broke out, in the first raid on Wilhelmshaven – flew a Blenheim and had at different times given me a whole lot of useful information about attack, defence and evasive tactics and I attribute our success in getting across without a single casualty to his unwitting help.

'Died on the first day of the war,' Edie sighed. 'God, that's sad.'

These last stages of pregnancy were making her emotional, and she was touched when John paused to stroke her cheek before he went on reading.

On one occasion an enemy machine came up astern at about
100 ft with the obvious intention of raking our decks. He came
down in a nice gliding dive, but I knew that he must elevate
some 10 or 15 degrees before his guns would bear. Calling my
son at the wheel to 'Stand by', I waited till as near as I could
judge he was just on the point of pulling up, then 'Hard-a-
port'. This of course threw his aim off completely. He banked
and tried again. Then 'Hard-a-starboard' with the same result.
After a third attempt he gave us up in disgust. Incidentally,
he was a sitter if I had a machine gun of any sort and funnily
enough, though the troops had rifles and ammunition,
everyone was apparently too interested in the manoeuvre to
think of using them.

Not least of our difficulties was contending with the wash
of fast craft, such as destroyers and transports. In every instance
I had to take the way off the ship and head the wash, other-
wise our successful little cruise would have ended in a bathe.
The effect of the consequent plunging on the troops down
below, in a stinking atmosphere with all ports and skylights
closed, can well be imagined. They were literally packed like
the proverbial sardines – even one in the bath and another
perched on the W.C., so that all the poor devils could do was
just sit and be sick.

'That's enough about seasickness.' It was more than a
year ago now, but Edie still didn't want to be reminded of
two days and nights sitting in her own vomit in a life-raft.

'Don't worry,' John said gently. 'If there's any more sick,
I'll skip over it.'

Arriving off the harbour I was first told to 'lie off'. With the help of a megaphone I told the authorities that I had 130 on board and that I was as likely to lie on my beam ends as anything. I was then told to 'come in'. I got her alongside a trawler at the quay and made fast, with no small relief. I heard afterwards that the impression ashore was that the 50 odd on deck was the extent of my load.

After I had got rid of those on deck I gave the order, 'come up from below' and the look on the official's face was certainly amusing to behold as troops vomited up through the forward and after companionways and the doors either side of the wheelhouse. As a stoker P.O., helping them over the trawler's bulwarks put it, 'Gods truth mate where did you put them?'

My intention had been to clear up the mess, get a couple of hours sleep and push off to Dunkirk again, but just then I heard an 'Ahoy there Sundowner' *from Kit Quentance. I was glad to see him safely back, and tired or not I joined him on* Cassandra *where we yarned till morning.*

'Surely that's not the end?'

John had fallen silent, and as she tried to peer over his shoulder at the memoir, he pulled it away from her. 'The rest seems to be about *Titanic*,' he said carefully, 'and it looks like pretty hot stuff. It won't do you any good if it makes you all excitable.'

'Oh Lord, I hadn't thought of that.' Oscar was looking at her worriedly. 'We don't want you going into premature labour, Eds.'

One of the babies chose that moment to start kicking, so she grabbed John's hand and pressed it over the drum of her abdomen. 'Feel that? Your children are as keen to hear this as I am, and I promise I'll be calm.'

'Well, if you're sure?' After giving her a searching look, he began to read again.

Needless to say, it was Titanic *we talked about. Quentance told me that while he was helping out with the lifeboats he had seen the Chief and me slipping away together and he claimed he'd spent his life wondering what was said. Of course the Chief and I had been to get the firearms along with the Captain and Murdoch, and after such a length of time, I couldn't see the harm in telling him. So I started by explaining about the speed trial, and how they'd put more steam on after Murdoch took over the Watch and planned to do so throughout that night. The owners wanted to make a show of getting into New York a few hours earlier than expected.*

'It's unbelievable,' Edie whispered. 'They were already making twenty-two knots. How could they have dreamed of going even faster?'

'If you're going to upset yourself I'm not going to read any more,' John said firmly. 'I mean it.'

'I'm not upset, just shocked.'

'Well don't be.' Edie dropped her head against the sofa-back to pretend she was relaxing as John began to read again.

The next thing Quentance wanted to know was why didn't Murdoch manage to avoid the berg? Then the whole sorry tale came out. I told Quentance that of course Murdoch did see the ice, or rather the white fringe round it. It was a blue-faced berg, and from his lower angle on the bridge, he spotted the thing a good while before the pair up in the crow's nest caught sight of it.

'Wasn't there some story that they'd have seen it if they'd had binoculars?' This time it was Oscar who did the interrupting.

'That was just a piece of nonsense.' Edie was dying to hear the rest but as she didn't want John getting anxious again, she forced herself to speak calmly. 'Binoculars restricted the lookouts' field of vision, so they always relied on their own eyesight. If glasses were used at all, it was only *after* an object had been spotted, and then only after the warning bells had been rung, never before.'

'Honestly, Eds, it's amazing the amount you know.'

'And I'll know a lot more if you shut up and let John finish.'

'"Murdoch immediately sang out Hard-a-Starboard, thinking he'd have time to Port Around." I'm sorry,' John broke off, 'you'll have to explain that one to me.'

'Of course I will.' Edie dug her nails into the palms of her hands to control her impatience. 'A port-around manoeuvre would be like drawing a C round the iceberg. First they'd turn to port to get the bow away, and then they'd swing back to starboard to clear the stern.'

'Thanks, and Oscar's quite right. You do know a lot.' He bent to give her a hug before picking up where he'd left off. '"I told Quentance that on the North Atlantic run in those days we were still using Tiller Orders, but the steersman had been serving the India route and up on the Baltic run. So Hitchins had been trained to Rudder Orders and his automatic reaction to Murdoch's urgency was to turn the wheel to starboard."'

The twins surged inside her as Edie let out a cry.

'What is it? Shall I get an ambulance?' Throwing Lightoller's papers aside, John was on his knees in front of her.

'I'm fine, it was just the surprise. My D.Phil. should be in the bag!' He and Oscar were both looking so worried, when all she wanted to do was shout for joy. It took a while to persuade the two men that she was all right, but eventually they stopped fussing over her as she told them what Lightoller's words meant. 'Hitchins turned the wrong way, it's as simple as that! When Murdoch gave his order, he moved the bow to starboard instead of to port.'

'But hang on a minute, Eds. Didn't you just say he was told to hard a-starboard?'

'Exactly. So he should have put the wheel over to port, and the bow would have gone to port.' Seeing that her husband was now looking as flummoxed as her twin, she tried again. 'You need to know the history to understand it. You see, sailors like Lightoller started their careers on the tall ships. Under sail, the tiller turned in the opposite direction to the wheel, or, to put it in landlubber terms, steering left turned the tiller right, and the bow to the left, do you see?' John's nod was rather half-hearted, so she tried to make it clearer. 'If the captain gave the order to hard-a-starboard, the helmsman turned the wheel to port. That pushed the tiller to starboard and the ship went to port. It's what they called Tiller Orders.'

'Tiller Orders. An order to steer one way turned you the other. I think I've got that,' Oscar said. 'Keep going, but slowly, please.'

'With steamships, steering's like driving a car. When you turn the wheel to the left, it turns the rudder left and the boat goes left.'

'But for heaven's sake, darling, *Titanic* was a steamship, wasn't she?' John laughed. 'So if Murdoch wanted *Titanic* to go to port, why did he say hard a-starboard?'

'Aha! Because *Titanic* sank during the transition from sail to steam. Since so many sailors had been trained on sailing ships, it was thought to be safer to stick to Tiller Orders so that the helmsman didn't turn the wheel the wrong way in an emergency. Murdoch gave the hard-a-starboard order, knowing that the helmsman would turn the wheel to port and *Titanic*'s bow would move to port too.'

'So what went wrong, Eds?'

'Plain bad luck, I suppose. Although Tiller Orders were still being used on the North Atlantic passage, in other parts of the world they'd already switched to Rudder Orders, where a hard-a-starboard order meant you put the wheel to starboard and that's the way the bow turned.' She shook her head ruefully. 'The helmsman at the time of the collision was a man called Robert Hitchins. He'd never worked the North Atlantic before, and he'd been trained to Rudder Orders.'

'My God. I understand now!' John reached over and took her hand. 'So when Murdoch called, "Hard a-starboard," Hitchins should have turned the wheel to port, and *Titanic* would have gone to port and avoided the iceberg.'

'Exactly. But Hitchins' instinctive reaction in an emergency was to revert to the Rudder Orders he'd been trained to. He turned the wheel to starboard. The wrong way!'

Her brother and husband both seemed to have been silenced, so Edie bent to reach the scattered papers of Lightoller's memoir. Scanning through to where John had left off, she read,

> Kit Quentance asked me what Murdoch did when he realised the bow was moving to starboard instead of to port, but I think he realised as well as I did that there wasn't a lot anyone could have done. Murdoch got the helm back over, but he'd lost too much time. The bow was just starting to swing to port when three bells rang from the crow's nest, but by then the iceberg was too close to avoid. The berg bumped along down the starboard bow and that was the end of it.
>
> By this stage it was dawn, and I still had to get Sundowner shipshape. Quentance and I went our separate ways, but before we parted I told him how grossly unfair the rumours about him had been, and that I'd made it clear at the enquiries that I'd given him a direct order to take charge of a lifeboat. Quentance simply said he never spoke about Titanic, and that it was far too late to persuade the world that he wasn't a coward.

So that's what happened!' Edie stared across at her twin as she finished reading. 'Kit was *ordered* into a lifeboat!'

Oscar got up to give her a kiss. 'Nothing cowardly in that. We know he was a good guy.'

Edie reached across and ruffled his hair. 'Good as gold.'

AFTERWORD

Good as Gold is more than fiction. Woven through the plot are facts about RMS *Titanic* that have been kept as secrets within my family for nearly a century.

This book tells what happened between the sighting of the iceberg at 11.36 p.m. on Sunday 14 April 1912 and the final shutting-down of the engines at 12.15 a.m. on Monday the 15th. During those forty minutes, decisions were taken that were to doom the unsinkable ship and those who died with her.

Not all the historical insights in *Good as Gold* are new. Kit Quentance's experience on *Titanic* mirrors the true story of Major Peuchen, the Canadian yachtsman who suffered life-long allegations of cowardice when all he'd done was to obey an order to take command of Boat 6. Similarly, the document sent to the fictional Oscar Quentance is based on a real Dunkirk memoir written by Commander Lightoller whose boat, *Sundowner*, was one of the Little Ships.

Commander Charles Herbert Lightoller was my grandfather. In April 1912 he was serving as second officer on RMS *Titanic* and showed great bravery during *Titanic*'s final hours, as portrayed by Kenneth More in the 1958 film *A Night to Remember.* My grandfather refused to leave on one of the last two lifeboats, despite being ordered to do so by one of his superior officers, and as a result he went down with *Titanic.* He survived through a lucky chance that brought him to the surface beside an upturned collapsible lifeboat, and as he discovered on reaching the rescue ship *Carpathia*, 'Apart from four junior officers ordered away in charge of boats, I found I was the solitary survivor of over fifty officers and engineers who had gone down with her.' (Commander Lightoller, *Titanic and Other Ships*, London, 1935: Ivor Nicholson & Watson, p. 254)

Four people knew the truth about the collision, three of whom were lost with the ship. Captain Smith, Chief Officer Wilde and First Officer Murdoch all having died, my grandfather was the only senior officer left alive, and the sole survivor who knew precisely why *Titanic* had foundered. From most of the world he kept this a lifelong secret, but there was one individual with whom he shared everything. The flysheet of his autobiography reads 'Dedicated to My Persistent Wife Who Made Me Do It'. The only person to whom he told the entire *Titanic* story was Sylvia Lightoller, my grandmother, hereafter referred to as Granny.

I was born in 1954, and in 1959, a few years after my grandfather's death, my parents, brother, sister and I moved to 1 Ducks Walk, Twickenham, where we lived with Granny until her sudden death from heart failure when I was sixteen. The house was on the Middlesex bank of the Thames, just upriver from the half-tide lock, and was built above

Richmond Slipways, my grandfather's marine-repair business. Neither house nor boatyard is there any longer, though a blue plaque remains.

COMMANDER CHARLES HERBERT LIGHTOLLER RNR. DSC*

1874 – 1952

RICHMOND SLIPWAYS, 1 DUCK'S WALK

- COMMANDER LIGHTOLLER WAS THE SENIOR SURVIVING OFFICER OF THE TITANIC IN 1912. GOING DOWN WITH THE SHIP, HE TOOK CHARGE OF AN UPTURNED LIFEBOAT AND WAS THE LAST SURVIVOR TO BE RESCUED.

- IN THE FIRST WORLD WAR, HE SERVED WITH THE ROYAL NAVY, COMMANDING THREE MTB/DESTROYERS AND ROSE TO THE RANK OF COMMANDER RNR. HE WON THE DSC IN 1916 AND WAS AWARDED A BAR TO IT IN 1918 AFTER SINKING A U-BOAT.

- IN 1940 COMMANDER LIGHTOLLER TOOK HIS MOTOR YACHT SUNDOWNER TO DUNKIRK AND RESCUED 127 MEN FROM THE BEACHES. SUNDOWNER IS PRESERVED AT THE MARITIME MUSEUM IN RAMSGATE.

- IN 1947 IN PARTNERSHIP WITH AN OLD FRIEND AND HIS SURVIVING SON, HE TOOK OVER THE SMALL BOAT BUILDING BUSINESS OF RICHMOND SLIPWAYS. HE LIVED THERE ON THE BOATYARD AT 1 DUCK'S WALK WITH HIS WIFE SYLVIA UNTIL PASSING AWAY PEACEFULLY ON 8TH DECEMBER 1952.

LUX VESTRA - "LET YOUR LIGHT SHINE"

THIS PLAQUE WAS PRESENTED TO THE LONDON BOROUGH OF RICHMOND UPON THAMES BY THE TWICKENHAM PARK RESIDENTS' ASSOCIATION

For a few years, life was very happy. Our Dunkirk survivor, *Sundowner*, was moored at the end of the garden. She was too big to pass very far upriver, but she did take us across the Channel to Ostend and Boulogne and, once, north through the French canals right from Marseilles to Calais. We swam in the Thames, had picnics on the mid-river eyots and rowed the boatyard dinghy in and out of the piers of Richmond Bridge. Granny was hindered by a dislocated hip and couldn't spend much time on the water, but she was a great provider of proper tea when we got back home.

Everything changed when my brother Charles, named after our grandfather, developed cancer and my parents vanished to be with him in hospital. My sister, being older, came back from school far later than I did, so when I got home I would go straight to Granny's end of the house. During the year Charles took to die, I spent most afternoons in a trio over the tea table with my grandmother and her best friend, a White Russian refugee called Princess Carina Barclay de Tolly.

As Princess Carina was deaf, she didn't take much part in the conversation, but Granny and I talked endlessly, often about *Titanic*, so that by the time I was ten I was an expert in subjects like false funnels, Wellin davits and watertight bulkheads. That same year, I took the Eleven Plus to determine which senior school I'd go on to. The essay set for the exam had to begin with the words 'The mist was coming down quickly and we had to slow down to a crawl ...' My effort was set in the North Atlantic. It involved an iceberg, wealthy passengers, and a ship without enough lifeboats.

When we weren't discussing *Titanic* or playing canasta, Granny's favourite card game, she would talk about her eventful life with my grandfather, which she relived with me. Despite its swoops between penury and plenty, theirs was the happiest of marriages from the moment he set eyes on her, a story she loved to tell me. It took place on the ship that was ferrying her between England and her home in Sydney, Australia. She was at the top of a gangplank, he was at the bottom. When he looked up and saw her face for the first time, he said to the sailor standing beside him, 'That's the girl I'm going to marry.'

My own parents' marriage was not so strong and didn't

survive for long after Charles's death. The savings that would have paid for him to go to Ampleforth were used to send my sister away to boarding school, and my mother took up a teaching career to help pay the other bills. Meanwhile, that Eleven Plus essay helped me win a free place at St Paul's Girls' School, and for a year or so I only saw Granny briefly after the long trek home to Richmond Slipways from my new school in Hammersmith.

But the following year, when I was twelve, I too became seriously ill. From then onwards, I spent long periods in Hammersmith Hospital and short ones taking advantage of that Eleven Plus place. The rest of the time I spent at home with Granny. This illness lasted until I was sixteen, and as I got older, so our conversations about *Titanic* became more adult. During those four years I learned in detail about the characters involved, the mistakes that had been made and the individuals whom my grandfather blamed most for the tragedy.

The fact that Robert Hitchins had turned the wrong way was a source of endless discussion, as was the switch from Tiller Orders to Rudder Orders which had caused him to make the error. Granny was clear that this had been a blunder, but the decision to get *Titanic* under way so soon after the collision was criminal, as my grandfather had often told her. We used to talk over and over again about those forty critical minutes between the sighting of the iceberg and the shutting down of the engines, even sketching out our own timetable of precisely what had gone wrong.

11.36 p.m.	First Officer Murdoch sees an iceberg a little less than two miles away. *Titanic* is heading towards it at about seven hundred yards per minute, giving him four minutes to steer her out of danger. Murdoch gives the order to hard-a-starboard.
11.37 p.m.	Quartermaster Hitchins makes his fatal mistake. The berg is now one and a half miles away.
11.38 p.m.	Murdoch corrects the error. The berg is now one mile away. Up in the crow's nest, Lookout Fleet spots the berg and rings three bells, meaning 'object dead ahead'.
11.40 p.m.	The bow has moved two points to port, sufficient to avoid a head-on collision but not far enough for Murdoch's planned port-around to succeed. *Titanic*'s starboard hull scrapes along the ram of the berg. A 'Stop' message is sent down to the engine room.
11.50 p.m.	Bruce Ismay reaches the bridge. Captain Smith tells Ismay he believes the damage to the ship is serious.
11.55 p.m.	A 'Slow ahead' order is given.
12.05 a.m.	A 'Stop' order is given.
12.10 a.m.	A 'Slow Astern' order is given.
12.15 a.m.	A 'Stop' order is given and the engines are shut down. The 'All hands on deck' order is given, and the crew begin to clear away the lifeboats.

Granny was quite clear that my grandfather had not always told the truth when giving evidence to the two inquiries, but in her view he'd simply done what he believed to be his duty. In the words Granny said to me time and time again, 'It was all about the insurance,' and while they were still on *Carpathia*, the chairman of the White Star Line had shown my grandfather where his duty lay. Due to certain exceptions in White Star Line's limited-liability insurance policy, Bruce Ismay had told him, if the company were found to be negligent it would be bankrupted, and every job would be lost. Rightly or wrongly, my grandfather decided that his first duty was to protect his employer and his fellow employees, and in his autobiography he made it clear that this was exactly what he had done.

> [At the inquiry] in London it was very necessary to keep one's hand on the whitewash brush. Sharp questions that needed clever answers if one was to avoid a pitfall, carefully and subtly dug, leading to a pinning down of blame on to someone's luckless shoulders . . .
> I think in the end the White Star Line won.
> (*Titanic and Other Ships*, p. 257)

Granny died when I was sixteen, and just months later my own health was restored and I returned to my interrupted education. Granny never asked me to keep our *Titanic* conversations secret, but whenever I talked about the tragedy with my mother, she ruled that everything must be kept strictly inside the family. A hero's reputation was at stake. Because of this, I never shared what my grandmother had told me.

Nearly forty years later, I was planning *Good as Gold*. With my mother and grandmother both long dead, I knew I was the last person alive with the specific knowledge I have of the *Titanic* tragedy. Before starting to write, I went through all the recorded evidence to double-check that the oral history Granny had given me also fitted the known facts. It does.

ACKNOWLEDGEMENTS

Andrew Obolensky and Jeff Peters shared their expertise in all things marine, Peter Obolensky provided the Russian translations and Michael Roche allowed me to use his lyrics.

My thanks go to them all.